KISSING THE PRINCE

"I would never do anything to harm you," Mikhail promised. "Nor would I do anything that you will regret. Do you trust me?"

"Yes, I trust you."

Mikhail kissed her again. He slid his mouth to her eyelids and lightly ran his lips across them. After drawing her chemise down, he removed his breeches.

Belle glided her fingertips across his chest. She heard the ragged catch of his breath and felt his heart beating beneath her palm.

"You are incredibly exquisite." His voice sounded husky.

Mikhail smoothed her shoulders and ran his fingers across her delicate collarbones. Then he caressed her arms from shoulder to hands. He lifted each hand to kiss, surprising her with his gentleness. His fingers made the return journey up the inside of her arms, his touch on the sensitive inside skin chilling her and igniting a flame in the bottom of her belly.

His intense gaze held her captive while his hand roamed along the silken skin of her neck, drifting down her body.

Belle moaned at the sensations he created. Her breath came in shallow gasps and her insides quivered and melted.

"Kiss me," Belle whispered, wrapping her arm around his neck. She wanted him closer and closer and closer.

His lips claimed hers in a kiss that consumed . . .

Books by Patricia Grasso

TO TAME A DUKE

TO TEMPT AN ANGEL

TO CHARM A PRINCE

TO CATCH A COUNTESS

TO LOVE A PRINCESS

SEDUCING THE PRINCE

PLEASURING THE PRINCE

TEMPTING THE PRINCE

Published by Zebra Books

Tempting the Prince

Patricia Grasso

ZEBRA BOOKS
Kensington Publishing Corp.
www.kensingtonbooks.com

ZEBRA BOOKS are published by

Kensington Publishing Corp.
850 Third Avenue
New York, NY 10022

All Kensington titles, imprints, and distributed lines are available at special quantity discounts for bulk purchases for sales promotion, premiums, fund-raising, educational, or institutional use.

Special book excerpts or customized printings can also be created to fit specific needs. For details, write or phone the office of the Kensington Special Sales Manager: Attn. Special Sales Department. Kensington Publishing Corp., 850 Third Avenue, New York, NY 10022. Phone: 1-800-221-2647.

Zebra and the Z logo Reg. U.S. Pat. & TM Off.

ISBN-13: 978-0-8217-8072-5
ISBN-10: 0-8217-8072-7

First Printing: May 2007
10 9 8 7 6 5 4 3 2 1

Printed in the United States of America

Chapter 1

London, 1821

He smelled her fear.

Shrouded in darkness and swirling fog, he watched her glancing over her shoulder when she reached the sickly yellow glow from the gaslight. She knew he was there. Somewhere. Lurking. He loved the hunt, especially when his quarry knew he was watching and waiting.

Rejecting him had sealed her fate. An insulting laugh and a toss of her mahogany curls had answered his proposition.

When she rounded the corner, he cut through the next alley to get ahead of her and leaned against the stone wall. Footsteps approached, heightening his anticipation.

She was almost here.

She would be his.

She would regret refusing him, if only for a moment.

Leaping out as she passed, he grabbed her from behind and slashed the blade across her throat. He pushed her to the ground and stood over her. The gurgling sounds of her struggle to breathe lessened, each beat of her heart pumping the life out of her.

Using his bloodied blade, he hacked a long length of her hair. Then he pressed a gold sovereign into the palm of her hand and closed her fingers around the coin.

"Thank you for an enjoyable evening, my dear."

The unmistakable aroma of horse droppings floated into the garden on a gentle breeze.

Belle Flambeau stood in her blossoming domain and sniffed the air, a smile touching her lips. The odor of horse dung from Soho Square shouted springtime.

Wisteria trees bloomed purple against the red brick house, while yellow tulips conspired with purple crocus to startle the eye with vibrant color. A fragrant lily of the valley ground cover reclined in front of the silver birch tree guarded by lilac, gardenia, rose, and pussy willow shrubs. Forsythia nodded in the breeze at their old friend, the purple pansy that lived in the shade beneath the oak tree.

The garden goddess promises minor miracles.

The clever business slogan pleased Belle. Her success in reviving plants had spread to the great mansions the previous season. Already, gardeners for those wealthy aristocrats had requested her services.

Belle narrowed her violet gaze on the pansy and walked toward the oak tree. The pansy's failure to thrive troubled her. Each day she snatched the pansy from death's grip but found it wilted again the next morning.

"Sister."

Belle glanced over her shoulder and saw one of her sisters walking across the grass. Bliss looked disgruntled.

"Why does Fancy insist on keeping the duke's identity a secret?" Bliss demanded, her voice shrill with anger.

"To which duke do you refer?"

"Our father, of course." Bliss rolled her eyes. "Investing would be easier if I knew which companies he owns." Her sister waved in the direction of the house. "The duke has always supported us in style. Why does our company need to pauperize him? If he retaliates, the Seven Doves will fail, and we will live in the poor house."

Belle placed her hand on her sister's shoulder. "Calm yourself."

Bliss took several deep breaths and then asked, "Is your touch making me feel better?"

Belle gave her an ambiguous smile. "Fancy will never forgive Father because, as the eldest, she remembers the relationship they shared."

"You're only a year younger," Bliss said. "Don't you have memories?"

"When I think of Father," Belle answered, "I see a tall, dark-haired gentleman holding Fancy on his lap."

"Did he never hold you?"

"At first I was too young to share his lap with Fancy." Belle shrugged, feigned nonchalance masking her remembered hurt. "When you and Blaze arrived, I suppose I was too old. The man could only hold one baby in each arm."

"Being born between the oldest and a set of twins is not the most auspicious position," Bliss said. "Being ignored could not have been pleasant."

"I enjoyed Nanny Smudge's attention." Belle lifted a rectangular gold case from the basket looped over her forearm. "Search for the duke with the initials *MC* and a boar's head crest."

Bliss shook her head. "Admitting ignorance of one's father's identity is humiliating. Does your illegitimacy bother Baron Wingate?"

Belle paused before answering, squelching the rush of irritation. None of her sisters could resist the opportunity to insult her future husband. "Charles understands that we cannot control our origins."

"I worry the baron will hurt you."

"I appreciate your concern." Belle watched Bliss disappear

into the house and turned to the ailing pansy. All thoughts of healing the flower vanished with her sister's concern.

I refuse to become love's victim, Belle told herself. *Like Mother.*

Gabrielle Flambeau, the daughter of a French aristocrat, had escaped the Terror when the citizens slaughtered her family. A penniless countess, her mother had won a position in the opera and caught the eye of a married duke. Together, her mother and her anonymous father had produced seven daughters.

The Flambeaus had wanted for nothing. Except the duke's love and attention.

The daughter had learned hard lessons from the mother, though. She refused to die broken-hearted.

Charles Wingate loved her and accepted that she intended to go to her marriage bed a virgin. She would never consider becoming any man's mistress.

Turning her thoughts to the pansy, Belle knelt in the dirt and set her wicker basket beside her. She reached for the white candle and its brass holder. Next came a tiny bell, followed by the *Book of Common Prayer.*

Finally, she lifted the gold case engraved with the initials *MC* and a boar's head. The case contained Lucifer matches and sandpaper to light her healing candle.

Belle traced her finger across the initials *MC.* A gentleman's accoutrement, the case had been left behind fifteen years earlier, and her father had never returned for it. A wealthy duke could easily replace one gold case, and she had cherished this memento of her father.

Hearing the door open again, Belle saw Blaze and Puddles, the family's mastiff, entering the garden. Blaze headed in her direction while Puddles raced around sniffing for a particular place.

"Are you practicing your hocus-pocus for the season?" her sister asked.

Belle smiled at that. "The garden goddess cannot perform minor miracles without a bit of showmanship."

"Good Lord, the stench from Soho seems stronger than usual today," Blaze remarked, pinching her nostrils together for emphasis. "What is wrong with that sorry-looking pansy? Is it choking from dung stink?"

"I revive the pansy every afternoon and then find it wilted again by morning," Belle said. "I cannot understand its problem."

"The garden goddess fails to save a flower's life?" her sister teased. "This could ruin your business."

The black-masked mastiff loped across the garden toward them. Reaching the oak tree, the dog lifted his hind leg perilously close to the pansy.

"Puddles, no." Down came the leg, and Belle rounded on her sister. "Tell Puddles to conduct his business against the stone wall, not near my pansy."

"Sorry." Blaze gave her a sheepish smile and then knelt in front of the dog. She stared into the mastiff's eyes for a long moment and then patted his head. Puddles bounded across the garden to the stone wall and conducted his business there.

"Thank you." Belle relaxed and teased her sister. "If my pansy dies, I will consider you and Puddles its murderers."

Blaze crouched beside her. "Listen, Puddles dislikes Baron Wingate."

Belle gave her a rueful smile. "Charles has disliked your dog since the day—"

"Puddles lifted his leg to the baron because he doesn't trust the man."

"I will not listen to another word against Charles." Her sisters' disapproval of the baron irritated Belle. "None of you, including Puddles, needs to like Charles since I am the one marrying him."

"If you say so." Blaze returned to the house, the mastiff following her.

Banishing all disturbing thoughts, Belle gave her attention

to the pansy. She lifted her right hand to make the beginning blessing but heard the door slam behind her.

Another visitor? Her pansy would expire before she could revive it. Perhaps ignoring whomever—

"Belle." The voice belonged to her youngest sister, who did not sound especially happy.

Raven plopped down on the grass beside her. "I need your advice."

Belle leaned back on her haunches. "What is the problem?"

"Constable Black may ask me to use my special gift to help with that Slasher investigation."

"Do you mean the one the newspapers have dubbed the Society Slasher?"

"My problem is Alex," Raven said, referring to their neighbor, the constable's assistant.

"A brick is more sensitive than Alexander Blake," Belle said, waving her hand in a dismissive gesture.

"I want to help the constable," Raven said, "but Alex makes me feel . . . *young*."

"You *are* young." Belle studied her sister for a long moment. "You told him you loved him, didn't you?"

Raven nodded, her misery etched across her face. "How do I behave around Alex?"

"Men want what they cannot have." Belle touched her sister's hand. "Treat Alex with chilly politeness and icy disdain."

"Be careful with Baron Wingate," Raven said before leaving. "I cannot trust the man."

Belle took a deep, calming breath and hoped her other three sisters did not interrupt. Then she prepared to heal the pansy.

As Nanny Smudge had taught her, Belle began with the magic blessing. She touched her left breast, her forehead, her right breast, left and right shoulders. Finally, she touched her left breast again.

After removing a Lucifer match and sandpaper, Belle lit

the white candle. Then she waved the tiny bell above the pansy, its tinkling sound breaking the garden's silence.

Belle placed her fingers against the pansy. "Ailing, ailing, ailing. Pansy, my touch is sealing, and thy illness is failing. Healing, healing, healing."

Taking the *Book of Common Prayer,* she held it over the pansy and whispered, "It is written. It is so."

Belle extinguished the candle's flame and made the magic blessing to complete the ritual. The pansy perked up almost immediately.

A hand touched her shoulder.

"Enough interruptions," Belle exclaimed, whirling around. "Charles, what a surprise."

Baron Charles Wingate stared at her, amusement lighting his brown eyes. "What are you doing?"

Belle blushed at being caught kneeling in the dirt. "My pansy needed tending."

The baron offered his hand to help her rise. When she reached for it, he dropped it to his side. "Your hands are dirty."

"This is dirt, not dung."

Charles shook his head in disapproval. "Playing in the dirt is unseemly behavior for a baroness, not to mention whispering to flowers."

"Ooops, you just mentioned it," she teased him, rising without his assistance.

"I do not consider that amusing. Once we marry—"

"Really, Charles, you are much too particular." Belle put her hands on her hips. "Do not forget we met when your gardener hired me to revive that rosebush."

"Darling, I don't mean to scold." He smiled, suddenly amenable. "Your meeting with my fastidious mother concerns me."

"Concerns or worries?" Belle touched his arm, trying to soothe him. "I will behave properly."

"Promise you won't mention working for money." Charles brushed the dirt off his sleeve where she had touched.

Belle smiled at that. "I promise."

"Do not mention gardening, either."

"My lips are locked." She pretended to button her lips together.

"Above all else, do not mention your sister singing in the opera. Mother dislikes such women."

Belle lost her good humor. Fingers of unease touched her spine. Was he embarrassed by her family?

"If you cannot be expensively attired," Charles continued, "then be certain your gown is modest."

Belle narrowed her violet gaze on him and brushed an ebony wisp off her forehead, leaving a smudge. "Are you implying—?"

"I have a sterling idea," Charles interrupted. "We could contrive to mention your father."

Belle gave him a blank stare. Was he serious? Or had he bumped his head, rattling his brain?

"You know, sweetheart, the duke?"

"That could prove awkward," Belle said, "since I do not know which duke sired me and my sisters."

"Doesn't His Grace support you and your sisters?" Charles sounded annoyed. "His Grace's barrister must mention him when he delivers your monthly allowance."

"Percy Howell calls my father *His Grace.*"

"You said your sister knows the duke's identity."

"Fancy refuses to name him."

"Then we will mention your deceased mother was a countess, albeit a penniless French refugee," Charles said. "We can only pray that your anonymous noble bloodlines and your incredible beauty sway Mother into approving our union."

Belle's irritation rose, inciting her to sarcasm. "I will pass the whole evening in prayer."

"I must leave now," Charles said, reaching for her hands.

"Mother doesn't like waiting." He lifted her hands to his lips but dropped them again when he saw the dirt.

"Where are you going?" Belle asked when he walked in the direction of the alley exit.

"That disreputable dog growled at me." And then he disappeared into the alley.

The baron's snobbishness made Belle uneasy. She feared his mother was worse. After all, the woman had raised him. Beneath that haughty exterior beat the heart of a decent man. If only she could snatch him away from his mother's influence.

Belle sighed, knowing that was impossible. She only wished Charles was not so concerned with appearances.

One mile and a world away from the Flambeau residence stood the great mansions in Grosvenor Square. Offensive street odors did not dare assault aristocratic nostrils in this enclave of the wealthy. Here, fragrant gardens masked the occasional whiff from passing horses.

Prince Mikhail Kazanov sat at his thirty-foot dining table set with the finest porcelain, crystal, and silver. Perched on the chair beside his was his four-year-old daughter, Elizabeth.

Mikhail stared at his plate, his grim expression mirroring his mood. Instead of beef, the prince saw his former sister-in-law's coy eagerness. The roasted potatoes bore a striking resemblance to his former mother-in-law's determined look.

He felt hunted.

His year of mourning had ended the previous month. Lavinia, his late wife's younger sister, had made her come-out two weeks earlier and immediately targeted him for her husband.

Even his former mother-in-law had become dangerous company. At the opera the previous evening, Prudence Smythe had reminded him that Lavinia had come of age and then proceeded to extol her virtues.

He had barely escaped entrapment. Thankfully, his brother

Rudolf had seen his panicked expression during intermission and interrupted the woman's dialogue.

Lavinia and Prudence Smythe were not alone in their ambition. Every maiden and widow in London was bent on tempting a prince into marriage.

He wanted a wife to give him an heir, and his daughter needed a loving stepmother. The society ladies of his acquaintance were shallow and greedy, unfit to mother his daughter.

"Daddy, your elbows are resting on the table."

"Excuse my lapse in manners, Bess."

Mikhail sliced a piece of beef, raised it to his lips, and then glanced at his daughter. Elizabeth had stabbed a piece of beef with her fork and raised it to her lips.

He winked at her. She winked in return. Slowly, he chewed the beef and swallowed. His daughter did the same.

Mikhail set his knife and fork on his plate and reached for his wine goblet. Elizabeth set her fork on the plate and reached for her lemon water.

Lifting his napkin, Mikhail dabbed at each corner of his mouth. His daughter lifted her napkin and dabbed at her mouth.

Mikhail leaned close to her and puckered his lips. Elizabeth puckered her lips, too, and gave him a smacking kiss.

"Thank you, Bess. I needed that kiss."

Elizabeth gave him a dimpled smile. "You are welcome, Daddy."

"What should we do before visiting Uncle Rudolf?"

"I want to go to Bond Street."

That made him smile. "What do you want to purchase?"

"I want a mummy," Elizabeth said, her disarming blue eyes gleaming with hope. "Cousin Sally got a new mummy, and I want one too."

His heart ached for his only child. "The Bond Street shops do not sell mummies."

Her expression drooped.

Mikhail lifted her delicate hands to his lips and proceeded

to kiss each of her tiny fingers. Then he pretended to gobble them, eliciting her giggles.

"Daddy, does the stork bring mummies?"

A smile flashed across his features. "Who told you about storks?"

"Cousin Roxanne said storks bring babies so I thought—" Elizabeth lifted her small shoulders in a shrug.

"Come, Bess, sit on my lap." When she did, Mikhail wrapped his arms around her. He wanted to protect her and make her dreams and wishes come true. "Tell me about this mummy you want."

"The best mummies know lots and lots of stories," Elizabeth said.

"Bedtime stories *are* very important." Mikhail nodded in agreement. "Anything else?"

"My new mummy will like laughing and playing in the garden."

Except for his brothers' wives, no lady of his acquaintance played in the dirt. Finding this mythical mummy could take years.

"My mummy will make tea parties for me." Her blue eyes sparkled with excitement as she warmed to her topic. "And happiness cakes too."

"Happiness cake?" he echoed.

"Cousin Amber makes happiness cakes for her little girl." Elizabeth placed the palm of her hand against his cheek. "Mummy will love me."

Mikhail turned his head and kissed the palm of her hand. "I love you, Bess."

"I love you, Daddy." She gazed into his dark eyes. "Mummy will love you too."

Julian Boomer, the prince's majordomo, appeared in the doorway and hurried to his side. "Your Highness?" The man shifted his gaze to the little girl and then arched a brow at him.

"Bess, tell Nanny Dee you will be leaving in a few minutes." Mikhail kissed her cheek and let her slip from his lap.

"Nanny Dee is gone for the day."

"Tell Nanny Cilla to wash your face," he instructed her. "I will wait in the foyer."

Mikhail watched his daughter disappear out the door. Then he looked at the majordomo.

Boomer passed him a calling card. "Ladies Prudence and Lavinia request an interview."

Mikhail groaned, his expression long suffering. He was not safe in his own home. His daughter's mythical mummy had better appear soon, or he would fall to the husband hunters.

Boomer cleared his throat. "I told them you had left for a business meeting, and Princess Elizabeth had gone with you to her tea party."

Mikhail grinned at the man. "You are worth your weight in gold."

"Thank you, Your Highness," the majordomo drawled. "Would that gold be literal or figurative?"

Mikhail laughed, rose from his chair, and clapped the man on the back. "Boomer, I do see a hefty raise in your future."

Belle Flambeau sat alone in the coach that Sunday afternoon and fumed, her anger directed at the baron and his mother. Charles knew she felt nervous but had opted to send his coach instead of escorting her himself, and Belle had no doubt his mother had done this purposely to prove her influence over her son.

Insensitive and disrespectful were the most appropriate words to describe Charles Wingate at the moment. Sending his coach insulted her. She would tell him that when they were alone.

Knowing she had one chance to make a good impression, Belle had taken more than an hour to dress for the occasion.

Her high-waisted, white gown had been embroidered with pink flowers beneath her bosom and around the hem. Her sisters had decided she appeared pleasingly virginal.

Belle ran her palm across the worn leather seat cushion. She wondered the reason the baron did not refurbish his carriage or purchase another.

The coach halted in front of a town house in Russell Square, a neighborhood more familiar with barristers than barons. The liveried coachman opened the door and helped her down.

When she banged the knocker, the majordomo opened the door. He stared at her, his expression haughty.

"I am Miss Flambeau," Belle said. "Baron Wingate is expecting me."

The majordomo stepped aside to allow her entrance. "The family is taking tea in the drawing room."

Belle gave the foyer a quick scan. She had expected something more lavish, but this foyer was lacking when compared with her own. She followed the servant to the stairs.

"You will wait here," the majordomo ordered, whirling around.

Belle looked at him in surprise. The servant's attitude stoked the flame of her simmering anger.

Would the Wingates keep a countess, a duchess, or a princess waiting in the foyer? The baron's mother had engineered this to make her feel inferior, and if that was true, she doubted this meeting would have a happy outcome.

Making a good impression did not seem so important now. Self-respect demanded she return insults in kind.

"Come now, miss," the majordomo said, returning to the foyer. "Do hurry. The baroness dislikes waiting."

"*I* dislike waiting, especially in foyers."

When she stepped inside the doorway, Charles smiled and crossed the room. "I'm glad you've come." He escorted her across the room. "Meet my family."

A man resembling the baron sat in a highbacked chair. His long legs stretched out, and a cane rested against the side of the chair. His expression registered boredom.

The middle-aged woman on the settee was another matter. Mild distaste had etched across her face.

"Mother, I present Miss Belle Flambeau," Charles introduced them. "Belle, my mother and Squire Wilkins, my half brother."

"I am pleased to make your acquaintances." Belle looked from the mother to the half brother, who was perusing her body.

Lifting his gaze to hers, Squire Wilkins rose from the chair and reached for his cane. "A pleasure to meet you, Miss Flambeau." With that, he left the drawing room.

"Please be seated."

Belle glanced at his mother and then chose the highbacked chair. Charles sat beside his mother on the settee.

The drawing room held an air of genteel shabbiness. Age had yellowed the armchair's doily, and the chair beneath it appeared threadbare. Even one of the teacups was chipped.

The Flambeau residence was more comfortably and expensively furnished. Her anonymous father had taken good care of them.

"My son did not exaggerate your beauty," the baroness said.

"Thank you, my lady." Belle sent Charles a serene smile, masking the knot of nervousness gripping her body.

"Beauty fades," the baroness said, "and couples—"

"Indeed, beauty does fade," Belle agreed, giving her a pointed look. She knew the baroness would not appreciate that comment, but the woman's expression screamed disapproval. Belle did not appreciate being treated like an inferior, and self-respect demanded reciprocity. Perhaps she should leave now before the situation worsened.

The baroness flushed with obvious anger. "As I was about to say, couples need more than love for a successful marriage."

Belle flicked a glance at Charles and wondered at his silence. "I would agree with you," she said, "but riches do not guarantee a happy marriage."

The baroness gave her a frigid smile that matched the coldness in her eyes. "Tell me about your family."

Belle had prepared herself for this particular topic. "My late mother was a French countess, and my father is an English duke."

"Can you prove that?"

Belle had not prepared herself for that unexpected question. "I do not carry birth or baptismal certificates in my reticule."

"How about a marriage certificate?" the baroness asked, her tone sneering.

"Mother, I object to this," Charles found his voice. "She cannot help—"

"Be quiet, Charles. This needs discussion." Then the baroness looked at Belle. "Your parents never married, which makes you—"

"—the daughter of a French countess and an English duke," Belle interrupted.

"Please, Mother," Charles whined.

The baroness ignored him. "I mean no disrespect."

"Of course you don't," Belle drawled, her voice dripping sarcasm. She could not decide who was more despicable, the mother or the sniveling son.

"Mother," Charles whined again. "I asked you to—"

"Be quiet," Belle snapped, surprising him. Ready for battle, she refused to cower or retreat. "What about your family, my lady?"

The baroness dropped her mouth open in surprise.

"I mean no disrespect," Belle said, "but my blood is a mingling of the French and English aristocracy, which I would not wish to dilute." She looked at the baron. "Didn't you tell me your maternal grandfather was a vicar and your mother's first husband a squire?"

The older woman found her voice. "You impertinent piece of baggage."

Belle bolted out of her chair, startling the other woman, and looked at the baron. "I want to leave now."

"The coachman will drive you home," his mother said.

Charles had stood when Belle did. "*I* will escort Miss Flambeau home."

The coach ride to Soho Square was completed in silence. Belle stared out the window without seeing anything. She had expected the baroness to oppose the match but refused to be intimidated. The baron's behavior was an entirely different matter. His failure to defend her had been a surprise, and she should reconsider their relationship. His mother would never approve of her, and a less than loyal husband was unacceptable.

"Darling, we have arrived." Charles walked her to the front door and raised her hand to his lips. "I apologize for Mother. You should not have argued with her, though. Now we will need to placate her before moving forward with our betrothal."

Belle managed a smile but refused to apologize for her behavior. The baron would need to choose—her or his mother.

"May I come inside?" he asked.

"That would be too tempting," she said in refusal. "My sisters are gone for the day."

"I did mention to Mother that Prince Stepan was picnicking with your sisters." Charles gave her a wry smile. "I had hoped that would impress her."

Belle unlocked the door. "Good day, Charles."

He grabbed her hand again. "I promise to speak to Mother."

Belle stepped into the foyer. Turning around, she smiled at the baron once more before closing the door.

Seconds later someone grabbed her from behind. When she tried to scream, a hand covered her mouth, and only muffled squawks came out. Her attacker yanked her against his muscular frame, and she kicked out wildly.

Something sharp stung her cheek, and she bit the massive hand covering her mouth. With a masculine yelp, the man pushed her away, and she landed facedown on the floor, the breath knocked from her body.

Belle turned her face in time to see her assailant hurrying down the hallway toward the rear of the house. When she tried to stand, Belle saw the droplets of blood where her face had hit the floor. She touched her right cheek and stared in a daze at her bloody fingers.

The bastard had sliced her cheek.

Chapter 2

She would carry a scar.

Always. Forever. Endlessly.

Belle sat alone on the parlor sofa the next morning. She closed her eyes against the pain emanating from her right cheek.

The sounds of passing carriages and muted voices wafted into the parlor through the open windows. The breeze toyed with her waist-length, ebony mane, which she wore loose that day lest someone besides her sisters enter the house.

"What can't be cured must be endured," Nanny Smudge would have said.

Now she knew the veracity of her nanny's words. Some things in life could never be undone, and scarring was one.

The best seamstress in the family, Raven had stitched her from cheekbone to mouth. Her sister could stitch her flesh but never mend her heart.

No man would want her now. She would never marry. She would never bear children. She would never enjoy her own loving family.

Long, lonely years stretched out in front of her. She felt more wilted than her pansy.

Belle shifted her gaze to the door when it swung open. Her elder sister stepped inside.

"Baron Wingate wants to see you," Fancy said.

That surprised Belle. "How does Charles—?"

"Prince Stepan visited him this morning," Fancy said, "but you do not need to see him or anyone else for that matter."

Belle studied the Aubusson rug for a long moment. "I prefer this unpleasantness finished."

"How do you know the baron will—?"

"I know Charles." Belle gave her a resigned smile and drew the curtain of her hair forward to cover her wound. "Charles will not want a scarred wife."

"If he loves you, the scar will not matter." Fancy slipped out the door.

Charles appeared a moment later. "Oh, my poor dearest." He sat beside her and reached for her hand. "I feel so guilty."

"Do not blame yourself." Belle patted his hand and wondered why she was comforting him.

"I am relieved the villain did not violate you," Charles continued. "I could not have borne that insult, and Mother would never allow me to marry a tarnished bride."

"Slashing my face *is* a violation." Anger balled her hands into fists in her lap.

Mother. Mother. Mother. She was heartily sick of that overbearing, pretentious woman masquerading as a loving mother.

"Let me see the damage." Charles reached to draw the hair away from her face.

Belle grabbed his wrist, stopping him, and fixed her violet gaze on his. Only a man in love would want her now.

"Prepare yourself," she said, keeping her gaze on his expression. "I am no longer the most beautiful of seven beauties, as you once said."

"Nonsense, dearheart. You will always be—"

Belle drew her hair away from her cheek. His expression went from smiling confidence to surprise and then revulsion.

She knew what he was seeing. Her stitches ran from her right cheekbone almost to the corner of her mouth. The wound was raw, the stitched skin puckered and red and dotted with clotted blood droplets.

"You will recover." His expression and tone did not inspire confidence, and his gaze skittered away from hers. "I blame myself for not escorting you inside."

Belle knew the time had arrived to test the baron's intent. "Our being alone would have been too much of a temptation. I want nothing to prevent me from coming to you a virgin on our wedding night."

Silence. Prolonged silence. Prolonged, awkward silence.

Charles cleared his throat and looked away, his gaze fixing on the French doors leading to the dining room. "Well, dearest, the fact is"—he hesitated—"Mother believes we would not suit. She cannot accept that your mother and father—" His voice trailed off.

Belle wanted to weep, to rail against an unkind fate, to strike back. "I have more nobility in my baby toe than the vicar's daughter has in her whole body."

"If your father would acknowledge you," Charles hedged, "perhaps Mother would reconsider her opinion."

"If my father acknowledged me," Belle countered, "I would never stoop to marry a mere baron."

Belle heard smothered chuckles from the hallway. Fancy and Prince Stepan were eavesdropping.

"I am asking for time to change Mother's opinion," Charles said. "If our love is true, a few more weeks will scarcely matter."

Charles is a coward, Belle decided. *He hides behind his mother's skirt as an excuse not to marry me and offers false hope to avoid an emotional confrontation.*

"Take all the time you need," Belle said. "I will be reconsidering my own feelings for you, of course."

Charles stood and looked down at her. "As you wish."

Once he'd gone, Belle could not contain the tears that flowed.

She knew the baron and his mother were not worth her tears. Did she really desire a husband who put his mother first?

Only . . . Her heart ached with the knowledge that no man would marry a scarred woman. She had looked forward to nurturing her own children. Now she would need to content herself with nieces and nephews.

Her future appeared darker than the unlit hearth. Like her ailing pansy, she needed a miracle.

Nanny Smudge had always believed that miracles happened every day. She prayed her nanny was correct. Only a miracle would give her a husband and children.

"Sister?" Raven crossed the parlor and sat beside her. "I heard Charles visited. How do you feel?"

Belle gave her a wobbly smile. "As well as can be expected, I suppose."

"The baron would never have made you happy," Raven said. "You will meet a man who will love you for who you are, not how you look."

"If you say so." Belle touched her sister's arm. "Thank you for stitching my face."

"I could not allow Fancy to sew you."

"Fancy *is* the worst seamstress in London," Belle agreed.

"You mean in England," Raven corrected her. "Constable Black and Alex have questions if you feel well enough."

"I will speak with them."

After crossing the parlor, Raven opened the door and beckoned to the waiting men. She returned to the sofa and held Belle's hand in a gesture of support.

Belle sent her a grateful look. Between the fine stitching and emotional support, Belle did not know how she would have coped without her baby sister. Perhaps her sister's special gifts made her wiser than the others.

Two men walked into the parlor.

Amadeus Black was London's most famous constable, providing his services for not only the city officials but also the wealthy. Dressed completely in black, he cut an imposing figure at more than six feet tall.

Beside the illustrious constable stood Alexander Blake, their neighbor and constable in training. As tall as his mentor, Alexander also made an imposing figure, but his natural expression was more pleasant than somber.

Belle sensed her sister's tension with Alexander in the room. She glanced at her and nearly smiled in spite of the pain that movement would cause.

Apparently, Raven had taken her advice to heart. Her sister was looking at Alex, an expression of icy disdain on her face.

Belle flicked a glance at Alex. He was looking at her sister like a starving man at a feast. Perhaps her sister's hopes and dreams would come true.

"I present Constable Black," Alexander introduced her.

"I am pleased to meet you," Belle said.

"I wish we could have met in different circumstances," the constable said.

"Please be seated," Raven said.

"I hope you will soon recover," the constable said, sitting in the chair across from her.

Alexander sat in the wing chair near the sofa. "Time will heal the scar."

Belle said nothing. She would be too old to marry by the time her scar faded.

Amadeus leaned forward in his chair. "Tell me what happened."

"He grabbed me from behind, muffled my scream with his hand, and flicked his blade down my cheek. When I bit his hand, he fled down the hallway to escape out the back."

"Do you think you left teeth marks?" the constable asked.

"I believe so."

Amadeus Black nodded at Alexander. "You will need to shake all those hands."

"Is your assistant required to walk through London searching for bite marks?" Raven asked, her amusement apparent.

"Nothing so boring as that, brat," Alexander answered.

"The Marquis of Basildon has reconciled with the Duke of Essex," Constable Black explained, referring to Alexander and his grandfather. "The entre into society will expand our investigative ability."

"Should we call you *my lord?*" Belle teased him.

Alexander smiled. "I would never require that of you."

"I thought you would never forgive your grandfather for his treatment of your parents," Raven said, her tone disapproving.

Alexander cocked a dark brow at her. "Sometimes, brat, necessity demands change." He looked at Belle, asking, "Did the villain say anything?"

Belle shook her head. "No."

"Did he place a gold sovereign in your hand?" Amadeus Black asked. "Or cut your hair?"

"No."

"Can you remember anything about him?" Alexander asked.

Belle leaned back against the sofa and closed her eyes. "I-I felt a ring on his finger when he covered my mouth. He pushed me to the floor after I bit him. And . . . umm—"

"Take your time." The voice belonged to Amadeus Black.

"He was tall and dressed like a gentleman, his gait swaying slightly from side to side." Belle opened her eyes and looked at the two men. "I cannot recall anything else."

"You have done exceptionally well," Constable Black said. "I want you to write everything down, no matter how trivial, including your emotions. Sometimes people remember little things later."

"Do you believe the Society Slasher attacked her?" Raven asked.

The two men exchanged a meaningful look. Then the constable told them, "The Society Slasher has never attacked his victims in a house."

"Or left a victim alive," Alexander added. "Your assailant may want us to believe he is the Slasher."

Belle looked from Alexander to Constable Black. "I don't understand."

"I could be mistaken," the constable said, "but I believe he targeted you specifically."

He wished his wife had been an orphan.

Her lack of a family would have saved his obligatory visits to his former in-laws. If he had ignored her calling card, Prudence Smythe would have descended upon him like one of the fabled furies.

Mikhail paused in his dressing for the evening and rubbed his throbbing temples, a by-product of taking tea with his former mother-in-law. First, Prudence had hinted that he needed a wife to give him an heir. Then had come the lecture about her granddaughter needing a mother. Finally, he had been required to listen to a litany of Lavinia's virtues.

A fictional business meeting had cut the litany short. Fortunately, he had escaped out the door before becoming betrothed to his former sister-in-law.

Mikhail reached for the white cravat and stood in front of the cheval mirror to tie it. Then he reached for his black evening jacket.

Another obligation loomed before him, the Duke and Duchess of Inverary's ball. If his brother hadn't married Her Grace's niece, Mikhail would not bother attending. He had not enjoyed socializing since his year of mourning had ended and husband-hunting season had begun.

Nobody ever refused an invitation from the Duke and Duchess of Inverary. Which meant dozens of prince-hungry brides-in-waiting would surround him like she-wolves sensing a fresh kill. Good Lord, how much longer could he last before one brought him down?

Walking into his daughter's bedchamber, Mikhail nodded to Nanny Dee and sat on the edge of the bed. Then he kissed his daughter good night.

"Are you going out, Daddy?"

"I am beginning my search for your new mummy at the Duke of Inverary's ball."

That made her smile. "You told Grandmama a lie today."

"I never tell lies."

"You said we needed to leave for a business meeting," she reminded him.

"Oh, that." Mikhail smiled at her. "That was an *excuse,* not a lie."

Elizabeth frowned. "What is the difference?"

"I will explain when you are older," Mikhail said. "Will you trust me until then?"

"Yes, Daddy."

Mikhail gave her another good night kiss and an exaggerated wink.

Elizabeth winked in return. "Don't forget the happiness cake, Daddy."

"I would never forget the cake."

Mikhail blew her another final kiss. Then he left the bedchamber and walked downstairs to the foyer.

The majordomo opened the door for him. "Enjoy your evening, Your Highness."

"Thank you, Boomer."

"Happy hunting," the man drawled. "Or should I say evading?"

Seated inside his coach, Mikhail leaned back against the soft leather. The trip would take longer by coach than on foot. How absurd to ride two blocks.

His coach waited in the line of carriages for thirty minutes. Finally, Mikhail climbed down and hurried into Inverary House. The sooner he made an appearance, the sooner he could retreat to safety.

"Good evening, Tinker," he greeted the duke's majordomo.

"Good evening, Your Highness." Tinker caught his eye, adding, "Are you prepared for tonight's hopeful horde?"

Mikhail grinned at his wit. "Are you related to Julian Boomer?"

"Boomer is an amateur when compared with me." Tinker leaned close. "The hopeful look hungry, Your Highness."

"Thank you for the warning."

Tinker turned toward the assembly, announcing, "Prince Mikhail Kazanov."

The Inverary ballroom was an enormous, rectangular chamber. The orchestra—cornet, piano, cello, two violins—played at one of the short ends of the room. Small tables, chairs, and pedestals had been positioned around the dance floor. Crystal chandeliers hung overhead.

A glittering throng of society's elite crushed together on the dance floor and its periphery. The women wore a rainbow of colors as well as precious gems on necks, arms, fingers, and ears. The gentlemen dressed in their formal black, a background for the ladies' beauty.

Mikhail spied his brothers on the far side of the room and stepped into the crowd, slowly wending his way in their direction. He spoke to a few acquaintances, smiled a greeting to others, waved to a few, but ignored the unmarried females.

"I would present Miss Fancy Flambeau," Prince Stepan said.

Mikhail smiled at the petite opera singer. "I have enjoyed your performances."

"Thank you, Your Highness."

Mikhail noted her beauty, ebony hair, and violet eyes. He understood the reason his baby brother was enamored, but she looked anxious.

"There is no need for nervousness," Mikhail said. "I guarantee the predators are hunting me tonight."

The opera singer seemed to relax, her face losing its pinched expression. "Why would predators hunt you, Your Highness?"

"Since Stepan is escorting you," Mikhail answered, "I am

the only unattached prince in attendance. I can hardly wait for our cousins to sail into London."

Prince Rudolf sidled up to him. "Do not turn around, brother, but the Blonde Brigade, accompanied by chaperones, is headed in your direction."

Mikhail's pained expression made his brothers laugh. The Blonde Brigade, as he had dubbed them, was the three most aggressive husband hunters: Princess Anya, the Russian ambassador's niece; Lady Cynthia Clarke; and Lavinia Smythe, his former sister-in-law.

"Good to see you, Mikhail." Princess Lieven, the Russian ambassador's wife, flicked a disapproving glance at Fancy Flambeau.

Mikhail knew Princess Lieven's tongue could draw blood. In an effort to prevent the opera singer any distress, he diverted the princess's attention by offering her his hand. "Would you like to dance, Princess?"

"Thank you, but I am resting at the moment." The princess pushed her niece forward. "Anya would love to dance."

Mikhail knew he'd been caught but, accepting defeat gracefully, turned to the young blonde. She placed her hand in his and gave her rivals a triumphant smile.

Mikhail guided Anya onto the dance floor. He moved with the easy grace of a man who had waltzed a thousand times.

After noting his brother escorting the opera singer to safety, Mikhail dropped his gaze to the princess in his arms. Her expression was sultry adoration.

"What is your opinion on literature?" Mikhail asked, remembering his daughter's mummy requirements.

Princess Anya looked confused.

"I mean books."

Still, the princess seemed bewildered.

Mikhail arched a dark brow at her. "Stories?"

Her expression cleared. "I adore stories."

Could she even read? Or did she need someone to read to her?

"How many stories do you know?" he asked.

"I-I do not know any. Do you?"

"I know enough."

Princess Anya fluttered her eyelashes at him. "Perhaps you would care to tell me stories sometime." When he grunted instead of answering, she changed the subject. "What do you think of Cynthia's gown?"

"What do I—?" Her question confused him. "I had not noticed her gown." He shifted his gaze to the lady in question. "It covers her."

"Willow green is *last* year's color," Anya said. "Do you think Cynthia has the worst fashion sense?"

Mikhail knew nothing about fashion. "Do *you?*"

Princess Anya nodded. "Most definitely."

When the waltz ended, Mikhail realized he would need to dance with each member of the Blonde Brigade. He did not want to give any particular maiden his attention.

Mikhail stepped onto the dance floor with Cynthia Clarke. He gave her a polite smile as the waltz began.

"You dance divinely, Your Highness."

"And so do you."

Cynthia smiled at him, her expression worshipful. "We do fit together perfectly."

Mikhail changed the topic. "What is your opinion on gardens?"

"I love flowers."

"How interesting," he murmured. "Have you ever *tended* a garden?"

"Tended?" Cynthia looked puzzled. "Do you mean digging in the dirt?"

"That is precisely what I mean."

"Tending gardens is for servants," Cynthia informed him. "No lady would dig in the dirt. If your gardener is having problems, tell him to hire the garden goddess. She promises minor miracles."

"Who is the garden goddess?"

"She is a woman—*not a lady*—who earns her bread advising gardeners."

"And does this garden goddess perform minor miracles?"

"I did hear Mother say her roses had never looked more beautiful." Cynthia gave him a calculating look. "I realize Lavinia was your sister-in-law, but—do you think her bodice is a bit low cut for a maiden?"

"I had not noticed." Mikhail glanced toward the lady in question. "Do *you* think the bodice is cut too low?"

Cynthia nodded. "Most definitely."

After delivering Cynthia to her mother, Mikhail turned to his former sister-in-law. "Shall we dance?"

Lavinia stepped into his arms as if she belonged there. "I am disappointed I missed you and Bess this afternoon."

"Bess missed her Aunt Livy."

She gave him a flirtatious smile. "Did you miss seeing me too?"

"Both Bess and I enjoy your company." Mikhail pretended to misunderstand her meaning. "What is your opinion on baking, Livy?"

"Baking?"

"You know, cakes and such."

Lavinia chuckled, a throaty seductive sound. "I have never stepped one foot into any kitchen, as you well know."

"Ah, yes." Mikhail grinned. "I do recall you prefer life's luxuries."

Mikhail and Lavinia swirled around the ballroom. He caught several smiling glances cast at them and realized society was coupling them and probably expecting an announcement. He could feel Prudence Smythe tightening the matrimonial noose around his neck.

"Anya believes she knows you better than I," Lavinia said. "She may be Russian, but I am family."

The noose got tighter, making breathing difficult. He must remember never to be alone with Lavinia.

"Do you think Anya is too forward with gentlemen?" Lavinia asked.

"I had not noticed." That put a satisfied smile on her lips. "Do *you* believe Anya is too forward?"

Lavinia nodded. "Most definitely."

Mikhail escorted Lavinia back to their group. He was beginning to wonder if his daughter's mythical mummy existed.

Escape time had arrived. On his way out, Mikhail nodded to the majordomo.

"Leaving so soon, Your Highness?" Tinker drawled.

"I am on my way to White's." Mikhail winked at the man. "No ladies allowed."

Tinker smiled at him. "Every fox needs a bolt-hole."

Her damn cheek itched. Even the salve her sister had given her did not ease the itch beyond a few minutes. She needed a good scratch, not a salve.

"Put your hand down."

Belle looked across the table at her youngest sister. "I was not—"

"Do not lie," Raven interrupted, making their sisters smile. "I will remove the stitches after breakfast, and the itch will ease."

A gentle breeze wafted into the dining room through the open windows and flirted with the French lace curtains, carrying the sweet perfume from the garden. A vase of fragrant lilacs perched on the table amid a special breakfast of eggbatter-fried cinnamon bread with blueberry preserves, sausage, and coffee.

Belle glanced at Fancy, sitting at the head of the table and wearing a troubled expression. Her sister cleared her throat, as if to speak, but then speared a piece of sausage.

Ignoring her sister's distraction, Belle looked across the table. "Why did you cook this special breakfast?"

Raven gave her a one-shoulder shrug. "I woke early."

Like her older sister, her youngest sister seemed preoccupied too. Belle wondered what they knew that she did not.

"I have important news," Fancy announced, and then hesitated.

Belle set her fork on the plate. She touched her sister's hand, murmuring, "The problem cannot be as dire as your expression."

Fancy looked at each sister in turn. "Our father wants his daughters to live with him."

"You mean us?" Nothing could have surprised Belle more. She glanced down the table. Her sisters appeared as surprised as she. Even the dog had cocked his head to one side.

"Our father has decided to acknowledge us and . . . *et cetera*." Fancy paused, a bright smile for her sisters. "Prince Stepan will help us move this afternoon. Only pack essentials and objects of particular value."

"Who *is* our father?" Raven asked.

Belle winced at that. How sad for a man to sire seven daughters and only one knew his identity.

"Magnus Campbell, the Duke of Inverary, is our father," Fancy answered, "and he wants us to move into his mansion on Park Lane."

"That is London's most exclusive address," Belle exclaimed. "What is *et cetera*?"

Fancy let her gaze drift around the table. "*Et cetera* means His Grace will find us husbands as befitting a duke's daughters."

"Husbands?" Blaze echoed. "I prefer a horse or a monkey." All the sisters laughed at that. "And what will happen to Puddles?"

"His Grace is acknowledging Puddles too," Fancy answered her.

"What does his duchess say about this?" Belle asked.

"Her Grace is his second wife, married after Mother died," Fancy told them. "Her Grace is childless and wants to mother us."

"She sounds like a good woman," Sophia said, "but we do not need a mother."

Serena gave her twin a placid smile. "If it makes her happy—"

"What do we call them?" asked Bliss, a stickler for details.

"Gawd, I will need to scribble all the titles on the palm of my hand," Blaze grumbled. "Our father will be Grace and his wife Gracie."

Serena clapped her hands. "I like that, sister."

"So do I," Sophia agreed.

"I think you're rude," Bliss told her twin.

Blaze looked at her. "I think my brilliant idea threatens your intellectual genius."

"If it wasn't for my intellectual genius," Bliss countered, "we would not own a successful business."

"And if it wasn't for my special gift with animals," Blaze reminded her, "we would not have raised the money to start the company."

Belle covered her mouth to keep from laughing. Not only did she not want to encourage the bickering, but moving her face muscles pained her injured cheek.

"What will happen with our Seven Doves Company?" Bliss asked.

"Our plan to pauperize the duke moves forward," Fancy said.

"If we eavesdrop on his business meetings," Bliss said, beaming with excitement, "we will make a great deal of money."

"Accepting his hospitality and then pauperizing him is reprehensible," Belle argued.

"We cannot repay his kindness by cheating him in the marketplace," Raven agreed.

"Where was *his* kindness when Mother was weeping for him?" Fancy demanded, her voice rising in anger. "Where was *his* kindness when he did not show his face at her funeral? Where was *his* kindness when he ignored us for fifteen years?"

All the sisters were silent. Though their father had supported them, his barrister had dealt with their material needs. Their father had walked out the door fifteen years earlier and had never seen them again.

Belle knew Fancy was more hurt than angry. Her sister's heart ached as much as her own cheek. Seeking to soothe, she reached for Fancy's hand.

Fancy slumped in her chair, depleted of anger. "The duke was not surprised by our various talents and interests. I suppose Nanny Smudge kept him informed about our lives."

"There, you see?" Belle managed a faint smile, though the movement pained her. "Our father *was* interested in us."

Her sisters remained silent, their expressions doubtful.

"We have two half brothers," Fancy said.

Surprise replaced their doubtful expressions.

"The Marquis of Argyll is the duke's legitimate heir, and Prince Rudolf Kazanov is his son out of wedlock."

"Grace certainly had a roving eye for the ladies," Bliss said into the silence.

"Humph," Blaze snorted, making them smile. "Grace needed more than an eye to sire eight children on the wrong side of the blanket."

"Could there be others?" Raven asked.

All the sisters looked at her in silent surprise. There was no way to know the answer to that, but the possibility of other unknown siblings existed.

"What if we don't like living on Park Lane?" Sophia asked.

"We can return home," Fancy answered.

"Grace owns this house," Serena reminded them.

"What if Grace forces us to remain there?" Blaze asked.

Bliss nodded, agreeing with her twin's concern. "We should discuss what to do if that happens."

Belle peeked at Fancy, who appeared ready to explode again. "Sisters, let's clear the breakfast dishes and pack our belongings," she said, taking charge. "Raven, I want these stitches removed now."

"I'll fetch the scissors." Raven left the dining room, followed by both sets of twins carrying plates.

"I want to speak privately." Belle watched Fancy close the dining room doors. "I want to stay in Soho with you."

"How do you know I refused to move?"

"I know how unforgiving you can be."

"Listen, the duke blames himself for your injury," Fancy said. "If you don't move, he will blame me, and the others will also refuse to move."

"I will not venture into society," Belle said. "Nor will I ever marry."

"You can hibernate inside his mansion as well as here," Fancy argued. "I will care for your garden."

"No! You will murder my plants." Belle sighed, surrendering to the inevitable. "I will tend my own garden. Will you tell my clients the garden goddess has moved to Park Lane?"

"I promise." Fancy hugged her. "A good husband is waiting in your future."

"What man desires a scarred woman to wife?"

"A man who loves her truly."

Belle gave Fancy a resigned smile. "Miracles do happen every day, I suppose."

Chapter 3

Soho Square seemed a lifetime ago. She belonged there, not at a Park Lane mansion.

Belle stood at the window in her bedchamber at Inverary House. Accustomed to sharing a chamber with Fancy and Raven, Belle had passed several restless nights. The room was too big, which made her lonely.

The bedchamber had been decorated in antique white, gold, and blue. A curtained bed perched on one side of the room, opposite the windows that overlooked the garden. A Grecian chaise lounged with indolent beauty in front of a white marble hearth. A mahogany tallboy, a hand-painted privacy screen, and a cheval mirror framed in scrolled gold stood among lesser pieces of furniture.

A bedchamber fit for a princess. Too bad, she was no princess.

Belle stared at the garden below her window and itched to inspect the duke's plants, shrubs, and trees. Digging in dirt and tending plants always relaxed her.

Lilacs scented the air. Their distinctive perfume told her those particular plants enjoyed good health.

Her father was trying to make amends for years of emotional neglect. That much was true, but she would have felt more comfortable if there weren't so many people. Or if she hadn't been injured.

Servants lurked down every hallway and around every corner. Pity leaped at her from curious gazes.

She despised that emotion. Pity demeaned her worth. Lord, she would prefer facing indifference or hatred.

Belle felt a paw touch her leg. Puddles sat beside her, his black eyes doleful and yearning.

The duchess had taken her sisters shopping for new wardrobes. Since she was not stepping into society, she needed no new gowns. She had refused to accompany them and inherited the dog for the afternoon.

"Do you want to go out?" Belle asked the mastiff.

Puddles barked, recognizing the word *out*.

Belle crossed the chamber to the bedside table for her magic basket. She would be prepared if any plants needed her ministrations.

Before leaving the chamber, Belle stood in front of the cheval mirror to inspect her cheek. Her facial wound was healing. Though her sister had managed tiny stitches, she would be scarred for life. How many stitches would mend her heart?

Belle wore her ebony hair loose, cascading to her waist. She looped the left side behind her ear and arranged the right side to hide her wound as best she could.

"Come, Puddles."

Keeping her gaze fixed on the carpet, Belle walked down the third-floor corridor to the stairs. She did not make eye contact with passing servants and hoped the curtain of her hair shrouded her cheek.

"Good afternoon, Miss Belle."

"Good day, sir." Belle glanced at the majordomo, standing in the foyer. "I am taking Puddles into the garden."

Tinker dropped his gaze to the mastiff. "I see."

"Is that permissible?"

"Since Master Puddles prefers the garden to the water closet," Tinker drawled, "I assume His Grace will allow it."

Belle smiled at that.

"Oops, I made you smile." Tinker winked at her. "And blush too."

Belle and the dog left the foyer and headed toward the rear of the mansion. When she stepped outside, relief surged through her. The garden was deserted.

Sniffing here and sniffing there, Puddles zoomed around like a newly freed felon. Belle paused to admire the idyllic scene and heavenly perfume, noxious street odors noticeably absent.

A fountain bubbled and gurgled in the middle of the garden. Red and yellow tulips circled it in a whimsical game of ring-around-the-rosy.

Purple wisteria leaned against the brick mansion as if blooming had proved tiresome. Several trees—elm, silver birch, oak—provided privacy from the rear alley. A profusion of blooming flowers added rioting colors while shrubbery and hedges lined the far end of the expanse. A path meandered around the garden, inviting a leisurely stroll, and stone benches appealed to the weary.

With her magic basket looped over her arm, Belle inspected every plant and shrub and tree. Nothing escaped her, and all seemed well. Even the pansies at the base of the white birch appeared healthy.

Belle wondered how her own pansy was faring. Lonely, perhaps. She would go to Soho the next day to verify its health and tend her garden.

Setting the basket down, Belle sat on a bench. The garden's artfully arranged color and form pleased her. Even the weather cooperated, white baby's breath clouds dotting a bluebell sky.

"Belle?" The Duke of Inverary walked toward her. "May I join you?"

The corners of her lips turned up in a polite smile. "You do own the bench, Your Grace."

"I do not want to intrude on your privacy."

Belle did not believe that for one millisecond. Since meeting him, she had reached several conclusions. Born and bred to lead, her sophisticated father always couched an order beneath the charming veneer of suggestion or request. He was a stubborn and determined man, unaccustomed to disobedience in others.

Her gaze met his. "Please, join me."

The Duke of Inverary sat beside her. The mastiff dashed across the garden and wagged his tail, the duke's devoted admirer.

Her father looked exactly as she remembered, tall and darkly handsome. Though, fifteen years had salted his temples with silver.

"Your garden is healthy, Your Grace."

He arched a dark brow at her. "Using my title is a bit formal between father and daughter."

"I do not feel a closeness," Belle said. "We scarcely know each other."

Did he really expect more from her and her sisters when they were virtual strangers? Relationships demanded time and careful nurturing. Sharing a bloodline did not guarantee love and loyalty.

"Your sister will not forgive my past mistakes," he said. "Are you angry too?"

"I am not Fancy."

Her father reached for her hand. "Will you forgive me?"

"My forgiveness cannot ease your conscience." Belle threaded her fingers through his. "You must forgive yourself."

"Smudge said you were wise beyond your years," her father said, referring to her deceased nanny. With his free hand, he pushed her hair away from her face. "I apologize for failing to protect you."

Belle did not want anyone, including her father, to see her

wound. She dropped her gaze to their entwined fingers, her face heating with embarrassment.

"Do not blame yourself for another's actions." She looked at him, but his gaze had fixed on a point behind her, a faraway look in his eyes.

"I can still see you peeking at me from behind Smudge's skirt." He looked at her, returning to the present. "You heal plants?"

Belle nodded. "God blessed me with a special talent."

"My Aunt Bedelia had the same gift," he said, and then changed the subject. "Tell me about Baron Wingate."

"Charles and I did not share intimacies," Belle said. "His mother did not approve a match between us and questioned my parentage—"

Her father winced at that.

"—and I returned the favor by questioning hers," she continued. "I told the baroness I did not want to dilute my pure aristocratic blood with a vicar's daughter."

The Duke of Inverary grinned. "You inherited my Campbell pride."

"So did my sisters."

"You can marry Wingate if you want," her father said. "No man would refuse a family link with me."

"No, thank you." Belle gave him an impish smile. "I've already told Charles if you acknowledged me, I would not stoop to marry a mere baron."

The duke chuckled. "Being an aristocrat is as much attitude as title and wealth."

"We Flambeau sisters have attitude in abundance, if nothing else."

His gaze dropped to her basket. "What is that?"

"The garden goddess cannot perform minor miracles without her magic tools," Belle told him. "I intend to continue my gardening business."

"I can afford to support my own children." Irritation tinged his voice. "I do not want my daughter working for money."

Good Lord, her father sounded like Charles.

"Then I will charge my clients sticks and stones," Belle said, making him smile. "I heal plants for love, not money."

"Do you accept payment for your services?"

"Yes, I do."

"You are working for money, child."

"I heal plants for love," Belle repeated, "and I accept payment for services. Then I donate the money to the poor."

"You give money away?"

"I do not need money," Belle drawled, her tone haughty. "My father is a wealthy duke. Besides, my share of the company gives me enough—" She froze, alarmed by what she'd almost revealed.

Her father was still smiling, but his dark eyes shone with curiosity. "To what company do you refer?"

"You will need to ask—"

"I am asking you."

"Your lips say *ask,*" she told him, "but your tone says *demand.*"

"Belle." His voice held a warning note.

"I cannot say."

"Cannot or will not?"

Belle held her hands palms-out in a silent gesture for understanding. "Bliss knows money and can explain everything to your satisfaction."

Her father stared at her for several long moments. "I will speak to Bliss when she returns from shopping. Which reminds me that you refused to accompany them."

"I am not going anywhere," Belle explained, "so I do not need new gowns and geegaws."

"Of course, you will be going out," her father said. "Roxie and I will introduce you to society, and you will eventually meet a suitable gentleman."

"Only a blind man would marry a scarred woman," Belle said. "Do not persuade any gentleman into a match with me."

"I would never do that." The duke lifted his arm and made a sweeping gesture at the garden. "You perform minor miracles every day, child. Why do you believe no man will marry you?"

"I would need a *major* miracle to find love now."

Her father shook his head. "You will marry a man who will love you for yourself."

Now he sounded like her sisters. She wondered if attitudes were hereditary. Her sisters and her father could never understand. Saying a gentleman would love her for herself was easy. Finding this mythical husband would prove impossible.

"Your Grace?" Tinker hurried toward them. "Your business associates have arrived."

Her father stood, asking, "Will you walk with me?"

"I want to sit here for a while and savor the sunshine." Belle folded her hands on her lap. "I will ponder the nature of miracles."

He needed a miracle.

Mikhail leaned back on the leather cushion inside his coach, mired in London's weekday traffic. He should have gone directly to his business meeting. Instead, he'd taken his daughter to Bond Street to prove that shops did not sell mummies.

Looking for particular traits in a prospective mate was easy. Finding this mythical wife would prove impossible. Baking and digging and laughing and loving were unusual activities. Beauty and money and pedigree meant nothing to his specific needs and would not make his daughter happy.

"Your Highness?"

Mikhail focused on his coachman holding the door open. He climbed down and grinned at his baby brother waiting for him in front of Inverary House.

"Showing your face to the duke is incredibly brave or incredibly foolish," Mikhail teased him. "This morning's *Times* mentioned a foreign royal seen leaving a certain opera singer's residence before dawn."

Prince Stepan blanched. "Do you think His Grace read the gossip?"

"What do *you* think?"

"I was protecting—"

"Save your explanation for Inverary."

The front door opened before they could knock. The duke's majordomo stepped aside, allowing them entrance.

"His Grace was asking your brothers if you would be attending," Tinker told Stepan. "I understand he is anxious to speak with you."

The two princes started up the stairs to the second-floor study. Mikhail glanced over his shoulder and exchanged smiles with the majordomo. With his droll sense of humor, Tinker was a treasure. Unless, of course, the man's barbs were directed at him.

Mikhail knocked on the study door and then walked inside, his younger brother following him. The Duke of Inverary sat behind his desk. Princes Rudolf and Viktor lounged in chairs near the desk.

Nodding at the duke and his brothers, Mikhail crossed the room and dropped into a chair near the windows. Stepan sat beside him.

"Baby brother, His Grace desires a word with you," Prince Rudolf said.

"I believe His Grace wants more than one word," Viktor amended.

Mikhail sent Stepan a sympathetic look. He would protect his baby brother as he had done his whole life.

Stepan turned to the duke, his mask of innocence only a baby of the family could produce. "How may I help you, Your Grace?"

The Duke of Inverary slammed a folded newspaper on the desk. "Explain that."

"Fancy and I have shared no intimacies," Stepan assured him.

"You are ruining my daughter's reputation."

"I want to marry her, but she dislikes aristocrats."

The duke had the good grace to flush. Out of all his natural daughters, Fancy refused to forgive his emotional neglect. The twit had inherited his own stubbornness.

"I was protecting Fancy from an insane admirer who deposited decapitated roses on her doorstep," Stepan said.

"Decapitated roses?" Mikhail echoed.

Stepan nodded. "That was not the first threat either."

"Be more discreet in the future," the duke said. "Keep your hands and other body parts to yourself."

"Tell your driver to wait for you in the alley," Viktor advised him. "That is what Regina and I—never mind."

Rudolf poured whisky into two crystal glasses and passed them to his youngest brothers. "Shall we discuss business?"

"Stepan, you promised to dissuade the Seven Doves owners against a price war," Rudolf said.

"Six agree to cease this nonsense." Stepan shrugged apologetically. "The seventh wants to pauperize His Grace."

The Duke of Inverary banged his fist on the desk. "I want that bastard's name."

Stepan gave the duke a sheepish smile. "I gave my word to remain silent."

Mikhail gulped the aged whisky, which burned a path to his stomach. Setting the glass on the desk, he stood to stretch his legs and wandered to the window.

A young, ebony-haired woman sat on a bench. A mastiff lay on the bench beside her and rested its enormous head on her lap while she stroked it. From this distance, the woman appeared petite with near-perfect features.

"Is that one of Inverary's daughters?"

Stepan joined him at the window. "Belle Flambeau, the second oldest."

"Your daughter seems lonely," Mikhail said, looking over his shoulder at the duke.

Inverary rose from his chair and crossed the study to stand beside them. "Belle lost her suitor because of the damn facial scar," the duke said. "She refuses to see anyone, insists on staying home, and declines her pin money."

Mikhail was silent, as were all the Kazanovs. A woman who refused spending money was suffering a severe malady.

"Belle is a beauty," Stepan said, "but the slash on her cheek cut into her soul."

The duke's daughter would appreciate a marriage offer and make a family for Bess and me, Mikhail thought. A scarred woman would understand that gowns, gossip, and expensive geegaws were unimportant. She would love a husband for himself, not his title and wealth.

Mikhail turned to the duke, his words surprising all. "I will marry her."

"You want to marry Belle?" Inverary looked stunned. "I will tell her your offer."

"No."

Mikhail whirled around. A young woman stood at the opposite end of the study.

"Raven?" The Duke of Inverary approached her. "What are you doing here?"

"I-I-I fell asleep," she answered. "Your voices awakened me."

The minx is an incompetent liar, Mikhail thought, his lips quirking in amusement. Pretty, though. Did the sister in the garden resemble her?

The Duke of Inverary put his arm around the girl and escorted her to the chair in front of his desk. The duke leaned back against the desk, his size intimidating, and stared at her for several long moments.

"Now tell me the real reason you were hiding behind that chair," Inverary said.

"I wasn't—"

"Raven." The duke's voice held a warning note. "I didn't fall to earth in the last rain shower."

Guilty embarrassment colored her complexion scarlet. Folded on her lap, her hands trembled visibly.

Mikhail struggled against laughter. Her behavior reminded him of his own boyhood. Though he did not doubt that Magnus Campbell was more benevolent than Fydor Kazanov.

"I was eavesdropping," Raven admitted. "Bliss asked me to take notes."

"Your Grace and brothers, I present one of the owners of the Seven Doves Company," Stepan said, drawing everyone's attention. "Guess the identity of the other six."

"His daughters are the business rivals undercutting our prices?" Surprise dropped Mikhail into his chair. He scooped his whisky off the desk, gulped a healthy swig, and set the glass down again.

"Seven children floated a viable company?" Prince Viktor said, his tone incredulous.

"Where did you get the capital for investments?" Prince Rudolf asked.

"Are my daughters pauperizing me with the allowance I gave them?" the duke demanded.

"We would never do that," Raven assured her father. "Using your money would be unethical."

Mikhail leaned close to her. "So is undercutting your own father's prices."

"Tell me about the Seven Doves Company," the duke said, his tone amiable.

"You will need to ask—"

"I am asking you." His tone wasn't quite so amiable.

"I know nothing about business," Raven said, "but Bliss can answer all your questions. Besides, isn't Belle's happiness more important at the moment?"

The Duke of Inverary stared at his youngest daughter long enough to make her squirm. "We will set aside our business discussion until this evening when six of the seven doves will be present."

"Answer one question for me," Prince Rudolf said. "If you did not use your allowances for the initial investments, where did you get the money?"

Raven glanced at the eldest prince and then gave her father an impish smile. "We won the money at the thoroughbred races."

Three princes and one duke stared at her in surprise. Only Prince Stepan appeared unfazed, already knowing the details.

"Blaze communes with animals," Raven explained, and then waited for their laughter to subside. "She and Bliss, our mathematical genius, dressed as boys and went to the races. The thoroughbreds told Blaze"—the men laughed—"which horse would win, and then our friendly next-door neighbor would place the bet."

Her father stared at her for a long moment. "Did Blaze ever pick a loser?"

"Never."

He smiled. "Blaze will be attending the races with me this year."

Prince Rudolf cleared his throat. "I would accompany you."

"You are welcome to join us."

"Why do you object to my marrying your sister?" Mikhail asked her.

"I do not object," Raven answered, "but Belle will refuse if she believes you pity her."

"We will meet by accident, and I will charm her into marriage." Mikhail winked at Raven, making her blush.

His three brothers laughed at his confidence. He sent them a quelling look.

"Belle refuses to meet visitors," Raven reminded him.

"Roxie owns a cottage on the far side of Primrose Hill," the duke spoke up. "I guarantee my wife will persuade Belle to recuperate there for a few days."

"She could fear another attack and refuse," Raven said.

Pondering the problem, Mikhail sipped his whisky and then set the glass on the desk again. "Belle can take the dog for protection."

"Where and when and how you meet is irrelevant," Raven argued. "My sister will believe you pity her unless you can convince her of your love."

"Mikhail cannot fall in love if he never meets her," Stepan said, "but if he meets her, he will need to look at her."

"If he looks at her," Viktor added, "she will think he pities her."

"A blind man could meet the lady without seeing her scar," Rudolf said.

Prince Stepan vetoed that. "You cannot expect Mikhail to blind himself just to—" He stopped talking when his brothers turned astonished gazes on him.

"I will pretend being victimized by robbers," Mikhail said, smiling at his own ingenuity, "and I will feign temporary blindness and amnesia."

"Memory loss is easy," Raven said, "but Belle will know you can see."

"I have had long practice unfocusing my gaze in those boring university classes."

"No wonder you performed so poorly," Viktor remarked.

"You can wear those spectacles that protect eyes from the sun," Stepan suggested.

"That could work," Raven said. "How will you prove that robbers attacked you?"

Prince Rudolf chuckled. "We will need to batter him."

Prince Viktor nodded. "A few bruises will convince your sister."

"Three cousins arrived from Moscow last night," Rudolf said. "Drako, Lykos, and Gunter will gladly help."

"Your living with Belle will ruin her reputation," Inverary said, reconsidering.

"I will marry her by proxy before I go there."

The Duke of Inverary flashed him a satisfied smile. "Welcome to the family, Mikhail."

"Fancy dislikes aristocrats," Raven said. "She will tell Belle if she discovers our scheme."

"I will take Fancy to Rudolf's estate on Sark Island." Stepan shifted his gaze to the duke. "She would never forgive me if I married her by proxy, but you may announce our betrothal as soon as we sail out of London."

"How long can you keep Fancy at Sark?" Mikhail asked.

"Two or three weeks, perhaps."

"Fancy will not go willingly," the duke said.

"I know several herbs that promote sleep," Raven said. "You must contrive to get them into her."

"Our plans are settled then." Stepan smiled at Mikhail. "After our marriages, will we be brothers-in-law or brothers?"

"Sometimes your idiocy amazes me," Mikhail told him.

Stepan grinned at the insult and gestured to Raven. "Did I mention our future sister-in-law moves objects with her mind?"

Mikhail looked from his baby brother to his future sister-in-law. Then he burst into laughter.

Perched on the edge of the desk, his glass tipped onto its side and spilled its contents. Too late, Mikhail leaped out of the chair and stared at the whisky staining his trousers.

"Oops," Raven said, gaining his attention. And then she winked at him.

The sleepy hamlet on the far side of Primrose Hill appeared idyllic, the bustle of London proper seeming miles away. Secluded by shrubs and trees, the timber-framed cottage at the end of the lane consisted of a large common room and two small bedchambers.

The common room served as kitchen and parlor. Both sides had its own hearth, one for cooking and the other for comfort.

It isn't Park Lane, Belle thought, her sweeping gaze surveying her surroundings, but the cottage would suit her simple needs. Here she could savor quiet moments away from prying eyes while her cheek healed.

"If you change your mind," Raven said, standing at the kitchen table to empty a box, "I can bring Puddles for your protection."

Belle joined her sister there. "Puddles would lick the villain to death."

"I can see the newspaper headlines now," Raven said, smiling. "Guard dog slobbers criminal to death."

Belle giggled. "Villain drowns in saliva."

Raven laughed at that. "Well, Puddles does sound ferocious when he barks."

In spite of her sister's good humor, Belle sensed something troubling her and read the anxiety crouched in her eyes. She pushed the thought aside and opened a box containing several Jane Austen novels borrowed from the duke's library.

Raven lifted two bottles out of a box. "Spirits."

"I don't need whisky and vodka," Belle said. "What is that?"

"Lunettes de soleil." Raven passed her the spectacles with darkened lenses. "His Grace sent these to protect your eyes from the sun while gardening."

Belle set the spectacles on her face and looped the wires over her ears. She smiled when the spectacles slipped to perch on the tip of her nose.

"Apparently, our father's head is wider than yours," Raven said. "No doubt, all that arrogance makes a fat head. How long are you planning to stay?"

"I need to regain my inner balance." Belle noted her sister's anxiety again. "What disturbs you? Has Alexander Blake upset you?"

"No." Raven's smiled seemed forced. "I will return with more supplies in a few days."

"Cook sent enough food to feed *two* people for a month."

"Don't fret about safety," Raven said, ignoring her comment. "Father's agents are patrolling the area."

"That is unnecessary." She hadn't meant to create work for anyone.

"Guarding you—discreetly, of course—allows His Grace a peaceful night's sleep." Raven hugged her. "Take care of yourself."

Belle walked her to the door and waited until Raven climbed into the ducal coach. She lifted her hand in farewell as the coach turned in a U.

Alone for the first time in her life, Belle finished unpacking her clothing in one of the bedchambers. At one point she found several articles—bedrobe, breeches, shirt—that did not belong to her.

One of the maids had mixed someone else's belongings with hers. Some poor footman would be searching for his bedrobe tonight.

Two steps brought Belle across the chamber to the window. The small expanse of garden had been neglected for years.

Today she would inspect her new domain to diagnose its problems. Tomorrow she would heal the damage and set things right. Too bad she could not heal her own damage and set herself right.

Belle left the cottage and stepped into the bright sunlight. Nary the hint of a cloud to mar the heavenly blue sky.

She would enjoy this time of solitude. That is, if she did not succumb to loneliness. She did not fear an attack. Unless, of course, the villain had followed her from Park Lane.

Belle strolled the perimeter of the miniscule garden, bordered by woodland. The lawn was a sea of weeds. Only the hardiest of plants had survived years of neglect.

And then Belle spied a solitary pansy cringing beneath a silver birch tree. She dropped to her knees and touched it, her lips moving in a silent prayer.

"Help."

Belle sat back on her haunches and stared at the pansy. This could not be happening. Flowers did not speak English.

"Help."

Belle lifted her head and listened, trying to decide the direction of the call. Her nerves rioted in high alert.

"Help."

Belle whirled around. Her lips parted in an O of surprise.

A man, bloodied and battered, staggered onto the property and grabbed the oak tree. He clung to its trunk like a drowning man.

Without hesitation, Belle raced to his aid. She looped his left arm over her shoulders, her right arm circling his back. Though he stood more than a foot taller, she was determined to save him.

"Lean on me," Belle said. "I can nurse you better inside."

Holding him steady, Belle started toward the cottage, but her legs buckled beneath his weight. Her load lightened before she went down as if unseen hands were keeping the man and her standing.

They reached the door by slow degrees. Only his occasional stumble and accompanying groan of pain hindered their progress.

Droplets of sweat rolled down Belle's face by the time they reached the sofa. Belle pressed him back against the cushions and dropped to her knees.

"Close your eyes," she said, her soothing tone a balm. "Breathe slowly and evenly."

The injuries appeared superficial. His bottom lip was bleeding and would swell. Severe bruising marred his cheekbones, and he had the beginnings of two black eyes.

Even battered and bloodied, the man had the dark good looks that women found intriguing. Belle would bet her last shilling this man had the ladies swooning in his path.

"What I can see does not appear life-threatening," Belle assured him. "Do you hurt anywhere besides your face?"

"Everywhere." He moaned in pathetic emphasis.

"Do you have sharp pains around your upper torso?"

"No."

"That means no cracked ribs," she said. "I'll wash your wounds. What's your name?"

He opened his eyes, dark and unfocused. "I cannot see you."

That alarmed her. "Do you see black only?"

"The world is a nauseating blur."

Belle reached for his hand. "Blurry means your blindness is probably temporary."

Only a blind man could love a scarred woman. That thought popped into her mind before guilt banished it.

"I am Belle Flambeau. Who are you?"

"I-I-I cannot remember."

That startled her more than his inability to see clearly. "Your memory will return with your vision. What shall I call you?"

"Mick seems familiar."

"Mick it is, then." Belle gave his hand an encouraging squeeze. "I am going to leave your side for a few minutes to warm water and fetch salve."

His grip on her hand tightened. "Will you bring a cloth to cover my eyes? I do not want you looking into my sightless gaze."

"I need to clean your injuries first." Belle placed the palm of her hand against his cheek. "Trust me to ease your pain."

Chapter 4

His bride wore pigtails.

Fighting a smile, Mikhail watched her from beneath half-closed lids. She was gentle and kind and calm and capable. No society lady of his acquaintance would consider rescuing a battered stranger.

Even Lenore would not have rushed to his aid. His late wife shared several of her mother's and her sister's failings.

Mikhail shifted his body, every muscle protesting the beating he had suffered. His brothers and his cousins had held nothing back. Someday his daughter would appreciate his sacrifice to obtain a suitable mummy. He hoped his bride would eventually cherish the extreme lengths he had taken to marry her.

Belle set a pot of water to heat over the hearth's flames. Then she grabbed a few linens and a jar.

Mikhail snapped his eyes shut when she turned around. A moment later, he sensed her presence beside him, and a linen cloth touched his lips.

"Hold this to stop the bleeding," she instructed him.

Mikhail did as told but opened his eyes a crack when she walked away. The natural sway of her hips appealed to him.

Once the water boiled, Belle poured it into a bowl. Then

she looped a basket over her arm and carried the bowl of steaming water toward him.

"Sit up, Mick." When he did, Belle perched on the edge of the sofa and lifted the linen. "The bleeding has almost stopped."

Belle dipped a fresh linen into the steaming water and washed his face, her touch light. She began with his forehead and worked her way lower, being extra careful around his blackening eyes and bruised cheekbones.

Pausing in her task, Belle studied his face. And then wished she hadn't.

Belle knew she was in trouble. Even battered, her patient was the most handsome man she'd ever seen with his black hair and strong angular face. A dimple dented the middle of his chin, softening his stark masculinity.

Charles Wingate was a vague, unpleasant memory. She could not conjure his face in her mind's eye.

There was only this man. And they were alone. He seemed familiar, though. "Have we met before?" she asked him.

"I would have remembered meeting an angel." His voice was husky, sending a shiver down her spine.

Belle blushed all the way down to her toes. Her patient was a flatterer.

"What shall we do about me?" Mikhail asked. "Will you hang FOUND signs all over London?"

Belle laughed at that. "The chamomile salve will help you heal." She dipped her finger into the jar of salve and then coated his cut lip. "You speak with an accent."

"Do I?"

Belle nodded before she remembered he couldn't see her. "Are you foreign?"

"I cannot remember who I am."

"Sorry." Belle blushed at her blunder and reached for the *lunettes de soleil.* She set them on his face, saying, "These spectacles will shield you from prying eyes."

"I did not mean you were prying," he said. "Only, I felt uncomfortable."

Belle touched his cheek. "I don't like people looking at me either."

"You sound beautiful."

"If you lie back against the cushion, I will ease your pain," Belle said, ignoring his compliment.

Mikhail watched her openly from behind the spectacles' dark lenses. His brother had spoken truthfully. His bride was beautiful, both outside and inside. Ebony hair, violet eyes, and a generous heart. The scar was a minor distraction that would fade with time.

Raising her hand, Belle performed an unusual blessing. She touched her left breast, forehead, right breast, left and right shoulders, and left breast again.

When she leaned close, her sensuous rose scent teased him. She placed her hands on each side of his head, and her lips moved in silent prayer.

"What are you doing?" he asked.

"Shhh, I am easing your pain."

Strangely, Mikhail did feel better. *Witchcraft* popped into his head, but he discarded that as too silly to consider.

"I do feel better. How did you accomplish that?"

An ambiguous smile touched her lips. "All things are possible with prayer."

"You asked the Lord to relieve my pain, and He answered your prayers?"

"If you feel better, then my prayers were answered."

Mikhail smiled, though the movement hurt him. "I have never known anyone whose prayers were answered."

"There is a first time for everything."

Belle stared at him for a long moment, so long he suspected she knew his ploy. She stood and disappeared into a bedchamber. Returning to the common room a moment later, she clutched a bedrobe.

"Take your clothes off."

That startled him. "I beg your pardon?"

"Your shirt and breeches need washing," Belle explained, a blush staining her cheeks. "This robe will fit you."

Mikhail did not move to take it from her. "Does the robe belong to your husband?"

"I am unmarried."

"Brother?"

"No."

"Lover?"

Her answer was an embarrassed squeak. "No."

By God, his bride blushed more than any woman he'd ever met. "And you will wash my clothing?" Mikhail sounded as surprised as he felt. He'd always had servants to care for trivial matters.

"I do not have a maid," she answered.

This was going to be fun and well worth a few bruises. "I will need your assistance disrobing," he said, and watched her blush again.

Belle stared at him, having failed to foresee this complication, and then gave herself a mental shake. She was a healer. He needed healing.

"Belle?"

"I will help you undress." Her words rushed out before she could stop them. She dropped the black bedrobe and sat on the edge of the sofa.

She *could* do this. She *would* do this. She *wanted* to do this.

Mustering her courage, Belle leaned close and unfastened the top button. Her fingers dropped to the second button. And then the third.

She paused, her violet gaze on his muscled chest. The matting of dark hair made him appear so . . . so . . . *masculine*.

"Is something wrong?" His voice sounded choked.

Her gaze flew to his face. She suffered the uncanny feeling that he was watching her every move. That was impossible, though.

"I have never seen a man's chest," she admitted.

"As you said, there is a first time for everything." He reached for her hand. "If you feel too uncomfortable, I will undress myself. Somehow."

"I can do it." Belle finished unfastening the buttons in a rush of movement. She spread the shirt wide with the palms of her hands, baring him to her mesmerized gaze. Without thinking, she glided her hands across his chest to his shoulders. His skin was warm and smooth, the muscles beneath pure steel.

Mikhail sat up, his chest mere inches away, his breath mingling with hers. Belle trembled with excitement, her belly melting in response to his movement, her breasts feeling heavy.

Danger, danger, danger. The alarm flashed through her mind.

Leaping up, Belle composed herself. She removed his shirt and helped him slip his arms into the bedrobe's sleeves.

"You can manage the breeches while I make us supper."

Belle fled to the kitchen side of the common room. She felt flushed as if she'd passed a hot summer's day in front of an oven.

After starting the porridge, Belle brewed birch tea laced with herbs promoting sleep. She kept her back on her patient while preparing supper. She knew what he was doing, though. She had never been more aware of another person in her entire life.

Belle had never been completely alone with a man. She and her sisters had been born on the wrong side of the blanket, but their virtue had been carefully guarded as befitting a duke's daughters.

Across the common room, Mikhail itched to laugh out loud. He had forgotten how skittish virgins were.

Wrapped in his bedrobe, he relaxed against the cushion and watched his bride. They would eat supper alone. Like commoners.

Mikhail had never realized the simple pleasures shared by commoners. Poverty did have a few benefits to it. Privacy and . . . and . . . He would consider the other benefits later.

Belle carried a tray holding a bowl of porridge, a cup of birch tea, and a spoon. A towel lay across her arm.

She set the tray on the table. "Sit up, and I will feed you."

His expression registered surprise. And then he smiled, inciting butterflies in the pit of her belly to take flight.

"What did you cook?"

"Oatmeal porridge. You need something bland but filling."

Belle sat on the edge of the couch and placed the towel across his lap. She dipped the spoon into the bowl and scooped a bit of porridge. When she lifted the spoon to his lips, she questioned her own sanity.

The man was temptation. Watching the spoon slip between his lips was a gentle, breath-catching torment.

Shielded by the spectacles, Mikhail kept his gaze on her while he ate. He read the emotions playing across her face. His bride was attracted to him and confused by the unfamiliar yearning.

Desire was a stranger to her. Until now. That made him exceedingly happy.

When he swallowed the last dollop of porridge, Belle placed the cup of birch tea in his hands. "The herbs in the tea will make you drowsy."

Mikhail sipped the tea and relaxed against the cushion. "Tell me about yourself, Princess."

Belle blushed, her smile unconsciously flirtatious. "I thought I was an angel."

"You *are* an angel, Princess."

"You are a flatterer, sir. Close your eyes, and I will tell you a story."

That perked him up. His daughter wanted a mummy who knew bedtime stories. "Do you know many stories?"

"Dozens and dozens and dozens," she answered. "Some are meant for children, but yours is for adults."

"You will make an excellent mother."

"I hope so." Belle patted his hand and began her story. "Many years ago in a country across the sea lived a noble family. The lord loved his lady, and both adored their three sons and seven daughters.

"Gabrielle, the seventh daughter, passed her first ten years basking in the sunshine of unconditional love. Her family cherished her, her nanny loved her, and even the farmers looked forward to her visits.

"And then Evil roamed the land with his friends, Terror and Death. The three disguised themselves as patriots and destroyed anyone who disagreed with them.

"Gabrielle's nanny took her into the woods, dressed her in peasant's clothing, and hid her in a trunk. A farmer, still loyal to the family, drove the nanny and her trunk in his cart all the way to the sea.

"An English ship carried the nanny and her charge to safety. Gabrielle stepped onto English soil and began a new life. . . ."

"Is the story true?" Mikhail asked.

"I will let you decide that for yourself."

"What happened to little Gabrielle?"

"You will need to wait until tomorrow evening for that." Belle lifted the empty teacup from his hands. "Close your eyes and sleep while I finish my chores."

"What story would you have told to a child?"

"Boy or girl?"

Mikhail smiled, though the movement pained him. "You have an extensive repertoire."

Belle carried the tray to the kitchen. She felt her patient watching her, which temporary blindness made impossible, and sensed when he dropped into sleep.

Before seeking her own chamber, Belle succumbed to the urge to get one last peek at her patient. She watched him sleeping, his lips slightly parted, and wondered how his lips would feel pressed against hers. Her gaze slid lower to the supple skin bared by the edges of the bedrobe, and the fluttering in her belly returned.

Only a blind man would marry a scarred woman.

Nanny Smudge had spoken truthfully. Miracles *did* happen every day. And this man was hers.

Fear rolled off her like waves surging toward shore.

She knew he was there. Somewhere. Lurking in the night. Watching. Waiting.

He loved the hunt, especially his quarry's fear. Closing his eyes for a moment, he imagined a droplet of sweat rolling down the valley between her breasts.

Charging him for her services had sealed her fate. She had not acknowledged the honor of his choosing her.

Mother was correct. All women were whores, deserving punishment for their sins.

He cut down an alley in order to get ahead of her. Approaching footsteps heightened his anticipation.

She was almost here. She would be his. She would regret insulting him by making him pay.

When she neared his hiding place, he stepped out of the shadows. She stopped short, her expression registering surprise and fear.

"I want you again."

"Ya'll need to pay agin, m'lord."

He reached into his pocket and passed her two one-pound notes. "A gold sovereign is yours when I've finished."

She folded the notes, stuffing them between her breasts, and followed him into the alley. Wearing a smile, she dropped to her knees in front of him.

Grabbing her hair, he yanked her head back and slashed the blade across her throat. Then he waited for her heart to pump the life out of her body.

Using his bloodied blade, he hacked a length of her hair and pressed a gold sovereign into the palm of her hand, closing her fingers around it. "Enjoy your sovereign."

Alexander Blake paid the driver and climbed out of the hackney in London's unsavory East End. Easy prey for the Society Slasher, another prostitute had been butchered, and he would bet his last shilling the scene would lack substantial evidence.

Dying is best done in winter, Alexander thought, *not on a spring day that promised perfection.*

Though the hour was early, a crowd had gathered near the mouth of the alley. Their voices were hushed whispers. Untimely death affected people that way.

At six feet tall, Alexander had no problem pushing his way through the crowd. The nauseating stench of unwashed bodies and the River Thames assaulted his nostrils. He was glad he hadn't bothered with breakfast.

The constable's runners held the curious back. They recognized Alexander and let him pass.

Amadeus Black stood near the blanket-covered lump and raised his hand in greeting. Barney, the constable's aide, had fixed his attention on the alley like a hound searching for a scent. A petite, young woman wept quietly, her sniffling as hushed as the crowd's whispers.

"I'm glad you got here so quickly," Constable Black said.

Alexander nodded, his eyes on the flies hovering above the lump's blanket. He slid his gaze to the sniffling girl. "Who is she?"

"Miss Tulip Woods is a friend of the victim," Amadeus told him. "Speak to her before inspecting the body."

"Is there something special about her?"

"You tell me."

Alexander approached the girl. She didn't look like any whore he'd ever seen. She was younger than Raven Flambeau, no more than fifteen or sixteen. Dark mahogany hair framed an angel's face. Her eyes were unusual, one blue and the other green. A sprinkling of fine freckles added to her innocent appearance.

Reaching into his pocket, Alexander pulled his handkerchief out and offered it to her. When she hesitated, he said, "It's clean."

Miss Tulip Woods accepted his offering.

Alexander studied her a moment longer, thinking she looked vaguely familiar. Intelligence shone from her eyes, not the usual dullness that life on the streets created.

"You found the body?"

"Ruby never came home last night so I went out early looking for her," she answered.

"Do you live nearby?"

"Yes."

"Where and when did you last see Ruby?" Alexander asked, trying to remember where he had seen her before.

"I saw her near Dirty Dick's," she answered. "Ruby was walking into the alley to entertain a gentleman."

"You saw Ruby and this gentleman?"

Tulip nodded. "The gent was her last client of the night, and then she was coming home."

"Can you describe the man?"

Tulip chewed on her bottom lip and dropped her gaze to the ground. "I didn't get a clear look at his face."

Alexander decided Miss Tulip Woods was not telling him the whole truth. "Do you remember anything about him?"

"He dressed in gentleman's clothes," Tulip answered. "I think Ruby called him Buck or Chuck, but she might have said suck or f—"

"Wait here while I speak to my colleague." Alexander crossed the short distance to the constable. "Tulip Woods is a ringer for our last victim. Instinct tells me the chit is hiding something."

"Always trust your instincts," Amadeus said. "Take a peek at the dead girl and tell me what you see."

Pulling his gloves on, Alexander walked to the lump and drew the blanket away from her face. His mouth dropped open in shock. He replaced the blanket and returned to the constable's side.

"Ruby arranged our last victim's funeral," Alexander said. "What are you thinking?"

Amadeus Black rubbed the back of his neck. "Except for Miss Tulip Woods, the connection eludes me."

"If the Slasher saw Tulip, she could be in danger," Alexander said. "We should keep a guarded eye on her."

"Who will guard her?"

"Leave this to me." Alexander crossed the alley to speak to the girl. "Ruby arranged the funeral for our previous victim, a girl who looked like you. Do you have an explanation for that?"

Her lips quivered as she fought fresh tears. "Your previous victim was Iris Woods, my twin. Ruby made the arrangements to spare me the duty. My sister's death was a shock."

"The constable and I fear for your safety," Alexander said. "We are taking you into protective custody."

"You're jailing me?"

"You will be staying in a safe house." Alexander looked over his shoulder and gestured to Barney. "Escort Tulip to her residence, guard her while she packs, and bring her here."

Barney smiled at the girl. "Tulip? What a pretty name. My wife loves tulips." He guided her through the crowd.

"You aren't keeping her in Soho?" Amadeus asked.

Alexander grinned. "My grandfather will shelter her."

The constable laughed and shook his head. "I cannot believe you would place the little ragamuffin in the Duke of Essex's home."

"Tulip Woods will become an honored guest," Alexander said, "or I will disown him. He needs me more than I need him."

"Inspect the body while she's gone."

Alexander drew the blanket off the lump. He circled the body once and then crouched beside it. Like the others, her throat had been slit and a length of hair taken as a souvenir of his kill.

The dead girl lay on her left side. Her right arm stretched out, her left arm mostly hidden by her body.

Alexander opened the fingers of her right hand and lifted the gold sovereign. He was about to stand when he realized the dead girl clutched something in her left hand. Gently, he turned her on her back and pried the fingers open.

Alexander inspected the metallic object, a gold button engraved with the letters *CW.* "We have evidence." He passed it to the constable.

"How careless of him," Amadeus said, a relieved smile appearing on his face. "We have narrowed our suspect list to those men whose initials are *CW.*"

Alexander drew the blanket over the girl. "I'll pay for the burial."

"I knew you would," Amadeus Black said. "You have paid for all the Slasher's victims."

"I don't like to see women hurt," Alexander said, and then shrugged. "I can afford the expense, and it's the least I can do besides capturing the monster."

"Ask the Duke of Inverary if he will allow Raven to help us," Amadeus instructed him. "I would know what she senses from the gold button."

"Do you really believe in that hocus-pocus?" Alexander asked with a smile.

"I believe in anything that will catch a killer."

"I'll stop at Inverary House after I deliver Tulip to my grandfather."

Barney returned with a bag in each hand. Behind him walked Tulip, carrying two bags, all she possessed in the world.

"You've a lot of baggage for a squirt of a girl." Alexander reached for the bags Barney carried.

Tulip refused to relinquish the two bags she clutched. She looked at the constable, asking, "What about Ruby?"

"Alex is paying for the funeral," Constable Black told her.

Alexander smiled at her. "I am Alexander Blake."

"Blake?" Tulip sounded surprised.

"Have you heard of the Blakes?"

"No, never."

Alexander narrowed his gaze on her. Why would she refuse knowing the Blakes when she had heard the name before? This was becoming more interesting by the moment.

Morning had aged into the usual weekday quagmire of coaches and pedestrians. Riding from one end of London to the other took longer than thirty minutes.

Alexander watched Tulip, who appeared surprised by the

gradual change from the East End's squalor to Park Lane luxury. That told him she was not a native Londoner.

"How old are you?" he asked.

"How old do I look?"

Cripes, Alexander thought, answering questions with questions sounded like his grandfather.

The hackney halted in front of his grandfather's Park Lane residence. Alexander helped her down and carried two bags while she carried the others.

"Is this your home?" Tulip asked.

"No, squirt, my grandfather lives here."

The front door opened to reveal a tall, dignified older man.

"Are you his grandfather?" Tulip asked.

"Good heavens, no."

Ushering her inside, Alexander said, "Twigs is my grandfather's majordomo. Twigs, meet Tulip Woods. Tulip, sit here until I send for you."

Tulip sat on a chair against the wall. She had three bags at her feet and one on her lap.

"His Grace is breakfasting in the dining room," Twigs said, hurrying down the corridor.

His grandfather sat alone at the head of a twenty-foot table. Alexander took the seat on his right.

"What can I serve you?" Twigs asked.

"Coffee."

"Why don't you eat?" his grandfather asked.

"The Slasher's latest victim stole my appetite," Alexander answered.

"You haven't forgotten the Winchester affair tonight?"

"I will be attending with you as planned."

His grandfather nodded. "Use the opportunity to start looking for a suitable bride. Maybe one of those Flambeau girls now that Inverary has acknowledged them. A union between Inverary and Essex would be the marriage of the decade."

Alexander conjured Raven's image in his mind. Her courtesan lips teased and taunted him.

"I see you have someone in mind."

Alexander lifted his cup and sipped the coffee. "You see too much."

"Raven Flambeau would make an excellent bride," his grandfather said.

Alexander gave him a sidelong glance. "She's too young."

"Young women make the best brides," the older man said, "because they don't have time to hone their wiles. Unfortunately, living with the Duchess of Inverary will quickly change her." His grandfather chuckled. "Roxanne Campbell was always a vixen and too smart for her own good, but Magnus can control her."

"Constable Black wants Raven Flambeau to help with our Slasher investigation," Alexander told his grandfather. "If she agrees, I'll need to get her father's permission. Life was simpler before he acknowledged his daughters."

"How could that young woman help a murder investigation?" the duke asked.

Alexander grinned at the old man. "Raven has the Sight."

The Duke of Essex look astounded. "Do you believe in that nonsense?"

"Amadeus Black believes in anything that helps him solve a crime," Alexander answered. "We need your assistance too."

His grandfather cocked a brow at him. "I suspect I will not like this."

"A witness may have seen the perpetrator," Alexander said, ignoring the comment. "I need you to give her refuge in your home."

That certainly startled the old man. "You want to install a doxy in my home?"

"Tulip is fifteen years old."

"What kind of blasted name is Tulip?"

"Her name." Alexander hoped he sounded as displeased as he felt. "If you will not do me this favor, I will disown you."

His grandfather stared at him for a moment. "You get your ruthlessness from me." He pursed his lips. "Where is she?"

Alexander gestured Twigs to fetch Tulip. "Promise me you won't frighten her."

"How can a harmless old man like me possibly frighten—?"

Twigs returned at that moment and announced, "Miss Tulip Woods."

Looking uncertain, Tulip stepped into the dining room. She clutched that one bag as if fearing a thief would steal it.

Alexander beckoned her forward.

Twigs headed toward the sideboard, saying, "I'll bring your breakfast, Miss Tulip."

"Am I required to feed her too?" the duke growled.

"Are you planning to starve me?" Tulip challenged.

"Did I say that?" the old man snapped.

Alexander felt like laughing. His grandfather may have met his match.

"Grandfather, I present Miss Tulip Woods. Squirt, meet His Grace, the Duke of Essex."

"Make your curtsey, girl," his grandfather said.

"Curtsey to you?"

"No, curtsey to my butler."

With the girl's breakfast in hand, Twigs turned toward the table at that moment. The old majordomo looked ready to explode when she curtsied to him.

"Is she simple?" the duke asked.

Tulip sat at the table. "Are you calling me simple?"

"Was I speaking to you?"

"You were ranting and raving, not speaking."

His grandfather banged his cane on the floor and shouted, "I never rant and rave."

Tulip gave the old man a satisfied smile. She had rested her case without uttering a word.

Alexander grinned. "She is *not* simple."

The duke rubbed his forehead. "What did I ever do to deserve this?" He glanced at the girl. "Are you going to eat those eggs or watch them grow mold? Give Twigs your bag. One of the maids will unpack it."

"Twigs can unpack the other three," Tulip said, hugging the bag to her chest. "No one touches this one."

Alexander stared at her clutching the tapestry bag to her breast like a baby. Whatever it contained could prove interesting. He would need to peek inside at first opportunity.

"No one will touch your bag," he assured her.

Tulip looked from him to his grandfather to the majordomo. Then she set the bag on the floor beside her.

"If the food grows cold, missy," the duke warned, "you won't get more."

Tulip sat ramrod straight. After placing the napkin on her lap, she lifted her fork and began eating.

Speaking to his grandfather about inconsequential matters, Alexander watched the girl without seeming to do so and kept his face devoid of expression.

Miss Tulip Woods was an enigma. She resembled the Slasher's last victim, profession unknown, and was a friend of his latest victim, clearly a prostitute. Her attitude and table manners shouted duchess, not doxy.

He would bet London Bridge that her tapestry bag contained all her secrets. Its contents would answer the question, duchess or doxy.

"I need to leave now," Alexander said to his grandfather, "but will see you this evening." He slid his gaze to the girl. "Enjoy your visit, Tulip, and I will see you soon."

Leaving Essex House, Alexander walked another block to Inverary House. His thoughts shifted to Raven Flambeau.

Weeks earlier, Raven had professed her love for him. Caught off-guard, he had responded badly, and her attitude since then had been darker than the north-facing window at dusk.

If he had seen her declaration coming, he would have been more sensitive to her feelings. Adding insult to injury, he'd told her she was too young for love and the little sister he'd never had.

Now he'd begun to view her differently. Her ebony hair and violet eyes were pretty, but her vanilla scent appealed to him as did her nicely developed figure. Her lips featured in his lewd dreams.

And that made him feel guilty.

Raven had always been everyone's baby sister. She wasn't a child any longer, though. He knew that for certain.

Reaching Inverary House, Alexander climbed the front steps. The door opened before he could knock.

"Good morning, my lord." Tinker, the duke's majordomo, stepped aside to allow him entrance. "Miss Raven has been anticipating your arrival."

"How did she—?"

"I know because . . . *I know.*" Sitting at the bottom of the grand staircase, Raven stood and walked toward him.

Alexander struggled to keep from perusing her assets. "We found evidence with our latest Slasher victim," he said. "Constable Black requests your assistance. With His Grace's permission, of course."

Raven gave him a long look. "Do you actually believe in my—how did you phrase it—my hocus-pocus helping to solve crimes?"

"If hocus-pocus could solve crimes," Alexander said, his smile clearly displeasing her, "magistrates would learn incantations instead of law."

"How entertaining life must be for the perpetually witty like you," Raven said, her face expressionless. "I daresay, your most appreciative audience is your own reflection in the mirror."

"Will you help us?"

Raven pressed a finger across her lips as if trying to recall her social schedule. "That depends upon the day and the hour."

Alexander cocked a brow at her. He could not decide if she was purposely contrary or had a full social schedule. Neither appealed to him.

"You will need to give me advance notice."

Alexander inclined his head, unable to mask his displeasure with her attitude. "Are you attending the Winchester ball tonight?"

"Perhaps."

"Will you honor me with a dance?"

Satisfaction leaped at him from her disarming violet eyes. She pursed her lips, making his groin tighten with need.

"I will consider it."

Without another word, Alexander walked out the door. His grandfather was correct. The Duchess of Inverary was teaching Raven the most effective methods of tormenting men.

Chapter 5

Someone was humming a waltz.

Mikhail awakened the next morning to the sound of his bride humming in the kitchen. The delicious aromas of brewing coffee and freshly baked bread wafted through the air, teasing his stomach into a growl.

Opening his eyes a crack, Mikhail noted the sunshine streaming through the window into the cottage. He donned the *lunettes de soleil*.

"Good morning." Belle approached and stood beside the sofa. "I trust you slept well."

She wore an old gown, threadbare and frayed, something no society lady of his acquaintance would wear to scrub floors. That is, if such a lady would consider scrubbing floors.

Mikhail knew he had never seen a more beautiful woman, her beauty glowing from within. A tattered gown or scarred cheek could never diminish her. He wished he knew magic words that would make her understand how desirable she was.

"Your tea is potent," he said, and then yawned.

"Let me help you rise." Belle blushed crimson, adding, "I placed a pot in the other chamber for your convenience."

Mikhail felt his own complexion heating with a flush. He had not considered the logistical reality of forced intimacy.

Belle guided him into the second bedchamber. "Call me when—" She blushed again.

He flushed. Again.

Mikhail knew embarrassment was unnecessary between husband and wife. The problem was the wife didn't know they were married.

"Who will clean it?" he asked.

She looked surprised. "I will clean the pot."

That embarrassed him even more. Besides, she was now his princess, and princesses did not clean chamber pots. He couldn't quite mask his irritation when he said, "You are no chambermaid."

"The maid quit last week."

He grinned. "Touché, Princess."

"Call me when you're finished," Belle said, placing the pot into his hands. She left the room, the door clicking shut behind her.

Mikhail stared at the door for a moment, a smile flirting with his lips. His wife was the most amazing woman, taking adversity in stride. She was humming again as she moved around the common room. He hoped she was happy enough for humming when she learned of their marriage.

Why was he worrying? Belle Flambeau would be ecstatic when she learned of their marriage. What woman would not be happy? She would have an exalted title and fabulous wealth and, of course, an exceedingly handsome husband.

In the kitchen, Belle placed the hot, crusty rolls on a plate. She carried a pan of warmed water, soap, and towels to the table near the sofa.

Caring for her patient felt natural. Since Fancy had no patience, she was the one who had helped Nanny Smudge care for her five younger sisters.

"Belle!"

Returning to the second bedchamber, Belle took her patient's hand and guided him to the sofa. Then she lifted the spectacles off his face.

"What are you doing?" he asked.

"I cannot wash your face while you wear those." Belle dampened a cloth and began to wash his face, gently around his injuries. Black stubbles of beard gave him a rakish look. "You will not shave for a few days."

My, my, my. His wife was the bossy type. She had better lose that tendency fast.

Mikhail did not want her attention on his face lest she realize he could see as well as she. "I can see better this morning," he said, trying to divert her attention.

He could have kicked himself when she lifted a hand to her injured cheek. "I can see vague shapes but no details," he amended himself.

Belle relaxed and dropped her hand. "Wash your face then," she said, placing the cloth into his hand. "I have prepared Nanny Smudge's specialty for strengthening a body."

"Who is Nanny Smudge?"

"She was my nanny who passed away last year."

Belle disappeared into the kitchen section of the common room and returned with a sandwich. "Eat that while I put breakfast on the table."

Mikhail took a bite, chewed, and swallowed. "Bread and butter and a sprinkling of cinnamon, huh?"

"Nanny's medicinal herb is added to the butter and cinnamon," Belle said. "You will eat that sandwich each morning and evening until you regain your strength."

Yes, indeed, his bride had a bossy streak. He took another bite. "What else is for breakfast?"

"Porridge."

"Again?"

Belle laughed at his dismayed tone and appeared in front of him. "We'll sit at the table for this meal."

Mikhail popped the last bit of sandwich into his mouth. Then he stood and let her guide him to a chair at the kitchen table.

"We have rolls, scrambled eggs, fried kippers, and coffee," Belle said. "Shall I feed you?"

"I will feed myself." Mikhail reached for a roll and then asked in surprise, "Did you bake the bread?"

"Cook quit last week too."

Mikhail gave her his most charming smile, knowing the devastating effect it had on the ladies. If his bride made all this breakfast, could she——? "Can you bake a happiness cake?"

"Happiness cakes are my specialty," she answered. "I make hugs and kisses cookies too."

"Are you making a joke at my expense?"

"Why would I joke about cookies and cake?" She sounded sincere.

Mikhail made no answer. He was too busy counting his blessings in choosing a bride his daughter would love.

They ate in silence. Mikhail ate most of the meal with his eyes closed to ensure enough spills and drops to convince her of his blindness.

Afterward, Belle cleaned the remnants of breakfast away and washed his breeches and shirt. Protected by his spectacles, Mikhail watched her work and admired her graceful movements. His bride was curvaceously slender, not too fat and not too skinny.

She disappeared into her bedchamber and returned with garments. "These breeches and shirt should fit."

"Who owns them?"

"I live with my father most of the time," Belle explained. "One of the maids mixed a footman's belongings with mine."

"Maids?" Mikhail feigned surprise. "Who is your father?"

"I prefer he remain anonymous."

"With maids and footmen, he must be a wealthy man."

Belle shrugged. "I suppose so."

"You sound unimpressed."

"Money does not guarantee happiness."

Her sentiment made him smile. His wife was a *real* woman, not an expensive accessory. "Why are you staying here?"

"I wanted a few days of privacy."

He grinned. "And then I dropped in."

"Staggered, more likely." She was blushing again. "Shall I help you dress?"

"I think I can manage." Laughter lurked in his voice. "Close your eyes."

Mikhail smiled when she snapped her eyes shut. Closing his own eyes in case she peeked, he slipped into the breeches and then doffed the bedrobe. He slipped his arms into the shirtsleeves.

"Will you fasten the buttons for me?" Mikhail asked, rising from the chair.

Belle blushed and reached for the first button. She stood so close, he was tempted to yank her into his arms and kiss her senseless.

For her part, Belle felt the urge to glide her fingers across his muscled chest. She could not imagine what was wrong with her. No man had ever affected her so strongly.

Mikhail watched her changing expression. His bride desired her prince but was too inexperienced to know it. Seductive innocence wrapped around her like a gossamer shawl.

Too embarrassed to look at him, Belle looped her small basket over her arm and reached for his hand. After guiding him out the door, she brought him around the cottage to sit beneath an oak tree. "Relax while I tend a few suffering plants."

The morning was alive with late spring's scents, sounds, and sights. Lovestruck doves were billing and cooing. Across an expanse of mostly weeds, a wren dove into its nest hole, and several sparrows fluttered past.

Mikhail breathed deeply. The world smelled green and fresh. He could not remember the last time he sat beneath a tree and did nothing but enjoy the day.

Belle knelt in the dirt in front of a dying pansy and lifted several items from her basket. She made an unusual blessing and then lit a candle. Placing her hands on either side of the pansy, she began whispering.

"Are you talking to me?" Mikhail called.

Belle answered without turning around, "I am coaxing this pansy back to life."

"My brother talks to plants too."

Belle whirled around so fast she fell on her rump. "You have a brother?"

"I cannot remember," Mikhail lied, "but I suppose I must if I said that." He fixed a pained expression on his face, adding, "You cannot imagine how frustrated I feel."

Belle left the pansy to sit beside him beneath the oak. "Your memory will return in bits and pieces until all your memories come rushing back. Your vision is already returning. Perhaps you need only wait a few more days for your memory."

"I pray you are correct." Mikhail gave her his charming smile, hoping to divert her from his brother. "Perhaps when my memory returns, we will know where I get my accent. Could I possibly—?" He hesitated. "I want to know what you look like. Would you permit me to touch your face?"

Belle bit her bottom lip in indecision. She feared him touching her cheek. "My face is scarred."

"Does it hurt?"

"Only when I look in a mirror." *Or think of my bleak future.* Mikhail reached for her hand. "Tell me about the scar."

"Someone attacked me," Belle told him. "I suppose I am lucky to be alive, but I do not feel especially lucky."

"You know who you are."

Belle stared at him. He was correct, of course. There were worse things in life than carrying a scar on her face. The scars people could not see were always worse than superficial ones.

Like her mother. She had lost her entire family in the Terror, and her insecurity had never allowed her happiness.

Belle took a deep, quivering breath. She reached for his hands and raised them to her face.

Good girl, Mikhail thought, *allowing me to do this means you will recover.*

Closing his eyes, Mikhail ran his fingertips across the smooth expanse of her forehead. He followed the arch of her brow with the tips of his index fingers. His thumbs glided down the bridge of her delicately boned nose and across her cheekbones. He caressed the curve of her ears and then slid his fingers down to feel the curve of her heart-shaped face. One thumb caressed the fullness of her lips.

Mikhail heard her breath catch when his fingertips glided across her cheeks, passing over her scar. He dipped his head, his lips hovering above her, and whispered, "So very lovely." His mouth covered hers in a sweetly passionate first kiss.

Belle had never felt like this before. A flame ignited in the pit of her stomach, her lower regions warming and melting.

His lips were firm and warm, enticing her to respond. She leaned into the kiss, pressing her own lips against his.

Mikhail drew back, murmuring, "So sweet."

Putting his arm around her shoulders, Mikhail drew her against his muscular frame. Her forget-me-not violet eyes were glazed with budding desire.

"I could not resist your beauty," he told her.

"I am not beautiful anymore."

"You are more beautiful than you can imagine."

His words were a balm to her aching soul. If only Mick could grow to care for her before he regained his sight, perhaps he would see past her scar to the woman beneath.

"Thank you for the gift of your first kiss."

Belle had never allowed Charles to kiss her, fearing he would think her wanton. How could Mick know that? Was she an incompetent kisser?

"How did you know it was my first kiss?"

"You are incredibly sweet."

That answer was less than satisfying. If she kissed incorrectly, she wanted to know. On the other hand, she could not practice kissing.

"If I had a memory," Mikhail said, "I would tell you my life story. Alas, my memory is hiding, but I would love to know about you."

"What do you want to know?"

"What were you saying to that pansy?" Mikhail shifted his gaze to the flower and was surprised to see it had revived to a healthy color.

"I was praying for the pansy," Belle answered. "I have a talent for growing plants. Whenever the gardeners in the great mansions have a plant problem, they send for me, and I never let them down."

"Gardeners consult you?"

"The garden goddess promises minor miracles," Belle said, her pride evident.

"I have heard of the garden goddess," Mikhail said without thinking.

"Where did you hear about me?"

"I-I cannot remember. What does your wealthy father say about your vocation?"

"I don't think he likes it," Belle admitted. "He insists he can afford to care for his children, but I do this for love. Not money."

"Do you volunteer your services?"

"I charge my clients a fee and give the money to the poor."

"You give money away?" Mikhail could not mask his surprise.

Belle laughed, a sweetly melodious sound. "Those were my father's words too." Without thinking, she touched his chin with one finger. "I bet the ladies love your dimple."

Mikhail cleared his throat. "I cannot remember."

A disturbing thought popped into Belle's mind. What if Mick had a wife waiting somewhere? "We should not kiss again," she told him. "You could be married."

He shook his head. "I do not remember any wife."

"You don't remember anything."

Damn, damn, damn. Mikhail cursed his luck. Their relationship had been progressing, but now he would need to find a way to convince her that he had no wife. Why hadn't he foreseen this?

Hours later, Mikhail was still cursing circumstances. He sat on the sofa and listened to his wife cleaning the kitchen after supper. How could he maneuver around the fact that he might have a wife somewhere? His brothers would enjoy a good laugh at his predicament.

Mikhail knew he needed to work quickly. He had two weeks to win his bride's love and consummate their marriage. After that, Stepan and Fancy would return to London, and the eldest Flambeau sister had an unpredictable temperament.

Relaxing against the cushion, Mikhail plotted his strategy. He needed to regain his sight before consummating their marriage. Belle needed to know he thought her face desirable.

He would regain his sight and court her. She deserved a courtship. In present circumstances, they could not enjoy a society courtship, but he would indulge her with gifts later.

Belle would respond to his wooing, and they would consummate their marriage. He would regain his memory after they became husband and wife in fact as well as name.

Too bad he lacked his older brothers' forcefulness and his younger brother's charm. Being caught by birth between Viktor and Stepan, the family baby, was not the most auspicious position.

"Belle, are you going to finish Gabrielle's story?" Mikhail called.

He heard her crossing the kitchen to the sofa. She sat beside him, lifted his hand, and placed the bread and butter sandwich in it.

"Eat that while I talk," she ordered.

Mikhail was not hungry but, to appease her, bit into the

sandwich. He glanced at the bread and butter, saw small black specks like pepper, and wondered which medicinal herb it was.

"Ten-year-old Gabrielle Flambeau and her nanny escaped the Terror," Belle began. "One of the émigrés who had left France with his fortune before the Terror gave Gabrielle and Nanny rooms in his house.

"Nanny became a surrogate mother and the only family Gabrielle had. Both did odd jobs to earn their keep, and Nanny earned extra money by sewing for others.

"Gabrielle grew into a beautiful young woman with black hair and violet eyes and a sweet expression. Her happy expression was merely a thin veneer, for she never forgot her slaughtered family and always felt alone in the world.

"Her faithful Nanny aged and sickened. Loyal to her surrogate mother, Gabrielle eased the older woman's passing by remaining at her bedside until Nanny breathed her last.

"Poor Gabrielle found herself alone again. She would need to start another new life. . . ."

"Where did she go?" Mikhail asked. "What did she do for life's necessities?"

"You will need to wait until tomorrow to learn that," Belle told him.

Mikhail groaned. "Did she find happiness?"

"Nothing would ever compensate for her family's slaughter," Belle said. "Even the daughters she bore could not erase that memory."

"How sad."

That earned him a kiss. Belle leaned close and planted a kiss on his cheek. "Good night, Mick. Call me if you need anything."

"Oh, my darlings, how enchanting you look." The Duchess of Inverary inspected her five stepdaughters like a general

before her troops. Indeed, the duchess was leading her fledgling warriors into their first battle with the opposite sex.

Raven's gown was petal pink silk with a high waist, scooped
neckline, and short melon sleeves. She wore matching petal pink
slippers and long, white kidskin gloves.

Peeking at her sisters, Raven decided the duchess had a
certain flair for color and style. Even Blaze's bold red hair
complemented the pale yellow silk gown.

"Listen carefully." The duchess imparted her wealth of
wisdom. "Men do not always think about sex. For a few brief
moments each day, gentlemen obsess about money and power."

Tinker, the duke's majordomo, made a suspicious squawk-
ing sound. When the duchess shifted her gaze to him, he gave
her a solemn look but appeared to be struggling to maintain
that serious facade.

"Do not believe anything that any gentleman tells you," the
Duchess of Inverary continued. "Men are prone to lying even
about unimportant things like the time."

Raven and her sisters looked at each other and giggled.

"Roxie, do not sour my daughters against men," the Duke
of Inverary said, walking down the stairs.

The Duchess of Inverary gave her husband a dimpled
smile. "I would not dream of doing that." She rounded on the
five sisters and amended herself, "Forget what I said. Believe
everything a gentleman tells you."

"No." The duke whirled around. "Men will say anything to
persuade a young lady in"—his complexion reddened—"just
follow Roxie's advice, and you will do well."

Raven bit her lip to keep from laughing when she heard
Blaze mumbling to her twin, "Papa ought to know. In his day,
he—"

The Duke of Inverary rounded on her sister, an unamused
expression on his face. Blaze gifted him with her most innocent smile.

A short time later, Raven and her sisters followed the duke

and duchess into the Earl and Countess of Winchester's ballroom. The countess was the duchess's niece.

The ballroom was enormous. Hundreds of scented beeswax candles lit crystal chandeliers, the prisms sparkling like fireflies on the darkest night.

Hushed voices conversed, mingling with muted laughter. The orchestra provided a melodic backdrop to this aristocratic communion.

Society appeared so very cultured and dignified. Its sham gentility nauseated Raven.

"The Duke of Essex," the earl's majordomo announced. "The Marquis of Basildon."

Raven watched Alexander Blake and his grandfather walk into the ballroom. Alexander was the most handsome man she'd ever seen, especially in his formal evening attire, but she could not forgive him for scoffing at her love or treating her like a silly child.

Speaking with one of his grandfather's cronies, Alexander lifted his gaze and caught her watching him. She turned her back, conveying her feelings to him.

Raven spied three gentlemen headed in her direction and sidestepped behind her father in an effort to make herself invisible. She had previously met the three young gentlemen and had no desire to dance with them.

"Miss Raven," William Castlereigh called.

She stepped back apace, for this gentleman sprayed when he spoke.

"I saw her first," Claude Wakefield complained, drawing her attention to his squint.

"May I have this dance?" Winston Cranmore asked before his friends could.

Raven looked at him, noting his twitching nose. Lords Spray, Squint, and Twitch were less than appealing, but she did not want to hurt anyone's feelings.

"My stepmother has warned me to grant no more than two

dances to any gentleman," Raven said, flashing them a warm smile. "I daresay I should begin the evening by—"

"—by dancing with an old family friend," said Prince Rudolf, materializing beside her.

The prince took her hand in his and led her onto the dance floor. She stepped into his arms, and they circled the dance floor.

"Thank you for rescuing me," Raven said.

"The pleasure is mine," Rudolf said. "I could not let those dashing three lead you astray."

Raven laughed at that. She shifted her gaze to those not dancing, trying to discover Alexander's whereabouts.

"Are you looking for someone?" Prince Rudolf asked.

Raven blushed. "I apologize for my inattention."

The prince smiled. "You did not answer my question."

At that moment, Alexander stepped onto the dance floor with Princess Anya, the beautiful blond niece of the Russian ambassador. Seeing them, Raven felt her heart sinking at the sight of a beautiful princess dancing with the man she loved.

By accepting his grandfather's inheritance, Alexander was destined to become a duke one day. He was a very attractive catch, even for a princess.

"Two can play that game, little one," Prince Rudolf said, his gaze following hers.

"I beg your pardon?"

"We will apply the economic law of supply and demand," Prince Rudolf told her. "Leave the details to me. You need only smile and pretend you are having the most wonderful evening of your life."

"I can manage that."

Prince Rudolf escorted her off the dance floor when the music ended and returned her to her stepmother. Raven saw Alexander walking toward her.

Prince Drako, the eldest Kazanov cousin, reached her first and offered his hand. She latched onto it like a falling woman and took the dance floor with him.

The prince drew her into his arms, and they swirled around and around the ballroom. She admired the prince's dark good looks and noted the longing glances the other ladies were sending in his direction.

Raven, however, was immune. His thirty years were much too old and too sophisticated for her taste. "Thank you for rescuing me, Your Highness."

"Dancing with you is my pleasure," Prince Drako said. "Besides, damsels in distress are my specialty as long as the damsel does not fall in love with me."

"I am in no danger of that," Raven assured him. "You are much too elderly to suit me."

Prince Drako smiled. "You have crushed my ego."

"I doubt your ego is so easily crushed."

Prince Drako laughed. "And now you imply that I am conceited."

At the waltz's end, Prince Drako escorted her to their group. A beautiful young woman was chatting with the duchess.

"Drako, darling," the Duchess of Inverary drawled, "I want you to meet the Contessa de Salerno. Though her deceased husband was Italian, Katerina is a native of Moscow."

Prince Drako bowed over the contessa's hand. "I am surprised we never met."

Removing her hand from his, the contessa gave him a warm smile. "My good luck was bound to change sometime." Without another word, the contessa walked away.

Prince Drako stared at her retreating back for a long moment. A smile flirting with his lips, the prince followed the contessa.

"I knew Drako would be interested in the contessa," the Duchess of Inverary said.

"That may be true, Roxie," the duke replied, "but the contessa did not seem interested in the prince."

The duchess dismissed his words with a wave of her hand. "The Contessa de Salerno is a brilliant strategist."

Watching the prince's reaction and listening to her step-mother proved an invaluable lesson for Raven. Attitude meant everything when dealing with gentlemen who, apparently, enjoyed suffering.

Raven scanned the ballroom, searching for Alexander. She spied him walking toward her, a determined look on his face.

"Miss Raven?" Prince Lykos, another Kazanov cousin, offered his hand. "Will you dance with me?"

"I would love to dance with you." Raven placed her hand in his, savoring the expression of irritated surprise on Alexander's face.

Enjoying the moment did not last long, however. Her stomach flipped in dismay when she spied him dancing with Cynthia Clarke.

Next Raven danced with Prince Gunter, the third Kazanov cousin. Alexander retaliated by dancing with Lavinia Smythe. Raven accepted her next dance with Prince Viktor Kazanov. And Alexander disappeared. Waltzing around the ballroom with the prince, she scanned the faces, but Alexander was nowhere to be seen.

When she returned to her stepmother's side, Raven found her sisters had disappeared somewhere. Not for the first time in her life, Raven wished she had a twin. Then she need not stand here feeling conspicuous. The twins had always stuck together, and she had been the odd one out. Though, Fancy and Belle made certain she felt part of them. Both sisters were gone from this scene for a while.

"Raven Flambeau?" Baron Charles Wingate approached her.

"Yes?" She hoped the baron was not planning to request a dance.

"I wondered how Belle was feeling."

Raven arched a brow at him. "Why?"

"You will not believe me," the baron said, "but I care deeply for your sister."

"You are correct," Raven said. "I do not believe you."

"I wish to rectify my mistake."

"What do you mean?"

"I have persuaded my mother to approve a match with Belle," the baron said. "I want to resume our courtship."

"Belle has gone away for a rest," Raven told him, "but I doubt she will want to see you again."

The baron looked contrite. "I hurt her terribly."

"On the contrary, Belle has never felt better," Raven lied, giving him an innocent smile. "She is considering a recent marriage proposal."

"Who offered for her?" the baron demanded.

"I cannot reveal that," Raven said, "but if I were you, I would set my sights on another lady with less status than a fabulously wealthy duke's daughter."

The baron's complexion mottled with anger. "I demand to know—"

"Are you ready for our dance?"

Raven placed her hand in Alexander's, saying, "Have a good evening, Charles."

Stepping onto the dance floor, Alexander pulled her into his arms and placed a hand in the center of her back. Raven placed her left hand in his and gave him her right hand to hold. Together, they swirled around and around the ballroom.

Raven felt she was living a dream, a real fairy tale. Only the man and the music existed in her dream. The rest of the world faded away.

"What did the baron want?" Alexander asked.

"Wingate has changed his mind about marrying Belle," Raven answered. "Apparently, Mama Wingate decided a connection to my father would be good for her."

Alexander nodded and, when the music ended, escorted her to her stepmother. "Good evening, Your Grace."

The Duchess of Inverary smiled at him. "What a pleasure

to see you taking your rightful place beside your grandfather, my lord."

"Thank you, Your Grace." Alexander turned to Raven. "I hope you will honor me with another dance tonight."

Raven fixed a disappointed expression on her face. "I am sorry, but none of my other dances are free."

Alexander narrowed his gaze on her. "Another time, then." With that, he walked away.

"Bravo, my darling," the duchess drawled. "I am proud of you taking my lessons to heart."

Raven grinned at her stepmother. "And I am lucky to have such a wise stepmother."

"Bless you, child."

Chapter 6

Creak, creak. Creak, creak. Creak, creak.

He loved his rocking chair. Its rhythmic motion soothed, reminding him of his boyhood.

Long fingers moved in a rhythm of their own, weaving three lengths of hair into one thick braid. He fastened the end with a scarlet ribbon and inspected his handiwork.

Scarlet ribbons for scarlet ladies. He giggled at his own wit and reached for three more lengths that needed braiding.

Mother said all women were whores. He needed to punish those whores for tempting him.

Creak, creak. Creak, creak. Creak, creak.

Belle finished dressing and looped the sides of her hair behind her ears. The scent of flowers called her to the window, and she paused to survey the scene outside.

Hidden in the trees, a feathered orchestra serenaded her. Singing larks heralded the perfect morn. Doves cooed and blue jays shrieked. Sparrows fluttered from branch to branch and tree to tree.

The noise outside contrasted with the silence inside the cottage. Her patient was still sleeping.

For his sake, Belle hoped Mick would regain his sight but dreaded losing him. She wished he was unmarried, but his good looks made that doubtful. A steady job would be welcome too.

Belle decided to make breakfast before awakening him. She walked into the common room and stopped short.

The sofa was empty. The *lunettes de soleil* lay on the table.

Belle tapped on the second bedchamber's door. "Mick?"

No answer.

The front door opened, startling her. She whirled around.

"I can see again," Mikhail announced, stepping into the cottage.

"What wonderful news." Belle managed a smile and unlooped the hair on the right side of her face, drawing it forward to hide her cheek.

Mick would reject her now. If she could keep him from seeing her cheek, she could postpone the inevitable. Rejection was not her preferred morning meal.

"I will make us a special breakfast." Belle crossed the common room to the kitchen and reached for a bowl. "You will still need your medicinal bread and butter until your memory returns."

Silent and watching, Mikhail leaned against the kitchen table. He could hardly believe the change in her demeanor.

A wave of protectiveness surged through him, his heart aching for his bride's pain. She needed him. He would convince her of her beauty, defeat her insecurity, and ease her heartache.

"Belle?"

She did not pause in her work, refusing to look at him. "Yes?"

He heard the forced cheerfulness in her voice. "Come here, Belle."

"We won't be eating if I pause to chat." She cast him a sidelong smile, her right cheek hidden, and reached for the bread.

Mikhail crossed the kitchen in two strides and placed his hands on her delicately boned shoulders. She stiffened at his touch but did not resist when he gently turned her to face him. He tilted her chin up and then pushed the ebony hair away from her cheek.

Belle sighed, resigned to the inevitable. When he remained silent, her violet gaze traveled from his chest to his dimpled chin to his dark eyes.

Dark gaze met violet. Mikhail dipped his head and claimed her lips in a slow, sweet kiss. He drew back and, without taking his gaze from hers, caressed her scarred cheek with a fingertip.

"You are lovely, more than you can imagine."

"You do not need to say that." Her bottom lip quivered in her struggle against the tears glistening in her eyes. "I know how I look."

Mikhail wrapped his arms around her and drew her against the hard, muscular planes of his body. "You will never heal until you let the pain go." He added in a voice hoarse with emotion, "Weeping will relieve your pain, my love."

The words *my love* spoken by this sensitive, handsome man broke the dam of Belle's emotions. She hid her face against his chest. Her anguish swelled until she could control it no longer.

Sobs shook her body. The sounds of her despair wrenched his heart. He hoped he would never hear such misery again in his lifetime.

Gradually, her sobs subsided and finally stopped. "Thank you for being so kind." Her voice was a mere whisper.

Mikhail grabbed a linen and wiped her tear-streaked face. "Blow your nose, and then we can begin our new lives together."

Belle lifted her gaze to his. Like glimpses of sunshine on a mostly overcast day, hope shone through eyes clouded with pain. "Together?"

"Heaven's loss of an angel is my gain." Mikhail brushed ebony wisps off her forehead and temples. "I will keep you close forever."

She gave him a worried look. "What if—?"

He placed one long finger across her lips, silencing her. "Eat now and worry later."

Belle managed a faint smile. "I'll make us eggbatter-fried bread."

"What can I do to help?"

"Sit at the table," she answered, "and I'll serve you your medicinal sandwich with your coffee."

Taking his chair, Mikhail watched her moving around the kitchen. He admired the graceful economy of her movements.

Belle set a pan of water over the hearth to boil. Then she placed a container of ground coffee, a stirring spoon, and a strainer beside their cups.

Grabbing a knife, Belle sliced yesterday's bread. When she glanced at him over her shoulder, he gave her an exaggerated wink, which made her blush.

Belle dropped several spoonfuls of coffee into the boiling water and stirred for a minute. Leaving it to steep for a few minutes, she spread butter on two slices of bread and reached for a small jar.

Taking the pan off the hearth, Belle poured the steaming coffee into their cups through the strainer. She delivered their coffee to the table and then set his medicinal sandwich in front of him.

Belle took two bowls from the cupboard. Humming to herself, she cracked an egg over the copper bowl and shifted its contents back and forth between the eggshell halves until all the egg white was in the bowl.

"What did you say was mixed with the butter?" Mikhail asked.

Belle dropped the yolk into the second bowl. "This and that."

"Precisely what is this and that?"

Belle turned around, her smile puzzled. "I added cinnamon to mask the taste of the black medicine."

Mikhail stared at his sandwich. "The black spots are moving."

"Spiders *do* move, silly."

Mikhail dropped the sandwich on the table, his dark gaze snapping to hers. "You have been feeding me black spiders?"

"Bread and butter, garnished with black spiders, works miracles."

Mikhail leaped off the chair, his hand covering his mouth. He bolted out the door.

Belle raised her hand to her throat when she heard the sounds of retching. She whipped the sandwich off the table and placed it out of sight.

Mikhail walked into the cottage a few minutes later. He took a large swig of coffee, swishing it around in his mouth before swallowing, and then looked at her.

Belle read the anger in his expression. She opened her mouth to speak but closed it again when his gaze narrowed on her.

"You may want to pray over the flowers out front," he told her.

"I can cure your nausea."

"No!" His hands flew up, warding off her suggestion. "Have you ever eaten Nanny Smudge's medicinal spider sandwich?"

Her gaze skittered away from him. "Spiders don't agree with me."

"Humph."

"Someday you will laugh about this." Belle gave him a brilliant smile. "Shall I make us breakfast?"

"I will wait for lunch," he refused. "Eat your own breakfast while I erase the taste of spiders from my mouth with whisky."

"I will wait for lunch too."

Belle hadn't the heart to eat in front of a nauseated man. After finishing her coffee, she reached for her magic basket and stood. "Will you join me in the garden?"

Mikhail followed her out.

Belle paused at the spot where he'd vomited and shook her head. "Prayers will not help that flower."

"Perhaps a spider sandwich would help?"

"Spiders really do—"

"Never feed people anything you would not eat yourself."

They circled the cottage to the rear garden.

She admired the blue canopy of sky, so rare in London's spring. He admired her admiring the sky.

Strolling the perimeter of the small expanse, Belle smiled with satisfaction. What her prayers had achieved pleased her. Heroic healing of biblical proportions, considering its state only a few days earlier.

Belle paused at the pansy, which looked much better but not cured completely. She knelt on the ground in front of it, and Mikhail crouched beside her.

"Tell me about your gardening business," he said. "How did you start it?"

"I walked to Hyde Park one day last spring," Belle answered. "On the way home, I passed through Grosvenor Square."

"Grosvenor Square sounds familiar."

She gave him a sidelong glance. "Boorish aristocrats live there."

"Boorish?"

"Most aristocrats believe they are better than we common folk," she told him. "The bigger the title, the bigger the boor."

Mikhail laughed at that. "Do you dislike aristocrats?"

Belle gave him an unconsciously flirtatious smile. "No, I dislike arrogant boors."

"Ah, I understand."

"The tulips on the square's island called to me in distress," Belle continued.

"Did anyone else hear them?"

Her violet gaze narrowed on him. "Do not be impertinent."

"I apologize," he said, laughter lurking in his voice.

"Ignoring those tulips would have been cruel," Belle said. "Dozens of tulips needed my attention. I touched each tulip in turn and prayed for its health. A gardener from one of the mansions saw my success and asked for my help, which I gladly gave. Word spread about my unique ability, and other gardeners, employed by the wealthy, were soon asking for help too."

Mikhail peeked into her basket. "Do you need these to heal the plants?"

She gave him an impish smile. "Showmanship dazzles them."

"Will you give me a demonstration?"

"The garden goddess promises minor miracles."

Belle focused her attention on the pansy. Then she touched her left breast, forehead, right breast, left and right shoulders before touching her left breast again. Opening the gold case, Belle used the Lucifer matches and sandpaper to light the white candle. Next she shook a tiny bell above the pansy.

Placing her fingers on each side of the pansy, she chanted, "Ailing, ailing, ailing. Pansy, my touch is sealing and thy illness is failing. Healing, healing, healing." She waved the *Book of Common Prayer* over the flower, saying, "It is written. It is so."

After concluding the healing session with another blessing of herself, Belle sat back on her haunches and waited for the pansy to revive. She glanced at Mikhail. "I need not do any of that except touch the flower, focus on its health, and pray."

He nodded in understanding. "Showmanship is good for business?"

"Quite so."

Lifting the gold case, Mikhail ran his finger across the initials *MC*. "What is the significance?"

"That belonged to my father once," Belle answered. "Nanny Smudge gave it to me."

His dark gaze fixed on hers. "Explain."

"My parents never married," she told him. "I had not seen my father for fifteen years before my recent move into his home."

Mikhail thought of his own daughter and could not imagine ignoring her existence for fifteen long years. "You missed his loving attention."

Belle gave him a rueful smile. "I never had his loving attention."

"Explain, please."

She sighed. "It is unimportant."

"On the contrary, I think this is very important," Mikhail said.

"I remember my older sister sitting on his lap," Belle said, "and the next year he was holding my younger, twin sisters. Being born between the first and a set of twins is an unenviable position."

Mikhail leaned back against the oak tree. "That scenario seems familiar."

"Do you remember something?"

"No."

Belle gestured to the tiny expanse of grass. "Will you help me weed?"

"I will watch you weeding."

On her knees, Belle began pulling weeds from the neglected grass. "Weeds choke plants," she said without looking at him.

Mikhail admired her rounded backside as she worked. "I like this view of you."

Whirling around, Belle fell on her rump. Her complexion was tomato red.

"You are more entertaining than Drury Lane players," Mikhail said. "Can I persuade you to sit in the shade and tell me more about Gabrielle?"

"Very well." Belle sat beneath the oak tree, his thigh so close she could feel his body heat. "After her nanny's death, Gabrielle won a position in the opera. Her beauty caught the attention of a charming duke, and they fell passionately in love. The duke loved Gabrielle as best he could, but he"—she blushed with embarrassment—"he had a wife."

"Wife?" Mikhail echoed. "I remember something."

"And?" Belle could not mask her anxiety.

"My wife died."

"Did she?" A relieved smile touched her lips and then disappeared in an instant. "I mean, I am sorry for your loss."

Mikhail struggled against the urge to laugh in her face. He had never seen anyone less sorry than she. What a genius he was to have solved the problem of whether or not he had a wife. Now there was no reason for her to refuse his persuasive advances.

"Do you remember anything else?"

"I know she sickened and died," he answered. "I cannot recall her name."

Belle patted his hand. "Your memories of her will surface."

"Perhaps hearing more of Gabrielle's story will help me remember."

"When she became pregnant with their first child," Belle continued, "the duke sent her Nanny Smudge."

"Your Nanny Smudge?" Mikhail feigned surprise. "Gabrielle is your mother, and Nanny Smudge helped her raise you and your sisters."

"Gabrielle helped Nanny Smudge raise us," Belle corrected him, and then fell silent for a long moment. "Do you think Gabrielle would have found happiness if he'd married her?"

"No one can say what might have been." Banishing the suddenly melancholy mood, Mikhail stood and pulled her to her feet. "I will teach you to protect yourself. Do you want to learn?"

"Yes."

Mikhail turned her back on him. "If someone grabs you from behind—"

Belle whirled around. "What if someone attacks from the front?"

"Cowardly assailants will always walk past in order to surprise you from behind."

"What if he isn't a coward?"

"Any man who attacks a woman is a coward," Mikhail told her. "I will demonstrate." He turned his back on her and said, "Now grab me."

Belle stepped close to press herself against his back. His body heat seeped through their clothing, his clean masculine scent making her knees wobble. She slipped her arms beneath his and wrapped them around his body. "Like that?"

Mikhail could feel her breasts pressed against his back and questioned his own sanity. "That is good if you want to make love."

She leaped back a pace. "I don't understand."

Wearing a smile, Mikhail faced her and planted a kiss on her lips. "Every person's vulnerability is eyes, neck, and groin."

The word *groin* colored her cheeks scarlet. Belle felt her face flaming but could not prevent it. No man had ever used that word in her presence.

"You blush so prettily." Mikhail showed her his back again. "Grab me from behind without the hugging."

When she did as ordered, Mikhail said, "First strike back with your elbow to his stomach." He demonstrated the movement in slow motion, being careful not to hurt her. "Then stomp on his foot. When he drops his arms—"

"What if he doesn't drop his arms?"

"Trust me, Princess. The villain will drop his arms if you hit him hard enough.

"Should I run away then?"

Mikhail shook his head. "You want to incapacitate him so he does not give chase. When he drops his arms, whirl around and punch his neck dead center." He showed her the movement and then continued, "He will grab his neck. Using your knee, smash his groin."

Belle blushed again.

"There is no blushing in combat, Princess." Mikhail winked at her. "Groin smashing will double him over. Poke his eyes with your fingers and run like the devil is chasing you. Understand?"

"I suppose so." Her expression said the opposite.

"Remember, Princess. Elbow to stomach, stomp to foot, fist to neck, knee to groin, and fingers to eyes."

Belle stood with her back to him. Guiding her movements, Mikhail demonstrated the defensive routine several times from beginning to end. Her delicate body, rounded buttocks, and sensuous rose scent made his legs wobble and his groin sensitive. He stepped away from temptation, ordering, "Perform the movements for me."

Over and over and over, Belle went through the routine's steps. Before too long, the five defensive steps became one fluid motion.

Panting from her exertions, Belle could feel the sweat rolling down the valley between her breasts. The back of her neck was damp, and moisture dotted her upper lip and temples.

Mikhail lifted her magic basket and gestured to return inside. "You have earned a rest."

Belle nodded, too hot and tired to speak, and wondered when he had gone from guest to master. Giving orders to one's hostess was improper, but she had no strength to correct him.

Turning away, Belle sauntered in the direction of the front door. Without warning, strong arms grabbed her from behind.

In a flash of movement, Belle elbowed her attacker's stomach and stomped on his foot with all her might. Whirling around, she landed a punch to his neck and kneed his groin.

Mikhail fell backward onto the ground before she could poke his eyes. His face reddened, his breathing came in gasps, and he clutched his groin.

"I never poked my fingers in—"

Belle realized he was hurting and dropped to her knees. "I am so sorry."

Mikhail held his hand up, gesturing that all would be well. "Excellent," he gasped, doubled over on his side. "You are a fast learner."

Belle smiled, pleased with her accomplishments. Taking the initiative, she leaned down and touched her lips to his, kissing him tentatively at first and then more boldly.

Mikhail slipped his arms around her, holding her tight against his body. He returned her kiss and teased the crease of her mouth with his tongue.

Belle parted her lips, allowing him entrance to her mouth. He surprised her by slipping his tongue inside.

Placing the palms of her hands on his shoulders, Belle pushed him away. She leaned over him, asking, "Do you surrender to my greater strength?"

His dark eyes lit with amusement. "I surrender, Princess. Help me up now."

When she stood and offered him her hand, Mikhail yanked her down on top of him and rolled to the right, pinning her beneath him. He claimed her lips in a long, leisurely kiss. Nose to nose with her, he asked, "Do *you* surrender?"

She gave him a flirtatious smile. "I will consider it."

Mikhail helped her up and slipped his arm around her shoulders in easy camaraderie. "Have you ever considered opening a restaurant, Princess? I believe London's boorish elite would consider spider sandwiches a delicacy."

A royal summons would give him less anxiety than the request to appear at Inverary House. The nicely worded note suggested invitation, but its true meaning shouted the duke's demand. *Or else*.

Alexander Blake pushed an errant lock of shaggy brown hair off his forehead. He reached for the knocker, but the door opened to reveal the majordomo, who stepped aside allowing him entrance.

"Good afternoon," Alexander greeted the man. "I have an appointment."

"His Grace is expecting you," the majordomo said. "Please follow me, Lord Blake."

Alexander had no idea what the duke wanted, but a wise man did not dare to offend the illustrious Duke of Inverary. The man had more highly connected friends who owed him favors than any aristocrat in the realm. Even more than his own grandfather, who was on a first-name basis with the royal family.

Tinker knocked on the door of the second-floor study and walked inside. "Lord Blake has arrived, Your Graces."

Alexander stopped short, the study's occupants catching him by surprise. Magnus Campbell lounged in a leather chair behind his desk. His duchess perched on a chair to his right and poured tea into delicate-looking, porcelain teacups. Three chairs stood in a row in front of the duke's desk. His own grandfather sat in the middle chair, his cane resting against its arm.

"Alexander, how wonderful to see you again." The Duchess of Inverary greeted him with a dimpled smile.

She was a notorious, meddling matchmaker. Her husband and his grandfather wore smug smiles. This trio boded ill for his peace of mind.

"Come and join us," the Duke of Inverary said.

Pasting a smile onto his face, Alexander crossed the study. He nodded at the duke and accepted a cup of tea from the duchess. "Good afternoon, Grandfather."

The Duke of Essex gestured to the chair on his right. "Sit here."

Intending an early escape, Alexander lifted the teacup and sipped the steaming liquid. "I'll stand if you don't mind."

"We *do* mind."

"Grandfather." His tone was purposely long-suffering.

The Duke of Essex grabbed his cane and whacked the arm of the vacant chair. *"Sit."*

Accustomed to his grandfather's theatrics, Alexander assumed a bored expression. "If you feel that strongly. . . ." He sat in the vacant chair.

The study was comfortable in its masculinity. The chairs were upholstered in leather softer than a lady's lap. The other furniture had been created in dark woods, and crammed into custom bookshelves, books lined the walls.

The only touch of femininity was the present duchess's portrait hanging above the summer-darkened hearth and a vase of roses placed on an occasional table. A gentle breeze blew aromatic garden perfumes through the open window to mingle with leather, ink, and parchment scents.

"These young swains respect nothing," his grandfather was complaining. "I cringe to think of the realm's moral decay when our children and grandchildren reach a venerable age."

"You will never see the decay," Alexander said, his tone dry. "Why waste your few remaining years worrying about things you cannot change? Besides, change could prove beneficial for England."

"Change?" the Duchess of Inverary echoed. "That very *change* is what my husband wishes to discuss."

Alexander gave the duke his attention. "What changes concern you, Your Grace?"

"I worry about the change in my youngest daughter's reputation," Inverary answered.

Uh-oh. A woman's loss of reputation heralded a man's loss of bachelorhood. "I don't understand."

"Constable Black and you would consult with Raven regarding the Society Slasher?"

"Yes, Your Grace."

"That sounds absurd if you ask me," the Duke of Essex interjected.

Alexander glanced at his grandfather. "Nobody is asking you."

"Humph, do you see that?" his grandfather asked Inverary. "I told you these young bucks respect nothing."

"Perhaps they are not beyond redemption." The Duke of Inverary drew Alexander's attention, asking, "Do you believe in hocus-pocus?"

"Do *you* believe in it?"

The duke smiled. "I asked first."

Stalling for time, Alexander sipped his tea and pondered on an ambiguous answer. "Constable Black is willing to listen to anything that could solve this case."

"And you?"

Was Inverary trying to trap him into an indiscreet answer? If so, what was his purpose?

"Constable Black is teaching me his most effective investigative techniques," Alexander said, "and I am learning not to discount anything on face value."

Inverary relaxed in his chair. "A very good answer, Blake."

"He never answered your question," the Duke of Essex observed.

"My Aunt Bedelia had the same gift as Raven," Inverary said.

That surprised Alexander. "Do *you* believe?"

"Like the constable, I believe in keeping an open mind," the duke answered. "We Highlanders are sensitive to such things."

"Highlanders are heathens," the Duke of Essex said.

The Duke of Inverary turned a displeased expression on the other duke.

"Present company excluded," came the older man's amendment.

"I know Raven helped with the last investigation," Inverary said, "but traipsing around town to crime scenes will ruin her."

"I can guarantee her safety," Alexander assured him.

"Her safety is not an issue." The Duke of Inverary gave him a meaningful look, which Alexander chose to ignore.

Raising his teacup to his lips, Alexander glanced at the duchess. Her dimpled smile told him that she knew something he did not. That definitely boded ill for him.

"On the other hand," the Duke of Inverary continued, "your grandfather and I have concluded that a betrothal between you and Raven would solve the problem."

The scheming old man had been busy. Only a marriage and a great-grandson would satisfy him. Without a doubt, his grandfather would cling to life for a hundred years waiting for a great-grandson. Or haunt him if denied by death.

Alexander opened his mouth to refuse the offer but closed it again without speaking. His first reaction of refusal was provoked by spite only.

Conjuring her image, Raven Flambeau paraded across his mind's eye. He saw her provocatively petite body. He saw her huge violet eyes in her angel's face. He saw her courtesan lips, pouting for kisses and other sensual activities.

Appearing too eager would be ill-advised since he and his grandfather argued about marriage with nauseating regularity. Moreover, he needed to assume a reluctant facade with the bride-to-be or look foolish because of his previous comments of her being an immature brat. His prospective bride had been decidedly cool toward him of late.

The Duke of Inverary cleared his throat, intruding on his thoughts. Given another moment of silence, his own grandfather would probably beat him with that cane.

Keeping his face expressionless, Alexander fixed his gaze on the duke. "I agree to the match."

"Oh, how exciting," the Duchess of Inverary exclaimed. "Think, Magnus. We have two future princesses and a future duchess. *So far.*"

"Calm yourself, Roxie." Inverary looked at his future

son-in-law. "Welcome to the family, but Roxie and I need to settle Fancy and Belle first."

"Which will merely take a week or two," the duchess added.

Alexander nodded in understanding. Too bad, intimacies would also be postponed.

"Why aren't you arguing?" his grandfather demanded, staring at him in surprise.

Confounding the old man felt good. "Do you want me to argue?"

"Do you actually want to marry the girl?"

Alexander struggled against a smile. "Do *you* want me to marry her?"

"Damn you." The Duke of Essex banged his cane on the floor. "Do *not* answer my questions with questions."

Ignoring the old man's frustration, Alexander warned Inverary, "Raven may not agree to the match."

"I can handle my own daughter," the duke said. "She will accept the match."

"Raven is more beautiful than an exotic butterfly," Alexander said, "but she is also more cantankerous than a camel."

A confident smile touched the older man's lips. "Well, lad, you may need lessons on handling strong-willed women."

Chapter 7

"Does Papa know you will be assisting the constable in the Slasher investigation?"

"Are you planning to blackmail me for your silence?"

Raven and Blaze Flambeau sat together in their father's garden. Puddles scurried here and there to sniff every blade of grass, flower, and tree trunk.

Blaze assumed an injured expression. "Do you think I would make you buy my silence?"

"I know the workings of your mind," Raven said. "Your allegiance can be bought."

Blaze gave her an impish smile. "I will keep the secret if you accompany Puddles outside for one week."

"Puddles may prefer your company to mine," Raven said. "Ask him."

"Come, Puddles!"

The brindled mastiff dashed across the garden to sit in front of Blaze. She leaned forward and stared into his eyes.

"Damn, damn, damn."

"What is wrong?" Raven asked.

"Puddles prefers me," Blaze answered, and burst into laughter.

Raven laughed when her sister did. The mastiff raised his head and howled, which made them laugh even more.

"Both Fancy and Belle will soon be happily married," Blaze said on a dreamy sigh.

"And princesses too," Raven reminded her.

"Do you think true love will ever happen to us?" Blaze asked.

"All good things come to those who wait," Raven answered. "Or so Nanny Smudge always said."

"I miss Nanny Smudge."

"So do I."

"Miss Raven."

The two sisters looked over their shoulders toward the garden door. Tinker, the duke's majordomo, hurried down the cobblestone path.

"His Grace wants to speak with you in his study."

"Thank you, Tinker." What sinful transgression had she committed to warrant an audience with her father?

"Uh-oh." Blaze gave voice to her sister's thoughts. "What have you done now?"

"I do not recall anything."

"You may take Puddles along for your protection."

Raven smiled at that. "I don't believe that will be necessary."

"Walk slowly," Blaze advised her.

Raven took her sister's advice. Five minutes passed before she reached the foyer. Climbing the stairs to the second floor wasted another five minutes. If her father hadn't been angry before, he would be now. Her pace slowed as she neared the study. She tried to recall breaking any rules, but her mind drew a blank. Where was her psychic ability when she needed it?

After tapping on the door, Raven stepped inside without waiting for permission. "You wanted—?"

Raven stopped short and stared in surprise at Alexander Blake and his grandfather, the Duke of Essex. Apparently, she would not be receiving a dressing down, but the reason for her presence eluded her.

"Oh, my darling Raven," the duchess gushed. "We have wonderful—"

"Roxie, please." Her father's voice held a warning note.

"Magnus, darling, I cannot contain my enthusiasm."

The Duke of Inverary patted his wife's hand. "Try harder, dear." He shifted his gaze to Raven and beckoned her forward.

Wearing a puzzled smile, Raven crossed the study. She flicked a nervous glance at the two visitors.

Alexander wore a sneaky smirk. His grandfather was inspecting her as if he considered her for sale.

"Sit here, child." The Duke of Essex gestured to the chair on his left.

Raven arched an ebony brow at the old man. "I prefer standing."

That simple statement incited several reactions. Alexander chuckled, his grandfather dropped his mouth open in surprise, and the duchess gave her a dimpled smile.

Her father laughed and glanced at Alexander. "She sounds like you."

"No doubt, a match made in Heaven," the Duke of Essex muttered. "My vengeance will be complete if he sires a child who speaks to him the way he speaks to me."

The Duke of Inverary smiled. "Children can be a curse as well as a blessing." He looked at Raven, saying, "We must discuss a matter of some importance. Please sit."

Raven accommodated his request. She sat in the vacant chair, took several moments to arrange her skirt, and only then lifted her gaze.

"I worry for your good reputation," her father said without preamble.

To what was he referring? Was he going to give her a dressing down in front of Alex? She would die of embarrassment if he did.

"I know you helped Constable Black and Alexander with their previous investigation," her father continued when she remained silent. "They would like permission to use your gift with the Slasher investigation."

Raven flicked Alexander a satisfied smile. Apparently, her hocus-pocus proved necessary when *his* limited logic failed. "Yes, Papa. I know they *need* my expertise."

Raven heard Alexander muttering indistinct words and curled her lip at him. There he sat, sipping his tea, safe and smug in his narrow-minded logic.

"Do you want to help the constable?" Her father drew her attention.

Raven struggled against the laughter bubbling up. She managed to keep her face expressionless when she answered, "I consider helping them my civic duty."

"Humph," Alexander muttered, sounding like his grandfather. "Civic duty runs in this family."

Raven felt her irritation rising. Alexander was behaving strangely for a man who needed her help.

Her father spoke then, drawing her attention again. What he said nearly felled her. "In that case, Alexander and you will become betrothed," he announced.

Raven dropped her mouth open in shock. "I-I . . ."

"Do not feign surprise, brat," Alexander shot at her. "You have been angling after this for a long, long time."

Raven snapped her head around and narrowed her gaze on him. The teacup in his hand exploded, sending shards of porcelain and hot tea everywhere.

With a yelp of surprise, Alexander leaped out of the chair and glared at her. "You did that," he accused.

The Duke of Inverary chuckled. "Aunt Bedelia did the very same thing to Uncle Colin once."

Raven sent Alexander her sweetest smile. "Surely you cannot believe my hocus-pocus caused that . . . *accident*."

"That was no accident."

"Thinking that does not make it so."

"It does in your case."

The Duke of Inverary cleared his throat. "From your tone, I assume you do not accept this match."

"Papa, I did not say that."

"Well, girl, what do you say to becoming my grandson's duchess one day?" the Duke of Essex asked.

Raven glanced at her stepmother and then repeated the Contessa de Salerno's words to Prince Drako, "I say, my good luck has run out."

Essex sent the duchess a disgruntled look. "Roxie, the chit is learning your wiles."

"All my stepdaughters are apt students," the Duchess of Inverary said. "We helpless females need some protection."

Alexander rose from his chair and took three steps toward his almost betrothed. Crouching down to be eye level with her, he took her hand in his, asking, "What *do* you say, brat?"

Raven could cheerfully have throttled him, her violet gaze telling him so. No woman desired an indifferent marriage proposal. She wanted moonlight and roses and whispered words of love. On the other hand, a betrothal would provide many opportunities to torment him.

Pasting a sweet smile on her lips, Raven shifted her gaze to her father. "I accept the match."

Alexander gave her hand a squeeze and then stood. He turned to shake her father's hand.

"Welcome to the family," the Duke of Inverary said.

"Thank you, Your Grace."

The Duchess of Inverary clapped her hands together. "How wonderful," she gushed. "Aren't you excited, sweeting?"

"Absolutely thrilled," Raven drawled in a bored tone.

Ignoring her insult, Alexander turned to his grandfather. "Are you happy, Your Grace?"

The Duke of Essex flicked his future granddaughter-in-law

a sidelong glance. "I will be happy once she delivers your heir."

Bolting out of her chair, Raven rounded on the old man. "If you think to browbeat me with your obscene demands, Your Grace, I urge you to reconsider. I lack your grandson's patience."

The Duke of Essex laughed at that. "I like her spirit."

"I will leave you to the contract particulars," Alexander told the two dukes. "I want to speak privately with my fiancée."

Alexander opened the door and ushered Raven into the corridor. She refused to look at him, merely marched toward the stairs.

"Wait one moment," Alexander ordered, his hand on her arm forcing her to stop. "I apologize for my behavior. My grandfather's constant pressure to marry and beget the next generation irritates me in the extreme, but I did not intend for you to suffer the brunt of my displeasure."

Raven stared into his brown eyes, uncertain whether to believe him or not. She nodded finally without actually forgiving him.

"Amadeus and I will soon be calling on you for your impressions," Alexander said, starting down the stairs to the foyer. "We found evidence at the last crime scene."

"Do you believe in my gift?" Raven asked.

"My skepticism cannot prove your gift does not exist." Alexander smiled at her. "You did explode that teacup in my hand."

He sounded astoundingly reasonable. For a skeptic, that is. Was the observation sincere or the means to keep the peace?

"At the last crime scene, I met a young woman—a child really—and placed her into protective custody at my grandfather's," Alexander told her. "Tulip Woods lost a sister to the Slasher and may have seen his face. I wondered if you would consider befriending her."

A young woman from the lower class living at his grandfather's? "How old is Tulip?"

"Fifteen or sixteen."

"And Tulip needs a friend?"

"She may be lonely without anyone to share her thoughts."

"Your grandfather could never be mistaken for a gracious host." Raven inclined her head, granting his request. "I will meet Tulip and offer my friendship."

"Promise not to explode any more teacups." Alexander winked at her. "I don't want her learning your bad habits."

"Is Tulip a paragon of femininity?"

"The chit is a mouthy squirt who has even bested my grandfather."

Raven smiled. "I like her already."

When they reached the front door, Alexander lifted her hand to his lips. "A ruby and diamond betrothal ring, I think, to symbolize my fire-and-ice fiancée."

Raven stared at the closed door after he'd gone, a smile playing on her lips. She dropped her gaze to the hand he'd kissed and recalled her nanny's words. *All good things come to those who wait.*

The mouthwatering aroma of whitebait and mushrooms frying in truffle oil wafted across the cottage, beckoning him. His growling stomach answered the call.

"I am starving."

Belle glanced over her shoulder at him. "All good things come to those who wait."

Sitting at the kitchen table, Mikhail raised his glass of whisky and saluted her wisdom. Or did the wisdom belong to Nanny Smudge?

Fires crackled in both of the common room's hearths, chasing away the evening chill. Overhead, the rhythmic beat of steady rain pounded on the roof.

Mikhail felt simple contentment. A warm room, a glass of

whisky, and a lovely bride to cook him supper. What more could any man desire?

His wife was a beauty, even without the artificial accoutrements of ravishing gowns and priceless jewels. And her inner beauty surpassed her near-perfect exterior. Here was a woman who appreciated what was truly important in life.

Tonight he would persuade her into making love, and their marriage would be consummated without her being aware of it. Should he reveal his true identity and their marriage immediately afterward? No. He would play with the amnesia until they needed to return to society. The more intimacy they shared, the easier her transition from maiden to wife. *And mother*.

"Mick?" Her voice drew him from his thoughts. "Here is a bite to tide you over."

Mikhail focused on her and then dropped his gaze to the plate. *A bread and butter sandwich.* He snapped his gaze to hers, his expression a revolted grimace.

Belle dissolved into giggles. "If you could only see yourself."

Her giggles, more than her prank, brought a smile to his lips. "Be warned, Princess. I intend revenge."

Belle pushed her hand in front of his face and shook it with great exaggeration. "See how frightened I am."

Mikhail grabbed her hand and pretended to gobble her fingers like he did to his daughter. Which made her laugh even harder.

Releasing her hand, Mikhail allowed her to return to the hearth. His daughter would be pleased with her new mummy. How amazing to have found the rare woman who could pass the mummy test.

His bride knew dozens of bedtime stories for boys and girls and adults. Laughing and dirtying her hands in the garden delighted her. She could bake happiness cakes as well as hugs and kisses cookies, and all women enjoyed gossipy tea parties. Most important, loving Bess and him would come easily to his chosen princess.

Belle served the fried whitebait and mushrooms. Sitting opposite him, she said without preamble, "I wonder what employment you had before your amnesia."

"I wish I could remember." Mikhail swallowed a piece of whitebait.

She gazed at him through violet eyes that gleamed with budding love. "Does carpentry seem familiar?"

"No."

"Farming?"

He sipped his whisky. "No."

"Merchant?"

Mikhail shook his head. "What if I am an earl, a duke, or a prince?"

Belle laughed at that outrageous idea. "Our friendship would end if that proved true."

Uh-oh. "You would end our association if I was a wealthy aristocrat?"

She gave him a flirtatious smile. "Do not forget handsome too."

Mikhail grinned. "Why would you refuse friendship with an aristocrat?"

Belle set her fork on her plate, her expression bordering on grim. "I do not trust those conceited boors," she answered. "I would always want my gardening business. Besides that, I have no desire to step into high society."

"Most women would marry a wealthy aristocrat because he *is* a wealthy aristocrat."

"I am *not* most women."

"I appreciate that," Mikhail said. "You are the most unique woman I have ever met."

"How do you know?" Belle asked him. "You cannot remember what happened before you staggered into my yard."

Mikhail laughed and raised his glass in salute. "*Touché,* Princess."

After all traces of supper had been cleared away, Mikhail and Belle sat on the settee and gazed at the mesmerizing flames in the hearth. He rested his arm behind her on the back of the settee.

Belle snuggled against his masculine frame and rested her head on his shoulder. His nearness excited her, his strength protected her, and his clean masculine scent enticed her.

"Tell me more about Gabrielle," Mikhail said.

Belle dragged her gaze away from the hearth and looked at his strong profile. "Gabrielle's story is finished, only her legacy remains."

He turned his head to look at her. "Tell me her legacy, then."

"Her seven daughters, of course."

Mikhail lifted her hand to his lips. "You are part of her legacy, Princess."

"Quite so." Belle held his hand, entwining her fingers through his, and spoke about her sisters. "Fancy is the eldest, recently debuted with the opera, and is a physical medium."

"What is that?"

"Through her five senses, Fancy is aware of spirits," Belle explained, watching for signs of disbelief. "My sister sniffs cinnamon whenever Nanny Smudge is with us, and many nights our mother's weeping has awakened her."

"Your sister senses ghosts?" Skepticism lurked in his eyes.

"We are not freakish."

He squeezed her hand. "I could never think that of you."

"Bliss is a mathematical genius," she continued, "and Blaze communicates with animals."

Belle glanced sidelong at him and caught his smile. She was not surprised. Most men possessed the sensitivity of a brick.

"Serena sings opera even better than Fancy. She also plays the flute and loves trees." She hesitated for a millisecond. "Her moods affect the weather."

Ignoring his chuckle, Belle said, "Sophia is the family

artist and sees people's auras, colors surrounding a person that change with mood or illness. Raven, the youngest, has visions and can move objects with her mind, especially when she is angry."

"You certainly enjoy a lively family." With one hand, Mikhail turned her head to face his. "And you, Princess, heal plants and other living creatures."

Her violet eyes clouded with pain. "I am a healer who cannot heal herself."

"Give yourself time, Princess." Mikhail planted a kiss on her temple. "All creatures need time to heal."

"You are correct, of course." She managed a smile for him. "So there are Gabrielle's daughters."

"Daughters," Mikhail echoed, as if recalling something about his life. "I remember my daughter Elizabeth, Bess for short."

His statement surprised Belle. "Do you know who you—?"

"How is she faring without me?" Mikhail interrupted, his worry evident in his voice. "Did I leave a four-year-old alone?"

"I am positive you make an excellent father," Belle assured him, "and you would have left someone caring for her. Bess is only wondering what is keeping you from home."

Mikhail leaned close, his lips hovering above hers. "I do not know what I would do without you."

Belle stared mesmerized as his handsome face inched toward hers. He was going to kiss her, and she was going to let him.

His lips were warm and firm and oh-so persuasive. She leaned into his kiss, savoring the incredible feeling of his mouth covering hers.

Mikhail wrapped his arms around her, holding her against his unyielding body. His right hand circled her small back, pressing her against him, while his left hand at the back of her head kept her immobile.

Belle slid her hands up his chest to wind around his neck. Leaning into him, she felt her breasts swell heavily with her desire and her nipples tightened.

"Open your mouth," Mikhail whispered hoarsely. He flicked his tongue across the crease of her lips, which opened for him, allowing him entrance inside to taste her sweetness.

Their kiss was long and langorous, smoldering with passion.

Belle had never felt like this before. The heady sensations he was creating seduced her. Reason vanished and instinct surfaced.

"I want us to share our hearts, our minds, our bodies." Mikhail stood then, his dark gaze holding hers captive, and held his hand out. "Trust me, Princess."

Her gaze slid from his dark eyes to his offered hand. Nervous indecision made her hesitate, her white teeth worrying her bottom lip, her expression tense.

She loved him. She wanted him. She hoped his feelings for her proved true.

Had her mother felt like this when faced with her father's passion? Was she making the same mistake her mother had made? Suddenly, she understood her mother better than she ever had. If her mother had felt like this, then she'd had no other option but to love her father.

Mikhail crouched down in front of her and traced a long finger down her scarred cheek. "What would you do if you were not afraid?"

Belle sighed, her whole being relaxing at his words. Her lips turned up in a shy smile, and she placed her hand in his.

Mikhail gave her hand a gentle squeeze and then led her into the bedchamber. After closing the door behind them, he turned to face her.

Belle stood there, huge violet eyes mirroring her apprehension. Her body trembled visibly.

He had forgotten how skittish virgins were. He wanted her badly but knew that slow was the only way to proceed.

Mikhail drew her toward him and wrapped his arms around her quaking body. He kissed her leisurely until she clung to him.

"When do we remove our clothing?" Belle asked, her strain apparent in her voice.

Mikhail hid a smile. Her innocence tugged at his heartstrings. "We disrobe when the moment seems right."

Relief etched itself across her sweet expression. She looked like a woman whose execution had been postponed.

"I would never do anything to hurt you," Mikhail said, and then kissed her.

All the while, Mikhail unfastened her buttons. The gown dropped to the floor and pooled at her feet. His shirt followed her gown.

Belle placed the palms of her hands on his chest, feeling his muscles and the light matting of black hair. "Yours is the first naked chest I have ever seen."

"Mine will be the only naked chest you will ever see," Mikhail told her. "I do not want my wife peeking at any other man."

That made her smile.

"Let us sit on the bed." Mikhail removed his boots and hose. Then he slipped her shoes off her feet and tossed them aside.

Mikhail drew her back on the bed and lay beside her. He kissed her again, his tongue slipping inside her mouth.

Emboldened, Belle returned his kiss in kind. Then she surprised him by imitating him and slipping her tongue inside his mouth.

His fingers slid up her petal-soft cheeks. Mikhail ran his hands through her thick ebony hair and then down the delicate column of her neck. He pushed the straps of her chemise off her shoulders and drew it down to her waist.

Belle blushed scarlet. The air on her naked breasts made her feel indecent, especially the way he was looking at them.

"I would never do anything to harm you," Mikhail promised. "Nor would I do anything that you will regret. Do you trust me?"

"Yes, I trust you."

Mikhail kissed her again. He slid his mouth to her eyelids and lightly ran his lips across them. After drawing her chemise down, he removed his breeches and noted that his bride kept her gaze above his waist.

Belle glided her fingertips across his chest. She heard the ragged catch of his breath and felt his heart beating beneath her palm.

"You are incredibly exquisite." His voice sounded husky.

Mikhail smoothed her shoulders and ran his fingers across her delicate collarbones. Then he caressed her arms from shoulder to hands. He lifted each hand to kiss, surprising her with his gentleness. His fingers made the return journey up the inside of her arms, his touch on the sensitive inside skin chilling her and igniting a flame in the bottom of her belly.

"Your breasts are perfection," Mikhail said, his eyes caressing them. "Your nipples are a dusky pink that darkens with your arousal."

His intense gaze held her captive while his hand roamed along the silken skin of her neck, drifting down her body. He avoided her breasts, building anticipation, until he slid his fingers up to caress each in turn. One finger circled her breast, moving ever closer to its center, until it touched the sensitive tip.

Belle moaned at the sensations he created. Her breath came in shallow gasps and her insides quivered and melted.

His lips and tongue mimicked his hand, swirling around the flesh of her breasts, moving closer and closer to its center. He touched the tip of her nipple with the tip of his tongue and heard her gasp of pleasure. Flicking his tongue out, he wet her nipple and then blew on it.

"Kiss me," Belle panted, wrapping her arm around his neck. She wanted him closer and closer and closer.

His lips claimed hers in a kiss that consumed. He stroked her belly and felt her quivering.

Belle felt as if she were floating on a cloud. Every muscle in her body relaxed. Every nerve in her body rioted.

Mikhail slipped his hand between her legs and held her there. He pressed the palm of his hand against her.

Belle responded with pure instinct. She moved her hips in a wavy motion, seeking his hand, pressing herself against it.

Toying with her, Mikhail touched her moist heat in a feathery light caress. "Will you make yourself mine, Princess, and allow me to make myself yours?"

Her lids fluttered open, and she looked at him through violet eyes dazed with desire. "Yes," she whispered.

Mikhail spread her legs and knelt between them. Wrapping his arms around her lower body, he raised her buttocks and positioned himself. Slowly and gently, he thrust himself forward a little at a time and then out. Each movement brought him deeper inside her. Finally, he thrust deeply and buried himself in her.

Belle felt consumed, overwhelmed, surrounded by his manhood. She felt no fear or pain.

They moved together, slowly at first. Catching his rhythm, Belle met him stroke for stroke and leaned into him when he grinded himself against her.

Mikhail slipped his hand between their bodies and caressed her most sensitive spot, catching her unaware. Belle flew over the edge of arousal into a mindless, sensual paradise. His thrusts becoming shorter and faster, Mikhail followed her there. He groaned and emptied his seed inside her quivering body.

Recovering himself, Mikhail fell to one side and pulled her into his embrace. "You were wonderful," he whispered, pressing a kiss on her temple.

Belle sighed, a dejected sound that made him look down at her. "I was saving myself for my husband."

"You *did* save yourself for your husband," Mikhail said. "We will marry as soon as I regain my memory."

"Do you really mean that?"

"Princess, I would never lie to you."

She relaxed in his arms. Silence.

"Mushrooms," Belle exclaimed, drawing his attention. Your *you-know* resembles a mushroom." She blushed and pointed below his waist. "See, there is the mushroom cap and there is the stem."

Mikhail dropped his gaze from her face to his groin. Then he shouted with laughter and hugged her. "Princess, you are an Original."

Chapter 8

Sunshine always lifted her spirits. Today proved an exception, though. Seven consecutive days of rain had meant seven long days of lovemaking, but the sun's rays would put an end to that.

Humming to herself, Belle opened the door to invite the morning's fresh air inside. She loved sunshine but, during the past week, had developed a fondness for stormy days of seclusion.

Rain delivered wonderful moments. Her mother's smiles. Green gardens. Making love with Mick.

Belle set two steaming cups of coffee on the table. Next came two bowls of porridge and a jar of honey.

Mick made her happy, happier than she'd ever been in her life, including those days when her unscarred face turned gentlemen's heads in her direction. She loved him. Once he'd regained his memory, they would marry and live happily ever after. No doubt, she would also love his daughter.

Wiping excess soap off his face, the object of her thoughts wandered into the kitchen. He sat at the table, saying, "I am developing a taste for your porridge."

"Don't forget the honey." Belle dipped her spoon into the honey jar and drizzled it slowly on her porridge. Catching his eye, she licked the coating of honey off the spoon before beginning the porridge.

"Compared with you, the honey tastes bitter," Mikhail said, and winked at her.

Belle blushed, but his compliment pleased her. She dipped her spoon into her porridge and lifted it to her lips, pausing to blow on it before eating.

Flicking a glance at Mick, Belle realized he was lost in his own thoughts. Her gaze drifted across the cottage. Sun streamed into the common room through the window, tiny dust motes dancing on air.

Belle watched Mick eating his porridge but pretended lost in her own thoughts. He seemed distant, his cheerful banter noticeably absent. Was he reconsidering his feelings for her? Would the sunshine see him revoke his love and his intention to marry her? Would he leave her today?

Mikhail finished his porridge and set his spoon in his empty bowl. He stood then, surprising her into a puzzled smile. Two steps brought him to her side. He leaned close and planted a kiss on her lips. "Mmm, you taste like honey."

Returning to his chair, he announced, "I have news to share with you."

Belle rested her spoon in the half-eaten bowl of porridge. Nervous, she flicked the tip of her tongue out to lick the honey off her lips.

"You drive me wild when you do that."

"Is that your news?"

Mikhail stretched his hand across the table. Belle placed her small hand on his open palm, and his long fingers closed around it.

"We can marry whenever you want," Mikhail told her. "I remember who I am."

The sunshine had brought them luck.

Belle smiled, her violet eyes sparkling brighter than the

day's sunshine. She had waited for this moment since first setting eyes on him.

"Who are you?"

"I am Prince Mikhail Kazanov."

Belle snatched her hand back, her expression mirroring her dismay. "Are you related to Prince Stepan?"

"Stepan is my brother." Mikhail ignored the warning signal of her distancing herself. "Rudolf, Viktor, and Vladimir are also my brothers."

"Who is Vladimir?"

"Viktor's twin still lives in Moscow."

Belle dropped her gaze, and her stomach revolted with nausea at this development. Bad luck had brought a prince into her life. *And her bed*.

"Princess?"

"I cannot marry you."

"Are you rejecting me or your bowl of porridge?"

Verging on tears, Belle summoned her reserves of inner strength. She lifted her gaze from his chest to his dimpled chin to his invitingly chiseled lips and aristocratic nose. The look in his dark eyes was forbiddingly cold.

"I cannot marry you," Belle said, her misery apparent. "You are a prince and . . . I am what I am."

Mikhail reached across the table to touch her hand, his black gaze holding hers captive. "I want you for my wife and stepmother for my daughter."

Belle closed her eyes, her heart aching. What ill luck had sent her an unsuitable man to love and who loved her in return. To be so close and so far from paradise. She wanted— *no, needed*—anonymity. Marrying a prince precluded that.

Belle lifted her hand from his and hid it on her lap. "I cannot marry you."

"You cannot or will not marry me?"

Belle heard the anger in his voice. She was hurting him and

herself. Better to suffer the pain now than later when managing it would be more difficult.

"I would marry you," Belle said, "but I can never be a society wife. If we were the only two to consider . . ."

"Marriage *is* between two people," Mikhail argued. "One society wife was more than enough. I do not want another."

"You say that now," Belle countered, "but later you will change your mind and wish you had married an aristocrat."

"Your sire is a duke," Mikhail reminded her, "and your mother was a countess in her own right. Very few can claim such an aristocratic bloodline.

Belle touched her right cheek. "I am scarred."

"Damn it." Mikhail banged his fist on the table, the force shaking their bowls and cups. "You are more beautiful than any woman I know. You radiate beauty."

Radiate beauty? Like the Madonna? Radiating beauty meant from the inside out. Which meant her scar was a distraction. She could live with that but not in public.

Belle knew she could not cope with society. A handsome, wealthy, titled aristocrat would always attract beautiful women. She would never survive a foray into society and outface all those rivals.

"I could never quit my gardening business," Belle argued, after searching her mind for an excuse. "All those plants need me."

"I need you." Mikhail closed his eyes, visibly struggling to compose himself. "What if you carry my child?"

Belle gasped, her face draining of color. She had not considered that eventuality.

"I believed you were a commoner." Belle ignored the possibility of pregnancy. "Of all the men in London who could have staggered into my garden, I saved a *damn* prince."

"Princesses do not curse."

"I am no *damn* princess."

Mikhail stood at that and headed for the door. She expected

him to slam it, but he exhibited herculean control by clicking it quietly shut. Which made her feel even worse.

More angry than he'd ever been in his life, Mikhail marched down the lane. The sunshine had gone out of his day. Of all the women in London who desired a prince, he had married the only one who had no desire to wed an exalted aristocrat.

Mikhail nodded a greeting at the driver of a coach parked in front of the last cottage. He advanced on that cottage and, without knocking, threw the door open.

Startled by the sudden invasion, three men saw him and leaped to their feet. Julian Boomer, his majordomo, had delivered breakfast to his two bodyguards, Fredek and Grisha.

"Your Highness, we did not expect you," Boomer exclaimed.

"*Sukin syn,*" Mikhail snapped.

Boomer looked at the two enormous bodyguards. "What did His Highness—?"

"I said *son of a bitch.*"

Mikhail reached for the vodka bottle and gulped a healthy swig, which made him shudder like a dog shaking off rain. He took a deep breath, feeling a bit calmer.

"Tell Johnny to take Fredek and Grisha home," Mikhail instructed his majordomo. "Then deliver the Duke of Inverary a message. Tell His Grace to send a coach to the cottage this afternoon. And tell him"—he flushed—"my wife refuses to marry me."

A sharp glance at his long-time bodyguards discouraged their smiles. Mikhail looked at Boomer, adding, "No one is to inform my wife that she is my wife."

"Yes, Your Highness." Boomer coughed, choking back laughter.

Mikhail gave him a venomous look. Cursing in Russian, he left the cottage and marched down the lane again.

Pausing outside the cottage, Mikhail schooled his features

into a pleasant expression. Anger would alienate his wife, which would be a mistake. From this moment forward, he would court his wife and coax her into marriage. She already loved him. Persuading her into marriage would not be so difficult. The problem was two weeks had not been enough time to build her trust. Once he had done that, their lives would be ships sailing on the calmest of seas.

Mikhail opened the door and stepped inside. "Belle?"

She turned around but remained silent, her gaze downcast.

"I apologize for losing my temper," he said. "I am unaccustomed to a woman's rejection."

Belle snapped her gaze to his. "Is that a fact?"

Mikhail grinned as if he'd made a joke. "What I mean is I admire you."

Her expression relaxed.

That was better.

"I worry for my daughter," he said. "Would you be amenable to meeting Bess?"

Now Belle smiled. "I would love to meet your daughter."

That was much better. His daughter would help him coax his wife into marriage.

The Duke of Inverary sent his coach that afternoon, his instruction to return home without delay. Belle hoped no one had died and nothing was wrong with any of her sisters.

She sat on the leather cushions inside the ducal coach, oblivious to their comfort. Opposite her sat Prince Mikhail. He seemed tight lipped for a man who wasn't angry.

Belle had never felt more miserable. She loved him but needed to marry a commoner. He could not understand her position, finding her rejection of his proposal incredible and insulting.

Uncomfortable with the prince's unhappy expression, Belle stared at the scenery outside the coach's window.

People scurried here and there, hurrying about their week-day business. Fair and foul scents from flower gardens to horse droppings mingled nauseatingly and wafted on the breeze. Her nose twitched at the sickening scents, and a ca-caphony of voices and noises assaulted her ears.

Belle felt sickness rolling in her stomach. Horse droppings and nerves were a combustible combination. Would she reach Park Lane without embarrassing herself?

"You are the only woman in London who would refuse a prince," Mikhail said, breaking the silence.

Belle kept her gaze riveted on the world outside the coach. "I am certain you are correct."

"You are the only woman in history to refuse a prince," he muttered.

"Do not exaggerate." Belle dragged her gaze from the pass-ing scenery to look at him. "I wish you would understand."

"The circumstances of your birth mean nothing," Mikhail said, making a sweeping gesture to dismiss her concerns. "The scar is a matter of no consequence."

"My scar is no tiny matter to me," Belle cried, "and I can't even grow a beard to hide it."

Mikhail chuckled at the image her words conjured. Belle bit her bottom lip to keep from smiling. Given a choice, she would prefer the scar to a beard.

"No woman has ever rejected me."

The prince sounded boyishly petulant. Men were wonder-ful creatures . . . as long as they were getting their own way.

"I am happy to add to your life experience." The coach halted in front of Inverary House. "You do not need to accom-pany me inside."

"Refrain from giving me orders," Mikhail said. "That per-ogative belongs to a wife."

Mikhail climbed out of the coach and then assisted Belle. With his hand on her back, he ushered her up the stairs.

The door opened, and Tinker stepped aside, allowing them

entrance. "Welcome home, Miss Belle and Your Highness," the majordomo greeted them. "Their Graces are taking tea in the parlor."

Mikhail nodded at the older man. "Thank you, Tinker."

Belle felt the prince's hand touch her back again, gently urging her up the stairs. She dreaded her father's reaction when he learned they'd been closeted at the cottage. In many ways, life had been easier before being acknowledged.

"Let me do the talking," Mikhail whispered.

They stepped into the parlor. Her father and her stepmother were sitting near the white marble hearth. With them was Rudolf Kazanov, the prince's eldest brother.

"Welcome home, darling," the Duchess of Inverary called. "Good to see you, Mikhail."

"Brother, I have been worried," Rudolf spoke. "Where did you disappear for two weeks?"

"I will explain as soon as Her Grace pours us tea." Mikhail gestured Belle to sit on the empty settee and then sat beside her.

The duchess passed the prince a cup of tea, who in turn passed it to Belle. She gave him a wobbly smile of thanks and accepted it with a trembling hand.

Feeling apprehensive is normal in these circumstances, Belle thought. If her father had any inkling of the shared intimacies, he would insist on marriage. In spite of disagreeing on the subject of marriage, she trusted the prince not to force the issue.

"I called you home to prepare for the wedding," the Duke of Inverary said.

"Wedding?" Belle squeaked in surprise.

A smile of immense satisfaction appeared on his face. "Prince Stepan and Fancy will be married on Monday."

That shocked Belle, who was well acquainted with her sister's dislike of aristocrats. "Fancy agreed to marry an aristocrat?"

"Theirs is such a romantic tale," the duchess exclaimed, giving them her dimpled smile. "Imagine, our Fancy will be a princess."

Mikhail cleared his throat, and Belle's anxiety grew. Feigning nonchalance, she lifted the teacup, but her hand shook as if she'd developed palsy. She set the teacup on the table in front of her.

"Are you hungry, darling?" the duchess asked, offering a platter of toast served with a pâté. "Try Cook's wonderful sardine and anchovy pâté."

Belle looked at the pâté, its fishy aroma revolting. Her hand flew to her throat, and she struggled against nausea.

Closing her eyes for a moment, Belle took a deep breath. "I have an aversion to the pâté's ingredients." Her voice sounded weak even to her own ears.

The duchess set the platter on the table in front of Belle. "The sardines or the anchovy?"

"B-B-Both." Tearing her gaze from the offending platter, Belle studied her hands folded on her lap.

"Your Grace, we must discuss a matter of importance." Mikhail cleared his throat again and said, "Two weeks ago I was beaten and robbed."

"You were what?" Prince Rudolf exclaimed. "Where did this happen?"

"Let me finish," Mikhail said, gesturing for silence. "Suffering from temporary blindness and amnesia, I staggered into a garden on the far side of Primrose Hill."

"I found His Highness," Belle interjected, and then blushed when her father looked at her.

"Your daughter saved my life," Mikhail told him.

"Well done, Belle."

"What a coincidence that your daughter found my brother," Rudolf remarked.

Belle glanced at the elder prince. His lips were twitching as if he struggled against laughter. Or suffered from a tic.

"What a small world," the duchess agreed. "How lucky to survive the brigands' beating."

Mikhail nodded at that and then continued, "I regained my sight after a couple of days, but my memory took longer."

"Did you and my daughter pass two weeks alone at the cottage?" the Duke of Inverary asked.

Belle knew what was coming but refused to be coerced into marrying any man. She loved the prince, but her peace of mind demanded a reclusive life. She wanted no part of society. Her experience with the baron's mother had convinced her of that.

"Your Grace, I have proposed—"

"I assure you, Papa," Belle interrupted, "nothing illicit happened between us."

Glancing sidelong at the prince, Belle noted his surprised expression and managed a humorless laugh. "Papa, His Highness was at death's door and unable even to feed himself."

The Duke of Inverary stared at her, making her fidget. "What tasks *could* His Highness perform?"

"Nothing of consequence." Belle stood, intending to escape. "Since the matter is settled, I will retire to my chamber."

Mikhail stood when she did. "I will walk you to the stairs."

At the end of the corridor, Belle paused at the staircase and turned to the prince. She had refused to marry him, but facing their separation was proving difficult. Too bad they couldn't have remained at the cottage.

Mikhail tilted her chin up and waited for her to lift her gaze to his. Her eyes were violet pools glistening with tears. That gave him hope for their future.

"Princess, you are an incompetent liar," he chided her, a faint smile on his lips.

She looked worried. "Do you think my father believed us?"

"I will cover for you if he asks," Mikhail said. "Your father will never know you lied."

"Why would you do that?" Belle asked. "If my father knew . . ."

"I will not force you into marriage," Mikhail answered. "When we marry, you will willingly walk down the aisle to me."

Belle knew she did not want to lose him permanently. "I will reconsider your proposal."

Mikhail recognized desire in her eyes and her reluctance to leave him. He lifted her hand to his lips. "You promised to meet my daughter."

"I haven't forgotten."

"I will miss you, Princess."

She missed him already. "When will I see you again?"

"I will definitely see you at our siblings' wedding."

"That is several days away," she complained.

"Perhaps you will see me sooner." Turning away, Mikhail left her standing there and retraced his steps to the parlor. He dropped onto the settee, his expression grim.

A glass appeared in front of his face. "You need this."

Mikhail looked at his brother's offering, muttering, "A merciful God created vodka to ease a man's journey." Lifting the glass to his lips, he emptied it in one gulp.

The Duke of Inverary cleared his throat. "I realize you have the right as her lawful husband to . . . um . . . consummate the marriage."

"Say no more, Your Grace." Mikhail held his hand up. "We did not consummate the marriage"—he noted the older man relax—"because my wife does not know I married her."

When his brother passed him another vodka, Mikhail noted the incredulous smirk. Rudolf did not believe the lie. Only a loving father would believe such a fairy tale.

"That damn scar makes Belle insecure," Mikhail told them. "I will kill the monster who sliced her."

"What is your plan to convince her to marry you?" the Duchess of Inverary asked.

That was a very good question. He wished he knew the answer.

"I will persuade her."

"You could not win her agreement during the previous two weeks," Prince Rudolf said, smiling. "Stepan is enjoying better luck than you."

"Belle has agreed to meet my Bess," Mikhail said, ignoring his brother's insult. "Perhaps she would accept a role as governess, bringing her into contact with me on a continuous basis."

"My daughter will not sleep at your house until society knows you are married." The duke vetoed that idea.

"Helping with Bess during the day would not be improper," Mikhail said. "Belle would be doing me a favor, and I promise not to besmirch her reputation."

The Duke of Inverary considered that alternative. "I suppose it would be acceptable, but I prefer your daughter visit Belle here a few days each week too."

Mikhail inclined his head, acquiescing to his father-in-law.

"Darling, I possess expertise in relationship strategies," the Duchess of Inverary drawled. "A dab of jealousy could work a miracle."

"No."

"No?"

"My wife suffers from insecurity," Mikhail said, "and I will not hurt her feelings by giving my attention to another woman."

"I commend your rare sensitivity," the duchess said, "but persuading her into a society marriage could take a while."

"All good things come to those who wait," Mikhail repeated his wife's words.

The Duchess of Inverary rolled her eyes. "I will pray for your success."

Mikhail grinned at her. "Miracles happen every day, or so my wife says."

* * *

"I see a miracle."

Belle stood in front of the gold-framed cheval mirror inside her bedchamber. She turned her head one way and then the other to study her scarred cheek. Her sister's theater cosmetics hid the scar. Almost. Only the tiniest flaw was visible.

Hope swelled within her breast. Her bottom lip quivered with sudden emotion.

"Nanny Smudge spoke truthfully." Belle whirled around and gave her sisters a wobbly smile. "Miracles *do* happen every day."

Fancy perched on the edge of the table set in front of the Grecian chaise where Raven sprawled. Both sisters were smiling.

"You look more beautiful than ever," Fancy said.

Raven nodded in agreement. "I cannot believe how our lives are changing."

Belle looked at her eldest sister. "I could not believe the news of your impending marriage."

Fancy blushed. "I am pregnant."

Belle had not considered the possibilty of a baby until Mikhail mentioned it. "How did you know—?"

Fancy interrupted with a laugh. "I had no idea. Stepan and the duchess recognized the symptoms."

"What are the symptoms?" Belle glanced at her youngest sister, who was watching her, and blushed.

"I suffer nausea, dizziness, and tiredness," Fancy answered. "I have the urge to smash the culprit's face for making me feel so ill."

Belle wandered across the chamber to gaze out the window. Lush summer had arrived once the rains had ceased, and a profusion of primary and pastel colors painted the duke's garden. Her thoughts were not on flowers and plants, though. She had been nauseated, dizzy, and tired these past few days. However, she did not harbor even the slightest urge to smash Mikhail's face. Did that mean she had escaped pregnancy?

"How does *it* feel?" she heard Raven asking behind her.

Belle turned around, saying, "How do you think nausea, dizziness, and tiredness feels?"

Raven laughed. "I wasn't asking about pregnancy. Come here and listen to Fancy tell me how—*you know*—feels."

Crossing the chamber, Belle pushed Raven's legs out of the way and sat beside her on the settee. "Does everyone suffer all those pregnancy symptoms?"

"Oh, no. Are you pregnant too?"

Belle looked from Fancy to Raven. Neither sister seemed surprised. "I don't have the urge to smash Mikhail."

"After years of vowing not to end up like our mother," Raven said, "both of you fell backward for an aristocrat."

"What about *your* betrothal?" Fancy snapped. "You did not refuse the Marquis of Basildon, did you?"

"I did not fall on my back for him."

"These are early days yet," Fancy said, "and you have not been left alone with him."

Belle agreed with her elder sister. "Alexander will expect it once the betrothal is official."

"What Alex expects and what Alex gets are totally different," Raven told them. "He may expect intimacy, but he will get torment."

The three sisters burst into laughter. The door opened, drawing their attention, and the duchess strolled into the bedchamber.

"My, what a happy group," the duchess said. "I need a private word with Belle."

Fancy and Raven left the chamber, the door closing behind them with a click. The Duchess of Inverary sat on the settee and patted Belle's hand.

"Mikhail insisted you shared no intimacies," the duchess said, "but I am not as easily fooled as your father."

Belle opened her mouth to defend herself. She snapped it shut again when her stepmother held her hand up.

"Do not bother denying it," the duchess drawled, her dimpled smile appearing. "I will not ask because you would only deny it if you *had* been intimate."

Belle dropped her gaze to her hands folded in her lap. The Duchess of Inverary was nobody's fool.

"Darling, heed this warning," the duchess said. "Certain young ladies desire a royal husband. Princess Anya, Cynthia Clarke, and Lavinia Smythe would give the devil their first-born to be in your enviable position. Dubbed the Blonde Brigade, these three have been pressing for a marriage offer from Mikhail since the poor man came out of mourning."

Belle paled at the mention of rivals for the prince's affection. She lifted a troubled gaze to her stepmother.

"Mikhail adores you," the duchess said, "but if you refuse his offer, he *will* marry again." She shrugged her shoulders, letting that disturbing possibility hang in the air like a dark cloud.

"I told him I would reconsider his offer," Belle said.

"That was a wise move," the duchess said. "Do not make the prince wait too long, darling, or you may find this golden opportunity gone, snatched away. Another young lady would not hesitate accepting the prince's offer."

Chapter 9

"Welcome home, Your Highness."

"Thank you, Boomer," Mikhail greeted his majordomo. "My daughter?"

"Princess Elizabeth is waiting in the—"

"Daddy!"

Mikhail laughed and hunkered down when he saw his daughter dashing across the entry foyer. She threw herself into his open arms, burying her face against his neck.

"I missed you Daddy."

"I missed you too."

"I missed you three," Elizabeth said, holding three fingers in front of his face.

Mikhail smiled at that. "Bess and I will take tea in the parlor," he instructed the majordomo.

"Yes, Your Highness."

Lifting his daughter into his arms, Mikhail carried her across the entry foyer. French doors led to a carpeted inner foyer where an alabaster Atlas held an enormous replica of the world and a spiral staircase climbed to the upper floors.

Mikhail loved the second-floor family parlor more than any other room in his town mansion. The comfortable room invited relaxation and encouraged intimacy, both of which brought a family closer. Three upholstered settees formed a U around a white marble hearth, a low, square table within easy reach from any of the settees. Inlaid with flower swags, a mahogany desk perched in front of the windows. An Aubusson carpet in shades of blue, gold, cream, and black covered the floor.

Mikhail placed his daughter on the settee facing the hearth and joined her there. A vase of roses sat on the table, their scent reminding him of Belle.

Slipping his arm around her shoulders, Mikhail drew his daughter into a snuggle. He had loved his only child at first sight, and she'd held him in thrall since her entry into the world. Fatherhood had proved surprisingly satisfying, and he looked forward to his wife filling their home with their children.

"What did you bring me, Daddy?"

"My little greedy one." His daughter was a typical female. Lonely when he went away, he ingratiated himself into her good graces by bringing her tokens. Surprises, she called them.

Boomer walked into the parlor and set a tray on the table. "Will there be anything else, Your Highness?"

"No, thank you, Boomer." Mikhail handed Elizabeth her glass of lemonade and waited while she drank. "Tell me what you have been doing, Bess."

After handing her father the glass, Elizabeth placed her index finger across her lips. "I attended a tea party."

"What is the gossip this week?"

"Princess Sunshine and the Earl of Goodness loped to Greta Green," she answered, making him smile. "Cousin Roxanne said Sunshine *needed* a husband but would not explain. What does that mean, Daddy?"

"I will explain when you are older." Mikhail gave her a sideways hug. "I promise Cousin Roxanne does not know what it means either."

"Grandmama and Aunt Livy visited me." She pursed her lips, a frown marring her sweet expression.

Something was bothering her. "And?"

Elizabeth looked at him through her mother's blue eyes. "Can an aunt be a mummy too?"

"I suppose so," Mikhail answered, and offered her a coconut cookie. "Uncle Stepan is an uncle and a brother."

Elizabeth shook her head, refusing the cookie. "Grandmama asked me if I would like Aunt Livy for my new mummy."

Mikhail kept his expression placid for his daughter's sake but could feel his temper rising. His former in-laws were using his daughter to get an offer of marriage. "How did you answer Grandmama?"

Elizabeth rolled her eyes, the same way she'd seen him do to Stepan. "Aunts cannot be mummies."

His lips twitched, but he managed to swallow the bubble of laughter trying to escape. He could imagine his mother-in-law's chagrined expression.

"Did Aunt Livy say anything?"

Elizabeth shook her head.

"What did Grandmama say?"

"She said pre-pus-your-us."

"Preposterous?" Mikhail grinned and dropped a kiss on the crown of her head. "Sit on my lap, Bess." When she did, he wrapped his arms around her. "Can you keep a big secret?"

"Yes, Daddy." Excitement sparkled in her blue eyes, and she pretended to button her lips.

"I found us a new mummy." Mikhail laughed when she clapped her hands. "Our new mummy knows hundreds of bedtime stories, digs in the dirt, and laughs all day. Not only can she make a happiness cake but hugs and kisses cookies too."

Wonder widened her eyes, and her smile was pure ecstasy. "Where did we get her?"

"Heaven sent her."

Elizabeth touched his cheek. "God answered my prayers."

Turning his head, Mikhail kissed her hand. His daughter's sentiment reminded him of Belle, who also believed that God heard and answered prayers. Perhaps He did answer prayers.

"One tiny problem needs fixing before we bring her home," Mikhail told her. "Our new mummy does not know I picked her. So we must convince her to live with us."

A frown troubled her brows. "How do we do that?"

"We give her all our love."

Elizabeth laughed. "That is easy, Daddy."

"Tomorrow I will take you to meet her," Mikhail said, "but you need to know something else. Mummy has a red mark on her cheek because a bad man hurt her once. She thinks people will stare at the mark. Can you pretend there is no mark on her cheek?"

Elizabeth nodded. "I can kiss her cheek and make her feel better."

"Nanny Dee and Nanny Cilla will help you choose a pretty pink gown for tomorrow." Mikhail wondered if warning Bess about the scar had been wise. Would Belle think he'd coached his daughter not to mention it?

"I want to pick my gown now," Elizabeth said, slipping off his lap.

"Very well." Mikhail hid a smile. If she was a tad older, she would have demanded to purchase a new gown.

Bess walked toward the door but changed her mind. Returning to him, she said, "I want a kiss, Daddy."

Mikhail gave her a kiss and a hug.

She walked away again. Looking over her shoulder, she gave him an exaggerated wink.

He returned her wink. Women were born with the knowledge of Eve.

Before his daughter disappeared out the door, Boomer appeared. "Your Highness, Lady Smythe requests—"

"Spare me, Boomer." Prudence Smythe marched into the parlor. "Announcing family is quite unnecessary."

The word *family* evoked an inner cringe. His former mother-in-law wanted to discuss a matter of importance, and he knew what it was.

Prudence Smythe leaned close to his daughter. "Give Grandmama a kiss."

Elizabeth planted a peck on her grandmother's cheek. "I cannot visit today, Grandmama, because I need to choose a pretty gown for tomorrow. I am meeting my new mummy." She put a finger across her lips. "Shhh, keep the secret."

Mikhail watched his former mother-in-law's expression change from patronizing patience to grim determination. Telling Bess about Belle had been a tactical error. More precisely, a blunder. He should not have expected a four-year-old to control her excitement.

Thirty-two years of impeccable manners brought Mikhail to his feet as Prudence advanced on him like Napoleon marching on Russia. Prudence would go the way of Napoleon into total defeat.

"Where have you been for two weeks?" Prudence demanded, sitting on the settee to his left.

Mikhail cocked a black brow at her. He answered to no one, especially a former mother-in-law. On the other hand, kindness cost nothing.

"I had business outside London."

"You should have mentioned you were leaving," she scolded him.

"I did not disappear into vapors," Mikhail said. "My brothers and my staff knew I had gone."

"Nobody told me," Prudence snapped.

Ignoring her peevishness, Mikhail reached for his teacup and silently counted to ten. He sipped the steaming brew and then set the cup on the table, his movements slow, stalling for time before he faced her wrath.

"Why were you looking for me?" he asked.

"I want no more of your shilly-shallying," Prudence told him. "You need a wife, an heir, and a stepmother for Elizabeth."

Mikhail narrowed his black gaze on her. She would not make his remarriage easy. Unless, of course, the bride was her daughter. He had hoped to postpone the explosion until Belle was ensconced in his home.

"Elizabeth adores her Aunt Lavinia," Prudence said, "and society has been awaiting the betrothal announcement since her come-out."

Mikhail supposed there was no kind way to dash her royal dreams. Brutal honesty was needed in this situation.

"Society will be waiting a long time for that particular announcement," Mikhail said, noting the rush of blood to her face. "I am not offering for Lavinia."

"She expects marriage," Prudence told him.

"I have never given her or you any encouragement in that direction," Mikhail said. "I do have another young woman in mind."

"Cynthia Clarke?" Prudence could not contain her fury, the names sounding like curses. "Princess Anya?"

"Neither of them interests me."

"Who is this interloper?"

Mikhail stared at her for a long moment, deciding how much information to give her. Only the truth would do. His mother-in-law would badger him until she knew who had foiled her plans. Belle was safely ensconced at her father's and could not be hurt by the woman's venom.

"Belle Flambeau is the Duke of Inverary's daughter and—"

"You cannot mean one of his bastards by that French whore," Prudence cried.

Her choice of vocabulary annoyed him. "Do not utter that sentiment in my presence again."

With a sinking feeling in the pit of his stomach, Mikhail realized what his wife feared. He had not understood because he had been raised a privileged prince, one of society's eligible elite. Mikhail did not doubt that society would accept his wife eventually. How much pain would Belle endure before all settled? The Flambeau sisters would support each other during their introduction into society, but his wife was a special case. She suffered more insecurities than her sisters.

"Belle lives with her father and has his acknowledgment," Mikhail said. "Believing women should be productive, she has chosen to continue her gardening business. You do know the definition of *productive?*"

"Gardening?"

His former mother-in-law's scandalized tone spoke for her attitude, and Mikhail now wished he hadn't mentioned the gardening business or succumbed to using sarcasm.

"Marry Lavinia and"—the older woman blushed—"take the girl for a mistress."

"I thought I had made my intentions clear," Mikhail said. "Belle is the kindest, most loving woman I ever met. And she would be that way even had she never been scarred."

"Scarred?" Prudence echoed. "What do you mean by scarred?"

Mikhail wished he hadn't said that either. He hadn't meant to mention the scar lest anyone misunderstand his motive for marriage. Avoiding further statements seemed sensible.

"I plan to court Miss Flambeau and marry her," Mikhail said, ending their conversation. "Nothing you can say or do will persuade me otherwise."

Prudence Smythe stood, which brought him to his feet. Grim determination etched across her features, giving her a pinched expression. "I will never allow my granddaughter to be mothered by that illegitimate tart." Without another word, she marched out of the parlor.

With a groan, Mikhail dropped onto the settee and closed his eyes against the beginnings of a headache. He had no doubt that Prudence Smythe would create problems, and he could be facing a united Blonde Brigade and their mamas.

Mikhail did not care about himself. His only concern was preventing his wife from hurting.

He needed vodka. Drinking spirits would not solve his problem, merely numb his brain for an evening.

Several hours later, Mikhail left his home for White's Gentlemen's Club and, he hoped, his brothers' and his cousins' commiseration. The interview with Prudence Smythe had drained him, and he had no plan for protecting Belle.

A refuge for London's masculine elite, White's Gentlemen's Club was located on St. James Street. The lighting was dim, the voices muted, and the chairs comfortable.

Mikhail entered the exclusive establishment through the door beside the famous bow window and immediately spotted his brothers and cousins. Perhaps, if all seven put their heads together, a plan could be formulated to frustrate the female forces set against his wife.

Dropping into a chair, Mikhail gestured Prince Rudolf to pour him a vodka. He downed it in one gulp and shivered as the spirits burned a path to his stomach.

Prince Viktor set a shot glass of whisky on the table in front of him. Prince Stepan refilled the vodka glass.

Mikhail belted the vodka down and chased it with the whisky. The alcohol's kick made him shudder, but he felt almost human again. "Good evening, brothers."

He turned his attention to the other three men, Princes Drako, Lykos, and Gunter. Black eyed and black haired, all the Kazanovs bore the same family resemblance. "Good to see you, cousins."

"You do not look especially happy," Prince Drako remarked. "For a newly married man, that is."

Three brothers and three cousins chuckled, which made them less than endearing. Long ago, he had learned never to show any weakness with this group or suffer the consequences.

Mikhail shrugged, feigning cool indifference. "Why are you not chasing *la contessa?*"

"Drako is giving *la contessa* time to miss him," Prince Lykos answered for his elder brother. "Are you here to give your bride time to miss you too?"

Six princes laughed again.

Mikhail smiled at his cousin. "I heard that Miss Blaze Flambeau interests you, Lykos."

"So?"

"On my way here, I spied the Marquis of Awe entering Inverary House."

Lykos arched a black brow at him. "And?"

"And my sweet bride told me the Highlander was also interested in Blaze," Mikhail answered.

Prince Lykos cursed in Russian. Then he stood and walked out of White's.

Mikhail smiled at his remaining relatives. Tormenting his cousin had lifted his spirits.

"Who interests you?" Mikhail asked Prince Gunter.

"I know who does *not* interest me," the younger prince answered. "That trio of blondes stepped through the gates of hell, vampires ready to sink fangs into any suitable man."

"Those three are prince hungry," Drako agreed. "Avoid being alone with them."

The mention of the Blonde Brigade reminded Mikhail of Prudence Smythe. He worried what the old witch would do.

"Brother, what troubles you?" Rudolf asked.

"You mean, besides his wife not wanting to marry him," Viktor amended.

All the Kazanov princes laughed. Except Mikhail, who re-filled his vodka and whisky glasses.

"I have endured a confrontation with my former mother-in-law, who wants me to marry Lavinia." Mikhail gulped the vodka and then downed the whisky. "Prudence will create problems to prevent my marrying Belle."

"Even Prudence Smythe cannot prevent an action that has already happened," Stepan said.

Prince Drako nudged Stepan. "I have missed your unique talent of stating the obvious."

All the Kazanov princes laughed.

"Be kind to Cousin Stepan," Gunter said. "He will soon become someone's father."

That surprised Mikhail. "Fancy is pregnant?"

Stepan smiled. "My seed hit its target."

"That must be the reason she is amenable to marriage," Mikhail teased his baby brother.

Stepan's smile grew into a grin. "I am not the Kazanov with an unconsummated marriage."

More laughter from the princes.

"Of course my marriage was consummated," Mikhail said.

"In that case, perhaps your seed also hit its target," Rudolf said, pouring everyone a vodka. "We need a toast."

The princes raised their glasses. The eldest at the table, Rudolf did the honors. "To marriage and motherhood."

The princes gulped their vodka. Rudolf dropped his empty glass on the carpet and stomped on it, drawing the attention of the room's occupants. The younger princes followed his lead.

"Bring more glasses," Rudolf called.

Mikhail shook his head. "Belle would have told me if she was pregnant."

"Perhaps Belle needs to be told." Stepan leaned close, adding, "Like her sister."

Mikhail bolted out of his chair. "I need to—"

Viktor reached out and jerked him back into his seat. "You cannot visit Inverary and ask if his daughter is pregnant."

"I *am* her husband."

"She does not know that," Drako reminded him.

"His Grace knows."

"Brother, do you really want Magnus Campbell to know you lied to him this afternoon?" Rudolf asked him.

Mikhail relaxed in his chair. "I will speak to the duchess tomorrow."

Prince Rudolf nodded in approval and smiled. "A wise decision, brother."

He hated foreigners, his gaze fixing on the laughing Russian princes. White's should not welcome them into its bastion of exclusivity. That damn Duke of Inverary had sponsored them, or they never would have been allowed through the door.

Gulping his whisky, he slipped a hand into his pocket and touched the gold sovereign. That made him smile.

The days of rain had ended. The nights of hunting would begin. Tonight.

He stood and walked toward the door. One of the filthy foreigners rose from his chair as he passed their table.

Masking his hatred, he gave the Russian a broad smile. "Good evening, Your Highness."

Prince Mikhail Kazanov looked at him, his black gaze glittering with cold contempt. "Good evening."

They should have known the Slasher would strike once the rain ceased.

Alexander Blake climbed out of the hackney. Passing coins to the driver, he surveyed the scene and then headed in the direction of the people gathering along the riverbank near Wapping Stairs.

The morning was aging toward noon. The cries of the sea-gulls assaulted his ears as did the blaring horns from the barges.

Shouldering his way through the crowd, Alexander nodded at the runners and approached the constable. His gaze shifted to the blanket-covered lump.

"Examine the body," Constable Black instructed him.

Donning his gloves, Alexander drew the blanket off the victim. One slash across her throat had bled her out. She appeared heartbreakingly young, probably near Tulip's age.

Alexander circled the body, never raising his gaze. Though emotion was an investigator's enemy, he could not suppress the outrage swelling within him. If he was lucky enough to get his hands on this monster— He banished that murderous thought and tried to focus on the scene.

Crouching beside her, Alexander lifted the gold sovereign from her hand. His heart wrenched at the sight of a cheap lady's fan, splattered with blood, attached to her wrist. Like the others, he had hacked her hair for a souvenir.

Alexander slipped the fan off her wrist. Covering her with the blanket, he returned to the constable's side. "Raven may glean something from the girl's fan."

"I brought the gold button and one of the sovereigns," Amadeus Black told him. "Hopefully, we will learn something interesting about our man."

"The girl doesn't appear to have much in the way of wealth," Alexander said. "I'll pay for the funeral."

Amadeus Black touched his shoulder. "You are a good man, my friend, but you cannot care for the world."

"I can pay for this girl's funeral, though."

Amadeus beckoned his assistant. "Barney, supervise the body's removal. Alex will pay for the funeral, but we need to stop at Inverary House. If Prosecutor Lowing asks, you do not know where we have gone."

Barney grinned. "You can depend on me."

* * *

At the opposite end of London, Raven finished brushing her ebony mane and tied it back with a scarlet ribbon. Then she walked downstairs to sit on the painted chair in the foyer.

"Good morning, Miss Raven."

"Good morning, Tinker." She gave the majordomo a bright smile. "I am expecting visitors."

Someone banged the knocker several times. Tinker opened the door and stepped aside. "Do come inside, gentlemen. Miss Raven is waiting."

"How did you—?" Alexander began, but then shook his head. "Never mind, brat. I know what you will say."

Raven stood, her violet gaze narrowing on him. No matter what she did, Alexander would never see the light of truth.

"You know what I will say?" Raven drawled, her tone an excellent imitation of her stepmother. "My, my, my. You may have hidden talents yourself."

Constable Black smiled at that. "Intuition is an investigator's friend."

"Intuition cannot testify against a criminal," Alexander said.

"Sometimes intuition leads to facts that may be used in court."

"We'll use my father's study for consultation." Raven led them upstairs and, gaining the study, sat on the upholstered settee in front of the black marble hearth. Alexander sat beside her while Amadeus Black took the highbacked leather chair.

"What is that?" Alexander pointed at the table where a washing cloth soaked in a pan of water.

"The objects sometimes make me uneasy," Raven answered, "and I need to wash the impressions off."

Alexander rolled his eyes at Amadeus. Raven caught the mocking gesture and glanced at the constable, who did not appear to see the humor in his apprentice's insult.

Catching him off-guard, Raven discovered Alex perusing her breasts. Slowly, he lifted his gaze to linger on her lips and then her eyes. The streaks of color across his cheeks pleased her.

"Shall we begin?" the constable asked.

Raven rubbed her hands together and reached for the bloodied fan. Closing her eyes, she took several deep breaths and invited the impressions.

"She's uneasy and wishing for a companion to escort her home. Apprehension chills her. A monster lurks in the darkness beyond the gaslight, more dangerous than the monster that lurked beneath her bed as a child. Dread churns her stomach. Fear. Panic. Bleeding . . . cold . . . tired."

Raven could not get rid of the fan fast enough. The only thing worse than feeling what the girl had felt was being the girl who had experienced it. Dipping her hands in the pan, she scrubbed the horror off.

"Excellent," the constable said.

"The victim's feelings do not give any clue to her murderer's identity," Alexander said.

Constable Black offered her a gold sovereign. "Try this."

"Give me the button too," Raven said, surprising both men.

Again, Raven rubbed her hands together and reached for the coin and the button. Holding them between her hands, she closed her eyes and waited. "Suppressed anger, exploding rage, punishing whores . . . Braiding, braiding, braiding. Scarlet ribbons for scarlet ladies."

"Describe him," Alexander whispered against her ear. "Focus on his face."

Raven heard his voice. When she pressed the gold button against the middle of her forehead, images formed in her mind's eye. "Fog and mist. Darkness and . . . Oh my God."

"Tell us what you see," Alexander demanded.

Raven opened her eyes, her complexion pale. She looked at the constable and then Alex. "I-I . . ."

"Did you see a face?" Alexander asked.

Raven nodded, shock preventing her from speaking.

"Can you describe the face?" the constable asked, excitement tingeing his voice.

"What does he look like?" Alexander asked, his arms encircling her, offering support.

"I saw a *she*." Raven looked from one to the other. "I saw Belle."

Chapter 10

She missed him.

Slipping into society frightened Belle. That had made her reject the prince's proposal in haste. Foolishly hasty, especially if she carried his babe. Which was possible, if not probable. Nausea, dizziness, and tiredness had dogged her for several days, but she had not suffered the urge to smash the prince's face for making her feel like this.

Would Mikhail propose again? Or would she need to humble herself by introducing the subject into a conversation?

A woman should never allow her man to gain the upper hand in their relationship. Or so the duchess had said. Humbling herself meant allowing Mikhail to gain the upper hand.

She would wait a week or two or three. If pregnant, she would tell him she'd changed her mind about marrying him. After all, she *had* mentioned she would reconsider his offer.

Early summer wore its most serene expression that afternoon. The sensuous scent of passionflower surrounded her, and she inhaled its smooth sweetness, more delicate than a rose.

Belle wandered the duke's garden to inspect her father's plants and shrubbery and trees. When she sat on a stone bench, Puddles dashed across the grass to rest his enormous head on her lap.

Her sister's theater cosmetics masked her scar almost completely. At least, enough to show herself at the wedding.

Miracles *did* happen every day. She should have listened to her nanny's wisdom.

Her stepmother's warning about rivals for the prince's affection stepped from the shadows to worry her. With beauty and breeding, the Blonde Brigade sounded formidable. What if one of them caught his eye? The fact that her sister was marrying his brother meant she and the prince would occasionally be at family gatherings. She would be devastated if he married another woman, forcing her to see them together.

All of society's maidens and widows wanted to marry her prince. How many of those ladies tempted him?

"Miss Belle." Her father's majordomo was advancing on her. "Are you receiving visitors today?"

"Who is it?"

"Sir Cedric Wilkins."

What business did the baron's brother have with her? "I will see the squire. Take Puddles inside with you."

The garden door opened a few minutes later, and Cedric Wilkins appeared. Leaning on his cane, he walked toward her.

Belle gave him a cordial smile. "Please, join me."

With his brown eyes and hair, Cedric Wilkins resembled his half brother. The features that seemed almost pretty on Charles appeared more masculine on the older brother.

Wilkins sat on the opposite side of the bench, a respectful distance from her. "You look surprised to see me."

"Yes, I suppose I am."

"I wanted to apologize for your injury," Cedric told her. "I regret your suffering."

"I appreciate your concern, sir." Belle blushed at the reference to her scar. "What happened was not your fault."

"For what my opinion is worth," Wilkins said, "I consider my brother's response to the attack reprehensible."

Belle stared at her hands folded on her lap. "Thank you for that."

Cedric Wilkins stood to leave. "May I call upon you sometime?"

Belle knew he was asking to court her. She lifted her violet gaze to his. "Sir Wilkins, you are a good, decent man but—"

"—but you could not consider a cripple," he finished.

Belle understood his suffering only too well. "Of course I would consider a gentleman who needed the aid of a cane, but adjusting to my scar has proved difficult. I am not ready to socialize."

"I wish you well." Cedric Wilkins retraced his steps down the stone path to the door.

Belle watched him disappear inside. He seemed lonely, but encouraging him would have been cruel. She loved her prince.

"Miss Belle." Tinker appeared again. "You have another visitor."

"Don't bother to announce me." Charles Wingate brushed past the majordomo.

His presence surprised Belle, and his confident smile grated on her pride. Seeing him with an objective eye, she decided he was too pretty and too perfectly dressed, as if he feared a strand of hair out of place. No wonder his fastidious self had not accepted her scarred cheek.

At first glance, Charles Wingate was a good-looking man. When compared to her prince, the baron was a dishcloth.

Belle felt nothing for him. Except contempt.

And then Charles stood in front of her. He remained silent for a moment, as if they'd seen each other the previous day and nothing had transpired to end their relationship.

Belle did not return his smile. "What do you want, Charles?"

"May I sit?"

Belle inched toward the edge of the stone bench and pointed at the opposite end. "Sit there."

"Are you punishing me by keeping your distance?"

Belle ignored his question. "What do you want?"

"You."

"I beg your pardon?" Surprise widened her violet eyes. She held up her hand when he started to slide toward her. "Stay there."

Charles stopped short and flashed her a winning smile. "I want to set a wedding date."

Belle arched an ebony brow. "Who are you marrying?"

"I love you." Charles slid to her side of the bench before she could prevent it and grabbed her hand. "Sweet Belle, will you do me the honor of becoming my wife and my baroness?"

Belle snatched her hand back. "No."

"No?" He looked genuinely bewildered. "We love each other."

He loves my father's money and influence.

"If you were the last man in the world," Belle said, enjoying this miniscule revenge, "I would seek refuge in a nunnery."

"You don't mean that," Charles said. "I hurt you, but since that day, I have persuaded Mother to accept that you will make an excellent addition to the Wingate family."

My wealthy father would make an excellent addition to the Wingate family.

"Why would I stoop to marry a mere baron," Belle asked, "when a prince has already offered for me?"

Barely suppressed anger mottled his complexion. "Who has stolen your affections?"

"You lost them yourself. Go away."

Charles stood and towered over her. "You loved me once and will love me again."

Belle watched the baron walk away. Her only regret was that Puddles was not present to bite him.

Every cloud had a silver lining, or so Nanny Smudge said. Her scar had saved her from marrying a sniveling, servile snake.

"Miss Belle."

She whirled around at the sound of the majordomo's voice. "Another visitor?"

"Two."

Prince Mikhail appeared, holding his four-year-old daughter's hand. Father and daughter walked toward her.

Belle dropped her gaze from the prince to the child and gave her a welcoming smile. The girl returned the smile, her sapphire blue eyes gleaming with anticipation.

"I present my daughter, Elizabeth," Mikhail introduced them. "Bess, this is Miss Flambeau."

"I am pleased to meet you," Belle said, and the girl's smile grew into a grin.

Bess had inherited her father's black hair and dimpled chin and her mother's sapphire blue eyes. "I am pleased to meet you, Miss Flambeau."

"You must call me Belle," she said, leaning close. "Like my sisters do."

"I wish I had sisters." Bess slipped her hand out of her father's grasp and into Belle's hand.

Belle accepted the gesture by gently closing her fingers around the smaller hand. "Someday you will get brothers and sisters."

"My new mummy will give—*oops*." Bess covered her mouth with her free hand and gazed at her father.

Belle felt her heartbeat quickening, her stomach rolling with nausea. Had the girl blundered by referring to a new mummy? Did that mean the prince had chosen another woman, possible one of the Blonde Brigade? Or had he warned his daughter not to use the word *mummy* because she had refused his proposal?

At the moment, Belle would have traded her healing talents for her sister's telepathy. Then she would know what the prince was thinking.

"I must attend a meeting upstairs," Mikhail said, ignoring his daughter's slip.

"Bess and I will use this time to become friends."

The prince hesitated for a fraction of a moment. "I will not be too long." Then he disappeared inside the house.

The naked joy on the girl's upturned face tugged on Belle's heartstrings. "Shall we walk around the garden?"

Bess crooked a tiny finger, beckoning her closer, and then planted a kiss on her scarred cheek. "My daddy said the bad man hurt you, but I made it feel better."

Belle struggled against the sudden tears welling up. The prince's daughter was so heartbreakingly eager for a mother. "Thank you, Bess. I do feel better."

With the girl clinging to her hand, Belle strolled along the stone path that circled the garden. She named the various flowers—wisteria and roses and passionflowers. Reaching the rear of the garden, they paused to sit on a stone bench.

A wren darted past and dove into a hollow in the elm tree. Squeaky peeps emanated from inside the tree.

"The wren makes its nest inside the elm's hollow," Belle said, pointing at the tree. "Her babies are chirping for food."

"What does the mother feed them?" Bess asked.

"Seeds and worms."

"Yuk, yuk, yuk."

Belle laughed at that and placed her arm around the four-year-old. "Have you ever heard the story about the King of Birds?"

"No." Adoration shone from the girl's eyes.

"Once upon a time," Belle began, "all God's winged creatures decided to have a contest. The bird who flew highest would be crowned the King of Birds. Naturally, the eagle became the favorite to win because he was bigger and stronger and always flew higher than the others.

"The appointed day dawned, and all the creatures hovered with flapping wings over the starting line. The race began when the cat meowed"—Bess laughed—"and, of course, the eagle flew up, up, up. Higher and higher and higher.

"All the birds thought the eagle had won. Unexpectedly, a

tiny wren appeared a few inches above the eagle's head. She looked down at all the creatures, including the eagle, and said, 'Behold, I am the Queen of the Birds.'

"The little wren won the contest by perching on the eagle's wing and then flapping herself a couple of inches over his head. She used her brain to win instead of her wings."

"Was the eagle angry?"

"He laughed at her trick." Belle touched the tip of the princess's nose with the tip of her finger. "Let the wren's victory be a lesson to you."

"What is the lesson?"

Belle laughed, and the princess laughed with her. "The lesson is, winners in life are the smartest, not the strongest. Brains beats brawn. Always."

"I know a riddle," Bess exclaimed. "What is better than an honor?"

Belle smiled and shrugged.

"*In her* is the answer, but I don't understand what that means."

"Did your daddy tell you that?"

Bess shook her head and laced her fingers through Belle's. "I heard Uncle Rudolf tell my daddy."

Belle glanced over her shoulder at the gurgling fountain. "My daddy built the fountain so the noise could mask the secrets we share."

"Tell me your secret," Bess whispered.

"My secret is pixies live in this garden."

The girl's blue eyes widened. "Where?"

"Look at the elm tree," Belle whispered against her ear. "The mushrooms beneath the tree are pixies. Whenever people look at them, the pixies disguise themselves as mushrooms."

Bess peeked at the mushrooms. "What if we eat the mushrooms?"

"Whoever eats a pickle of pixies will be stricken with laughter and fall on the ground," Belle told her. "Do you have a secret to share?"

Cupping her hands around her mouth, Bess whispered, "I love you."

Belle felt tears threatening again. "I love you," she said, "and that is no secret."

Resting her head against Belle's arm, Bess sighed in contentment. "Do you know any more secrets, Mummy?"

Mummy? What would the prince say if he heard that? On the other hand, a motherless child would respond to any female who gave her attention.

"I do know another secret," Belle said. "Girls are smarter than boys. No exceptions."

"Miss Belle." Tinker hurried toward them. "His Highness is leaving."

"Thank you, Tinker." Belle stood and held her hand out. "Your daddy is waiting."

A mulish expression appeared on the princess's face. "Let him wait. I want to stay here."

"Your daddy will cry if you send him away. I promise to see you soon."

"Tomorrow?"

"Tomorrow I need to watch my sister marry your Uncle Stepan," Belle answered, "but I will see you the day after that. With your daddy's permission, of course."

The Kazanov princes and the Duke of Inverary stood in the foyer. Their chatting stopped when Belle and Bess appeared, holding hands.

Prince Mikhail looked at Belle, his heated gaze making her blush, before giving his daughter his attention. "Did you enjoy your visit?"

"We shared secrets and saw pixies," Bess answered, her excitement apparent. "The wren won the contest, and girls are smarter than boys."

Four princes, one duke, and a majordomo snapped their gazes to Belle. She gave them her sweetest smile.

"Never tell boys we are smarter," Belle said, crouching beside the princess. "You will hurt their feelings."

The princes left, except Mikhail, and the duke returned upstairs. Mikhail lifted his daughter into his arms, smiling when she yawned and said, "Daddy, I want my nap."

"I promised Bess I will see her the day after the wedding," Belle said.

Mikhail peered at his daughter whose eyes were closing slowly. "You will be our guest. Will I see you at the wedding?"

A blush streaked across her cheeks. "I will be attending."

"Save me a dance." Mikhail winked at her and disappeared out the door.

Belle stood there, staring into empty space. If the prince only knew. . . . All her dances belonged to him.

Daringly gowned in ruby red, the Duchess of Inverary marched down the line of stepdaughters like a general before her troops. Immense satisfaction curled her lips into a feline smile.

Blush pink, lily lavender, violet whisper, willow green, and ice blue. Each Flambeau sister sparkled like a jewel in the perfect setting of a fabulous gown. Taken together, the vivid streak of color blended in harmony, a portrait created by one of the masters.

"In society, friends come and friends go," the duchess told them, "but enemies accumulate. Beware of smiles that could mask menacing thoughts and emotions. Never cut and run if faced with an uncomfortable situation. Consider insult an art form, and enjoy the discord."

The duchess stopped in front of Belle. "Darling, even healers must inflict pain on others sometimes." She gave her a dimpled smile, her critical gaze admiring the ice blue gown. "You look spectacular. I do possess impeccable taste and an eye for color."

Thirty minutes later, Belle sat in the front pew of St. Paul's Cathedral and listened to the words that would transform her sister from opera singer to princess. She was nervous about her first foray into society but felt more confident of her appearance than she had since the attack. The theater cosmetics covered her scar almost completely.

Belle dropped her gaze to the skirt of her ice blue silk gown, the finest she'd ever worn. Silk stockings embroidered with flowers, dainty slippers, and long white gloves completed the outfit. She felt like Cinderella on the way to the ball. Her own prince sat across the aisle beside his brothers and sisters-in-law.

Unable to stop herself, Belle peeked across the aisle at him. Mikhail was watching her. She blushed when he winked at her, and the corners of her lips turned up in a faint smile.

Her gaze drifted to an older matron and a young blonde sitting in the next pew down. Grim faces stared at her, making her uncomfortable.

Two other blondes sat nearby. Both wore identical, cold expressions.

"What is more interesting than your sister becoming a princess?" the duchess asked, her voice a mere whisper.

"Being cursed by three blond witches?"

"Don't worry, darling." The duchess patted her hand. "They have more to fear from you."

Becoming a princess was surprisingly easy. The ceremony was shorter than she imagined.

An hour later, Belle and Raven followed their sisters into the Inverary ballroom. Tables had been set on one side of the enormous chamber, and the other side was reserved for dancing. A small orchestra provided background music.

Violins caressed ears, expensive perfumes teased nostrils, and priceless jewels dazzled eyes. Silk, lace, and ostrich feathers abounded in the chamber. Air kisses mimicked true affection.

Belle noted the decorations, orange blossoms set against garlands of greenery. White roses and blue forget-me-nots in porcelain vases flaunted their beauty in the center of each table.

She pursed her lips, annoyed by society's insensitivity. What a pity the ignorant insisted on amputating flowers from healthy plants.

"You look tempting in blue."

Her prince stood beside her. "You look tempting all the time."

"Are you trying to make me blush?" Mikhail teased, a smile lingering on his lips. "Bess is eagerly anticipating tomorrow."

"God blessed you with a wonderful daughter."

"I think so." Mikhail gestured to the reception line. "Shall we walk through together?"

"This wedding excitement has wearied me," Belle said. "I would like to sit."

His hand on the small of her back, Mikhail guided her toward their table. "Your stepmother has put us in the company of friendly faces." He helped her into the chair and gestured to a footman for a drink.

"Did you notice my face?" Belle asked him. "Fancy's theater cosmetics cover my scar."

"You are a beauty with or without the cosmetics."

Raven and Alexander joined them as did Prince Viktor, Princess Regina, Prince Drako, and the Contessa de Salerno. The remaining four Flambeau sisters had been strategically placed at a table with four eligible bachelors.

"I present my brother Viktor and his wife, Regina," Mikhail made the introductions. "Over here are my cousin Drako and Katerina, Contessa de Salerno."

Belle gestured to the final two, saying, "My sister Raven and Alexander Blake, the Marquis of Basildon."

Dozens of footmen began serving the wedding feast. The scent of chicken made her queasy, and the poached salmon's pungent caper sauce sent her stomach into rebellion. Belle managed to down the blandest dishes and move the rest around on her plate, hoping no one would notice her lack of appetite.

Belle realized the more she spoke, the less she would be expected to eat. "Alexander is an associate of London's famous constable, Amadeus Black."

"Are you nearing an arrest in those Slasher murders?" Prince Viktor asked.

"We are investigating new clues," Alexander answered.

Hearing the word *slasher,* Belle touched her injured cheek in an unconscious gesture. She glanced at the next table and saw a young woman staring at her.

"Who is the blonde?" she whispered to the prince.

"Cynthia Clarke."

"Is she one of the Blonde Brigade?"

"You have heard of them." Mikhail grinned, amusement gleaming in his black eyes, and then changed the subject. "Regina is a published novelist."

"I have never met an author," Belle exclaimed. "What kind of stories?"

Princess Regina smiled. "I write romances like Jane Austen."

"I love romances," Belle said.

Raven nodded. "So do I."

"I adore their happy endings," the contessa agreed.

"One day in the future my wife will write a *real* novel," Prince Viktor teased her.

Four gentlemen smiled. Four ladies did not.

Prince Viktor rested his arm across the back of his wife's chair. "You do realize I was joking?"

Princess Regina gave her husband a sidelong glance. "Do you see me laughing?"

"If I thought you had no talent," Viktor said, "would I have bought you a publishing company?"

"You would have done *anything* to win my hand in marriage," Regina drawled. "You did want your son—"

"My love for you made me do whatever was needed to win your hand in marriage," Viktor interrupted. "I have never experienced even one unhappy moment since then."

Princess Regina smiled at her husband. "You say the sweetest things, my love."

Argument averted.

Belle watched their teasing byplay. That Prince Viktor allowed his wife a career fostered the belief the garden goddess would continue. If she married her prince.

"And who is the blonde at that table?" Belle asked, leaning close to the prince.

Mikhail's gaze followed hers. "Princess Anya is the Russian ambassador's niece."

"Katerina designs priceless jewel creations," Prince Drako said conversationally.

The Contessa de Salerno gifted the prince with a sultry smile. "Drako is flattering me in hopes I will discount my prices and save him a good deal of coin."

Drako lifted her hand to his lips. "My dear contessa, you know my pockets are deep."

"I designed your sister's wedding band," Katerina told the Flambeau sisters.

Belle felt doubly hopeful. Two princes valued two ladies who did not fit the high-society mold. Three princes, if she counted Stepan and Fancy.

"Raven is an amateur sleuth," Alexander dropped into the conversation. "She is helping with the Slasher investigation."

"How do you help?" Katerina asked.

"I-I . . ." Raven appeared at a loss for words.

"My sister gets impressions from objects," Belle explained, "and sometimes she has visions."

Prince Drako looked at Alexander. "Do you and the constable believe in such happenings?"

"The constable will believe in anything that solves a

crime," Alexander answered, "but I will remain a skeptic until Raven can name the guilty."

The Contessa de Salerno slipped an exquisite sapphire and diamond dinner ring off her finger. "What impression do you get of me?" she asked, offering her ring.

Raven rubbed her hands together and held the ring between her hands. She closed her eyes for a prolonged moment and then told the contessa, "Revenge will not breathe life into the dead."

The contessa seemed momentarily stricken, but recovered herself and murmured, "I will ponder your words."

"Upon whom are you seeking vengeance?" Prince Drako asked.

"The answer would surprise you."

"I hope not me."

The contessa gave him a flirtatious, sidelong glance. "Have you trespassed against me?"

"Is that an invitation?" Drako asked, a smile in his voice.

"You need not worry, Your Highness."

"And if I did?" Drako placed his arm across the top of her chair, leaned close to her, and said in a silken voice, "Tell me, *la contessa,* what form would your revenge take?"

"A poison pendant, perhaps?"

"Ah, yes, the Italians do possess a special expertise in poisons."

Belle wished she possessed the contessa's sophisticated confidence with gentlemen. Her attention and gaze wandered until she noticed a third blonde sitting two tables beyond theirs. Her stare was a sharp dagger.

"Lavinia Smythe, my former sister-in-law," Mikhail said, leaning close to her.

The Contessa de Salerno spoke, drawing their attention. "We have an author, a jeweler, and a psychic," she said, looking at Belle. "How do you pass your time?"

"I save lives," Belle answered without hesitation.

Everyone stared in silent surprise at her. Except Raven and Mikhail, who smiled.

"Are you a physician?" Princess Regina asked.

Belle blushed. "I save plants mostly."

"My sister has been blessed with healing hands," Raven said. "The garden goddess promises minor miracles by restoring health."

"Are you a gardener?" the contessa asked. "Or a healer?"

Prince Drako turned to the contessa. "Do you believe in that nonsense?"

The Contessa de Salerno looked from him to Raven and then Belle. "I believe some souls are blessed with special gifts. My talent creating designs with gems is a gift the same as healing hands."

"I wish I had ink and parchment," Princess Regina said. "I want to include this in my next story."

Everyone laughed.

After the main courses, the footmen cleared the tables and served cheeses and fruit accompanied by coffee, tea, and cordials. The orchestra played the waltz, first for the bride and groom and then for the bride and her father.

Prince Mikhail stood and offered Belle his hand. "Dance with me?"

Belle allowed him to escort her across the ballroom to the dance floor and stepped into his arms. His intimate smile warmed her, and she felt like a princess. They moved as one, swirling around the candlelit ballroom, the man and the music intoxicating her senses.

"You dance divinely," Mikhail said. "Did His Grace send dancing masters to instruct his daughters?"

"On winter evenings, the Flambeau sisters forced Alexander to help us practice our dancing in the event a handsome prince invited us to a ball," Belle answered, smiling at the memory.

"And here I am." Mikhail passed her to the duke when the music ended.

"I have always dreamed about dancing with my daughters," her father told her.

"And we practiced years for this moment."

"You do realize that His Highness cares deeply for you."

"I am considering his offer, Papa."

Prince Stepan partnered her for the next waltz. Whirling around the ballroom, Belle saw Mikhail dancing with Cynthia Clarke and felt her stomach flip-flop.

"Do not concern yourself," Stepan said, his gaze following hers.

Prince Rudolf invited her to dance and passed the time extolling his brother's admirable traits. When Belle spied Mikhail waltzing with Princess Anya, he said, "Pay no attention to obligatory dances."

Belle declined the next waltz with Alexander. She felt queasy and tired from her exertions. Belle left the ballroom for the ladies' withdrawing room. Dropping onto a chair, she closed her eyes and took deep breaths, willing the nausea away.

I am not pregnant, she told herself. *Queasy, dizzy, and tired are only three of pregnancy's symptoms.*

Once her stomach quieted, Belle returned to the ballroom lest her prince wonder where she had gone. If her stepmother knew about the nausea, she would inform the duke, who would suspect her prevarication. That word sounded less harsh than lies.

Her father and her stepmother were dancing and appeared a perfectly matched couple. Her own mother would have been too fragile for this crowd. Or would Gabrielle have found strength in the title of wife?

All her sisters were dancing too. Fancy and Stepan were making the rounds of their guests, probably intending to escape.

Belle scanned the enormous chamber for her prince. The queasiness returned when she spotted him dancing. His former sister-in-law moved as if she belonged in his arms.

Feeling conspicuously alone, Belle wished to be anywhere but there. *Never cut and run.* She recalled her stepmother's advice.

Lifting her chin, Belle decided to stay and fight for her prince. Lady Althorpe, her stepmother's crony, spoke with another older woman only a short distance away.

Belle started toward them but slowed as she drew near. The topic of their conversation brought her to a sudden halt but kept her rooted there.

"Will I see you at Roxie's luncheon?" Lady Althorpe asked.

"Of course, dear," the woman answered. "Lavinia and I will be attending."

"I haven't seen Lavinia all day, Prudence."

"She's dancing with Mikhail. Don't they look a perfect couple?"

Lady Althorpe appeared nonplussed. "I suppose so."

"Mikhail and Lavinia will marry before the year is out," Prudence said, her pride apparent in her voice.

Belle wanted to disappear. Her churning nausea returned, more virulent than earlier. Grim curiosity forced her to listen when she wanted to run.

"I never read the betrothal announcement," Lady Althorpe was saying.

"A mere formality." Prudence Smythe dismissed that with a wave of her hand. "Doesn't it make sense that Mikhail would marry his beloved late wife's sister?"

"Are you certain about that? I thought Roxie said—"

"Mikhail is besotted with my Lavinia." Prudence turned a displeased expression on the other woman. "He has been purposely pretending otherwise to make her jealous. Why, look at their smiles."

Shifting her gaze to Mikhail, who was smiling at the blonde, Belle struggled against the almost overwhelming urge to smash both their faces. Oh Lord, that was the fourth pregnancy symptom. She *was* carrying the prince's baby.

Prince Viktor materialized beside her. "Belle, may I have this dance?"

"I am sorry, Your Highness," Belle refused, her violet gaze mirroring her anguish, "but I need to retire upstairs."

Viktor looked alarmed. "Are you ill?"

"Too much excitement, I suppose." Belle managed a faint smile. "I will feel better once I have rested."

"Shall I fetch Her Grace?"

"No, thank you."

"Let me find Mikhail for you," Viktor said. "He will escort you upstairs."

"Don't bother your brother." She flicked a glance at the waltzing couples. "Mikhail and his fiancée are dancing."

And then Belle quit the ballroom.

Chapter 11

Should he knock? Or not?

Mikhail stared in indecision at the bedchamber door. Either his wife was feeling under the eaves or someone had undermined her confidence. All his coaxing and cajoling and persuading would need to begin again if she refused to show her face in society.

Without knocking, Mikhail opened the door and stepped inside. He saw her at once, sitting on the chaise in front of the dark hearth. Her small shoulders slumped in defeat. She looked so heartbreakingly alone, a downcast angel.

Mikhail spared a quick glance at the bedchamber, noting its feminine decor. A vase of roses—*her scent*—perfumed the air.

"Were you running away?" He watched her shoulders straighten, stiffening with pride.

Belle looked over her shoulder at him. "I consider my vanishing act an honorable retreat."

She was angry with him.

Mikhail crossed the chamber to stand in front of her. He shoved his hands into his trouser pockets and waited in silence for her gaze to meet his.

Though she was no longer a virgin, his wife wore her innocence like a gossamer cloak. She lacked the sophistication necessary to survive society's games, a dearth of stamina needed to outface the worst society could offer.

She was perfection. He would not change even one thing about her.

"Are you ill?"

Her gaze drifted upward from his legs to his chest to his face. Glittering anger leaped from her violet eyes, making him wary.

Belle rose from her perch on the chaise to confront him. "I have been queasy, dizzy, and tired," she said, her finger poking into his chest with each word spoken. "Now, Your Highness, I want to smash your face."

Her temper both amused and startled him. His black brows snapped together, but his lips quirked into a smile.

"Do you think pregnancy is funny?" Belle asked, her finger still stabbing his chest.

"Are you certain?" Her question caught him off-guard. "How do you know?"

"I am suffering those damn symptoms."

Mikhail swallowed his laughter and drew her into his embrace. "Marry me?"

Belle curled her lips at him. "Were you planning to commit bigamy?"

Mikhail did laugh at that. "What nonsense is this?"

"Have you forgotten your fiancée, Lavinia Smythe?"

"I am not betrothed to Lavinia."

"As good as," Belle countered. "I overheard Prudence sharing the happy news with Lady Althorpe."

Mikhail groaned and lifted her chin, his dark gaze holding hers captive. "On the night we returned from the cottage, I told Prudence I intended to marry you."

"Why would she lie to Lady Althorpe?"

"Prudence Smythe is a vicious old woman who wanted to hurt your feelings," Mikhail answered.

She looked puzzled. "What did I ever do to her?"

"You have stolen her daughter's chance to become a princess," Mikhail said. "Will you marry me?"

Belle sighed, and her small white teeth worried her bottom lip. Many Prudences abounded in society, but she did not want to end up like her own mother.

"Yes, I will marry you."

Mikhail held her tight against his muscular frame, inhaling her sensuous rose scent, savoring her body heat. Claiming ownership, his mouth covered hers in a lingering kiss that smoldered with passion.

Softer than a rose petal, her lips parted for him, inviting his possession. He slipped his tongue past her lips to explore the sweetness of her mouth.

"Lock the door," she whispered, "and join me in bed."

Mikhail gently set her back a pace. "I will not bed you in your father's home with several hundred wedding guests in the ballroom." He slipped his arm around her, guiding her toward the door. "We will speak to His Grace immediately."

"Do not mention the baby," Belle said, letting him lead her down the corridor to the stairs. "My father will know I lied."

"You concentrate on our firstborn," Mikhail said, "and leave the explanations to me."

Mikhail ushered her into the duke's study and to one of the chairs in front of the desk. "I will find Their Graces and return in a few minutes."

Belle stared into space. Was she doing the right thing? She didn't want the prince to marry her because of the baby, but he *had* proposed marriage their last day at the cottage.

That meant nothing, though. The prince had assumed the risk of pregnancy was great.

How could she compete against his late wife's memory? Would he measure her worth by his first wife?

Second best. She had always been second best only.

Born second, Belle had been sandwiched between two gifted sisters. She had stood in her older sister's shadow and then was overlooked because of the birth of twins. Fancy was the talented singer with an artist's temperament, and Bliss loved numbers, a mathematical genius whose judgment increased the Flambeau coffers.

Her own talents lay elsewhere, a place no one appreciated. Nurturing her younger sisters, listening to their problems, tending the earth's plants and trees.

Nobody mourned the death of a flower.

That was a sad fact of life. Which meant nobody appreciated her restoring a plant's health. Both aristocrat and commoner would certainly mourn if flowers vanished from this earth forever.

The door opened. The prince, her father, and her stepmother walked into the study.

"Here we are, my darling," the duchess greeted her, sitting in the chair beside the desk. "This secrecy has whetted my curiosity. You know how I love a good secret."

Belle gave her stepmother a sickly smile. Then she dropped her gaze to her hands folded on her lap, too embarrassed to look at anyone.

"So downcast, dearest?" the duchess said. "Tragedy cannot have struck on this glorious day when your sister has become a princess."

"Roxie, allow Mikhail to speak," the duke said.

"Of course, Magnus."

Mikhail dragged a chair close to Belle's and reached for her hand. Belle gave him a shy smile and then peeked at her father, his gaze fixed on their entwined hands.

"Belle did not want you to think badly of her," Mikhail told the duke, "so I protected her by concocting the lie regarding not sharing intimacies."

"How romantic," the Duchess of Inverary exclaimed. "Isn't that romantic, Magnus?"

The duke looked at his wife. "Quite."

"Belle has accepted my marriage proposal," Mikhail announced.

"*Two* princesses," the duchess cried, unable to contain her excitement.

"Calm yourself, Roxie, or you may not live to see her married." The Duke of Inverary looked at his daughter. "Belle, do you willingly agree—?"

"Don't be silly," the duchess snapped. "Of course, she agrees."

"Roxie."

"I do want to marry Mikhail but—"

"Belle." The prince's voice held a warning note. "Prudence Smythe gave her a problem today."

"Everyone has a problem with Prudence Smythe," the duchess said, dismissing the worry with a wave of her hand. "I can teach you to handle women of her ilk."

"Belle and I have another announcement." Mikhail lifted her hand to his lips, making her blush. "We are expecting our first child."

"I knew it." The duchess's dimpled smile appeared as she turned to her husband. "You owe me a diamond choker with matching earrings, bracelet, and dinner ring."

The Duke of Inverary rolled his eyes. Because of his own indiscretions, he remained silent about his daughter's succumbing to temptation. Offering the prince his hand, he said, "Welcome to the family, Mikhail."

"We'll plan the wedding for a week from Saturday," the duchess said.

"I don't want a big wedding." Walking down the aisle would give her hives.

"Darling, a big wedding makes a statement." The duchess turned to the prince. "A big diamond also makes a statement."

Mikhail grinned at the duchess. Only Roxanne Campbell could utter mercenary thoughts and remain loveable.

Belle suffered an awful feeling that a whirlwind had been released. Like Pandora and her box of swarming evils.

"We'll place the betrothal announcement in the Friday morning *Times*," the duchess was saying. "While the gentlemen golf down Pall Mall, the unlucky hopefuls and their mamas can vent their disappointment at my luncheon."

"Vent?" Belle squeaked, her nausea returning.

The duchess rose from her chair. "Trust me to protect you." She looked at her husband, saying, "We really must return to the reception."

Belle watched them leave and then looked at the prince. Now would come the test of his devotion. "What happens with my garden goddess?"

Mikhail leaned close, giving her an easy smile. "You can cure every plant and tree and blade of grass in the realm, my love."

Raven inspected her image in the cheval mirror the following afternoon. Deciding the best she could hope for was neat and clean, she left her bedchamber and descended the stairs to the foyer.

"Good afternoon, Tinker." She sat on the foyer chair.

"Good afternoon to you," the majordomo returned her greeting. "Are you visiting me or—?"

Someone banged on the door.

"I am expecting a caller."

Tinker opened the door and stepped aside. "Good afternoon, my lord. Miss Raven awaits your pleasure."

Alexander Blake walked into the foyer, his expression surprised. "How did you know—?"

"Intuition."

"Will you come to my grandfather's now?"

Raven gave him a smug smile. "I have been waiting for you, have I not?"

Park Lane seemed unusually deserted. A solitary carriage

passed, its horse faintly snickering. A symphony of birdsong wafted through the air, mingling with the scents of garden flowers, masking the smell of manure.

"Belle has accepted Prince Mikhail's marriage proposal," Raven told him. "They will wed in less than two weeks."

"What's the hurry?"

Raven gave him a sidelong look that spoke volumes.

"Oh." Before climbing his grandfather's front stairs, Alexander stopped short and grasped her arm. "Once you've met Tulip, I want you to take her to Inverary House on some pretext. I need to search her bedchamber."

Raven balked at the idea. "Your guest is entitled to privacy."

"Tulip has a small bag that she protects more than a mother with a newborn babe," Alexander said. "The bag could contain a clue to the Slasher."

"Is she the monster's accomplice?"

Alexander shook his head. "I believe she does not appreciate the importance of whatever is in the bag."

"If that is the case, why would she protect it?"

"A hunch tells me something momentous is stored inside the bag."

"So, my lord," Raven drawled, her voice dripping sarcasm, "you have an *impression* without tangible proof?"

"Touché, brat." Alexander inclined his head to acknowledge her wit. "Sarcasm does not become you."

"Hypocrisy does not become you," she countered, her tone haughty. "You cannot act upon hunches and then mock my impressions."

"Will you help me now," Alexander asked, "and debate this later?"

"Very well," Raven agreed with a resigned sigh. "Do not make subterfuge a habit."

The door opened, revealing an older man. The duke's majordomo stepped aside, allowing them entrance. "Good afternoon, my lord."

"Good day to you, Twigs. Where are my grandfather and Tulip?"

"They are lunching in the dining room."

"Together?"

"People who eat at the same table are usually considered together," the majordomo answered.

Raven covered her mouth, trying in vain to stifle a giggle.

"And you are?" Twigs asked.

"I am your most appreciative audience."

His lips twitched. "Thank you, my lady."

"Meet Twigs, my grandfather's uppity majordomo," Alexander said. "Miss Raven Flambeau is my betrothed."

"A pleasure to meet you," Twigs said. "I am relieved the marquis occasionally exhibits good taste."

Raven flashed the man a smile. "Thank you, Twigs."

The majordomo led the way down a long corridor. They followed him into an enormous dining room.

Two steps into the chamber, Raven stopped short. The grumpy old duke was laughing with a young woman. Alexander wore a startled expression too.

Twigs approached the duke. "Your Grace, the Marquis of Basildon—"

"I can see who is there," the duke snapped.

Twigs raised his eyes toward heaven and left the chamber, grumbling, "He never lets me announce anyone."

Alexander placed his hand on the small of Raven's back and ushered her toward the table. "Hello, squirt." He nodded at his grandfather, remarking, "You seem in a rare good mood."

Raven sat in the chair opposite the girl and smiled when Alexander said, "Meet Tulip Woods."

Delicately petite, Tulip Woods had lovely mahogany brown hair. Her most disarming feature was her eyes, one blue and one green.

"I am pleased to meet you," Raven said.

"Why?"

Surprised by the question, Raven looked from the smiling Duke of Essex to the girl. "Any friend of Alexander's is a friend of mine."

Tulip gave her a puzzled look. "What makes you think I'm his friend?"

Raven narrowed her violet gaze on the girl, taking her measure before speaking. "Since you are currently living in his grandfather's home, I would not consider you an enemy. *Would I?*"

Tulip grinned at the ending question and pushed a platter across the table. "Help yourself."

Raven knew she had just passed a test. She looked at the platter containing exotic nougats, sticky and nutty. Her own mother had always loved nougats, claiming the candy tasted like French sunshine.

Raven bit into a pistachio nougat. Her mother had been correct. The nougat *did* taste like sunshine. She didn't know about the French part since she had never been there.

"Tulip made these last evening," the Duke of Essex said.

Raven savored the candy, thinking the girl had talent.

"God blessed me with a special gift and a secret ingredient," Tulip said.

"What is it?"

"I keep my secrets."

Alexander reached for his second nougat. "Raven is marrying me."

Tulip looked at her. "Aren't you a tad young for marriage?"

"What makes you think I'm young?"

Tulip burst into tickled laughter. "I like you."

"You could use a change of scenery," Raven said, "and I live only a few doors down. Would you care to meet my sisters and dog?"

Tulip lost her smile at the word *sisters*. Her eyes filled with tears.

"I am sorry to remind you of your loss. Another time, perhaps?"

"I would like to meet your sisters," Tulip said. "How many are there?"

"Seven sisters, counting me," Raven answered. "You won't meet my oldest sister because Fancy married Prince Stepan yesterday."

"Your sister married a prince?"

Raven nodded. "My stepmother would like to meet you too."

"Why?"

Raven rose from her chair. "Why not?"

That made Tulip laugh again, and they walked toward the door. "What kind of dog?"

"Puddles is a mastiff." Then Raven drawled, "Do not ask how he earned his name."

Alexander watched them disappear out the door. He bit into another nougat and chewed slowly.

"What was that about?" his grandfather asked.

"I thought Tulip could use a friend, girlish confidences and all that." Alexander stood, saying, "A hunch tells me the squirt's bag will reveal her guarded secrets."

Alexander left his grandfather in the dining room. Taking the stairs two at a time, he hurried down the third-floor corridor and slipped into the girl's bedchamber.

He opened the armoire, the most likely hiding place, and found no bag. Then he checked beneath it, just to be sure. Next came the tallboy, two bedside tables, and the unlit hearth.

With growing frustration, Alexander turned in a circle and tried to imagine where a young woman would hide whatever should not be found. His gaze fixed on the bed, but he could not credit she would use so obvious a place. Still . . .

Alexander checked beneath the mattress. He dropped to his knees at the foot of the bed, lifted the coverlet, and peered underneath. Nothing there.

Without forethought, Alexander looked beneath the uphol-stered bench at the foot of the bed. And then he grinned.

Smart girl. Using needle and thread to fashion a makeshift sling, Tulip had fastened the bag beneath the bench's cushion.

Alexander stood and turned the bench onto its side. He would search the bag and then replace its contents. Tulip would never know.

Her bag contained six items: two documents, three etch-ings, and a slip of paper.

Alexander perused the two documents, his complexion paling at what was written. The three etchings dropped him onto the mattress, and the slip of paper confirmed what he could not believe.

This shocking complication catching him off-guard, Alexander heard a buzzing in his ears, and his head began to spin dizzingly. He took several deep breaths, needing a moment to digest this before speaking with his grandfather.

With the coachman's assistance, Belle alighted from her father's coach in Grosvenor Square. She smiled her thanks, climbed the front stairs of Mikhail's mansion, and knocked on the door.

"She's here!" Belle heard the girl's excited cry.

Prince Mikhail and Elizabeth were waiting in the foyer. The girl threw herself into Belle's arms.

"Welcome home," Bess cried.

Belle blushed, realizing the prince had shared their news with his daughter.

"I welcome you home too." Mikhail lifted her hand to his lips. "Unfortunately, I am needed at a business meeting but hope to return early."

"Before you leave," Belle said, "I want your permission for Bess to hostess a tea party on Thursday." She knew she had cornered the prince, especially when his daughter shrieked in joy.

Mikhail turned to his majordomo. "Send invitations to Viktor's and Rudolf's daughters."

"Yes, Your Highness."

Bess grabbed her hand. "Come, Mummy."

"Ahem . . ."

Prince Mikhail smiled. "Belle, I present Julian Boomer."

"A pleasure to meet you, Mr. Boomer."

"Boomer will do, my lady," the majordomo said. "Please accept my best wishes, and I look forward to serving you."

"I will see you soon." Prince Mikhail planted a kiss on her scarred cheek, his smile melting her insides.

"I want to show you our garden," Bess said, drawing her into the inner foyer. "That is my daddy's Atlas holding the world."

The prince's garden delighted Belle. A curving lawn path winded its way through a harmony of colors. Close to the mansion stood a wisteria, its violet-blue petals shrouding the ground beneath. Tulips rising from a carpet of red wallflowers surrounded the fountain up ahead, and a white gazebo stood in the rear of the garden. Small, but large enough to house a girl's tea party. A silver birch ringed by red tulips caught her eyes, old age wilting several.

"Come with me," Belle said. "Those tulips need my help."

Belle knelt in front of the tulips. Bending close, she placed two fingers on each side of one's stem and prayed in silence. She moved to the next tulip. And then a third. Again and again and again.

"What are you doing?" Bess asked. "Your lips were moving but no sounds came out."

Belle sat back on her haunches. "I was praying for God to save His tulips."

"Will He answer your prayers?"

"Only He knows that," Belle said. "Do you want to learn to toss your troubles away?"

Bess nodded. "What are troubles?"

"Troubles are problems that make you angry or sad."

"I have those," Bess said.

"Take a handful of dirt in both hands," Belle said, demonstrating her instructions. She watched the girl mimic her actions.

"Stand and face the garden door. Stare at the dirt and tell it all your problems."

"Let me think. . . ."

"Speak silently to the dirt."

Bess looked at her. "How can I speak and be silent at the same time?"

Belle swallowed the bubble of laughter threatening. "Look at the dirt and think your problems."

Silence.

"I'm finished," Bess whispered.

"Toss the dirt over your shoulders." Belle tossed her dirt, and Bess did the same. "Walk toward the door, but don't look back."

"We did it," Bess cried, her excitement tangible.

The garden door opened unexpectedly. A middle-aged woman stepped outside, her expression tense. Behind her stood Prudence Smythe.

"Go along with Nanny Dee," the older woman said, "while I speak with Miss Flambeau."

The girl's expression became mulish. "Grandmama, my daddy said—"

"Sweetheart," Belle interrupted, crouching eye level with her. "If you go with Nanny Dee, you can help with the tea party invitations."

The mulish expression vanished. "Don't forget the hugs and kisses cookies."

"I promise." Belle stood and watched Bess disappear inside. Then she looked at the older woman's pinched expression.

"What are you doing here?"

"I was invited," Belle answered. "And you?"

"I don't answer to the likes of you," Prudence Smythe said. "You are reaching above yourself and will be hurt."

"Are you worried about my feelings?"

"Do not be impertinent," Prudence snapped. "Marrying Mikhail would ruin his life, the least of which would be a reluctance to go about in society because of that scar."

Belle felt her face heating with a blush. Embarrassment or anger, she did not know. "The prince decides his own path in life," she countered.

"You are unfit to be his wife," Prudence continued. "If smart, you will set your sights lower."

Belle gave her an ambiguous smile. "Thank you for your opinion."

The older woman's face mottled in anger, and she grabbed Belle's arm. "Heed my warning or suffer the consequences."

"Heed *my* warning," Belle said, shaking the hand off. "Touch me again and suffer the consequences."

"Even Roxanne Campbell cannot change the rules of polite society whenever it suits her."

Belle flashed her a smile meant to insult. "I will certainly pass your sentiment along to my stepmother. However, the Duke and Duchess of Inverary make the rules that lesser people obey."

Chapter 12

"What would you do if the Slasher murdered *your* sister?"

Tulip sat between Raven and Blaze on a bench in the Duke of Inverary's garden, its carefully designed serenity spoiled by the girl's bitterness. Raven watched her stroking the mastiff's head, resting on her lap, and an uneasy feeling of foreboding settled over her like a dark cloud. On the surface, the question appeared rhetorical. What lay behind the casually spoken words?

"I suppose I would want justice for my sister," Raven said, sounding reasonable.

"Forget justice," Blaze said, making them smile. "I would seek revenge like being drawn and quartered or slitting his throat with a dull blade. The monster's agony would satisfy my sister's memory."

"What we send out returns to us," Raven reminded them.

"The Slasher deserves fear and pain returned to him," Tulip argued.

"I agree." Blaze sent Raven an arched look. "The Bible says to do unto others and all that."

"Alexander and the constable are doing what they can," Raven said, "but investigations take time."

"Women are dying," Tulip said. "I can catch my sister's killer but need help."

No, no, no. Raven rubbed her temples, soothing the beginnings of a headache.

"You can depend on me," Blaze said. "Puddles too."

Raven looked at Tulip and then her idiotic sister. Misgivings assailed her, and the drumming in her temples increased. No matter how foolproof the plan, something could go wrong.

"Baiting the Slasher is tickling the dragon's tail," Raven warned, her alarm rising.

"The Slasher is a coward, not a dragon," Blaze countered. "Besides, there are three of us and a vicious dog."

That made Raven smile. "Are you implying that Puddles is vicious? What will he do, slobber the man to death?"

"I do not fear him," Tulip said.

"Neither do I," Blaze added. "Puddles?"

The mastiff barked.

Blaze stared into her dog's eyes. "Be a bad boy."

Puddles curled his lips, showing his fangs. A low rumbling growl sounded in his throat and drool began dripping from the corners of his mouth.

All three laughed at the dog's performance. The mastiff sat down and wagged his tail, ruining the ferocious effect.

"I suppose three of us and a vicious dog would assure our safety," Raven relented. "What is your plan?"

"Do you swear not to tell Alex or the constable?" Tulip asked.

"If you did," Blaze said, "they would thwart our plans."

"I promise to keep the silence," Raven agreed, against her better judgment.

Closing her eyes, Raven touched Tulip's arm and waited for any impressions. *A scream in the night. A snarling dog. A fallen cloak.*

"Miss Raven!" Tinker hurried down the path toward them. "Her Grace requires your presence in the parlor."

Blaze grinned. "What did you do, sister?"

"Perhaps your stepmother doesn't want you associating with a commoner," Tulip said.

"Nobody is more common than the Flambeau sisters," Raven drawled, imitating her stepmother.

"That's true," Blaze verified. "Our father never married our mother."

"My father never married my mother either," Tulip told them.

"Trust me." Raven patted her arm. "There are worse things in life than being born on the wrong side of—"

Tinker cleared his throat, drawing the girls' attention. "Her Grace requires Miss Tulip to accompany you."

With a shrug of her shoulders, Raven stood and pulled Tulip to her feet. "There's no need to fear my stepmother," she said, noting the girl's anxious expression.

"I fear nothing."

Raven led her into the family parlor. Straight ahead stood an enormous, upholstered sofa in front of the hearth. Two chairs at right angles to the sofa enclosed the section into a U with a table in the center.

The Duchess of Inverary sat on one side of the sofa. The occupants of each chair brought Raven to a surprised halt. Alexander and his grandfather sat there.

Raven started forward, leading Tulip into the room. A vase of roses perched on the table as did the Worcester porcelain tea service. Had the Blakes come to tea?

"Sit here, my darlings," the duchess called. "Tulip, I want you between my wonderful stepdaughter and me."

Taking her seat on the sofa, Raven looked from her stepmother to the Duke of Essex and then Alexander. Something important was happening, but no impressions popped into her mind.

"His Grace and I came to Inverary House," Alexander said, "because we require the Duchess of Inverary's social expertise."

Raven could feel waves of tension pouring off Tulip. "Will you get to the point," she demanded, taking pity on the girl.

Alexander looked at her. "Be quiet, brat."

The porcelain teacup in front of him exploded, the hot liquid spraying the top of the table, the carpet, and him.

Ignoring the tea drenching his leather boots, Alexander pulled several sheets of parchment from inside his jacket. He unfolded each and laid them flat on the table in front of the two young women.

The first two documents certified the births of Tulip and Iris Woods. The next three were etchings. Tulip and her sister in the first, followed by their mother's image, and finally their father.

Moving closer to peer at the man's picture, Raven knew she'd seen him somewhere. Or did he merely bear a resemblance to someone she knew?

Raven glanced at Tulip. The other girl had paled a deathly white, her expression grim.

Alexander placed the last sheet of parchment on the table. It bore a London address.

Raven gasped, recognizing the address. She shifted her gaze from the address to the etching of the man to her new friend's ashen complexion. And then she knew.

"If you had presented yourself at that address," Alexander said, "your sister might still be living."

"Are you implying Tulip caused her sister's death?" Raven asked, slipping her arm around the girl's shoulders.

A second teacup exploded, startling Alexander. He shifted his gaze from the shattered porcelain to his betrothed's angry expression.

"Calm yourself, brat."

A third teacup exploded.

Alexander ran a hand down his face. Then he nodded at her, and his lips moved into a defeated smirk.

"I never meant to blame anyone for Iris's death," Alexander assured Raven. "*Please* calm yourself."

Nothing exploded.

Alexander looked at his half sister. "What do you say, Tulip?"

"Who gave you permission to snoop in my private property?" Tulip challenged, finding her voice finally. "You could not possibly have seen my papers accidentally." She looked at the duchess. "Send for the authorities. I want to press thievery charges against this man."

The Duke of Essex erupted in a bark of laughter. "My granddaughter takes after me, Roxie. Don't you think so?"

"I do see a resemblance, Bart."

"I commend your ingenuity in hiding these," Alexander said, gesturing to the parchments. "Would you ever have identified yourself to me or my grandfather?"

"Iris and I visited the Soho address several times," Tulip told him. "No one answered the door."

"Discovering a sister pleases me as much as discovering a granddaughter pleases our grandfather." After a pause, Alexander added, "I cannot fathom my father—"

"If my father roamed," Raven interrupted, "then so could yours. I pray the behavior is not an inherited weakness."

"And so do I," Alexander said.

The porcelain teapot cracked, leaking tea onto the table.

Alexander looked at his sister. "Why didn't you tell His Grace your identity?"

Tulip shook her head, indicating she had no answer.

"Make no mistake, Tulip, my home is now your home," the Duke of Essex said. "Which brings us to the reason for sharing this with the Duchess of Inverary. Beginning immediately, Her Grace will groom you for a lady."

"I am what I am," Tulip said.

"Nonsense," the duke said, and gestured to Raven. "Her Grace has performed miracles with the Flambeau girls."

"I beg your pardon?" Raven fixed her violet gaze on the old man.

The duke's cane, leaning against the chair, fell onto the floor.

The Duke of Essex looked at the Duchess of Inverary.

"Today's young misses have no respect for their elders. No sense of humor either."

The Duchess of Inverary turned to her newest charge. "Tomorrow, darling, we will shop for an appropriate wardrobe."

"How much will this cost me?" the duke asked.

"Do you want me to be a lady without the proper clothing?"

"Did I say that?"

"Your granddaughter does bear an uncanny resemblance to you," the duchess interjected.

The Duke of Essex grinned. "She does, indeed."

"Tulip will attend my ladies' luncheon this Friday," the duchess said.

"Ladies' luncheon?" Tulip grimaced in distaste. "I cannot promise to behave as properly as I am gowned."

"That attitude will serve you well when swimming amid society's sharks," Raven said, giving the girl a sideways hug. "And we will make our plans."

"Which plans are those?"

Raven heard the suspicion in Alexander's voice and flashed him her sweetest smile. "Our plans are not your business."

Lemon, vanilla, and cinnamon aromas scented the air inside the kitchen. Every servant who walked into the room paused to savor the delicious smells, murmuring a sigh of pleasure—which filled the baker with immense pride.

Using the thick pot holders, Belle removed the sheet of angel cookies from the oven. She'd thought Bess and her cousins would enjoy the tale that went along with the cookies.

Belle reached for the beeswax to coat another cookie sheet. She rolled the firm dough flat and, using her paper traces, began cutting Xs and Os for the hugs and kisses cookies.

"Miss Belle." Tinker paused inside the doorway and inhaled the mouthwatering aromas.

She smiled at the majordomo's rapturous expression. "Did you want me for something?"

"This arrived for you." Tinker passed her a sealed note. "The courier is awaiting your answer."

Belle broke the seal and read the missive. Someone needed the garden goddess's services.

"Tell the courier I will come this afternoon." Belle resumed tracing her Xs and Os, placing each on the baking sheet. After putting them in the oven, she gathered ingredients for meringues.

All females loved meringues. Even Marie Antoinette, the Queen of France, had been known to make her own meringues. At least, her own mother had said so.

Unannounced, Prince Mikhail appeared in the kitchen, shocking cook and staff who scurried away. Belle smiled as he sauntered across the kitchen.

The prince helped himself to a nut and cinnamon cookie. "Delicious. What is it?"

"You are eating an angel cookie."

Mikhail gave her a boyishly charming grin, his dark eyes alight with amusement. "The only angel in this kitchen is you."

Belle blushed. "I am glad you like it."

"Where are the famous hugs and kisses cookies?"

"Baking, and you may not peek at them."

Mikhail dropped his gaze to the eggs, sugar, and other ingredients on the worktable. "What masterpiece will this become?"

"I am making stuffed meringues."

"Do you mean whipped cream sandwiched between two meringues and topped with drizzled chocolate?"

Belle smiled and nodded. "I make the lightest meringues in London."

"I can hardly wait." Mikhail looked around the kitchen. "I have never entered a kitchen before today."

"Your lofty title has deprived you of life's simple joys," she teased him.

"I did enjoy cooking at the cottage."

"Your Highness, you enjoyed *watching* me cook at the cottage."

"Miss Belle." Tinker's voice reached the kitchen before his body. He burst into the room, saying, "I have another message for you. . . . Oh, I apologize for intruding."

Belle lifted the parchment out of his hand and read it. Someone else was calling for the garden goddess. "Tell the courier I will come this afternoon."

"Where are you going?" Mikhail asked.

"Some plants need my help," she answered. "The garden goddess promises minor miracles, you know."

"I see."

Belle read the prince's expression correctly. The thought of her visiting clients displeased him. He *had* promised she could cure every plant in England if she agreed to marry him.

"Is there a problem with my tending sick plants?" she asked.

Mikhail did not answer her question. "Boomer told me about Prudence Smythe's visit yesterday, and I want to apologize if she behaved badly."

"You need not apologize for that woman." Belle slid her hands up his chest to loop around his neck. She pressed a kiss on his lips, and then murmured, "I can handle Prudence Smythe."

"I will leave you to your baking." Mikhail grabbed another angel cookie and left the kitchen.

Belle returned to her cookies, the kitchen staff straggling back once the prince had gone. She removed the hugs and kisses cookies from the oven and set the meringues inside.

"I carry a special delivery for Belle," Blaze called, waving a sealed parchment in the air. "What is that delicious aroma?"

"Angel cookies." Belle opened the missive. A third person needed the garden goddess. "Tell the courier I will come this afternoon."

"I'll tell him for a cookie," Blaze said.

"Help yourself."

"Mmmmm." Blaze bit into the cinnamon and nut angel cookie. "Her Grace and Raven have gone shopping, and His Grace has left for the afternoon. Which means there are no drivers available, but I could drive you in the phaeton."

"Can you drive it?"

"The horse is a friend of mine." Blaze winked at Belle, making her laugh. "I'll tell him our destination and ask him to take us."

Two hours later, Belle looped her basket over her arm and waited for Blaze to bring the phaeton around. She had washed her face and dabbed the theater cosmetics on the scar but hadn't changed into a fresh gown. What did her gown matter when she would be kneeling in the dirt?

Belle hurried down the steps when her sister halted the phaeton in front of Inverary House. She climbed up on the seat, asking, "Are you certain about this?"

"Pumpkin and I reached an understanding," Blaze said. "Isn't that right, Pumpkin?" Strangely, the horse neighed at that precise moment.

Belle relaxed on the seat, feeling confident. Pumpkin sounded like a gentle name.

Blaze flicked the reins, and the phaeton lurched onto Park Lane, startling passing coachmen and horses. Belle made a grab for the side of the seat and held it in a death grip lest she topple off.

"I thought you could drive," she cried.

"Relax," Blaze said. "I need to get my feet wet, in a manner of speaking."

"We're going the wrong way," Belle said.

"I plan to turn in a U at Cumberland Gate," Blaze told her, "and then we will be traveling in the right direction."

"Will you do me a favor?"

"What?"

"Take the turn on four wheels, not two."

Blaze burst into laughter. "You have nothing to fear with me at the reins."

Ten minutes later, the phaeton jerked to an abrupt halt in front of a mansion. Belle scrambled down, silently cursing her own stupidity trusting her sister to drive carefully. The girl was a menace in traffic, and she was in no mood to placate anyone.

Belle knocked on the front door. The majordomo answered the call almost immediately.

He inspected her appearance and found her lacking. "Yes?"

"Your gardener requested my assistance." Belle waved the missive in front of her.

"Come inside." Then, "Wait here."

Five minutes passed and became ten. Ten minutes grew into fifteen.

Belle turned away, her hand on the doorknob. She heard someone say "hello" and whirled around.

Princess Anya, the Russian ambassador's niece, stood there. The blonde's blue gaze traveled from Belle's face to her gown to her shoes. And then the princess laughed.

Belle felt the blush heating her cheeks. This was the last thing she needed today.

"Mikhail will never marry you," Princess Anya said. "Though, if he cleans you up, he may make you his mistress. My God, you are a tattered peasant."

Princess Anya stepped closer, her frigid gaze fixed on Belle's cheek. Belle knew what she was seeing. Theater cosmetics could only hide so much and would fail to mask any mark under intense scrutiny.

"And that scar," the princess sneered. "Do you actually believe any man—especially a prince—would want to marry you?"

"Am I to assume your gardener does not require my services?" Belle asked. "You feigned a need for my skills in order to spew your hate."

Princess Anya gave her a sneering smile. "You do learn fast."

"If I were a flower," Belle said, opening the door, "I would prefer death to your company."

Outside, Belle climbed onto the phaeton and stared straight ahead. The princess's cruelty stung, making her morning nausea return for an afternoon visit.

"Hanover Square is my next appointment."

The phaeton did not move.

"Why do you look ill?" her sister asked.

"I am ill, damn it."

The phaeton lurched into traffic, causing a problem for the coach behind. "My driving is improving, don't you think?"

Belle burst into tears.

Blaze halted the phaeton at the intersection of Knightsbridge Road and Hyde Park Corner, blocking traffic. Cursing and shouting and shaking fists erupted from coaches behind.

"We're blocking other coaches," Belle said, composing herself.

"Let them wait," Blaze said. "You are more important to me than those blockheads."

"Thank you, sister." Belle managed a wobbly smile. "Please take me to Hanover Square."

Fifteen minutes later, Blaze jerked to a halt in front of a mansion. Belle climbed down and knocked on the door.

"The gardener is expecting me," Belle said, holding the missive up. "I am Miss Flambeau."

The majordomo stepped aside, allowing her entrance. "Wait here, please."

Several minutes passed. Belle suffered the suspicion that the scene at the Russian ambassador's home would replay here.

"You took your time answering my summons."

Belle turned to the voice. Cynthia Clarke, another member of the Blonde Brigade, was crossing the foyer.

"Why do you dress so raggedly?" the blonde asked, her expression extreme distaste. "Charles told me about that hideous scar."

"Does your gardener require my services?"

"The prince won't marry you," Lady Cynthia continued, as if she hadn't spoken. "Your only hope for marriage lies with Charles."

"Charles Wingate?"

"Do not misunderstand," Cynthia said. "Charles doesn't want to marry you but needs the money your father would settle on you."

The sting wasn't so sharp this time. The Blonde Brigade would be proven wrong when the *Times* announced her betrothal. Belle was happy her stepmother had ensured these harpies would need to face her at the Ladies Luncheon, the day they would learn of their defeat in winning the prince in marriage.

"If you will excuse me." Belle turned to the door, but the blonde blocked her escape.

"I'm not finished."

"Let me say this, Cindy." Belle gave her a chilling smile. "Step aside, or my stepmother will ruin not only your reputation but your mother's as well."

Outside, Belle climbed onto the phaeton. "Cynthia Clarke wanted to insult me. I wish I were a hexer instead of a healer."

"That's the spirit," Blaze said. "We must plan something special to give the Blonde Brigade at the luncheon."

"Do you mean in addition to the fact that the object of their affection is marrying me?"

Blaze smiled at that. "Your marrying the prince should be served as an appetizer only."

"My last appointment is Berkeley Square." Belle grabbed the side of the seat in preparation for takeoff.

Ten minutes later, the phaeton halted in front of a mansion. Belle climbed down and knocked on the door. Waving the missive, she said, "Your gardener is expecting Miss Flambeau."

"Yes, miss. Please come inside."

Belle stepped into the foyer. The man sounded as if this was a gardener's authentic call for help.

"Follow me, miss." The majordomo led her through a maze of corridors that ended at the garden door.

"Thank you, sir." Belle stepped into the garden and spied her man on the far side. Following the path, she advanced on him.

And then Belle saw the pathetic rosebush. Its leaves were brown, its petals unopened.

"Oh dear. This rosebush needs a miracle."

"Yes, miss. Can you save it?"

Belle gave him a smile meant to encourage. "I will do my best. Do you keep manure?"

"Yes, miss."

"Fetch me a bucket."

Belle knelt on the grass and opened her basket. She lifted her magic paraphernalia and a white handkerchief, pilfered from her father.

"Here it is, miss."

Belle pressed the handkerchief to her nose in response to the stink. "Set the bucket here, please."

After blessing herself, Belle reached for the gold case containing Lucifer matches and sandpaper. She set the white candle into the brass holder and lit it. Then she rang the bell in front of the rosebush.

Inching closer on her knees, Belle touched the bush with both hands. "Ailing, ailing, ailing. Rosebush, my touch is sealing and thy illness is failing. Healing, healing, healing."

Belle waved the *Book of Common Prayer* in front of the plant, saying, "It is written. It is so."

After blessing herself again, Belle placed all of her belongings except the handkerchief into the basket. Then she dragged the bucket closer.

Using both hands, Belle reached into the bucket and grabbed globs of foul-smelling fertilizer. She packed it around the plant's base. Again and again and again.

"Loop my basket over my forearm," Belle instructed the gardener. She stood, the handkerchief in hand.

"I brought a bucket of water for your convenience," the gardener offered.

Another voice spoke. "That will be unnecessary."

Belle turned around to face Lavinia Smythe. Had the Blonde Brigade conspired against her? Were the three declaring war?

"Well, well, well. If it isn't the little ragamuffin," Lavinia said, her tone a sarcastic sneer.

"You should be more careful," Belle warned, "or your face will freeze into that grimace."

"Better a grimace than an ugly scar." Lavinia looked her up and down insultingly. "Do you really believe Mikhail will marry you? My God, you reek of-of . . . that stench."

"I'm sorry you dislike the smell of horse shit." Belle moved to walk past the blonde. "I do hope you will forgive my stink."

And then Belle touched the other woman's arm in apology. Leaving behind a manure handprint and a shrieking blonde.

Chapter 13

"Welcome to my tea party." Bess's excitement was contagious.

Standing near the outer foyer's French doors, Belle smiled at Mikhail. The four-year-old stood with Boomer near the front door to greet her four cousins.

"Is that the new mummy?" the smallest whispered.

Bess reached for her cousin's hand and drew her forward, the others following behind. "Here is my Mummy Belle."

"I present my nieces," Prince Mikhail made the introductions. "Princesses Roxanne, Natasia, Lily, and Sally. Next week, Mummy Belle will become Princess Belle, and Princess Fancy is her sister."

"I am pleased to make your acquaintances," Belle said. "Bess, if you escort your guests to the garden, Boomer will serve us."

"Come, cousins." Bess led them through the French doors and past Atlas holding the world. "We will take our tea in the garden."

Prince Mikhail turned to Belle and lifted her hand to his lips. "Thank you for making my daughter happy."

"Making people happy is what I do best."

"Oh, I do hope so."

Once he'd gone, Belle followed her charges through the

foyer to the hallway leading to the garden door. She trailed behind them along the curving path to the gazebo.

With the eldest in the lead, the other four princesses paired off and held hands. Lord, they reminded her of the Flambeau sisters a decade earlier.

The day was idyllic for a garden party. No clouds blemished the sky's deep blue, and greenery framed primary- and pastel-colored flowers. Faint birdsong complemented the mood.

"Girls, do you see these plants?" Belle pointed to the purple flowers. "I want everyone to sniff the lavender."

In turn, each princess stepped forward and pressed her nose to the plant.

"Does the lavender smell clean and refreshing?" Belle asked.

Five little girls bobbed their heads in unison.

"A long time ago, Blessed Mary set baby Jesus' newly washed clothes to dry on a lavender plant," Belle told them. "When His clothes had dried, they smelled fresh and clean. And so did the lavender plant."

The five girls clapped at her story. Lily, the smallest, reached for the plant as if to pick it off the stem.

"If you carry a sprig of lavender," Belle added, hoping to discourage the amputation, "you will see ghosts."

The tiny hand dropped from the lavender.

Inside the gazebo, Boomer had set a round table and seven chairs. Bess had insisted they needed a seat for Uncle Stepan, who usually attended.

"You must introduce yourselves to me again," Belle said, "and tell me your ages."

"I am Princess Roxanne," the eldest said. "Six years old." Then she took charge, pointing to each girl. "My sister Natasia and cousin Sally are five, and my sister Lily is four years like Bess. Sally has a new mummy who is giving us another cousin this year."

"I hope we have a girl," Natasia said.

"So do I," Lily agreed.

Sally nodded. "Me too."

"Then she will come to our tea party." Bess looked at Belle. "Will you give us a new cousin too?"

"When I marry your daddy and live here," Belle hedged, "you must ask your daddy."

"Darling, Uncle Mikhail will need your cooperation," Princess Roxanne drawled, sounding like the duchess. "You *do* know where we get babies?"

Belle struggled against the laughter threatening. "I think I do."

"Daddy and Mummy go into the bedchamber and lock the door," Sally said.

"Then the stork drops the baby down the chimney into the mummy's belly," Natasia said.

"That is correct, sister." Roxanne took charge of the discussion.

Lily tugged on Belle's sleeve. "How does the baby get out of the mummy's belly?"

"Well . . ."

"Don't *you* know?" The question came from Roxanne.

"When the stork drops a baby into my belly," Belle answered, "I will let you know."

Princess Roxanne smiled. "You don't know either."

"Here are the refreshments," Belle said.

Boomer and two footmen crossed the garden. The major-domo carried a tray holding five crystal glasses surrounding a pitcher of lemon barley water. One footman carried a tray with a pot of tea and its accoutrements while the other carried the tray with cookies.

After serving her tea, Boomer passed glasses of the lemon water around. He served each girl a plate with a sampling of the cookies and then set the platter in the middle of the table.

"Enjoy your party, ladies," Boomer said. "I will return to refresh your drinks."

"What is he going to do to our drinks?" Sally asked.

"Boomer will bring more later," Belle told her. "The cinnamon and nut cookies are called angel cookies. The Xs and Os are hugs and kisses, and the meringues are stuffed with whipped cream."

Several moments of silence reigned while the princesses tasted each kind of cookie. Peace and contentment filled Belle. The girls, the garden, and the silence soothed her worries.

"Mummy Belle made these cookies," Bess announced, "and the bad man hurt her cheek."

Silence. Prolonged silence. Prolonged, uncomfortable silence.

The princesses were avoiding her stepdaughter's remark about the bad man. Most likely, their parents had ordered them to ignore the mark on her face.

"One of my sisters sings in the opera," Belle told them. "She owns pots of theater cosmetics, which she gave me to cover my scar."

Belle looked at their rapt expressions. Taking her napkin, she walked to the fountain and dipped it in the water.

"When I wash the theater cosmetics off," Belle said, "I want everyone to look at my scar. And then we can enjoy our tea party."

"But our mother said—" Roxanne began.

"Your mother feared you would hurt my feelings," Belle interrupted, "but I want us to talk about the scar if we want."

Belle raised the wet napkin to her face, almost laughing at their open-mouthed expressions. This needed doing, though, or the girls would never behave normally in her vicinity.

"Come closer," Belle said, once she'd wiped her face clean of cosmetics. "You may touch it if you want."

The five little princesses surrounded her, inspecting the long, red mark they'd been ordered to ignore. Princess Roxanne, their undisputed queen, leaned close then and kissed her cheek. The others followed her lead.

"All those kisses have made my face feel better," Belle said, the girls returning to their chairs.

Only Bess remained by her side. She wrapped her arms around Belle's neck, saying, "I love you, Mummy."

"And I love you."

"I love you too," Lily said.

"So do I."

"Me too."

Roxanne smiled across the table at her. "Ditto for me."

"Who loves me?" called a masculine voice.

"Uncle Stepan, you came to my tea party." Bess ran down the path to her uncle.

Prince Stepan lifted her into his arms and gave her a smacking kiss on her cheek. "I would not even consider missing my Bess's first tea party."

Reaching the gazebo, Stepan set her down. He turned to Belle and kissed her hand, making his nieces giggle.

Stepan sat in the chair reserved for him. Once the major-domo had served his tea, he helped himself to a cinnamon and nut cookie.

"My new mummy baked the cookies," Bess boasted.

"Those are angel cookies." Lily looked at Belle, asking, "Do angels eat them?"

Belle smiled. Stepan grinned. Lily's sisters and cousins giggled.

"When little children die," Belle told them, "Saint Peter greets them at the Gates of Heaven. He gives them one of these cookies to help them recover from their homesickness."

"Cookies do make everyone feel better," Prince Stepan said, helping himself to another. "Princess Roxanne, have you heard any gossip recently?"

"Well . . ." Roxanne waited until all eyes were upon her. "The Earl of Goodness dueled Captain Crude."

"Did either get shot?"

"Captain Crude hit a tree, and the Earl of Goodness fired in the air."

"Thank you, Princess." Stepan looked at five-year-old Natasia. "Do you know any gossip?"

"The Crown hanged the Earl of Rotten at Tyburn Hill," she answered him.

"That was my gossip," Lily cried. "Daddy told me."

"Then I will ask Sally while you think of something else."

Belle watched the youngest Kazanov brother, a smile on her lips. Like Mikhail, Stepan was made to be a father. She hoped her sister appreciated that.

"Princess Sunshine had Baby Boy Bunting," Sally was saying.

"What wonderful news," Stepan exclaimed. "Is the Earl of Goodness Baby Boy Bunting's father?"

Sally gave her uncle a shy smile. "Yes."

"Are you ready now?" Stepan asked Lily.

She nodded and pointed at Belle. "That lady is Bess's new mummy."

"That's my gossip," Bess cried. "You stole my gossip."

"Well, Natasia stole my gossip," Lily defended herself.

"Can you think of something else?" Stepan asked.

Bess placed a tiny index finger across her lips and paused for a long moment. "I know how the baby gets out of the mummy's belly."

"How?" Four princesses asked at the same time.

Bess looked at her cousins. "You will need to wait until next tea party for that gossip."

Belle and Stepan laughed. The four princesses laughed too.

"I will ask my mummy," Natasia said, "and that will be my gossip."

"Mummy won't tell you," Roxanne said. "I asked her already."

Stepan stood and pointed his finger at each niece. "I love you and you and you and you and you." Then he circled the table, giving each niece a peck on her cheek. Reaching Belle, he lifted her hand to his lips. "Can Fancy make those cookies?"

"Only if you are suicidal."

Stepan laughed at that and left the garden, calling over his shoulder, "I will see you next week, ladies."

Boomer materialized a few minutes later with a fresh pitcher of lemon barley water and a pot of tea. The princesses paused in their conversations to eat more cookies.

Belle's gaze wandered the garden from plant to plant and flower to flower. The garden's peacefulness pleased her, and living here would bring her happiness.

The garden door opening caught her attention. Her heart sank to her stomach at the sight of Prudence and Lavinia Smythe.

If this is paradise, Belle thought, *the Smythes are serpents slithering toward me.*

"Grandmama," Bess exclaimed, "I am having a tea party."

"So I see, Elizabeth."

"His Highness has gone to a business meeting," Belle told them. "I don't know when he will return."

Prudence Smythe gave her a frigid look. "We will wait."

The curtness in her tone was unmistakable. Casting uncomfortable glances at each other, the Kazanov princesses remained silent.

Lavinia Smythe sat in the chair Prince Stepan had vacated. Politeness brought Belle to her feet, offering the older woman her own seat.

Boomer served the women tea, murmuring, "I will fetch another chair."

"Don't bother about that," Belle said. "I have been sitting long enough."

"What are you doing here, Miss Flambeau?"

Belle looked at Lavinia. "I am helping Bess hostess her first tea party."

"Elizabeth has both grandmother and aunt," Prudence said. "She does not need you."

Belle itched to slap the old lady, but two things stopped her.

She had never struck anyone in her life, nor would she wish to upset the girls.

"Nevertheless, His Highness and Bess requested my assistance," Belle said. "Not yours."

"Taste these cookies," Bess said, breaking the tense silence that followed.

Prudence ate one of the meringues. "Delicious, Elizabeth. Boomer must give Cook our compliments."

"She baked them," Princess Roxanne said.

Prudence looked at the six-year-old. "Who baked them?"

"*I* baked the meringues," Belle answered.

"How bourgeoise," Lavinia said, her smile haughty.

"Mummy Belle makes good cookies," Princess Lily said.

"What did you say?" Prudence asked the four-year-old.

"When she marries my daddy," Bess explained, "Mummy Belle will be my new mummy."

"This slut will never marry His Highness."

Belle gasped. "How dare you use that word—"

"I knew Gabrielle Flambeau," Prudence snapped. "Like mother, like daughter."

"How frightening for Lavinia," Belle drawled in a perfect imitation of her stepmother.

Before either Smythe could retaliate, Princess Lily told them, "Mummy Belle will marry Uncle Mikhail, not His Highness."

"You cheeky minx," Prudence sputtered, clearly appalled by the child's forthrightness.

Lily looked at her eldest sister. "Minks? I don't have fur."

Princess Roxanne looked Prudence straight in the eye. "We are princesses," she imitated the duchess. "Respect the title."

Belle covered her mouth to keep from laughing. The six-year-old had learned outrageous impertinence from the Duchess of Inverary.

"What are you?" Princess Natasia asked.

Prudence Smythe stared at the five-year-old.

Princess Sally shook her head. "She is no princess."

Belle stepped into the fray. "You may be princesses," she scolded the girls, "but even princesses must show respect for old people—I mean, their elders."

"The slut is a bad influence," Lavinia said to her mother.

Bess pointed a finger at her grandmother. "I want you to go away."

Prudence rounded on Belle, blaming her for the children's impertinence. "You will never step foot inside this house once I report your impertinence."

"I doubt Mikhail considers impertinence criminal," Belle countered.

"Grandmama Nasty and Aunty Mean are ruining my tea party." Bess burst into tears, and Princess Lily burst into tears when her cousin did.

"Excuse us." Belle took both girls by the hand and led them away from the gazebo. Reaching the garden door, she crouched eye level to wipe their tears and then put her arms around them.

"Your grandmother and aunt did not intend to ruin your tea party," Belle said. "If I leave now—"

Bess clung to her. "Don't leave, Mummy."

"Next week your daddy and I will marry," Belle promised, "and we will have another tea party. Boomer won't let anyone inside except the invited."

Belle kissed each girl's cheek. "If you return to the gazebo and tell your grandmother 'sorry,' then I will tell you the story about the frog prince next time."

Once the girls calmed, Belle walked through the mansion to the foyer. She smiled at the surprised majordomo and reached for the doorknob.

"You aren't leaving?" Boomer asked. "Your coach has not returned for you."

"Walking two blocks to Park Lane will not cripple me."

"What about Princess Elizabeth's tea party?"

"Trust me," Belle said, "the tea party will run smoother in my absence." And then she walked out the door.

The return to Inverary House wasted ten minutes. Belle entered the garden via the alley gate instead of the house. Answering questions was impossible until she could contain her emotions. Nausea churned her stomach. Her baby disliked the Smythes too.

Belle wandered the garden, inspecting its plants. The lilacs, tulips, and forsythias had vanished with the end of spring. Red and white dianthus with their fringed petals and clove scent were blooming now as were the lupins and delphiniums.

Keeping her back to the mansion, Belle sat on the bench beyond the fountain. The Smythes troubled her as did the realization that marrying the prince meant a lifetime of seeing them.

Belle heard the garden door opening. Puddles whizzed by her in his search for a certain spot.

Blaze plopped down beside her. "How was the tea party?"

Belle burst into tears.

"That good, huh?"

Belle struggled to compose herself, her bottom lip quivering. "Mikhail went to a business meeting, and the Smythes appeared without invitation and ruined it."

"Why would they want to ruin a little girl's tea party?"

"The Symthes did not intend to spoil the party," Belle answered. "They wanted to insult and humiliate me. They called our mother and me *sluts*."

Blaze bolted off the bench. "I've a mind to—"

"Sit, please."

Blaze dropped beside her again. "Wiping yesterday's *you know* on Lavinia's gown made the situation worse." And then she laughed. "I wish I had seen that."

"I will be dealing with the Smythes until they or I die," Belle said. "I think I should tell Mikhail I've changed my mind."

"You can't change your mind now," Blaze told her. "The prince went to a lot of trouble to marry you—letting his brothers beat him, pretending blindness, faking amnesia . . ."

"What do you mean?"

Blaze froze, gaping at her sister's surprised expression. "Oops . . ."

"Beware of unmarried women cornering you in a compromising situation," Mikhail said, stretching his long legs out. He looked at his three younger cousins. "Once the *Times* announces my betrothal tomorrow morning, you will be the only bachelor princes in London."

"I would not refuse being cornered between the Contessa de Salerno's thighs," Prince Drako said, making them smile.

"I welcome female attention," said Gunter, the youngest.

Prince Lykos shook his head. "Mikhail is warning us against female entrapment, not attention."

Prince Viktor laughed. "A female's attention means entrapment."

The door opened, drawing their attention. Four-year-old Lily Kazanov walked into her father's study, a smile lighting her face.

"Has the tea party ended so soon?" Mikhail asked her.

Lily nodded and set a plate of cookies on the desk in front of her father. "I brought you a present, Daddy."

"Thank you, Princess." Rudolf lifted his youngest daughter onto his lap and gestured his brothers and cousins to help themselves to the cookies.

Lily touched her father's cheek. "Daddy, what is a slut?"

All seven princes turned startled gazes on the four-year-old. Perfectly relaxed, she rested her head against her father's shoulder.

"That is a bad word," Prince Rudolf told her.

"I thought so."

Mikhail straightened in his chair. "Did someone say that word at the tea party?"

"Grandma Nasty and Aunty Mean said Mummy Belle is a

slut." Lily lifted her dark gaze to her father's, adding, "Grandma Nasty called me a cheeky minks, but I don't have any fur."

Mikhail's anger ignited. He looked at his youngest brother.

"Everyone was happy when I left," Stepan said.

"Can you tell me what happened at the tea party?" Mikhail asked his niece.

"I walked into the house," Lily began. "Then I saw Bess and you and—"

Prince Rudolf chuckled. "Uncle wants to know what happened when Lady Smythe arrived."

"Who is that?"

All the princes smiled.

"Lady Smythe is Grandma Nasty," Rudolf said.

"Well . . ." Imitating her eldest sister, Lily waited until all eyes were fixed on her. "Aunty Mean sat in Uncle Stepan's chair, and Mummy Belle gave her chair to Grandma Nasty. Then the old lady called Mummy Belle a slut. Like mother, like daughter."

Mikhail's anger heated from simmering to boiling. "Anything else, Lily?"

"She said that Mummy Belle will never marry His Highness—whoever he is."

All seven princes smiled at that.

"Cousin Bess cried," Lily continued, "and I cried with her. Then Mummy Belle wiped our tears and went away, and we never saw her again."

"Thank you, Lily." Mikhail rose from his chair, nodding a farewell to the others.

His in-laws had ruined his daughter's tea party and hurt Belle's feelings. Now he had the unenviable task of consoling his two ladies.

Fifteen minutes later, Mikhail climbed out of his carriage and gestured his coachman to wait. He walked into the foyer. "Where is Bess?"

Boomer raised his brows. "The princess is sitting outside."

Mikhail stepped into the garden and saw his daughter sitting in the gazebo, her nannies nearby. She looked so heartbreakingly alone, reminding him of Belle sitting in the duke's garden.

With a flick of his hand, Mikhail sent the nannies away. He looked at his daughter, noting her red-rimmed eyes and swollen lids.

"Hello, Bess."

She lifted her gaze to his, her bottom lip quivering. "Hello, Daddy."

"Come here." Mikhail sat and lifted her onto his lap. She rested her head against his chest.

Aching love for his daughter swelled within him. He wanted to protect her, make her life perfect, ensure her happiness.

"Lily told me about the tea party."

Bess gazed at him through her mother's blue eyes. He touched her dimpled chin, his own legacy to her along with the black hair.

"Sometimes adults make mistakes," Mikhail said. "Grandmama and Aunt Livy behaved badly today."

"Will you spank them?"

Mikhail heard the hopeful note in her voice and wished he could do just that. "Grandmama and Aunt Livy are too big to spank," he said, "but I promise they will never misbehave again. Mummy Belle will give you another tea party, and Boomer will not allow your grandmother and aunt into the house."

"I love you, Daddy."

He hugged her tight. "I love you more, Bess."

Mikhail's second destination was Berkeley Square and the confrontation he had avoided for months. He found his former mother-in-law in the parlor, but Lavinia was absent.

"I want to speak to you," Prudence said when he walked through the door. "How dare you set that woman in my daughter's place. Why, I—"

"Listen to me," Mikhail interrupted her intended tirade.

"You ruined my daughter's first tea party and insulted my invited guests, including *that* woman."

"Elizabeth is my granddaughter."

"Bess is *my* daughter," Mikhail countered. "You will not presume upon a family connection again."

"What do you mean?"

"Visiting my home without an invitation is forbidden," Mikhail informed her. "You will send a note asking permission either to visit Bess in my home or invite her to yours. Boomer will refuse you entrance if you appear at my door."

"This is outrageous," Prudence snapped. "That woman has bewitched you. As I recall, her mother did the same to Magnus Campbell."

"You will abide by my wishes and demonstrate respect for Belle Flambeau."

Prudence stared him straight in the eye, a determined expression etched across her face. "I will not show respect I do not feel."

"Belle Flambeau is worth a hundred of you." Mikhail leveled a contemptuous look on her. "If you value your position in society, Prudence, you will pretend what you do not feel."

"Are you threatening me?"

"Consider my words a friendly warning."

Mikhail's final destination was Inverary House. Stepping into the garden, Mikhail paused near the door. Belle sat alone on a bench beyond the fountain, reminding him of his daughter.

The Smythes had ruined both Bess's and Belle's first tea party. He wished his in-laws were men so he could give them a good thrashing.

"I apologize for what happened," Mikhail said, sitting beside her on the bench. "I should have stayed home, but I thought—"

Belle turned to him on a sigh. "You should not shoulder the blame."

"I have consoled Bess," Mikhail said, raising her hand to his lips. "I went to Berkeley Square and informed Prudence that she must stay away unless invited. Being my daughter's grandmother does not give her license to consider my home as hers."

Her disarming violet eyes caught his, holding them captive. "Tell me the reason you schemed to meet me."

Uh-oh. Someone had blundered with a slip of the tongue. Mikhail hesitated for a long moment, wondering what she knew and what to answer.

"Your brothers beat you," Belle said, "and you pretended blindness and amnesia."

Thankfully, she didn't know they had already been married by proxy. If he was lucky, she would never discover that fact. At least, until they had been married twenty years.

Mikhail leveled his intense, black gaze on her and gave her his most charming smile. "One day I stood at your father's window and saw you sitting alone." He slipped an arm around her shoulders. "I wanted an introduction desperately, but your father said you refused all visitors."

He watched the play of emotions on her face. She did not look especially angry.

"I do not want a husband who is less than completely honest," Belle said. "Is there anything else you would confess to me?"

"Absolutely not." No hesitation there.

"I cannot understand the reason for such a drastic contrivance," Belle said. "You had only seen me once from a distance."

"I believe my reason is obvious." Mikhail cupped her chin and pressed a light kiss on her mouth. "I loved you at first sight. . . ."

Chapter 14

Love at first sight. A romantic elixir to soothe hurt feelings.

Belle could barely contain her smile. She had feared happiness would never be hers, especially since the assault. Even her morning nausea could not suppress the simple joy of loving and being loved in return.

What she had wanted most in life was hers. True love and her own family, one child inherited and one child on the way. She had all the ingredients for a perfect future, especially when mixed with her gardening business.

Nanny Smudge had been correct. Miracles *did* happen every day.

"Here you are, Miss Belle." Tinker served her a cup of black tea, plain toast, and scrambled eggs. "On behalf of His Grace's entire staff, I offer our best wishes for your forthcoming marriage."

"Thank you, Tinker." Her smile did appear then. She glanced around the breakfast table and caught her sisters and her parents smiling at her.

"Listen to this." Sitting across the table from her, Blaze read from the morning *Times*. "The Duke and Duchess of Inverary announce the betrothal of their daughter, Miss Belle Flambeau, and Prince Mikhail Kazanov."

"That should upset the horde of losers for the prince's hand in marriage," Serena said.

"The Kazanovs' royal cousins are visiting London," Sophia said. "Perhaps the disappointed hopefuls will leave Belle in peace and chase those three princes."

"The cousins have deep pockets," Bliss said. "Maybe *we* should join the chase."

"Dear Bliss, what a delightful attitude you have developed since moving to Inverary House," the duchess complimented her.

Belle smiled at her sisters' conversation. Yes, she felt nauseated and dizzy and tired. No, she was not looking forward to today's luncheon. But . . . out of all the women in London, Mikhail had loved her at first sight.

"I daresay the disappointed and their mamas will be on the warpath," the duchess remarked. "I was hoping a huge betrothal ring would deflect some venom, silencing the snakes."

"Did you tell Her Grace about yesterday?" Raven asked Belle, knowing she hadn't.

Belle looked at her father and stepmother. "Prudence and Lavinia Smythe ruined Bess's tea party, and"—she hesitated—"Prudence Smythe called me and my mother a slut."

The Duke of Inverary banged his fist on the table, rattling the silverware and his family. "Prudence will—"

"Darling, do not concern yourself with female frivolities," the duchess interrupted his beginning tirade.

"Frivolities?" the duke barked. "Calling my daughter and—"

"Trust me, Magnus. I can handle Prudence Smythe and will instruct my stepdaughters on dealing with others of her ilk."

Though grateful for their support, Belle wished Raven had minded her own business. Relating yesterday's fiasco had upset their father, which, in turn, upset their stepmother.

"You need to develop your backbone," Blaze said to her. "Certain situations demand fighting fire with fire."

The Duchess of Inverary looked down the length of the table at her husband. "Blaze has inherited your Highland temperament."

The Duke of Inverary grinned, his good humor restored. "Thank you, my dear."

"You are very welcome, *darling,*" Blaze drawled, imitating their stepmother.

Everyone laughed. Even the duchess gave Blaze a dimpled smile.

Blaze looked at Belle. "I will protect you from those serpents' tongues."

"Thank you, sister," Belle said. "I have never seen this poetical side of yours."

"I possess many talents unknown to the world at large." Then Blaze grew serious. "You can depend on your sisters to protect you."

Belle rolled her eyes. "I wonder how many favors I will do as repayment."

"Darling Magnus, isn't this heartwarming to witness your daughters' loyalty to each other?"

"That will be their Scots blood, Roxie. The damn French are prone to chopping heads."

"Good morning."

Belle knew who it was before she looked over her shoulder. Her love-at-first-sight prince had come to see her before joining the gentlemen golfing.

Eyeing him as he walked toward her, Belle thought how lucky she was. With his dark good looks, her prince was incredibly tempting. His face was handsomely chiseled, and his height gave him an imposing presence.

His heart pleased Belle most, though. His lean, hard physique hid a gentle heart. And he had loved her at first sight.

"Good morning." Belle blushed, knowing her family was watching.

Mikhail dropped into the chair beside her, his gaze on her bland breakfast. "How do you feel this morning, Princess?"

"I feel wonderful," Belle answered. "If I discount the nausea and dizziness and tiredness."

"You do not suffer from the fourth symptom?"

"I am saving all my smashing urges for Her Grace's luncheon."

Mikhail looked down the table at the duchess. "I would prefer Belle not to attend if you think there will be trouble."

"You need not worry about trouble," the Duke of Inverary told the prince. "Her sisters are prepared to protect her." He glanced at Blaze. "One is eagerly anticipating trouble and itching for a fight."

"The Contessa de Salerno created your betrothal ring." Mikhail drew a small box from his pocket and opened it.

Belle had never seen a more exquisite piece of jewelry. Set in platinum, a square-cut diamond sparkled at her from its bed of black velvet. Emeralds ringed the enormous stone.

"The diamond, like you, is a rare and priceless jewel," Mikhail said, slipping the ring on her finger, "and emeralds are considered love's emblem."

Belle looked from his face to the ring and his face again. She didn't know what to say, his words touching her heart.

His face inched closer and his lips touched hers. His taste and his scent were familiar. She had missed this intimacy since returning from the cottage.

"Your sentiment means more than the ring," Belle said, finding her voice.

"I have been practicing my speech since dawn," Mikhail admitted, making her smile.

"Darling, let us see the ring," the duchess said.

Belle held her hand up. Her sisters gathered around her, *ohhing* and *ahhing*. The duchess nodded her approval.

"The ring makes an enormous statement." The duchess looked at her husband. "Don't you agree, Magnus?"

"Yes, dear. The ring is very pretty."

"Very pretty?" the duchess echoed. "Those jewels cost a small fortune."

"Actually, the ring cost a large fortune," Mikhail said, his tone rueful.

Belle panicked at the exorbitant cost. "What if I lose it?"

"I will buy you another." Mikhail raised her hand to his lips.

"Oh, how romantic," the duchess gushed, making the girls giggle. "I can hardly wait to show certain people that ring. How delicious."

The duke looked down the long table at his wife. "Roxie, I want no trouble here."

The duchess gave him a dimpled smile. "Darling, would I cause trouble?"

"Yes."

"Very well, I promise to behave."

"Do not tire yourself out." Mikhail planted a chaste kiss on Belle's lips and whispered, "I am thankful our betrothal will be short."

Her smile was seductive. "You cannot possibly be more thankful than I."

Four hours later, Belle stood in front of the cheval mirror in her bedchamber to inspect her appearance. She wore a pale violet gown with short, puffed sleeves and scooped neckline.

The front view looked presentable, except for the red mark on her cheek. Her sister's theater cosmetics could not cover the scar completely, but she would learn to live with it. There was no other option.

Turning sideways, Belle studied her profile and pressed the palms of her hands against her belly. Which, thankfully, did not protrude. She could scarcely believe a tiny baby was growing inside her.

Raising her hand, Belle stared at her betrothal ring. Theater cosmetics did not matter. Her prince loved her even with the mark on her cheek.

Belle wandered to the window, knowing she was delaying going downstairs. She prayed for the strength to survive her rivals' spite.

On the other hand, perhaps her rivals should beware of her. She did suffer from the urge to smash someone.

Blaze, Raven, and Tulip Woods huddled together in the rear of the garden. The three were standing so close they appeared to be sharing secrets.

There was safety in numbers. She would use her sisters as a buffer against the Blonde Brigade.

Leaving her bedchamber, Belle walked down the corridor to the servants' stairs. Then she slipped out the garden door and walked toward her sisters, who did not hear her approach.

"Tulip, you look lovely in turquoise," Belle said, surprising them, "and I do believe the color will match both your blue and green eyes."

The girls whirled around at the sound of her voice. All three wore guilty expressions.

"What are you planning?" Belle was certain they were conspiring to create mischief at the luncheon.

"We will tell you if you promise to keep the secret," Blaze said.

"How can I promise silence if I don't know what you are planning?"

Raven shrugged. "Then we won't tell you."

"Is that real?" Tulip asked, pointing at the betrothal ring.

"Yes, I believe so."

Blaze turned to Tulip. "We must shadow Belle today and protect her from society's witches."

"Why doesn't she protect herself?"

"Our sister cannot force herself to hurt anyone's feelings," Raven answered.

"Belle did smear garden dung on Lavinia Smythe's sleeve," Blaze said.

Raven and Tulip laughed. Belle smiled, proud of what she'd done.

"I will keep your secret," Belle agreed. "Tell me what you are planning."

"The Slasher murdered my sister," Tulip said. "He must be captured and punished."

"We will catch the monster tonight," Blaze added.

Belle could not credit what she was hearing. If the constable couldn't catch the villain, how could her sisters? The only thing they would catch is trouble.

"One of us will dress to entice and walk the streets," Raven told her. "The other two and Puddles will protect the bait."

Belle could feel the color draining from her own face. Her knees felt weak, and she sat on a nearby bench.

"That is much too dangerous. Tell Alex—"

"You promised to keep our secret," Tulip interrupted her.

"I'll go with you."

"If you go, then Serena and Sophia and Bliss will want to go," Raven said.

"Besides, no pregnant women allowed," Tulip said.

"The prince would kill us if anything happened to you," Raven said.

"You wouldn't want to make the Blonde Brigade happy by dying before you married the prince," Blaze added.

"Very well," Belle agreed, albeit reluctantly, "but I will drown in guilt if anyone is injured."

Limited to one hundred guests, the Duchess of Inverary's Annual Ladies Luncheon was one of society's most exclusive invitations. Two violinists played background music at one end of the enormous ballroom while one hundred ladies greeted and gossiped with friends and located their seats.

Belle saw her stepmother as soon as she walked into the ballroom. Ignoring a duchess who sparkled was impossible.

Regal in a dark red gown, the Duchess of Inverary dripped diamonds. Several fingers bore diamond rings, diamonds by the yard draped her neck, cuffs fashioned with diamonds circled her wrists, and her earlobes glittered with diamond adornment.

"Belle darling," the duchess called from where she stood with Lady Smythe and the Contessa de Salerno. "Come here and thank the contessa for creating your exquisite betrothal ring."

Insult is an art form, Belle recalled the statement. Her stepmother was baiting Prudence Smythe.

Belle glanced at her sisters. Blaze was smiling at the prospect of creating trouble.

"Contessa, I cannot understand how genius improves itself," the duchess said, lifting Belle's hand to admire the betrothal ring. "You have done precisely that."

"I thank you for the praise, Your Grace." The contessa flicked a glance at Prudence and gave the duchess a knowing look. She turned to Belle. "Wear your ring in good health, and I offer you best wishes for your marriage."

"Thank you, Contessa."

The Duchess of Inverary looped her arm through Belle's. "Your noble mother would be so proud."

Unexpected tears welled in Belle's eyes. Except for her father, the duchess was the only member of society who had spoken kindly of her mother.

Belle glanced at her sisters. Raven and Blaze seemed touched by her words too.

The duchess looked at the older woman. "Isn't that the most gorgeous betrothal ring, Prudence?"

"Quite lovely, Your Grace." Prudence Smythe looked as if she'd sat on a tack. "However, a betrothal ring does not make a marriage. The prince may change his mind yet."

"Bite your tongue," the contessa said, her smile softening her words.

The duchess gave a throaty chuckle and turned a dimpled smile on the older woman. "I have a thousand pounds that says not only will the marriage take place but the prince will get his heir before a year ends."

Belle blushed at her stepmother's words. She wanted no one to guess she already carried the prince's baby.

"Tulip darling, you look lovely today." The duchess drew the girl forward. "Contessa and Lady Smythe, I present the Duke of Essex's granddaughter."

The contessa inclined her head. "A pleasure to meet you, Tulip."

"I didn't know Bart had a granddaughter," Prudence Smythe said, eyeing the girl with suspicion.

Belle watched Prudence, fearing her spiteful tongue would cut Tulip. *Another bastard* was leaping from the older woman's eyes, but Belle had misjudged the girl's toughness.

Tulip fixed her blue-green gaze on Lady Smythe. Assuming a haughty tone, she said, "You cannot expect to know all the insider *on-dits*."

Prudence Smythe narrowed her gaze on the girl. "I see she inherited Bart's temperament. If you will excuse me."

The Duchess of Inverary watched Prudence Smythe walk away. "Tulip darling, you show great promise." She gave them a feline smile. "Find your seats, my dears. Tinker is awaiting my signal to serve."

Belle sat at a table with friendly faces. Besides her sisters and Tulip, there were the Contessa de Salerno and Samantha and Regina Kazanov, her future sisters-in-law.

Deciding she would survive the afternoon, Belle let the conversation swirl around her. Among other things, their diverse topics touched on jewelry design, thoroughbred racing, and candy delights.

Though subdued, the Blonde Brigade sent her hate-filled looks. Belle suffered the uncanny feeling that the Brigade, former rivals of each other, were united and conspiring against her.

After the luncheon, the ladies drifted to the formal drawing room where coffee, tea, and desserts would be served. Here the ladies played cards, admired each other's jewels, and enjoyed the gossip.

The drawing room was formal but comfortable. One wall

had floor-to-ceiling windows while two other walls had white marble hearths. Above one hearth was the first duchess's portrait, and the present duchess observed all from her portrait above the second hearth.

The walls were burnished oak from floor to dado and papered a deep gold above that. Couches, chairs, and chaises in a mixture of textiles and jeweled colors stood on Persian carpets of red, gold, cream, and blue.

Old friends gravitated toward each other, sipping tea and gossiping. Young matrons discussed babies and housekeeping anecdotes. The younger unmarrieds congregated near one of the marble hearths.

"We should play Yes and No," Cynthia Clarke suggested. "The Chosen thinks of an object or person, and the others ask questions and guess what the Chosen is thinking."

Belle sat with her sisters, barely listening to the conversation. She would have preferred a nap but did not want anyone to suspect her condition.

"Princess Anya, you will be our first Chosen," Cynthia was saying.

The princess nodded. She paused for a moment and then said, "I have something in mind. You may proceed."

Cynthia pointed at Tulip. "You may start the questioning."

"Is it an object?" Tulip asked.

"Yes," the princess answered.

Serena came next. "Will we find this object inside the house?"

"Yes."

"Can I hold this object in my hands?" Sophia asked.

"Yes."

Bliss thought for a long moment. "Will I find the object in this room?"

"Yes."

"Can I wear it?" Blaze asked.

"No."

"Is it furniture?" The question came from Raven.

"No."

"Here are the footmen with our tea and desserts," Cynthia said. Then, "Is the object edible?"

"Yes."

Lavinia looked at Belle. "Is the object a *tart?*"

Princess Anya smirked at Belle. "Yes, a tart."

The Flambeau sisters gasped at the insult. Other ladies stopped talking and turned to watch.

Gesturing Blaze to say nothing, Belle remained silent, but a heated blush colored her cheeks. The losers could play their stupid games, but she was the woman wearing the prince's betrothal ring.

"Let's play Crambo," Tulip said, her voice sounding overly loud in the silent drawing room. "I say a phrase or a word, and each person must rhyme. *Hitch.*"

"Glitch," Serena said, helping diffuse the tension.

"Ditch" came from Sophia.

Bliss looked around the circle. "Twitch."

"Pitch," said Blaze, looking clearly unhappy.

"Rich," Princess Anya said with a smile.

Lavinia looked at Belle. "Witch."

The Flambeau sisters gasped, and all conversations stopped again.

Belle knew she had to fight back, or the Blonde Brigade would torment her. Her sister had been correct. There were situations that demanded fighting fire with fire.

Belle rose from her chair and stood in front of Lavinia. *"Bitch."*

"Breeding does tell," Prudence Smythe said into the shocked silence.

Belle turned her head to see a frigid gaze on the elder Smythe. "Like daughter, like mother."

Her sisters erupted into applause. Her future sisters-in-law sent her smiles of approval.

"Bravo," the Duchess of Inverary drawled.

Lifting her nose into the air, Belle quit the drawing room.

Raven slipped out the garden door, careful to close it behind her silently. No one must suspect she or Blaze were not in their bedchambers. Her sister had already escaped to fetch the town carriage and bring it around to the alley, where Tulip would meet them.

The scents of myriad flowers mingled in the darkness and perfumed the air. The night sky was clear overhead, its moon waxing.

Raven glided like an apparition through the garden to the alley stairs. She stepped through the gate and gasped in surprise.

Dressed in black, Tulip waited there. Surrounding the girl were her sisters. Belle, Bliss, Serena, and Sophia had also dressed in dark colors. Only Fancy was missing, residing with her husband, Prince Stepan.

Before she could say anything, Raven heard the town carriage rolling down the alley. Blaze halted the horses with an abrupt jerk. She placed the reins in the mastiff's mouth, whispered in its ear, and then climbed down.

"What the bloody blue blazes is this?" Blaze asked. "A party?"

"We want to help catch the killer," Sophia said.

"Everyone won't fit in the carriage," Tulip said.

"You need someone to stay with the carriage," Belle said, "or thieves will steal it."

"No pregnant women allowed," Raven said, "but we *do* need a guard for the carriage."

Blaze vetoed her own twin's participation. "Bliss is a genius with numbers but nothing else."

"We don't need to see evil's aura," Raven said, eliminating Sophia.

That left Serena only. "If the situation requires action, I can pelt the man with rain."

Tulip looked confused. "There's nary a cloud in the night sky."

"Trust me," Blaze said. "She can bring down the rain."

"Serena will accompany us," Raven agreed.

"I know self-defense," Belle said, making them smile. "Mikhail taught me at the cottage." She demonstrated as she spoke. "Elbow to stomach, stomp on foot, knee to groin, fist to neck, and fingers to eyes."

"If we don't find the Slasher tonight," Tulip said, "we'll practice the moves during the week." She opened her bag and produced a gown. "Ruby wore this to attract men."

"I will be the decoy," Raven said, grabbing the gown. When Tulip opened her mouth to argue, she added, "You can be the decoy next time."

"Why can't you be the decoy next time?"

"I'm holding the gown," Raven said.

She disrobed and pulled the dead prostitute's gown over her head. The scarlet gown had an indecently low scooped neckline and a tight-fitting bodice.

"I brought Papa's pistol," Blaze said.

"What if it misfires?" Belle asked.

"The pistol is unloaded."

Raven rolled her eyes. "Then why do we need it?"

"Puddles is *my* weapon," Blaze explained, "and the pistol is Tulip's weapon." She passed it to the girl. "She can bash the villain's brains."

"Where is my weapon?" Raven asked. "I'm the bait."

"The bait doesn't get a weapon," Blaze said, "because Tulip and I will be guarding you."

Tulip climbed onto the driver's seat with Blaze. Raven, Serena, and Puddles crammed together on a seat meant for two.

"We'll try Dirty Dick's in Bishopgate," Tulip said.

Leaving exclusive Park Lane, Blaze drove east. They followed the Strand to Fleet Street to Ludgate and Cannon Streets. Finally, the carriage turned onto Bishopgate in a unsavory section of the city.

"Stop here," Tulip said. "Dirty Dick's is a block away."

Tulip climbed down, and the others disembarked. Blaze and Serena changed places.

"Stay on this side of the street," Tulip told Raven. "Walk one block past Dirty Dick's and then turn around to walk back to the coach. Blaze and I will hide across the street."

Faced with being alone, Raven felt unexpectedly insecure. Brave words were easily spoken, but now she needed to put her words into action. "What if a gent tries to hire my services?"

"Refuse the bloke," Tulip said with a smile. "Last time I checked, England was a free country and prostitutes can still refuse."

"What if he won't take *no* for an answer?" Raven asked.

"Puddles will persuade him," Blaze answered.

Tulip, Blaze, and the mastiff crossed to the opposite side of Bishopgate. Raven sauntered down the street, her step slow and her nerves on high alert. Was the evening suddenly warm? Or was fear heating her?

Dirty Dick's sounded rowdy. She heard men's loud voices and women's high-pitched laughter.

Raven strode past the tavern and froze at the mouth of the next alley. Had something moved in the darkness? When nothing happened, she took a deep breath to calm herself and retraced her steps at a leisurely pace. Surely, streetwalkers would not rush around.

"Nothing yet," Raven whispered, reaching Serena with the coach.

Raven turned and walked up the street again, slowing her pace near the tavern's door. Up the street, down the street. Again and again and again.

Pacing back and forth was absurd. While she was outside, the Slasher could be inside prowling for his next victim.

Raven crossed the street and whispered, "Blaze?"

Tulip and her sister materialized from the blackness of the alley. "What is it?"

"I'm going inside to scout the tavern."

"Puddles and I will hide in the alley on the tavern's right," Blaze said. "Tulip and the pistol will hide in the other alley. If there's trouble, smash heads first and ask questions later."

Raven felt her heartbeat quicken while her guards assumed their new positions. She crossed the street and, standing in front of the tavern, took a fortifying breath and pulled her bodice down a bit.

The door swung open unexpectedly, smoke and odors and noise escaping. A tall, expensively dressed gentleman stood there. He reeked of gin and stale smoke.

"Well, well, well," he drawled. "Tonight is definitely my lucky night."

Raven gave him a smile, hopefully seductive. "I'm the lucky one, guv."

The door closed behind the gentleman, his smile leering. "I've been looking for you all evening, puss."

"Me?" Raven squeaked, and then lowered her voice. "I mean, me and my body have been lookin' for you all night."

The gentleman pulled a gold sovereign from his pocket and held it in front of her face. "I'll give you this, puss, if you walk down the alley with me."

The gold sovereign. A sign of the Slasher. Her heartbeat pounded in a frightened frenzy.

"Well, guv, you are a handsome gentleman." Raven placed special emphasis on the word and lifted the sovereign from his hand. "I'd love to walk down the alley with a gentleman like you. A gentleman like you makes a girl's life worth living."

The man put an arm around her shoulders and yanked her

against his body. Urging her around the corner into the alley, he shoved her against the wall and—

Wham. He crumpled at her feet.

Raven felt like crumpling beside him in relief. Her stomach was nauseated, and her legs felt weak. Bravado had proven more difficult than she'd imagined.

Tulip stood beside her, staring at the man, the pistol in her hand. Both heard rushing footsteps, and Blaze appeared with the mastiff.

"Is he dead?" Tulip asked. "Should we send for the runners?"

Blaze crouched beside the unconscious man, who was beginning to groan. "Rarely do drunks hurt themselves."

"How do we know he's the Slasher?" Raven asked.

"Take his knife before he wakes," Tulip said.

Blaze checked his outside and inside pockets. Nothing. She ran her hands down his body, avoiding particular parts, and then stood. "The gent's not carrying a blade."

"Which means he's not the Slasher," Tulip said.

Willing the pounding of her heart to slow, Raven dropped the gold sovereign on the man's chest. "I think we should go home now."

Chapter 15

"Turn in a circle, darling."

Standing in the nave of St. Paul's Cathedral, Belle did as her stepmother requested. Her father and her five unmarried sisters watched the duchess's final inspection.

Created in ivory satin and silk, Belle's wedding gown had a drop-waisted bodice and scooped neckline. Its bell-shaped sleeves precluded the need for long gloves and were sheer gossamer silk as were her stockings and veil.

Much to her stepmother's consternation, Belle had insisted she wanted no sophisticated, upswept hairstyle. Instead, her ebony mane cascaded almost to her waist like a bride of yore. All Belle needed to complete the look was a dagger at her waist. Foregoing the blade, she held a bouquet of orange blossoms.

The orange blossoms symbolized virginity—which was gone, given to the prince at the cottage. The flowers also served as a fertility charm—which was unnecessary, since she had already conceived.

"So exquisite." The Duchess of Inverary lifted her discerning gaze to the ebony mane. "Even with an old-fashioned hairstyle."

The Flambeau sisters giggled. The duke smiled at his wife.

"The wedding of the decade," the duchess gushed.

"I thought Stepan's and Fancy's was the wedding of the decade," Belle said.

The duchess gave her a dimpled smile. "Can there not be *two* weddings of the decade?"

The Flambeau sisters giggled again. The duke gave his wife another indulgent smile.

"Come, my darlings." The duchess led the girls away. "Since all the guests are seated, we can make our grand entrance."

The Duchess of Inverary glided down the aisle, nodding like a queen at friend and foe alike. Behind the duchess walked the unmarried Flambeau sisters, five chicks forming a single line behind their mother hen.

"Roxanne loves being the center of attention," the Duke of Inverary said, a smile lurking in his voice.

"You make a dynamic couple," Belle said.

"I want you to know I did love your mother and would have married her if I'd been free," her father told her. "Gabrielle would be so proud of you."

"Thank you, Papa."

After kissing each cheek, the duke drew the veil down to cover her face. He offered his arm, saying, "Your prince is waiting."

Belle placed her hand on her father's arm. They walked to the center aisle.

The music from two violins and an organ wafted through the air. Hundreds of candles lit the cathedral, their flickering casting dancing shadows on the walls.

"Are you ready?"

"Yes, Papa."

The Duke of Inverary stepped forward, taking his daughter with him. Belle could see the front of the church, adorned with white roses, their fragrance growing stronger with each step.

And then she saw Mikhail. With his dark good looks, the prince was breathtakingly handsome in his formal attire. More important, his heart was big and beautiful. And he was smiling at her.

Belle sent up a silent prayer that they would always be as loving as they were at this moment. Only five steps forward and he would be hers.

"That's my new mummy."

Belle heard Bess's exclamation and the congregation's amusement. She saw the prince send his daughter a smile.

"Wait," Belle whispered to her father.

She walked to the Kazanov side of the cathedral. The five princesses stood together in the front pew.

"Will you hold this for me?" Belle asked her stepdaughter, passing her the orange blossom bouquet.

Bess nodded, her smile bright, and lifted the bouquet from her hand. The four watching princesses squealed in delight.

Relatives and guests near the front were smiling. Those in the back were craning their necks to see what was happening.

"Who's that man?" asked Princess Lily, pointing at the duke.

Subdued chuckles erupted in the front of the cathedral.

"That man is my daddy," Belle answered.

"There's my daddy," Bess cried in excitement. "Hello, Daddy."

More laughter from the guests.

Belle looked over her shoulder to see the smiling prince blow his daughter a kiss. She returned to her father's side and finished the walk to her groom.

Before her father could turn away, Belle lifted her hand to touch his cheek, whispering, "I love you, Papa."

Without waiting for his reply, Belle faced Mikhail who asked, "Will you marry me now?"

"Yes, Your Highness."

Mikhail and Belle turned to the bishop. The ceremony was surprisingly short for one of life's milestones.

After the bishop pronounced them husband and wife, Mikhail lifted Belle's veil. He planted a kiss on each cheek and then claimed her lips.

"Ohhh . . ." The Kazanov princesses squealed again.

An hour later, Mikhail and Belle walked into the Inverary ballroom to receive their guests. On one side of them stood the Duke and Duchess of Inverary, and on the other side Prince Rudolf and Princess Samantha.

The head table was on one side of the chamber while several violinists played at the other end. Tables had been set between the head table and the musicians. Garlands of forget-me-nots pleased the eye, and the heady perfume of hundreds of roses— white, red, yellow—wafted through the air.

Belle stared in dismay at the rose centerpieces on each table. How many hundreds of plants had suffered for a decoration nobody noticed?

"If you smile," Mikhail whispered against her ear, "our guests will believe you are happily married."

"I *am* happy but—" Belle gestured around the room. "These flowers have been needlessly amputated."

Mikhail lifted her hand to his lips. "You are an Original, my wife."

"Why doesn't anyone mourn the death of a flower?" Belle asked. "Plants are the Lord's living creations, and He loves them as He loves us."

"Tell me, my love," Mikhail said, laughter lurking in his voice, "were those *real* orange blossoms or perfect imitations?"

She blushed at his teasing. "My stepmother insisted the orange blossoms would make a statement."

"How bloodthirsty of her."

Their guests began walking down the receiving line. The prince introduced her to the guests she did not know and her stepmother to others.

Prince Stepan and Princess Fancy stood in front of them. Fancy kissed her cheek and offered Mikhail her hand.

"I am anticipating your next tea party," Prince Stepan said. "Your cookies were delicious." He looked at his wife. "You should bake cookies too."

Fancy gave him a sidelong smile. "My talents lie elsewhere."

Prince Viktor and Princess Regina were next in line. "Welcome to the family," Regina said, "and I admire what you did at the luncheon last week."

"What was that?" Mikhail asked.

Belle leaned close and whispered, "I called Lavinia a bad name."

"Like daughter, like mother," Regina repeated her words.

"Remember Crazy Eddie?" Viktor asked his brother. "Someone found him in an alley with a sovereign on his chest. You know, similiar to that murderer's scenario."

"Was Eddie slashed?" Mikhail asked.

Viktor shook his head. "Drunk."

Belle knew the brothers were discussing the gentleman Tulip Woods had whacked. Thankfully, the man had sustained no serious injury.

Princes Lykos and Gunter were next in line. Both princes kissed Belle's hand in a courtly manner.

"I am feeling hunted," Prince Lykos said.

Mikhail smiled at his cousin. "The wolf becomes the hunted."

"The hunter becomes the hunted," Gunter added, referring to the meaning of his own name. "We may need to send to Moscow for a few of our younger brothers."

"If I could find a lady as lovely as your bride," Lykos said, "I would gladly place myself in her gentle hands."

Behind the two cousins walked the Contessa de Salerno and Prince Drako Kazanov. The contessa smiled at Belle, and the prince bowed over her hand.

"You make a beautiful bride," Katerina said.

Mikhail smiled at his cousin. "You could be the next Kazanov groom."

"I may require the help of Her Grace's expert relationship strategies," Drako said, glancing at the contessa.

The Duke of Essex and his grandchildren, Alexander Blake and Tulip Woods, reached the front of the receiving line. Belle introduced Mikhail to them and then smiled at her step-mother's never-ending matchmaking.

"My darling Belle is now settled," the Duchess of Inverary said to Alexander. "We may proceed with your betrothal."

"The contessa is designing a special betrothal ring for Raven," Alexander told the duchess.

"The sooner the boy marries," the Duke of Essex said, "the sooner I will see my great-grandson." The old man looked at Alexander, adding, "I can't live forever, you know."

"Bart, Tulip shows extraordinary promise," the Duchess of Inverary told the duke. "With my tutelage, Tulip will become one of society's great ladies."

Belle looked at Tulip and tried not to laugh. The girl appeared distinctly unimpressed with her future.

"Why do you say that?" the Duke of Essex was asking.

"I demand respect for myself and my friends," Tulip answered instead of the duchess, "and I use insult like an artist."

The duke chuckled. "She takes after me."

At the end of the line walked two of the Duke of Inverary's kinsmen. Ross MacArthur was the Marquis of Awe, and Douglas Gordon was the Marquis of Huntley.

Belle recognized the calculation in her stepmother's expression. These two gentlemen would not enjoy their bachelorhood much longer.

"I have seated you at a table with two of my stepdaughters," the Duchess of Inverary told the men. "Blaze and Bliss are delightful and lovely, and I knew you would enjoy their company."

"If they are as lovely as the new princess," Ross MacArthur said, "Dougie and I will consider ourselves fortunate."

Belle noted that the Blonde Brigade chose not to walk through the receiving line. Neither did their mamas.

Mikhail escorted Belle to the head table. The wedding guests found their seats, and the servants poured champagne into crystal flutes.

As he'd done for his youngest brother, Prince Rudolf stood for the first toast. "For more than a year, my brother and his daughter have lacked a loving anchor," the prince said, "and I thank Princess Belle for bringing joy into my brother's and my niece's lives."

Mikhail kissed Belle's hand and then rose from his chair to shake his brother's hand and make his own toast. "Several weeks ago, I stood at the window in His Grace's study and saw an angel sitting in his garden," he said. "I fell in love with my princess at first sight."

When her prince sat again, Belle moved her hand to his thigh and said, "I have missed you."

Mikhail slipped his arm around her and planted a kiss on her lips. "In a very few hours, our torment will be finished, and we can revel in each other for many years."

While the footmen began serving, Tinker approached the head table. He set a covered, silver platter on the table in front of Belle.

"His Highness requested this special dish prepared for you," the majordomo said.

Tinker removed the cover. On the platter lay a bread and butter sandwich.

Belle giggled and lifted the top slice of bread. Black pepper assumed the role of the spider.

"Are those you-know-what in the butter?" she asked her husband.

"Would I do that to you, my love?"

"Yes."

"I would," he agreed, "but I did not this time."

The Duke of Inverary had spared no expense. The guests were treated to a variety of delicacies like poached salmon, rump of beef, and roast duckling.

Belle ate sparingly of the bland offerings only, fearing nausea would ruin her day. She did not want any of society's witches to know she'd been pregnant on her wedding day.

Holding hands, Princesses Bess and Lily appeared in front of the head table. Both princesses gave their fathers adoring smiles.

"Hello, Daddy," Lily greeted her father.

"Hello, Sweetness," Prince Rudolf returned the greeting.

"Hello, Daddy," Bess greeted Mikhail.

"Hello, Precious."

"I am sleeping at Lily's house," Bess told her new step-mother. "I won't see you tonight."

"I will miss you," Belle said. "When you come home, we will plan your next tea party."

Bess clapped her hands in excitement.

Princess Lily rolled her eyes. "I hope Grandma Nasty and Aunty Mean won't be invited."

Belle suppressed a smile. "You need not concern yourself about that."

Still holding hands, Princesses Bess and Lily returned to their places. Guests were walking around, greeting friends before dessert was served.

Belle excused herself to go to the ladies' withdrawing room. Blaze stood outside the ballroom and walked with her.

"Did you enjoy meeting the Marquis of Awe?" Belle teased her sister.

Blaze curled her lip. "Do you mean the Marquis de Sade?"

Belle giggled. "What is wrong with him?"

"The man is arrogant and bossy."

"Darling, all men are arrogant and bossy," Belle mimicked their stepmother. "Your task is to humble them and trick them into doing what you want while still believing it was their own idea."

Blaze burst out laughing. "I doubt our dear stepmother could handle the exalted marquis."

Reaching the withdrawing room, Belle and Blaze paused before entering, feminine laughter drifting out to them. And then voices followed the laughter.

"Most likely, she's pregnant," a voice said.

"What other reason could there be for a rushed wedding," agreed a second voice.

"I refuse to call her *Your Highness,*" a third voice said. "Roxanne Campbell hovers around her husband's bastards like a hen protecting her chicks."

"Beware," warned a fourth voice. "No one crosses the Duchess of Inverary."

Belle knew the disappointed horde were venting their anger, probably at the Blonde Brigade's encouragement. She looked at her volatile sister who appeared battle ready.

"Do not mar my wedding day," Belle whispered, placing a restraining hand on her sister's arm.

Blaze gave her a reluctant nod. "We will take our revenge another day."

By unspoken agreement, the sisters walked upstairs to the water closet. When they returned ten minutes later, the prince was standing outside the ballroom.

"Is anything amiss?" Mikhail asked, his expression concerned.

Belle gave him a winsome smile while her sister disappeared into the ballroom. "Today I married the man I love. What could possibly be amiss?"

"I was looking for you and saw the Blonde Brigade and company leaving the withdrawing room," Mikhail said.

"Blaze and I went to the upstairs water closet." Belle stood on tiptoes and planted a kiss on his chin. "You worry about me too much, Your Highness, and I love you for that . . . among other things."

Mikhail wrapped his arms around her. "And I love you, Princess."

Two hours later, the prince's coach halted in front of his town mansion on Duke Street in Grosvenor Square. Mikhail climbed down first and then assisted Belle. Before escorting her inside, Mikhail called her attention to three points of interest.

"As you know, Stepan and your sister live directly across

the square," Mikhail said, "but you did not know that Viktor lives on Brook Street and Rudolf on Grosvenor Street, both facing the square."

"The Kazanov brothers live within walking distance from each other," Belle said, walking up the front stairs beside him. "We need never feel alone."

"Yes, we Kazanovs are within shouting distance of each other."

The front door opened before they reached it. The maids and footmen were lined up inside the foyer.

"On behalf of the staff," the majordomo said, "I offer you our sincerest best wishes."

"Thank you, Boomer." Mikhail put an arm around Belle and addressed the assembled. "I present my bride, Princess Belle."

The staff applauded and then dispersed. Only three men remained, the majordomo and two enormous men.

"Boomer, serve us tea and a snack in my chamber," Mikhail instructed his man. Then he turned to the giants. "Belle, I present Fredek and Grisha, my bodyguards and friends from Moscow."

"I am pleased to meet you."

"We pleasure meet you," Fredek said.

Grisha grinned. "You make prince happy. Yes?"

Belle looked at her husband. "I will do my best."

Taking her hand in his, Mikhail led her through the French doors to the inner foyer and up the stairs. Belle dropped her gaze to her hand in his and then peeked at his profile. This special man was now her husband, and she considered herself the most fortunate woman in the world.

The prince's bedchamber had been decorated in various red textiles, predominately ruby. The four-poster bed was huge, its coverlet and curtains matching. A chaise, two chairs, and an occasional table perched in front of a black marble hearth, and Persian area rugs hugged the polished hardwood floor.

"Relax, Princess." Mikhail ushered her across the chamber to the upholstered chaise and sat beside her. "You know there is nothing to fear."

"Where is my chamber?" Belle asked, unable to completely mask the fret in her eyes.

Mikhail slipped his arm around her shoulder. "I was hoping we could share this chamber."

The fret vanished, and her smile could have lit the mansion on the longest night of the year. Belle had hoped they would sleep together each night as they had done at the cottage.

"I will consider your smile an affirmative." Mikhail brushed his lips across her temples. "I love your scent of roses."

A tap on the door warned them of the majordomo's arrival. The older man deposited a tray with the teapot and accoutrements. Cucumber sandwiches, fruit medley, and cheeses accompanied the tea.

"Will you require anything else, Your Highness?"

"Privacy."

Boomer blushed and left the chamber.

Mikhail poured her tea and fed her a piece of cheese. "I noticed your lack of appetite earlier."

"I feared the nausea would return at an inappropriate moment."

Mikhail lifted her teacup out of her hand and set it on the table. Then he offered her a small box. "My wedding gift to you, love."

Belle opened its lid and gasped. Inside lay a butterfly pendant. Yellow diamonds on gold formed its body. The wings had been created in white diamonds, pink tourmalines, and amethysts. The jeweled butterfly was attached to a rope of diamonds and gold.

"You remind me of a butterfly flitting from flower to flower," Mikhail said. "Until the day I die, I will never look at a flower and see it the way I did before meeting you."

"Thank you, husband. I will cherish the necklace almost as much as my wedding ring." Belle looked into his dark gaze. "Those are the second loveliest words you've ever said to me."

"What are the first loveliest words?"

"I love you."

Mikhail claimed her mouth in a lingering kiss. Then he felt her hand caress his cheek.

"I have gifts for you."

"You are the only gift I want."

"Humor me," Belle said. "I am pregnant."

That made him smile.

"Where did Boomer put my belongings?"

"Walk through that door." Mikhail pointed across the chamber.

Mikhail watched her disappear into the connecting chamber. His hunger for her would soon be satisfied. The past two weeks had seemed like two years.

Belle returned to sit beside him. She handed him a long rectangular box. "This is first."

Mikhail looked from her smiling face to the box. He unfastened the long ribbon, removed the cover, and grinned. Inside was a hardwood walking stick with a gold lion's head.

Belle reached into a black satchel and passed him a small rectangular box. "This must be used with the stick."

Mikhail laughed and lifted the *lunettes de soleil* from the box.

"A blind man, especially a prince, should never leave home without his walking stick and *lunettes de soleil*," Belle said, and then drew a much smaller box from the satchel.

A heavy gold ring, topped with a star sapphire, reclined on a bed of black velvet. Mikhail slipped the ring onto the third finger of his left hand and planted a kiss on her lips.

"Three benign spirits named Faith, Hope, and Destiny form the sapphire's star," she informed him. "The contessa said these spirits bring the wearer good fortune."

"I feel lucky already." Mikhail reached for her, but she held him off.

"I have another gift." Belle produced a golden thimble and a glass container filled with white powder. "A thimbleful of finely ground frankincense drunk in white wine will help you retain your memory. No more amnesia."

Mikhail laughed, and then grew serious. "May I kiss you now?"

She lifted her violet gaze to his. "Yes, husband, kiss me."

His lips claimed hers in a gentle, lingering kiss. He wrapped his arms around her, holding her tight, one hand caressing the nape of her neck. She slid her hands up his chest to hook her arms around his neck, and their kiss deepened.

Heat flowed through Belle's body, his love and their marriage releasing her inhibitions. She returned his kiss with equal ardor, a hot langorous feeling seducing her senses.

He captured her whole being, her entire universe centering on his firm lips and muscular body. They were the only man and woman in the world. And she wanted more. . . .

Mikhail drew back and smiled at her dazed expression, tracing a finger down her cheek, her skin softer than rose petals. Without a word, he stood and offered her his hand.

Belle placed her smaller hand in his and rose from the chaise. She followed him across the chamber to their bed.

After another long passionate kiss, Mikhail began undressing her. He removed her wedding gown and placed it across a bench at the foot of the bed. Then he sat her on the edge of the bed.

Mikhail undressed her slowly, his lips savoring each inch of nakedness revealed. First, he removed her slippers and stockings and garters, kissing her feet and running his lips down the outside of her legs and then up the soft inner flesh. Then he slid the straps of her chemise down, taking the bodice with them, baring her breasts to his heated gaze.

Her breasts ached for his touch. And then his fingertips

were there, gliding across her sensitive nipples. She moaned softly, and his lips followed his fingertips.

"Come to bed," Belle whispered, her hands stroking the back of his head. "Please."

Mikhail disrobed where he stood, letting his clothing pool at his feet. Belle dropped her violet gaze from his chiseled features to his broad shoulders and muscled chest with its matting of black hair.

Dropping to his knees, Mikhail pressed his lips against her belly. Lifting his black gaze to hers, he said in a voice husky with emotion, "I adore you, my princess."

His simple words, spoken from the heart, touched her as no gift or gown or gem could.

Mikhail stood and, entwining his fingers with hers, pressed her back on the bed. His lips hovered above hers to whisper, "I love you." Then he dipped his head and kissed her, pouring all his love and need into that single stirring kiss. It melted into another langorous kiss. And then another.

"Will I harm the babe or you if I—"

"I need you inside me," she said on a sigh.

Mikhail moved between her thighs and entered her slowly. He slid deeper, inch by inch, until he was completely sheathed. And then he moved, slowly at first, his tempo quickening gradually.

Belle moved with him, meeting his thrusts with her own. She called his name, losing control, and melted into him.

Her pleasure excited him beyond all restraint. His thrusts became shorter and faster. He groaned and shuddered and spilled his seed deep inside her.

After a moment, Mikhail rolled away and pulled her with him. He imprisoned her within his embrace, and she rested her head against his chest.

Belle closed her eyes in sated sleep. She awakened in the morning to her husband sitting on the edge of the bed and watching her.

"Sit up and eat this." Mikhail handed her a slice of bread. "Eating bread before rising will help calm the nausea."

Belle bit into the bread. "Did my stepmother instruct you to do this?"

"No, Princess, I have experienced a woman's pregnancy before."

"I think we should tell Bess about the baby immediately," Belle said, "but I will defer to your wishes."

"We will tell her today." Mikhail handed her a cup of plain steaming tea. "Shall we leave for my estate today?"

"I would love that," Belle answered, "but I think we should remain in London to give Bess another tea party."

Mikhail smiled his approval. "What do you want to do on our first full day of marriage? We can ride in the park, picnic, shop, or whatever you desire."

Belle dropped her gaze to his groin, a seductive smile touching her lips.

His gaze followed hers. "We can do that too. . . ."

After passing the morning in bed, Mikhail and Belle decided on a light luncheon in the gazebo. Boomer served them cucumber sandwiches, miniature pastries, lemon barley water, and tea.

"Prudence and Lavinia will not be allowed inside this house without prior permission," Mikhail was saying. "Boomer has been instructed to allow no one inside this house today or tomorrow except in an emergency."

"Daddy."

Both Mikhail and Belle looked toward the house. Bess was running across the garden.

"Slow down," Mikhail called, and chuckled when his daughter continued running. He grabbed her and lifted her onto his lap. "I am a happy man, sitting with my two favorite ladies."

"Bess, do you want a cucumber sandwich?" Belle asked.

The four-year-old shook her head. "Daddy, you have something on your face that smells."

"I do?"

Bess giggled. "It's your nose, Daddy."

Mikhail chuckled. "Who told you that?"

"Uncle Rudolf."

"I should have known." Mikhail planted a smacking kiss on her cheek, making her laugh. "Mummy Belle and I have a surprise. We are going to have a baby."

Bess clapped her hands in excitement. "Is it a girl?"

"Only God knows what He will send us," Belle answered.

That made Bess frown. "The stork brings the baby, not God."

"God gives the stork our baby," Mikhail explained, "and the stork delivers the baby to us."

Her expression cleared. "How does the baby get out of the mummy's belly?"

Mikhail looked at his wife. "Mummy Belle?"

"When I find out," Belle told her stepdaughter and husband, "I will let you know."

Chapter 16

Dirty Dick's. One of my favorite haunts.

Who would satisfy his hunger that night? Blonde, brunette, or redhead?

Sitting in a dark corner of the crowded tavern allowed him to watch without being seen. Smoke hung in the hair as did the scents of gin and body odor.

No redheads were in attendance. Tonight's main course would be blonde or brunette.

Decisions, decisions, decisions.

He could not decide which whore would make the ultimate sacrifice for his pleasure. What would Mother advise? Whoever left the tavern first would win his loving attention.

His lips parted in a cold smile. Too bad the Blonde Brigade wasn't here. He would pay more than three sovereigns to add their hair to his collection. Besides, those three were little better than whores, their price being matrimony to a wealthy gentleman.

Someone was imitating his practices, which disturbed him. A drunk had been found in a nearby alley, a gold sovereign on his chest. There was a message in that.

Who had placed the coin there? Was this anonymous

person a woman? What a delightful thought. Too bad they could not hunt together.

Or was she mimicking him? If that proved true, he would punish her. Severely. If he could discover her identity.

He watched a pretty blonde wave good night to her friends and slip out the door. Noting in which direction she turned, he finished his gin and tossed a couple of coins on the table.

Not too many, though. He did not want to draw undue attention. After all, his handsome face placed him at risk.

He stood and then headed for the door. Not too fast, though. Calling the tavern's customers to his hurry was unwise.

Stepping outside, he paused and inhaled the unusually warm air. Perfect weather for hunting.

The night's silence pleased him. She would hear his footsteps as he stalked her. The thought of her fright tightened his groin, hardening him in arousal.

He decided to walk in the opposite direction from the whore and then double back on the other side of the street. Anyone watching would believe he'd had nothing to do with the blonde's demise.

Suppressing a giggle proved impossible. Mother would be so proud.

Dirty Dick's. The Slasher's favorite haunt.

That grim thought struck Alexander Blake with the impact of an avalanche. Several of the Slasher's victims had been found in an alley close to the tavern. Perhaps the constable could send a few runners each night to watch the tavern. Stalk the stalker.

The hackney halted beside a crowd gathering at the mouth of an alley. Alexander climbed down, calling to the driver, "Wait here, and I'll pay for your time."

With the assistance of the constable's runners, Alexander

pushed his way through the mob of curious spectators. His nostrils twitched, the odor of gin and body sweat assailing him.

Constable Amadeus Black stood alone. Several paces away lay the Slasher's most recent victim. Alexander knew the gruesome sight lying beneath the blanket.

"I sent Barney to fetch Raven." Amadeus gestured to a man standing nearby. "Jack Beadsley identified the woman as Opal Bowling. I waited for you before questioning him further."

"Tell us about Miss Bowling," Alexander said to the man.

"Opal was drinking down the block at Dirty Dick's," Beadsley said.

"Is Miss Bowling a prostitute?" Amadeus asked.

"Whoring is illegal," Beadsley said, making the two men smile.

"Did Opal leave the tavern with anyone?" Alexander asked.

Beadsley shook his head. "Opal went home alone about ten or eleven." He glanced at the lump. "I guess she never got there."

"Did anyone follow her out?" Amadeus asked.

Beadsley rubbed his stubbled chin. "I did see this gentleman drinking alone in a corner. The bloke left right after Opal." His expresion clouded. "I watched the gent walk in the opposite direction from Opal."

"If you saw him again," Alexander asked, "could you recognize him?"

"Well, the place was dark," Beadsley hedged, "but the gent appeared near six foot tall, brown hair. Lucille served his drinks and would've got a closer look."

"Where can we find Lucille?" Alexander asked.

"Most nights she's serving at Dick's," Beadsley answered, "but asking her questions there could cause a commotion."

Alexander nodded in understanding. Nobody liked a snitch.

"Do you know the Old Bailey?" Amadeus asked him.

Beadsley chuckled. "I been there a time or two."

"Could you escort Lucille to my office later today?"

Beadsley glanced at the blanket-covered lump. "Opal brung me whisky and hot stew when I come down with the ague last winter. I'll fetch Lucille and bring her down."

"If you don't show," Alexander warned, "we'll be looking for you."

"Lucille and me will be there," Beadsley assured them. "She'll come if I promise to walk her home after work."

"Bring her around noon." Once Beadsley had gone, Amadeus looked at Alexander. "What do you think?"

"I think the Slasher considers himself smarter than the rest of us."

Amadeus gave him a rare smile. "Why do you say that?"

"Walking in the opposite direction proves nothing," Alexander answered. "He could have doubled back."

"You are beginning to think like the criminals," Amadeus said. "Once you understand the criminal's mind, you can anticipate his next move and wait there to catch him."

"Thanks for the praise," Alexander said. "What do you think motivates him?"

Amadeus Black looked at the blanket-covered lump. "The Slasher is an insane bastard."

Dirty Dick's. One of the monster's favorite haunts.

Raven sat across from Barney in the hackney coach. She had known the constable would send for her this morning, but the victim's location jolted her.

Right place. Wrong night.

Raven wondered about the likelihood of the Slasher stalking his next victim from Dirty Dick's. She would ask Bliss to calculate the probability of that, but searching the monster's other haunts would be wise.

The hackney halted near the alley closest to Dirty Dick's.

Barney climbed down first and then offered her his hand. Leading the way, the constable's assistant cleared a path through the crowd at the mouth of the alley.

"Who's that?" one of the spectators asked.

"I dunno," answered a second, drawing Raven's attention.

"The constable's snatch?" suggested a third, eliciting laughter.

Raven narrowed her violet gaze on the odorous man. The bottle of gin he held cracked, dripping gin.

Approaching the constable, Raven stared at the shrouded corpse. She knew the Slasher's victims would appear more gruesome than the last investigation.

"I am grateful you could join us," Amadeus Black greeted her.

"Do you have the stomach for this?" Alexander asked her.

"If I can help to catch a killer," Raven answered, "I *will* stomach this."

The three approached the body, carefully avoiding a bloody footprint. The constable and she waited for Alexander to draw the blanket off the body. She closed her eyes against the sickening sight to compose herself.

Pulling his gloves on, Alexander circled the body and then crouched beside it. He pried the fingers of her hand open, revealing the signature gold sovereign.

"He slashes the throat," Alexander told her, "and then he hacks a length of her hair for a souvenir. I suppose he considers the sovereign a payment."

"She is holding something in her other hand," Raven told him.

Alexander looked at the constable and rolled his eyes. "Her other hand is hidden beneath her body."

"I can see that," Raven said, irritation tingeing her voice, "but look in her other hand anyway."

Alexander turned the girl onto her back and pried her fingers open. He saw a gold cuff link, initialed with the letters *CW.*

Raven gave him an I-told-you-so look. "Do you carry a magnifier?"

"Why do you need a magnifier?" Alexander asked, a sardonic smile on his lips. "Isn't your psychic ability enough?"

Raven curled her lip at him, which drew a chuckle from the constable.

"Here you are," Amadeus said, offering her the magnifier.

"Give it to Alex," Raven said. "Inspect the unbloodied side of her bodice, and you will find several strands of hair belonging to the Slasher."

Alexander did as told and then nodded at the constable. "The Slasher has brown hair."

"That corroborates what Jack Beadsley saw," Amadeus said.

"So the Slasher has brown hair and the initials *CW*," Raven said.

"Beadsley said the man stood six feet tall," the constable said.

"We'll make a list of tall, brown-haired society gentlemen whose name begins with *CW*," Alexander said.

"That does narrow our search." Raven paused and then listed the ones she knew. "Charles Wingate, Cedric Wilkins, Claude Wakefield, Winston Cranmore, Calvin Williams, Carleton Webster, Cyril Walker, Clarence White . . . The villain could be a woman like—"

Alexander burst into insulting laughter. Amadeus turned away, too polite to laugh.

"A woman could wear men's clothing," Raven argued. "The Rose Petal Murderer wore men's clothing. I think Charlotte Wingate is a likely candidate."

"Look at the size of those footprints," Alexander said. "No woman has feet that big."

Raven grabbed the magnifier and, kneeling beside him, examined the bloody footprint. "The recent weather has narrowed the suspect list even more. The perpetrator wears Marcello boots. Quite expensive too."

"What?" Alexander and Amadeus said simultaneously.

"Look at the M where the heel is," Raven said. While the two men peered through the magnifier, she told them, "Marcello always leaves his signature M on the bottom of the heel."

Alexander looked astounded. "How do you know this?"

"Darling," Raven drawled in a good imitation of the duchess, "my stepmother has shared her vast knowledge of useless information."

Both men chuckled. "Not so useless in this case," the constable said.

"I say Charlotte Wingate is masquerading as a man," Raven said.

"Is that an impression?" Amadeus asked.

Raven shook her head. "I have a feeling, not an impression."

"What is the difference?" Alexander asked.

"Explaining that abstraction to you would be like conversing with a stone wall," Raven said, her smile sugary sweet. "You possess less sensitivity than a brick, my lord."

Belle surveyed her husband's garden, an earthly paradise in the middle of London. Sensuous roses, the essence of summer, reigned like queens at this moment of the year. Vivid colors. Varied textures. Bewitching fragrances.

"Look, Mummy Belle."

Bess pointed at something across the garden. Focusing on the moving object, Belle realized a wren was fluttering on the ground.

Holding her stepdaughter's hand, Belle hurried toward the injured bird. Apparently, the fledgling had fallen and injured its wing, certain death.

Bess burst into tears at the wren's panic.

Belle looked from her sobbing stepdaughter to the flailing fledgling. She knelt on the grass, cupped the small bird in her hands, and closed her eyes. All her energy focused on the tiny wren.

"Ailing, ailing, ailing. Wren, my touch is sealing, and thy injury is failing. Healing, healing, healing."

Belle repeated the prayer. Again and again and again.

The fledgling tilted its head to one side and stared into her eyes. Its mother called, breaking the silent communion. And the fledgling flew.

"You did it, Mummy Belle," Bess exclaimed. "You saved its life."

"All things are possible with prayer," Belle said, her gaze on the fledgling sitting on the lowest branch of the silver birch tree. "Miracles happen every day."

"Your Highness."

Belle and Bess turned around. Boomer was walking toward them.

"Your Highness, these arrived for you this morning," Boomer said, passing her three sealed missives.

Breaking the seal on the first, Belle read the message. Then she read the second and the third. Three gardens in need of her help. None of the addresses belonged to the Blonde Brigade.

"Where is my husband?"

"His Highness has gone to a business luncheon at White's," the majordomo told her.

"Thank you, Boomer."

How fortunate for her that Mikhail had left for the afternoon. She suspected her husband would be less than enthusiastic about her continuing her gardening business, no matter that he had said otherwise. Men were notorious prevaricators when in pursuit of what they wanted. Now she would not need to tell him where she was going. If she enlisted her sister's help, her husband need never learn where she'd gone.

"Would you like to visit my sister?" Belle asked her stepdaughter. "We will walk to Park Lane."

"Yes." Bess looked excited by the thought of walking somewhere.

A short time later, Belle looped her magic basket over her

left arm, and her right hand reached for her stepdaughter's. They began their two-block journey to Inverary House, from Upper Grosvenor Street to Park Lane.

"Good afternoon," Tinker greeted them when they reached the duke's.

"We're visiting," Bess told the majordomo.

"I am thrilled to see you," Tinker told the girl.

"Is Blaze available?" Belle asked.

"Miss Blaze and Master Puddles are in the garden," Tinker answered.

Bess giggled. "Puddles is a dog, not a master."

Belle led Bess down the hallway to the rear of the mansion and outside into the garden. The mastiff spotted them first and loped across the grass, his attention on the little girl.

"Sit."

The mastiff obeyed his owner's command, but his tail swished back and forth, his gaze never leaving the child.

"Mummy Belle fixed the bird's wing," Bess said.

"Your Mummy Belle is very talented," Blaze said.

Bess bobbed her head up and down in agreement. Then she held her hand out to Puddles, who gave it a thorough licking.

"Will you drive the garden goddess to three clients?" Belle asked.

"Do you trust my driving?" her sister asked.

"Do I have a choice?"

Blaze grinned. "I'll get the phaeton."

Belle put Bess between Blaze and her on the phaeton. She moved her basket to her right arm and wrapped her left arm around her stepdaughter.

Blaze pulled out into Park Lane, their phaeton cutting in front of an enclosed coach. "Much better than last time, don't you think?"

Belle gave her an uneasy smile and wondered about her own sanity. "We're going to Trevor Place."

Blaze made a U-turn at Cumberland Gate and at the end of

Park Lane started down Knightsbridge Road. "Didn't we come this way the last time?"

"Princess Anya's home is near the corner of Knightsbridge and Trevor," Belle said, "but the Cranmore residence is on Trevor Place."

The phaeton jerked to an abrupt halt in front of Cranmore House, making Bess giggle. Belle gave her sister an unamused look.

"I did that on purpose," Blaze defended herself, "because I wanted to make the ride fun for Bess."

Belle climbed down from the phaeton and moved the basket from her right arm to her left. Then she helped her stepdaughter down. Holding the girl's hand, Belle led her up the stairs to the front door, which opened to reveal the Cranmore majordomo.

"The gardener is expecting the garden goddess," Belle told the man.

"Follow me, please."

Belle and Bess walked behind the majordomo to the rear of the mansion. One flight down brought them to the garden door.

Slipping outside, Belle paused to inhale the rich perfume of roses. There were sweetly scented wine-red apothecary roses, sugary-smelling Damask roses, and the distinctive tang of rugosas.

"What is the problem?" Belle asked the gardener. When the man dropped his gaze to the girl, she added, "My new stepdaughter."

"Ah, I see." He smiled at the four-year-old. "Are you helping your mother?"

Bess nodded. "She fixed the baby bird's wing."

"Your mother is a talented lady." The gardener led them across the grass to a rosebush.

Belle studied the plant but could see nothing amiss. She circled the bush, but it appeared healthy in spite of the recent dry weather.

"Lady Cranmore worried for this rosebush," the gardener

told her. "I could not see any sign of ill health, but she insisted on your opinion."

A wasted trip, Belle thought. She could not understand the woman's concern or insistence.

"Prayers are never wasted," she told the gardener.

Belle knelt in front of the rosebush, set the basket on the ground beside her, and removed its contents. She suffered the uncanny feeling of being watched but shook it off.

"Do you want to help?" she asked her stepdaughter, who nodded eagerly. "Ring the bell when I tell you. Can you do that?"

"Yes." Bess reached for the bell and gave it a couple of shakes. "I'm practicing."

Belle blessed herself and then lifted the Lucifer matches and sandpaper from the gold box. After lighting the white candle, she said, "Ring the bell, Bess."

The four-year-old rang the bell. Once, twice, three times.

Belle leaned close to the rosebush and placed her hands on it. "Ailing, ailing, ailing. Rosebush, my touch is sealing, and thy illness is failing. Healing, healing, healing."

Waving the *Book of Common Prayer* in front of the bush, Belle said, "It is written. It is so." Then she blew the candle out and blessed herself again.

After replacing her magic utensils in her basket, Belle turned to the gardener. "Keep the roses damp in this weather."

With her stepdaughter's hand in hers, Belle crossed the garden. The door opened before they reached it, and two women stepped outside. Caroline Cranmore and Princess Anya.

The Russian princess looked from Belle to Bess. Lifting her nose into the air, Anya walked past them without saying a word.

Belle hoped the princess would not mention this encounter to the Smythes. Prudence would be happy to inform Mikhail about her activities.

After lifting the four-year-old into the phaeton, Belle climbed up. "Princess Anya was visiting Caroline Cranmore."

"Did she say anything?" Blaze asked.

Belle shook her head. The thought persisted that Anya's presence had been no coincidence.

Blaze drove away from the Cranmore residence without cutting in front of any coach. Montague Place, their next destination, was located near Russell Square. They drove down Knightsbridge to Piccadilly, congested with traffic.

"Are you certain you can get us safely to Russell Square?" Belle asked.

"I am in complete control." Blaze shook her fist in the air when another coach pulled in front of them.

"What are you doing?" Bess asked her.

"I am waving to friends." Blaze looked at her sister. "Doesn't Cynthia Clarke live in Russell Square?"

"We aren't going that far."

Blaze halted the phaeton in front of the Williard mansion on Montague Place. "I told you my driving was improving. Even Pumpkin thinks so."

"Who's Pumpkin?" Bess asked.

"The horse."

"How do you know what Pumpkin thinks?"

"She told me," Blaze answered, making her giggle.

Belle had already climbed down and then helped Bess. Hand in hand, they walked up the front stairs. The Williard majordomo led them to the rear of the mansion and then outside, where the gardener waited.

"What is the problem?" Belle asked the man.

The gardener shrugged. "Lady Williard found several shriveled blossoms and insisted we send for you."

Feeling watched again, Belle circled the rosebush as she had at the Cranmore residence. She could see nothing wrong with the plant except the need for watering.

"I doubt the bush is ill," she told the gardener, "but I will pray for it."

As she had done at the Cranmore residence, Belle knelt on

the grass and removed her special utensils from the basket. She blessed herself, lit the white candle, and gestured her stepdaughter, who rang the bell.

Belle placed her hands on the rosebush and moved her lips in silent prayer. *Ailing, ailing, ailing. Rosebush, my touch is sealing, and thy illness is failing. Healing, healing, healing.*

She waved the prayer book in front of the bush. "It is written. It is so."

Belle blessed herself, packed her magic tools in the basket, and stood. "Be certain to quench the rosebush's thirst during this dry weather."

With her stepdaughter in hand, Belle retraced her steps through the Williard mansion. The majordomo opened the door, but Cynthia Clarke stood there.

Belle met the blonde's gaze but said nothing. She stepped aside, allowing entrance to the mansion, and then descended the front steps to the phaeton.

"Two rosebushes and two of the Blonde Brigade seem an unlikely coincidence," Belle said to her sister.

"Shall we forget the last request for your services?" Blaze asked.

"A plant may really need my help," Belle said. "Davies Street is on the way to Grosvenor Square."

Blaze merged with the traffic onto Oxford Street. "Isn't Davies Street near Berkeley Square?"

"Yes."

"Isn't the Smythe residence in Berkeley Square?"

"Yes."

"Do you still want to stop there?"

"Yes."

When they reached the Benchley residence, Belle climbed down from the phaeton. "Bess, stay here."

"I want to go with you."

"Very well." Belle helped the four-year-old out of the

phaeton and walked up the front stairs. The Berkeley major-domo led them to the garden.

"You need my help?" Belle asked the gardener.

The man seemed embarrassed. "Lady Benchley insisted this rosebush was ailing."

Belle circled the bush as she'd done at her two previous appointments. "I am happy to report this plant enjoys good health."

She grasped her stepdaughter's hand. "Come, Bess."

The two started toward the mansion. Feeling watched again, Belle glanced at the windows. Lavinia Smythe and Gloriana Benchley peered at her from the second floor.

Returning to the phaeton, Belle told her sister, "I do believe my husband and I are scheduled for our first argument."

"Was you-know-who at the Benchley's?"

"What do you think?"

"I think you should lie about today," Blaze said, turning the phaeton onto Oxford Road.

"Lying is naughty," Bess said.

"Saying *I don't remember* is not naughty," Blaze told her.

Bess looked at Belle, who nodded in agreement with her sister. "If you do not want to lie or tell the truth, say that you do not remember."

Bess laughed. "*I don't remember* means lying without telling a lie."

"We do not want your father to know where we went today," Belle said. "If your daddy asks, what do we say?"

"I don't remember!"

Blaze halted the phaeton in front of the Grosvenor Square mansion. Prince Mikhail was climbing down from his coach and waited when he saw them.

"I'm leaving my basket here," Belle whispered, setting it down. "Please return it to me tomorrow."

"You can depend on me, sister."

Belle smiled at her husband when he helped her alight from the phaeton. Then he lifted his daughter out too.

"Did you have a good day?" Mikhail asked the four-year-old.

"Yes, Daddy."

"Did Blaze take you and Mummy Belle for a drive?"

"Yes, Daddy."

"Where did you go?"

"I don't remember." Bess winked at Belle.

Mikhail seemed confused and shifted his gaze to his wife.

"Mummy Belle doesn't remember either."

Belle smiled at her husband's puzzled expression. "My sister treated us to a mystery ride."

Chapter 17

He had married the perfect woman.

Prince Mikhail stood at the window in his study overlooking the garden. He had tried to concentrate on paperwork, but the sound of his daughter's laughter had drawn him from his desk.

Belle Flambeau was everything he had wanted in a wife and mother of his children. Loving and nurturing, his wife would give him the family life he'd craved his entire life.

The Kazanov brothers may have been born with great wealth and an exalted title, but little else. His father had locked his mother in an insane asylum once her childbearing days had passed. There she had remained until Rudolf rescued her, fled to England, and given her a secure peace on his Sark Island estate.

Belle would be a balm to his mother's confused mind, and his mother would love her.

Prince Fydor Kazanov was as bad a father as he'd been a husband. He had given Vladimir, his heir, all his attention and none to Mikhail or his brothers.

Rudolf, Viktor, Stepan, and he had banded together to make their own family, which included their orphaned cousin Amber, now married to the Earl of Stratford.

Mikhail wanted a better family life for his daughter and any other children he sired, which was the reason he had never considered marrying Lavinia or any other shallow society miss. Good Lord, he would not marry his late wife again.

Women were strange creatures. They behaved in a certain manner before marrying but reverted to their true selves once the ring was on the finger.

Except Belle, his perfect wife.

A knock on the door drew his attention. "Enter."

Boomer walked into the study. "Lady Smythe's courier awaits your reply," he said, passing him a sealed missive.

Mikhail read the missive and then shifted his gaze to the older man. "If you were I," he said, "would you allow Prudence Smythe into your home?"

"May I speak honestly?"

"Please do."

"Lady Smythe is and always will be Princess Elizabeth's grandmother," Boomer answered, "but I would not leave her alone with Princess Belle."

"I appreciate your wisdom," Mikhail replied. "Inform the courier my answer is *yes.*"

Once the majordomo had gone, Mikhail returned to his desk and forced himself to concentrate on his paperwork. His thoughts soon wandered to his troublesome former in-laws.

Boomer was correct. He could not keep his daughter away from the Smythes, but he had no wish to pass his remaining days guarding his wife from their spite.

Mikhail could see no immediate solution to his problem. Perhaps the situation would change once Lavinia found a suitable husband.

An hour later, Boomer knocked on the door and stepped inside, announcing, "Ladies Prudence and Lavinia have arrived."

"There is no need for formality," Lady Prudence said, the two women brushing past the majordomo.

"Fetch Bess," Mikhail instructed his man.

"Wait one moment," Prudence said, stopping the majordomo. "We need a few private moments before Elizabeth arrives."

Mikhail inclined his head. "Wait five minutes before calling Bess."

Mikhail ushered his in-laws to the sofa in front of the darkened hearth. He sat in the upholstered chair beside them.

"What do you want to discuss?" Mikhail asked, fixing a polite smile on his face.

"Lavinia witnessed something quite distressing yesterday," Prudence answered, "and she brought it to my attention."

Mikhail shifted his black gaze to his former sister-in-law. Without a doubt, this quite distressing something concerned his wife. He should have known the trouble would not end with his marriage.

"If I wasn't concerned for Bess," Lavinia said, "I would not be telling tales."

Mikhail raised his brows. "I am waiting to hear these tales."

"That woman took my granddaughter to her gardening jobs," Prudence snapped, her tone scathing.

"That woman is a princess," Mikhail said, "and you would do well to remember it."

"Mama means no disrespect," Lavinia said, "but learning your wife took Elizabeth gardening has upset her."

Mikhail kept his face expressionless, a habit he had learned in society and at the gaming table. Behind the placid expression, his anger was simmering close to a boil. However, a husband and a wife should show a united face to the world.

"My wife answers to me, not you."

Prudence looked stunned. "What do you mean?"

Mikhail looked from one to the other. "Princess Belle had my permission prior to her excursion with *my* daughter."

"I had no idea," Lavinia said.

"How shocking," said Prudence.

"My wife and I consider her gardening charity work," Mikhail said, feigning a calmness he did not feel, "since she donates all proceeds to the poor."

"She gives money away?" Prudence exclaimed.

Lavinia managed a faint smile. "Then we need not distress ourselves further."

The study door opened. Bess ran into the room and then stopped short when she saw who sat there.

"Come here, Bess." Mikhail read the wariness in his daughter's expression and put his arm around her. "Grandmama and Aunt Livy want to speak to you."

"We apologize for our behavior at your tea party," Lavinia said.

"We want to take you to the Sweet Shoppe," Prudence added.

Bess brightened visibly at that. She clapped her hands together in her excitement.

"What will you choose?" Mikhail asked her.

She put her index finger across her lips as she'd seen him do when thinking. "I want walnut creams and molasses taffy. What do you want, Daddy?"

Mikhail placed his index finger across his lips and then winked at her. "I would like fig and raisin fudge."

"What would Mummy Belle want?"

"She likes orange and lemon creams." Mikhail stood then to escort them downstairs.

"We will certainly bring candy home," Prudence said, forcing a smile that did not reach her eyes.

Lavinia held her hand out. "Come, Elizabeth."

Bess slipped her hand into her aunt's. "My Mummy Belle is having a baby," she blurted, "and I want a baby girl to come to my tea parties."

Mikhail opened the door but did not quite meet his former mother-in-law's gaze, her expression more grimace than smile. He should have known that his daughter would spread the news. They walked down the winding staircase in silence, past Atlas holding the world, and through the French doors.

When the door closed behind the three, Mikhail instructed his majordomo, "Wait five minutes and then ask my wife to come to my study."

"Yes, Your Highness."

Gaining his study, Mikhail poured himself a shot of vodka and downed it in one gulp. He and his wife were scheduled for their first argument.

Mikhail stood behind his desk to keep the discussion formal. Distancing himself was smart because if he stood too close to his wife, he would kiss her instead of lecturing her.

A few minutes later, Belle paused outside her husband's door and summoned her courage. Boomer had whispered in her ear that the Smythes had visited and taken Bess out in their carriage. Belle knew that the Smythes—*God curse and rot them*—had squealed about yesterday's activities.

Belle squared her shoulders, tapped on the door, and entered without waiting for a reply. Her husband sat behind his desk, looking formal and stiff.

Thankfully, she had learned a few lessons from her stepmother. Now she would use those lessons to confound her husband.

Belle gave him her warmest smile as she crossed the study. Ignoring his gesture to sit in the chair in front of his desk, Belle circled around it and leaned close to plant a kiss on his cheek.

"Mmmm, I love your scent," she said. "I have missed you since breakfast."

His lips twitching pleased her. That meant he was very close to smiling, and a man could not smile and hold onto his anger.

"Sit over there, wife."

"I would prefer sitting on your lap, husband."

She could see him steeling himself against her, which meant he knew she was wheedling him. More consultations with her stepmother would help her marriage.

"We need to speak," Mikhail said, "and I cannot concentrate while you hang on me."

Belle straightened and sent him a hurt look. "Then I will refrain from touching you, of course."

As she circled the desk, she gave him a sidelong glance. Her husband wore a guilty look for hurting her feelings. He should feel badly and would feel even worse when she finished with him.

Belle sat in the chair and wasted a moment arranging the skirt of her gown, a stalling tactic Blaze had taught her. Then she lifted her violet gaze to his. "Where is Bess hiding?"

"Prudence and Lavinia have apologized for their bad behavior at the tea party," Mikhail told her. "Reparation was taking her to the Sweet Shoppe."

"I am relieved for Bess's sake." Belle sent him her most winsome smile. "I adore sweet shoppes but can never decide which candy I want."

"I sent for you to discuss *your* bad behavior."

Belle dismissed him with a wave of her hand. "I never behave badly."

"Where did you go yesterday?" he asked.

"You saw us arrive home," she evaded.

Mikhail gave her a stern look. "That is no answer."

"Bess and I walked to Inverary House," Belle hedged, "and my sister took us for a carriage ride. Blaze has been practicing her driving skills."

His expression told her he was becoming frustrated. "And where did your sister drive you?"

"Why do you ask? Is something wrong?"

"Answer my question," he said.

"Do you require details?"

"Details would be appreciated."

"We rode north on Park Lane to the Cumberland Gate where Blaze turned the coach—*excuse me*—turned the phaeton south."

"Belle." His voice held a warning note.

"You wanted details," she argued.

"You went gardening yesterday," he accused her.

"If you know where I went," she countered, "why are you asking me?"

Mikhail ran a hand down his face. Then he sat in silence and rubbed his forehead.

"Are you suffering a headache?" She started to rise. "I can help—"

"Sit," he ordered, and she sat. "I have a pain in the arse, not a headache."

Belle narrowed her violet gaze on him, letting him know how much that displeased her. "The Blonde Brigade engineered this whole fiasco and used my gardening weakness against me."

"Explain yourself. Please."

"I received three requests to heal three healthy rosebushes," she told him. "One of those blond witches was at each appointment."

"You told my daughter to lie to me," he said.

"That is completely false," she defended herself. "I explained that saying *I don't remember* is avoiding the truth without lying. Politicians say that all the time, and nobody calls them liars."

"My daughter is not a politician," Mikhail said. "Gardening is unseemly for my wife and daughter."

"You lied too," Belle said, pointing her finger at him. "You said I could cure every plant in England if I married you."

Mikhail looked surprised, caught by his own words. "Yes, I did but—"

"—but lying is different for you," she finished.

Mikhail said nothing.

"Was lying good for you because you wanted to marry me?"

His expression softened, and his lips quirked into a reluctant smile. "I wanted to marry you very much."

Belle ignored that lest she softened her attitude toward him. She intended to win this first argument. "I was saving lives, not gardening. Those blond—"

"They did not twist your arm and force you to take yourself and my daughter to perform menial labor," Mikhail interrupted her. "I do not want my daughter or you gardening for other people. Do you understand?"

She understood all right. Obeying was a different matter.

"Well?"

"I understand perfectly."

Mikhail relaxed visibly. "Now you can sit on my lap."

Belle rose from the chair. "I wouldn't sit on your lap to save my soul."

Whirling away, Belle marched across the study to the door. When he called her back, she ignored him and slammed the door behind her.

Slamming that door felt good. Her volatile sister Blaze had the correct attitude. Do not let anyone get away with anything at any time and never hold anything back.

Belle walked down the stairs and crossed the foyer to the door. She nodded at the majordomo when he opened the door.

"Shall I order you a carriage, Your Highness?" Boomer asked.

"No, thank you."

"If His Highness asks, what shall I tell him?"

"Tell him to go to hell."

Belle walked the two blocks to Inverary House. She banged

on the front door, seeing her husband's expression when he wanted her to sit on his lap.

"Your Highness, what a pleasant surprise," the majordomo greeted her.

"Good afternoon, Tinker. Is Blaze home?"

"Try the garden, Your Highness."

Belle hurried toward the rear of the house and down one flight to the garden door. Stepping outside, she called to her sister, "What is Puddles doing?"

Blaze walked toward her. "He is digging a hole."

"Do you think he could dig one large enough for a prince?"

Blaze burst into laughter. "My psychic ability tells me the Blonde Brigade squealed, and Mikhail took exception to a gardening princess."

"Prudence and Lavinia are determined to cause trouble," Belle said, "and Mikhail accused me of teaching Bess to lie. He assured me I could cure every plant in England if I married him. So, who is the real liar?"

"Calm down," Blaze said, drawing her toward a stone bench. "You'll give birth to a baby with cholic."

"My husband is setting down new rules."

"Tell him yes, yes, yes. Then do whatever you want."

"What if he finds out?"

"What if he *does* find out?" Blaze countered. "Will the sky fall on your head? Will the earth open to swallow you? Will the Thames rise up to drown you?"

Belle laughed. "Sister, you have the best attitude of all."

Blaze slipped her arm around her shoulder in easy camaraderie. "Trust me, sister. Prince Mikhail loves you enough to approve of your gardening."

"I don't know about that."

"He loved you enough to marry you twice."

Belle gave her a puzzled smile. "What do you mean?"

"Oops." Blaze looked across the garden, calling, "Puddles, you will be in trouble if you keep digging."

"Tell me what you know, Blaze."

"Mikhail married you by proxy before he went to the cottage."

Belle could not credit that. "I never signed anything."

"Sophia forged your name," Blaze said. "Please don't tell anyone I squealed."

"I will protect your identity," Belle promised, rising to leave, "and I thank you for giving me ammunition."

With her spirits high, Belle retraced her path through Inverary House and then walked the two blocks to Grosvenor Square. She climbed the front stairs, but the door opened before she could knock.

"Welcome home, Your Highness." The majordomo's lips twitched. "His Highness was asking for you. I relayed your message."

Belle smiled at that. "Thank you, Boomer."

"His Highness has sought sanctuary in his study."

Belle climbed the stairs to the second floor. Becoming upset had sickened her stomach and given her heartburn.

Without bothering to knock, Belle threw the door open with a violence she hadn't known she possessed. The door hit the wall, causing a painting to drop to the floor. Then the door ricocheted off the wall to close behind her as she crossed the room.

Her husband stood but did not appear especially happy. "I expected you would have calmed by now."

Belle stood in front of his desk, her hands on her hips. "So, you value honesty?"

"I do not respect lying."

"I know you lied about the blindness and amnesia," Belle said. "Tell me about the proxy marriage."

Mikhail stared at her for several long moments, enough time to make her fidget, and then walked around the desk. He grasped her upper arms and yanked her against his hard muscular planes, their bodies touching from chest to thigh.

"I fell in love at first sight," he said, his lips hovering above hers.

"You stole my right to choose my own husband," she countered.

"You love me."

"What if I hadn't loved you?"

"I am a handsome, wealthy prince." Mikhail gave her a charming smile. "What is not to love?"

Belle wanted to laugh at his arrogance, but amusement would only condone what he'd done. "You committed a serious fraud," she said. "I could ask for an annulment."

Mikhail dropped his hand to her belly. "I doubt annulment is a viable option, and you need my permission for a divorce."

Belle narrowed her gaze on him, reluctant to surrender the upper hand. "Your duplicity has sickened my stomach and given me heartburn."

"I apologize for that," he said. "Prudence catching me off-guard gave me heartburn."

"What did you say to her?"

"I told them I had given you permission."

Her husband had supported her.

A smile touched her lips, and she glided her hands up his chest to entwine his neck. "And do I have your permission?"

"I promised you could cure every plant in England," Mikhail said, and then claimed her lips in a lingering kiss. "And so you shall with one tiny stipulation."

"What would that be?"

"The garden goddess will leave my daughter home," he answered, "and she will take her silent partner instead."

She gave him a puzzled smile. "Who is my silent partner?"

"I will accompany you to your appointments," Mikhail answered. "With me by your side, I guarantee your gardening will create a trend in society. Everyone and her grandmother will be kneeling in the dirt to tend the roses."

Standing on her tiptoes, Belle planted a chaste kiss on his dimpled chin. "I love you, my prince."

"Are you happy I did not go to hell?"

"Incredibly happy."

She had a bad feeling.

Dressed in black, Raven opened her bedchamber door a crack and peered into the deserted corridor. She glanced over her shoulder at her bed where she had puffed a few pillows and drawn the coverlet up. If anyone opened the door, the bed would appear occupied.

Raven stepped into the corridor, closing the door behind her silently, and sneaked down the servants' staircase. Reaching ground level, she slipped out the garden door but paused to listen for sounds of possible witnesses to her escape. Nobody could know that Serena, Blaze, and she had left their chambers.

The night sky was clear, and a full moon shone, casting the garden in eerie light and shadow. The birds and insects were silent in sleep, shrouding the enclosed area in an auditory peace, only the bubbling fountain breaking the silence. Myriad flower scents mingled to perfume the still air and intoxicate the senses.

Satisfied that she was alone, Raven glided down the stone path past the fountain, the silver birch tree, and wisteria. She climbed the alley stairs and stepped through the gate.

Serena and Tulip waited there. Her sister had dressed in black like her, but the younger girl wore the deceased prostitute's clothing. The scarlet gown had a tight bodice and daringly scooped neckline.

The telltale sounds of horse and carriage rolled down the alley toward them. Coming into view, Blaze and Puddles sat on the driver's seat. Her sister brought the carriage to an abrupt halt.

Raven wondered if Blaze would kill them in the carriage before the Slasher was caught. Her sister needed more driving practice.

"Pumpkin, do not move," Blaze ordered the horse.

She climbed down, the mastiff at her side. Strangely, the horse stood statue still.

Raven turned to Tulip, saying, "I should play the decoy again."

"My sister was murdered," Tulip said, shaking her head. "I will play the decoy."

"We will definitely meet the Slasher tonight," Raven warned her.

That surprised Tulip. "How do you know?"

Skepticism runs through the Blakes like some families inherit the gout.

"I know," Raven answered, "because I know."

"Tonight, I avenge my sister's death."

"Did you bring Papa's pistol?" Raven asked Blaze.

Her sister passed her the unloaded pistol. "Bash his brains first and ask questions later."

"If something happens," Raven said to Serena, "a lightning bolt would be appreciated."

Serena smiled at the reference to her own special talent. "I will give that my best effort."

"Shall we try Dirty Dick's again?" Blaze asked. "His most recent victim came from that tavern."

"The Slasher won't chance returning to that tavern so soon after his last attack," Raven said.

"Let's try The Blind Beggar on Whitechapel Street," Tulip suggested.

Blaze and Raven climbed onto the driver's seat. Tulip, Serena, and Puddles squished together in the back.

Leaving the safety of Park Lane, Blaze drove the carriage east on Oxford Street toward London's unsavory section. Passing Bishopgate where Dirty Dick's was located, they traveled farther to Aldgate and then Whitechapel Street.

Blaze halted the carriage two blocks away from The Blind Beggar. Everyone climbed down except Serena, who took her place at the reins.

"The pistol and I will hide in the alley beside the tavern," Raven said to Blaze. "You and Puddles hide in the one on the other side." She looked up at the brilliant full moon. "Keep to the shadows at the mouth of the alley and do not take your eyes off Tulip."

"I know what to do." Blaze crouched beside the mastiff. "No heavy panting or the monster will hear us."

"Are we ready?" Tulip asked. "Let's go."

Together, they walked in the direction of the tavern. Raven slipped into the first alley, and Tulip waited with her until Blaze and Puddles disappeared into the next alley.

"My sister and I watched Ruby conducting her business," Tulip whispered, a smile in her voice, "so I know how to tempt a man. If only I had bigger bosoms. Don't attack until he grabs me."

Tulip yanked her bodice down an inch and sauntered toward the tavern, her body swaying enticingly from side to side. When she reached the next alley, Tulip turned with a roll of her hips and retraced her steps past the tavern.

"How am I doin', luv," Tulip whispered.

"Stay alert," Raven warned. "The Slasher is almost here."

Raven watched Tulip strolling toward the tavern, her slim hips swaying. Holding the unloaded pistol in a tight grip, she steeled herself for the worst.

The tavern's door opened, and a tall, well-built man stepped outside. Even from a distance, Raven saw he dressed like a gentleman—which did not necessarily make him the

Slasher. More than a few aristocrats slummed through the seedier side of town.

When the man ambled in Tulip's direction, Raven's breath caught in her throat, and her heartbeat quickened. Waves of demented anger and unholy hatred rolled off him. Raven knew he was the one.

"Step into the alley with me," Raven heard him saying, "and I'll give you a sovereign."

Tulip whirled around to confront him.

"You're dead," he exclaimed in a loud, shocked voice. "I killed you."

And Tulip opened her mouth and screamed.

"The Slasher . . ."

"Simple, senseless, stupid blockheads."

Raven had never felt more humiliated in her life, hot embarrassment staining her cheeks crimson. She stared at her hands folded in her lap and wished to be anywhere but here, receiving a dressing-down in front of an audience.

With his arms folded across his chest, Alexander Blake leaned against the wall in her father's study. Amadeus Black stood beside him while the Duke of Essex sat behind her father's desk and her stepmother in another chair nearby.

The Duke of Inverary paced back and forth in front of her and the others, sitting in a row. Puddles perched beside Blaze, the mastiff's head hanging in doggy shame.

Arriving at The Blind Beggar, Alexander and Constable Black had been stunned by their presence. And the first of several scathing lectures had begun, expounding on their dangerous, foolhardy risk taking.

Raven knew they were correct, though. She should have known better. She had seen the Slasher's handiwork.

Flashing her almost-betrothed a sullen glance, Raven dared him to laugh. Wisely, Alexander averted his gaze.

She and her accomplices had been dragged home like criminals. Her father had sent a footman to bring the Duke of Essex to Inverary House.

That four young ladies and one dog had nearly caught the Slasher was probably annoying Alexander. They had managed to get closer than he and the other professionals.

The Duke of Inverary walked down the line again, staring at each of them in turn. When her father dropped his gaze on the dog, poor Puddles whined in canine misery.

"You could have been killed," the duke continued his ranting. "Do you know more than the constables?"

Tulip snapped her head up. "Your Grace—"

"Keep your lips shut," Inverary barked. "I own boots older than you."

"Darlings, traipsing around London is *so* unladylike," the Duchess of Inverary drawled. "You must catch *husbands,* not murderers."

Raven bit her lip to keep from laughing, and a muffled squawk of laughter escaped Alexander. Even Constable Black was smiling.

The Duke of Inverary looked at his wife. "Roxie, please."

The duchess gave him a dimpled smile. "I am only trying to help."

"I appreciate the gesture, dear," the duke said, "but you are much too softhearted to deal with these miscreants." He looked at the Duke of Essex. "Do you have anything to add, Bart?"

"Listen here, Tulip." The Duke of Essex sounded stern. "I admire your ingenuity."

"Bart."

"However misplaced that ingenuity was, of course."

"Constable?"

"Your enthusiasm could have cost your lives," Amadeus Black told them. "Thankfully, you brought the mastiff along."

"Before being kicked in the gut, Puddles nearly tore the man's left hand off," Raven said. "Our suspect is a tall, brown-haired CW who wears Marcello boots and a bandaged left hand."

"He thought I was Iris," Tulip added.

"If you were that close," Alexander said, "you can identify him."

"I will never forget his face."

"If Tulip can identify him," Amadeus Black said, "then he can identify and silence her. Permanently."

"Bart, I think your granddaughter should remain in my protective custody," the Duke of Inverary said. "Guarding four simpletons is just as easy as three."

"Tulip is too damn fearless for her own good," Alexander said, "and Twigs is too old to follow her around."

The Duke of Essex looked at his granddaughter. "I will miss you, Tulip, but I agree with Alex."

Alexander looked at Raven. "If Tulip describes the Slasher, do you think Sophia could sketch him?"

"I know she could sketch him."

"Sophia should make two or three sketches," Amadeus said, "and we can show them around town, especially the taverns in the East End."

"Once we see his likeness," Alexander said to the Duke of Inverary, "Raven and I can make the rounds of social events. With your permission, of course."

"I will consider it."

"My husband and I prefer the betrothal contract signed," the Duchess of Inverary said, "before Raven appears by your side in public. Don't we, darling?"

"I agree with whatever you say, dear."

"Since Belle is settled now," Alexander said, "announce our betrothal in the *Times*."

Catching his eye, Raven sent Alexander her sweetest smile. Her future did not look so bleak, knowing she would soon escape Inverary House since her stepmother would not give him time to change his mind.

Raven knew she could manage her arrogant skeptic. And converting him into a believer appealed to her.

Chapter 18

"Life was simpler before marrying a prince," Belle said, crossing the bedchamber to the cheval mirror. "I dislike attending society functions."

"I wanted to retire to the country," Mikhail reminded her, "but you refused."

Her gaze on his reflection in the mirror, Belle watched him tying his cravat. "Let's leave tomorrow."

Mikhail reached for his jacket. "Disliking society is one of your many endearing qualities."

Belle frowned at her reflection in the mirror. She knew critical eyes would search for her flaws, but striving for perfection would always prove futile.

Her high-waisted silk gown in violet whisper had a low-cut, scooped neckline and short, puffed sleeves. Its skirt sported a scalloped flounce at the hem.

Decidedly out of fashion, her ebony hair had been brushed back into a knot at the nape of her slender neck. Hair styles and accessories, as her stepmother had chanted, could make or break a gown. Around her neck, she wore her jeweled butterfly attached to the length of diamonds. Belle wore no other jewelry, except for her wedding ring, but did carry a mother-of-pearl mirror fan.

"Be careful," Mikhail warned, walking toward her. "What will you do if the frown freezes on your face?"

Belle rounded on him and smiled. "What will *you* do?"

"I will love you, of course." Mikhail planted a chaste kiss on her lips and offered her his hand. "You are much too tempting to resist. Ready?"

"Oh dear, I've forgotten my cosmetics."

"You do not need the concealer."

She paled at the unsettling thought of foraging into society without that protection. "I want the cosmetics," she insisted, her expression mulish.

"Wait here."

Retrieving the cosmetics, Mikhail lifted the lid off the small pot and dabbed a dot onto his finger. Then he slid the concealer down the fading red mark and blended it into her cheek.

After wiping his finger on a handkerchief, he tossed it aside and looped her arm through his. "Are you ready now, Your Highness?"

She stood on tiptoes and kissed his cheek. "Quite ready, Your Highness."

The Earl and Countess of Winchester, their hosts for the evening, lived on South Audley Street, a mere two blocks from Grosvenor Square. Victoria Emerson, the countess, was Prince Rudolf's sister-in-law and the Duchess of Inverary's niece, hence the obligation to attend.

They wasted forty-five minutes traveling, fifteen minutes to reach the mansion, and another thirty minutes waiting in the coach line. Walking would have had them there thirty-five minutes sooner.

The Winchester ballroom had floor-to-ceiling windows on the shorter street- and garden-facing sides. Several violins, a cornet, and a piano played on one side of the room. Small tables and chairs circled the dance floor, leaving standing space to loiter. An archway connected to the card room.

Waiting in line to be announced, Belle scanned the crowd of London's sophisticated elite and felt like an outsider. The

Blonde Brigade was in attendance and, thankfully, her sister Fancy. At least she would see one friendly face in the throng amid a multitude of disappointed enemies.

Dressed in their finest, the ladies were colorful blossoms set against the hardy stems of their gentlemen's formal attire. Pink, lavender, ethereal blue, and spring green were the most prevalent colors this season, but several women wore basic black or red or yellow or white.

Expensive gems sparkled from feminine throats, wrists, fingers, and ears. Drop earrings dangled everywhere, making Belle feel positively naked without any earrings at all.

Fashionable red morocco reticules and mirror fans were much in attendance as were *Corsage a la Sevigne,* those wide waist ribbons with broad bows and long ends in back. Belle's own gown had no ribbons and a higher waist because she wanted no attention drawn to her gently swelling belly.

"Prince Mikhail and Princess Belle Kazanov," the Winchester majordomo announced them.

"I will never accustom myself to the title," Belle whispered, drawing her husband's attention.

"As time passes, you will not even hear the title," Mikhail promised, looping her arm through his. "I saw the family at the other end of the room."

They stepped into the crush and wended their way through the crowd. Her husband greeted acquaintances but never stopped for conversation. She smiled, pretending enjoyment.

"Darling, you look radiant," the Duchess of Inverary greeted her.

"Thank you, and a good evening to you," Belle returned her stepmother's greeting.

"As you see, your charming sister Fancy is here tonight," the duchess said. "What a coincidence that two sisters should dress their hair in unfashionable styles. Your sisters-in-law are disregarding the latest styles too."

"We won't take offense if you pretend not to know us," Belle said.

The duchess gave her dimpled smile. "Though provoked, I could never give my darlings the cut."

"Good to see you, sister." Fancy sidled up to Belle. "Stepan loved your cookies. When he asked me to bake him some, I told him to let me know when he wanted to die."

Belle giggled. "You could bake if you put your mind to it."

"How do you feel?" Princess Samantha asked her. "Have you passed the morning sickness?"

"I feel fine at the moment," Belle answered, "but mornings are a torment."

"Samantha and I are tormented in the mornings too," Princess Regina told her.

"Imagine four brothers and four pregnant wives," the duchess exclaimed. "I wonder if that vodka helps fertility."

"If that were true," Prince Rudolf said, "the Kazanovs would be the richest family in England."

"And Russia would be the most populated country," Viktor added.

Mikhail leaned close to Belle, whispering, "Dance with me?"

Belle placed her hand in his. Together, they swirled around the ballroom, she finding comfort in his arms. Her husband danced with the ease of a man who had waltzed a thousand times, which made her wonder who had partnered him for those nine hundred and ninety odd waltzes.

"You are the most beautiful woman I have ever seen," Mikhail told her.

"Are you taking lessons from Stepan?" Belle teased, referring to her brother-in-law's habit of outrageous compliments.

"I taught my baby brother everything he knows."

That made her smile. "Instead of a conventional tea party," Belle said, "I suggest taking Bess and the girls to your country estate for a few days."

"If you feel well enough," Mikhail replied, "Bess would certainly be thrilled."

Belle danced with each of her brothers-in-law and caught the sneering looks from the Blonde Brigade and their friends.

She had prepared herself in advance for that, knowing those three would never be counted as friends.

"I need to visit the withdrawing room," Belle told her husband.

"Look for me in the card room," he said.

"I'll go with you," Fancy said, walking beside her.

High-pitched chatter and giggles emanated from the withdrawing room. The closer they got, the louder the female voices sounded.

Conversation ceased when Belle and Fancy walked into the room where several unmarrieds had gathered. A tense silence hung like a storm cloud over all.

"Please do not allow our presence to stifle your gossiping about us," Fancy drawled, imitating the duchess.

Belle noted the embarrassed blushes on several faces. She supposed her sister's stage experience helped her outface anyone. Assume a role and play it to the end.

"The opera singer and the gardener," Lavinia Smythe sneered. "Don't get too close to them, ladies, or these imposters will contaminate you."

Most of the young women gasped at the insult. Apparently, most considered gossiping nasty but harmless fun. Open warfare was a different matter entirely.

Belle grasped her sister's arm, preventing an assault. She and Lavinia needed to settle their differences sooner rather than later. They could never be friends, but carrying a grudge was senseless.

"Lavinia and I must discuss a private matter," Belle said, looking at the ladies and then her sister. "You will excuse us, please."

The group hurried out of the room. Wearing an uncertain expression, Fancy paused before leaving.

"I can fight my own battles," Belle told her.

Fancy looked from Belle to Lavinia and then back again. "I will be waiting outside."

After her sister had gone, Belle rounded on Lavinia. "We need to make peace for Bess's sake," she said. "I know you are disappointed, but I am Mikhail's wife. Nothing will change that. I sincerely wish you a marriage as loving as ours."

"Mikhail doesn't love you," Lavinia said, a sneer marring her beauty. "He married you because your scar gave him a wife who preferred children and hearth to a full social schedule."

"You are lying," Belle accused her. "Mikhail and I married for love and will remain married no matter what you say or do."

The other woman's gaze mirrored her cold contempt. "You are fooling yourself," she insisted. "That necklace once belonged to my sister whom Mikhail considered a social butterfly."

Paling a sickly white, Belle felt the pitch and roll of beginning nausea. She refused to believe this witch's poison. And yet—

"Ask Mikhail," Lavinia suggested, her smile smug. "Though, he has proven himself a liar. He promised my sister to marry me and save her daughter from an unknown stepmother."

For the first time in her life, Belle suffered the urge to do violence to another person. She didn't like the feeling of a healer wanting to cause another bodily harm.

"Your malicious spite is pathetic." With those parting words, Belle turned her back and left the withdrawing room. She found her sister outside.

"Are you all right?" Fancy asked, falling into step beside her. "You look pale and heartsick."

Belle wanted—*no, needed*—to be alone to digest what Lavinia had thrown at her. Lies were mixed with the truth, she suspected. Which were lies? And which was the truth?

If she questioned him, Mikhail would tell her what he thought she wanted to hear. She needed the truth, regardless of the pain. Her father would know the truth. His willingness to share that knowledge was uncertain, though.

Finding her father, Belle gave him her sweetest smile. "May I have this dance, Papa?"

"I would love to dance with you."

Father and daughter stepped onto the dance floor. They

swirled around and around the glittering ballroom, fulfilling a girlhood dream.

"Tell me the reason Mikhail wanted to marry me," Belle said.

The duke's step faltered at the unexpected question. "Why, I—" She'd caught him by surprise. "The prince saw you sitting in the garden and asked for your hand in marriage."

That much was true, then.

"Did my husband marry me because of my scar?" Belle asked. "Or did he want me in spite of it."

"Mikhail did not share his motivation," the duke answered her, "and I did not ask him."

She knew he was lying. His evasion told her what she needed to know, and that made perfect sense. What father did not want to protect his child from pain?

Belle managed a smile for her father. "Then I will ask him for his motivation."

When the waltz ended, Belle excused herself by needing to visit the withdrawing room. Instead, she headed for the foyer.

Her loved ones had betrayed her. Love at first sight was a lie as was her father's lack of knowledge. She would gamble a fortune that everyone—*except her*—knew the truth. Her sisters, her father, her stepmother, her brothers- and sisters-in-law knew the reason her husband had married her. Even Lavinia Smythe had guessed the real reason.

Only she had been foolish enough to believe in love at first sight. Her husband had lied about his blindness and amnesia. He had lied by omission about the proxy marriage. He had lied about his reason for marrying her.

"Shall I send for your coach?" a footman asked her.

"No, thank you." Belle managed a polite smile. "I'll walk."

The footman looked shocked.

"I live two blocks away," Belle explained. "If Prince Mikhail asks for his wife, please tell him I've gone home. Only if he asks for me."

"Yes, Your Highness." The footman opened the door. "Enjoy your walk home, Your Highness."

Leaving the Winchester mansion, Belle walked in the direction of Grosvenor Square. She passed Adam's Row and Upper Grosvenor Street, and then another half block brought her into Grosvenor Square, arriving home ten minutes after leaving the ball.

Boomer opened the front door. "Welcome home, Your Highness."

Tears welled up in her eyes. "Thank you, Boomer."

"Where is His Highness?" The majordomo looked out the door, surprised by her solitary arrival. "Where is the coach?"

"I left both husband and coach at the ball."

Belle climbed the stairs to her bedchamber and pondered her position. She needed a couple of days away to think about her marriage and sort out her feelings. Though she was reluctant to abandon the little girl, feigning normalcy around Bess would prove impossible and confuse her stepdaughter.

After removing her gown, Belle laid it neatly across the bench and dropped the butterfly necklace on top of it. She donned a morning gown and grabbed a cashmere shawl, and then placed a change of clothes and a few necessities into a tapestry bag.

Belle sat on the edge of the bed. Should she leave a note? She wasn't running away, merely going home for a few days to nurse her emotional wounds.

Two blocks away at Winchester mansion, Mikhail tossed his losing hand of cards on the table and looked around the table at his brothers. "Dancing with my wife is free."

He left the card room in search of his wife. They would take one last waltz around the dance floor and then leave, their obligation done.

Mikhail entered the ballroom and scanned the dancers. No wife there. Locating his in-laws, he circled the dance floor but did not see his wife.

"Do you know where Belle is?" he asked them.

The Duke of Inverary nodded. "She retired to the with-drawing room."

Leaving the ballroom, Mikhail loitered in the corridor near the ladies' withdrawing room. He waited ten minutes and then returned to the ballroom.

"Are you certain she said the withdrawing room?" Mikhail asked the duke.

"I'll look for you," Princess Samantha said.

"I'll go with you." Princess Regina fell into step beside her.

Five minutes passed. And then another five. Mikhail was becoming concerned when his sisters-in-law reappeared without his wife.

That sent him into full panic. He did not know where she'd gone, but when he found her, he'd give her a blistering lecture for making him worry.

"Someone has been trying to cause trouble," the Duke of Inverary said, drawing him aside. "When I danced with her, Belle asked if you had married her because of her scar. You should ask the staff at the front door if she left."

Mikhail hurried to the foyer. "Have you been standing here all evening?" he asked the footman, who nodded. "Have you seen my wife, Princess Belle?"

"Her Highness asked me to tell you she'd gone home if you asked for her," the footman answered.

"How long ago was this?"

The footman thought for a moment. "Fifteen minutes or so."

Mikhail bolted out the door. His coach parked across the street surprised him. "Did you drive my wife home?" he asked his man.

"No, Your Highness," the man answered. "I thought I saw a woman who resembled her walking down the street, but she had disappeared by the time I got there."

She had walked home?

Mikhail could not quite grasp the concept of his pregnant princess walking home. If anything happened— He banished that horrifying thought.

"Meet me at the house."

His driver looked confused. "Don't you want to ride, Your Highness?"

"Running is faster." Whirling away, Mikhail dashed down Audley Street. He passed Adam's Row and Upper Grosvenor Street, reaching home in five short minutes.

Panting from his exertions, Mikhail burst into the foyer and then stopped short. His wife was walking down the stairs, a bag in hand.

This was bad. Worse than he'd imagined. Much worse.

Belle paused, her heart sinking at the sight of her husband, and then crossed the foyer to stand in front of him. Leaving would have been easier if he hadn't returned home.

"Why are you panting?"

"I ran home."

That surprised Belle. High society did not attend social events on lowly feet.

Belle studied his beloved face, his sharp angular features, eyes blacker than a fathomless pool, chiseled lips she yearned to kiss. And then Belle steeled herself against him, gathering her anger around herself like a cloak.

"Did my butterfly necklace belong to your first wife?" Belle demanded.

Mikhail gave her a blank stare. "What?"

Lavinia had lied about the necklace.

"Did you make a death-bed promise to marry Lavinia?"

Mikhail seemed bewildered. "What are you saying?"

Lavinia had lied about that too.

"Did you marry me because of my scar?" Her violet gaze captured his. Willing him to tell the truth. Willing him to prove the other woman had lied. Willing him to say the words she wanted to hear.

Mikhail paled, his black gaze skittering away from hers. Then his face flushed and darkened as the seconds ticked by.

Lavinia had spoken the truth.

Mikhail held his hands out in supplication. "Listen . . ."

"You listen to me," Belle snapped, pointing her finger at

him. "You used subterfuge and lies to trick me into marriage. I wonder what other lies have slipped from those lips."

Those lips tightened in anger. "I do not lie."

"Do not insult my intelligence."

"Walking home alone was not the smartest choice you have ever made."

"Neither was marrying you." Belle gave him a look filled with contempt. "You appreciated my sister's theater cosmetics, I bet. Then you could enjoy a scarred wife who preferred to hide her face at home, and the cosmetic concealer would mask the mark for an evening out."

"That is absurd," Mikhail said, his voice rising in anger. "You are using those cosmetics like a crutch. With or without the scar, I love you."

"With all these pretenses and lies, I cannot believe you," Belle countered, "and proving your love is impossible."

"Only a man in love would eat a spider sandwich," Mikhail shouted. "Is that proof enough?"

In spite of her anger and pain, the thought of him eating the spider sandwich tickled something inside Belle. She burst into giggles, recalling his revolted expression when he'd realized spiders laced the butter.

Mikhail gave her a lopsided smile and reached for her hand. "Please do not leave me."

"I need a couple of days to sort myself," Belle told him. "I won't be gone long."

"Why can you not sort yourself here?"

"You are here."

"What will I tell Bess?"

"The truth might be a nice change," Belle answered, "but a lie will suffice, and you do excel at them."

Mikhail released her hand. "You will come home."

"I promise."

Lifting her bag, Mikhail escorted her outside and helped her into his coach. "I will see you in a day or two."

Belle felt her heart wrenching at his dejection, but Lavinia

Smythe had caught her by surprise. If only he'd told her the real reason he'd married her. She wouldn't have liked it, but his subsequent profession of love would have been believable.

Mikhail watched the coach disappear around the corner and wished they had stayed home that evening. Her pregnancy would have been a good excuse not to appear at functions.

Sitting behind the desk in his study, Mikhail reached for the vodka and poured the colorless liquid into a shot glass. Then he downed it in one gulp, shuddering as the vodka burned a path to his stomach.

Belle had mentioned a death-bed promise and his late wife's jewels. Both accusations were lies, and the accusation about her scar was only partially true. He *had* fallen in love with her at second sight, when she rescued him that first day at the cottage.

Lavinia Smythe was behind tonight. The devil *did* have the power to assume a pleasing shape and mix lies with the truth.

Mikhail knew one thing for certain. He did not want to sleep without his wife. In order to convince her of his love, he needed to speak to her. Waiting until tomorrow or the day after that was unacceptable.

Mikhail marched downstairs. "I want another coach brought around."

"Yes, Your Highness." Boomer hurried down the corridor.

Fifteen minutes later, Mikhail was en route to Inverary House. Walking would have been faster, but he needed to give his wife a chance to calm down.

"Good evening, Your Highness," Tinker greeted him.

Mikhail brushed past the majordomo. "Please tell my wife I would speak with her."

Tinker gave him a blank look. "Her Highness isn't here. Would you like me—?"

Raven appeared at that moment. Puddles dashed down the stairs in front of her.

"Do you know where Belle is?" Mikhail asked.

"My sister is missing?" Raven asked, instantly concerned.

"Lavinia Smythe upset her tonight," Mikhail said, "and Belle insisted she needed to go home and sort herself."

"Home is Soho, not Inverary House."

"I do not want my wife staying in that house alone," Mikhail said, alarmed. "Will you pass the night with her?"

"I would do anything to escape this prison," Raven said, making the majordomo chuckle.

"I will explain what happened along the way," Mikhail said.

A short time later, the coach halted in front of the Flambeau residence in Soho Square. Mikhail climbed down and then assisted Raven.

"You will persuade Belle to return home?"

"Leave it to me." Raven patted his arm. "I guarantee your wife will be dining with you tomorrow."

"Thank you." Mikhail watched his sister-in-law disappear into the house and then climbed into the coach. His next stop would be Audley Street where he intended to behave badly for the first time in his life.

With grim determination stamped across his features, Mikhail marched into the Winchester mansion and headed for the ballroom. Though reluctant to cause a scene, he would not allow his former sister-in-law and her cohorts to harass his wife. Speaking privately had not solved the problem, hence the need for a public rebuke.

Mikhail located Lavinia in the crowd and started forward. Friends and acquaintances greeted him. He ignored all but his quarry.

"Lavinia."

She greeted him with her sweetest smile. "Good to see you, Mikhail."

"Is it?" Those two tiny words silenced conversations in their immediate vicinity.

Lavinia paled at his tone, and then an embarrassed blush colored her cheeks.

"You will not insult my wife or approach her again," Mikhail warned, his voice low but deadly serious. "If you do"—he gestured to their audience—"this discomfort will be the least of your troubles. Do you understand?"

"Perfectly."

Mikhail stared into her eyes a short moment before turning away. "God help the man who marries you."

Chapter 19

Mikhail stretched his long legs out and sipped his dram of whisky, feigning cool patience. He planned to ride to Soho Square as soon as Inverary's meeting ended. Unless, of course, Raven had persuaded his wife to go home. He would know all was well if his sister-in-law had returned.

"Your causing a disturbance last night surprised me," Stepan said.

Mikhail slanted his younger brother a smile and took another sip of his whisky. He wasn't in the mood for his brothers' jests and good-natured taunts, all his mental energy focusing on his wife.

"You have always been the most reasonable Kazanov," Viktor said.

"Even peacemakers lose their tempers," Drako remarked.

"Lavinia lost her composure and left the ball," Rudolf told him.

Mikhail grimaced and rubbed his forehead, regretting what he'd done. He had always disliked making others uncomfortable. Losing his wife was no excuse for ungentlemanly behavior. Lavinia was not responsible for his lies. He hadn't solved any problem, merely spread the misery around.

"You should not feel guilty," Rudolf said.

"I feel no guilt," Mikhail lied.

Rudolf smiled at him. "You have become quite an accomplished liar, brother."

"I have no doubt that escaping her punishment appealed to Raven," the Duke of Inverary said, "but you should have ordered Belle to stay home."

"Have you ever given your wife an order?" Mikhail asked his father-in-law.

The duke narrowed his gaze on him. "Yes, of course."

"Did Her Grace actually obey your order without complaint or argument or making your life a misery?"

The duke gave him a long look, clearly reluctant to answer the question. "I understand your point."

A knock on the door drew their attention. Tinker announced, "Constable Black and Lord Blake have arrived."

"Escort them here," the duke instructed, "and then fetch Sophia and Tulip with their sketches."

Upon entering the study, Amadeus Black and Alexander Blake shook the duke's hand and accepted the glasses of whisky that Prince Rudolf passed them. A moment later, Sophia and Tulip walked into the room.

Their sketch pictured a good-looking man, his features pleasant but nondescript. There were no identifying marks on his face, nothing to set him apart from others.

"He does look familiar," Mikhail said, "but I cannot put a name to the face."

"The villain is pretty rather than handsome," Tulip remarked, staring at the image of the man who had murdered her twin sister. "His mother must boss her baby monster around."

The princes, the constable, and the duke smiled at her simplistic opinion.

"Your Grace, Squire Wilkins requests an interview with Constable Black," Tinker said from the doorway, drawing their attention. "Apparently, the constable's assistant directed him here. The squire has important information regarding the Slasher."

Amadeus Black looked at the princes and the duke. "I suppose you want to listen."

"Escort the squire here," the duke instructed his man, and then looked at the two young women. "You may leave now."

"I have faced that insane murderer," Tulip said, her hands on her hips. "If you want me to leave, you will need to drag me away."

The Duke of Inverary and the Kazanov princes smiled at her bravado. At a nod from the constable, the duke said, "You may remain, but I want no outbursts."

Tinker escorted Squire Wilkins into the study. The squire stopped short when he saw the gathered group.

"Sit here," Mikhail said, standing to offer his seat.

Folding his arms across his chest, Mikhail leaned against the floor-to-ceiling bookcase to watch the proceedings. He noted the majordomo had left the door slightly ajar. If he yanked the door open, he would find the man eavesdropping.

"What is this important information?" Constable Black asked.

"I know the Slasher's identity," Wilkins said, casting an apprehensive glance around the group. "Before telling you, I must confess to a crime. On my mother's orders, I slashed Belle Flambeau's face."

"Bastard." In a flash of movement, Mikhail grabbed the squire with both hands and slammed him into the bookcase. Books toppled off the shelves, striking both men. Mikhail raised his fist to strike, but his eldest brother wrapped his arms around him, pulling him away.

"The law will take care of him," Rudolf growled, tightening his hold.

Every instinct urged Mikhail to shake his brother off and kill the other man. Gradually, his breathing slowed and he composed himself.

"Tell me the reason your mother wanted my wife hurt."

"Mother wanted Charles to marry a woman with money

and status," Wilkins answered. "She knew Charles would reject her if Belle's beauty was marred."

"I want Charlotte Wingate prosecuted," Mikhail told the constable.

"Justice will be done," Amadeus Black promised, and then turned to the squire. "Give me the information regarding the Slasher."

Cedric Wilkins reached into his pocket and removed a braided rope of blond, brown, red, and black hair. "I found this in my brother's bedchamber," he said. "I fear Charles may be your Slasher."

Alexander Blake showed him the sketch. "Is this Charles Wingate?"

"That is my brother," Wilkins verified, "but you won't find him at home."

"Where will we find him?" the constable asked.

The door burst open before Wilkins could answer. Puddles dashed into the room, followed by Blaze Flambeau, who glanced over her shoulder and smiled at someone in the corridor. "What is so interesting that Tinker is eavesdropping?"

"Baron Wingate is the Slasher," Sophia exclaimed.

"Charles Weasel Wingate?" Blaze looked flabbergasted. "You must be joking."

Tulip showed her the sketch. "Is this Charles Wingate?"

"Oh my God," Blaze cried, her face draining of color. "The baron was standing in the foyer a few minutes ago and begged to speak with Belle. I sent him to Soho."

"Don't scratch the hardwood floor," Belle cautioned her sister. "One, two, three . . . go."

Working together, Belle and Raven moved the dining room table against the French doors leading to the parlor. Then they began setting the armoire's crystal, china, and silver onto the table in preparation for cleaning.

There is nothing in the world like manual labor to take one's mind off problems, Belle thought, reaching for the silver polish and rags. Her sisters would laugh at her, but since leaving their Soho residence, she had actually missed the household chores.

"Mikhail loves you," Raven said without preamble. "I think you should go home."

Belle gave her sister a long look. "How can you possibly know what another person truly feels?"

"I know because I know," Raven answered, making her smile.

"My husband should have spoken truthfully," Belle argued. "He could have said he married me for my scar and then fell in love. Instead, I believed his love-at-first-sight nonsense."

"If your husband loves you now," Raven said, "does his initial reason matter?"

"I suppose not."

"Will you return to Grosvenor Square today?"

"Let's give the house a thorough cleaning," Belle suggested, "and then we'll walk home."

Raven looked at her as if she'd grown another head. "Why should we clean when Papa can order his servants to do it?"

"I do not feel a sense of accomplishment when others do the chores," Belle answered.

"Pardon me, sister." Raven rolled her eyes toward heaven. "I would not want to ruin your sense of accomplishment."

The sisters looked at each other and laughed. Then they worked in silence for a time.

A gentle breeze wafted into the room through the open window and flirted with the bottom edge of the French lace curtains. The fragrance of roses perfumed the room, drifting inside on the breeze.

"Tell me about the investigation," Belle said, reaching for a porcelain teacup.

"We know the Slasher has brown hair, the initials CW, and Marcello boots," Raven told her.

"Marcello boots?"

Raven nodded. "I recognized Marcello's unique mark in the blood."

Belle shuddered, her stomach flip-flopping with sudden nausea. She knew the fear the victims suffered, because she had been slashed too.

"Puddles bit him," Raven added. "The Slasher will be sporting a bandaged left hand."

Belle would have replied, but a knock on the front door drew their attention. "I'll answer that."

Expecting their visitor was Mikhail, Belle wiped her hands on a linen cloth and left the dining room. She hurried down the hallway to the foyer. Her mouth dropped open in surprise when she saw her visitor. Charles Wingate stood there, a sheepish smile on his face.

"I went to Grosvenor Square and Inverary House," Charles told her. "Blaze sent me here. I must speak with you. May I come inside?"

Belle assumed a polite smile, knowing she could not bring herself to slam the door on anyone's face, not even the baron. "Yes, of course, come into the parlor."

Charles sat on the upholstered sofa in front of the window. Belle dropped onto the chair nearest the door.

"What do you want to discuss?" Belle asked.

Before he could answer, Raven popped into the parlor. If the baron's presence surprised her, she did not show it.

"Baron Wingate, good to see you again," Raven greeted him. Her smile remained fixed, but her gaze drifted downward.

Watching her sister, Belle followed her gaze to the baron's bandaged left hand. Was Charles the Slasher? That was ridiculous. Charles was too much of a mama's boy. Mother would probably spank him if he misbehaved.

"Are those Marcello boots?" Raven asked him. "I've always admired your impeccable taste."

Baron Wingate smiled, pleased with the praise. "I imagine Her Grace is instructing you on the Quality."

"My stepmother has been a wealth of useful information," Raven agreed, "and I admire her immensely. By the way, what happened to your hand?"

Wingate held his left hand up and looked at the bandage. "A dog bit me."

"Are you in pain, Charles?" Belle asked, hoping her tone sounded normal. Every nerve in her body was trembling. She suffered the almost overwhelming urge to run for her life, but running incited predators to chase.

"My hand does throb," Charles was saying.

"I'll make us tea," Raven said. "I have mild herbs that will take the edge off the pain." Without waiting for his reply, she left the parlor.

Belle silently cursed her sister for leaving her alone with him. She struggled to remain seated instead of running out of the house.

"I heard what happened at the Winchester ball," Charles said, once her sister had gone. "I want to apologize for hurting your feelings."

"You cannot blame yourself for another's behavior," Belle said, managing a faint smile.

"Here we are," Raven called, entering the parlor. She set a tray on the table and passed the baron his tea. "Belle baked her famous angel cookies. Help yourself while I set more tea to steep."

Watching her sister, Belle could scarcely believe she'd been left alone with the murderer a second time. All this nervous tension could not be healthy for her baby.

Belle sipped the steaming tea and then set it on the table. Her hands were shaking too much to hold the cup without spilling its contents.

Five minutes passed in silence while the baron drank his tea and ate several cookies. And then another five minutes passed.

"Sister, help me carry this," Raven called from the kitchen.

"Excuse me, Charles." Belle gave him her most winsome smile. "Don't go away."

"I will wait for you, sweetheart."

Belle walked unhurriedly to the door. Rounding the corner, she lifted her skirt and dashed down the hallway to the kitchen. Two steps into the kitchen, her sister yanked her into the dining room and shut that door, using the elm coffer as a barricade.

"Charles is the Slasher," Raven whispered, moving to close the hallway door.

The baron stood in the doorway, preventing escape. Both women backed away to the far side of the room.

"Raven, you drugged my tea." Charles wagged his finger at her and staggered foward. His speech sounded slurred when he added, "You have guessed my secret."

The baron drew a dagger from inside his jacket, the blade's gleam taunting them. "You cannot imagine how quickly the body drains of blood." Walking on unsteady legs, he paused in the middle of the room to lean against the table.

"Do something," Belle snapped at her sister.

"What?"

"Drop the chandelier on his head."

Raven focused her gaze on the chandelier, willing it to drop. Several crystal goblets on the table exploded into glass shards.

Charles looked at the crystal, porcelain, and silver on the table and shook his head. "I should have known these expensive furnishings meant your father valued his daughters."

Two porcelain cups flew off the table and crashed into the wall above the marble hearth. The gilt-framed mirror hanging there cracked into several large pieces.

"The chandelier, stupid, not the china."

"I'm trying."

"I told Mother I wanted you but—" He glanced at the swaying chandelier over his head, his body swaying with it.

The champagne flutes exploded, startling the three of them. Behind the sisters, the dining room windows cracked as did the French door's glass panes. A teacup leaped off the table. Its saucer took flight, breaking the armoire's glass door.

"The chandelier, you idiot," Belle screamed.

In a flash of movement, Mikhail raced into the dining room. Alexander Blake was one step behind, followed by the constable and his runners as well as the princes and the duke.

Mikhail grabbed Charles from behind, wrapping his arms around his body and lifting him off the floor. He threw the baron against the dining room table, the blade falling from his hand.

Alexander yanked the baron's hands behind his back to chain his wrists together. Constable Black locked his ankles in leg irons. At a nod from the constable, the runners grabbed the baron's arms and dragged him ungently away.

Mikhail turned to Belle, all his love shining from his black eyes. She threw herself into his arms, sobbing, "Look at this mess. My mother's possessions are broken beyond repair."

"Did the baron cause all this destruction?" he asked.

Belle shook her head, her violet eyes swimming in tears. "Raven did it."

Mikhail tilted her chin up, and dipping his head, his mouth covered hers in a lingering kiss. "I feared we would not arrive in time."

"How did you know?"

"Squire Wilkins found irrefutable evidence and informed the constable." Mikhail tightened his hold on her, reluctant to let her go.

"I want to go home," Belle said, surveying the damage from within the circle of his arms, "but this mess needs cleaning and the windows repairing."

"I will send my staff to set the house right," the Duke of Inverary spoke up.

"I told you Papa would do that," Raven said. "Your sense of accomplishment threatened our lives. I doubt I will ever be able to do housework again."

"Tossing the crystal and porcelain at him saved your lives," Constable Black said. "Good thinking, Raven."

She shook her head. "I drugged his tea, and when he came after us, I tried to drop the chandelier on his head."

Alexander Blake burst into laughter. "Does the witch need more control?"

Raven did not take exception to the name *witch*. She rounded on him, a surprised smile on her lips. "Do you now believe—?"

"Your hocus-pocus is nonsense."

That wiped the smile off her face. She gave him a tight-lipped stare.

Alexander returned her grim look. Without warning, he grasped her upper arms and yanked her against his body. "Don't ever scare me like that again."

His mouth captured hers in a smoldering kiss. That melted into another. And then—

"Enough, Blake." The Duke of Inverary cleared his throat. "Raven is still being punished for sneaking out the other night. And you, Blake, will not kiss her like that again until the vows have been spoken."

Belle tilted her head back and gazed into her husband's black eyes. "I love you."

Mikhail put his arm around her shoulders and ushered her toward the door. "You believe me when I say I love you and have done since the first moment I saw you in the cottage garden?"

Belle gave him a serene smile. "Only a man in love would eat a spider sandwich."

* * *

Eight Months Later

He arrived on the second day of spring, robustly screeching his reluctance to enter the world. His enamored parents called him Vlad, which meant "prince of the world."

Holding his first son in his arms, the proud father announced his intention to pass his wealth of knowledge to this tiny miracle. His son would grow into a successful, admired gentleman.

Vlad's weary mother gave her husband a benign smile, knowing hers was the more difficult task. She needed to civilize and soften him without weakening his strength. Gardening would be the best tool for teaching him patience and responsibility and a reverence for God's creatures.

The first of many visitors arrived on the third day of spring. Smiling with anticipation, the five tea-party cousins filed into the bedchamber.

Princess Roxanne, their undisputed queen, was honored with the first close look and then frowned. "I thought the babe was a boy."

"Vlad is a boy," Belle said. "Prince Vlad Kazanov."

Natasha wore a pained expression. "Vlad looks like Genevieve and Gabrielle," she said, referring to her twin cousins born the previous day.

"All babies are pink and wrinkled," Mikhail explained.

"Vlad is yawning," Sally said.

"He is *so* precious," Roxanne drawled, sounding like the duchess.

"I always thought boys never cried," Bess told her cousins, "but Vlad never stops." She looked at her father. "I love Vlad even though he is a terrible crybaby."

"Vlad loves you too." Mikhail looked at his youngest niece. "What do you think, Lily?"

"I think Mummy Belle should tell us how the baby gets out

of the mummy's belly," Lily answered, and her four cousins bobbed their heads in agreement.

"I am sorry," Belle said, "but the stork made me promise to keep the secret."

"Do you know the secret, Uncle?"

Mikhail shook his head. "Mummy Belle would not share the secret with me." He stood then and crossed the chamber to the door. "Come, ladies. Vlad needs his sleep to grow big and strong. Boomer is waiting to serve Mummy Belle's angel cookies and stuffed meringues."

Closing the door behind the girls, Mikhail returned to sit beside Belle on the bed, and they watched the thrilling sight of their sleeping son. His every whimper and tiniest movement held them enthralled.

"How are you feeling, my love?" Mikhail asked, slipping his arm around her shoulders.

Belle gazed at him, her violet eyes gleaming with love. "I feel a trifle weak but abundantly happy."

"A spider sandwich works miracles for regaining strength."

Her giggles roused Vlad. Pushing her gown open, she offered him her breast and smiled when he latched onto a nipple.

"I love you, Princess."

"And I love you." Belle slid a hand down his body to caress him.

Mikhail brushed his lips across her temples. "What are you doing, my love?"

"Tempting my prince."

Please turn the page for an exciting sneak peek of

Patricia Grasso's

ENTICING THE PRINCE,

coming soon from Zebra Books!

London, 1821

Anticipation strummed through her, sharpening her senses. She could almost hear the rhythmic pulsing of her surging blood.

Tonight the prince and she would rendezvous. She had waited five years for this moment and intended to savor every scintillating second of her evening. Scandal would explode like Vesuvius erupting, scorching society.

Katerina Garibaldi, the Contessa de Salerno, studied her image in the cheval mirror. A feline smile of satisfaction touched her lips, lifting the corners of her mouth. Excitement enhanced her beauty, her dark eyes gleaming like the priceless jewels she created.

Two delicate diamond buckle pendants—her own creation—clipped the gauzy straps of her violet gown. Diamond pins glittered in her black, upswept hairdo like stars sprinkled across the midnight sky. She wore a diamond cuff-bracelet on her right arm, and diamond fan earrings dangled from her earlobes, precluding the need for a necklace.

She wanted to dazzle the prince, not blind him.

From somewhere behind her, Katerina heard the humming

of Nonna Strega, the widow she'd brought from Naples. The only other sound was the cicadas singing in the darkness of the garden below her window.

Katerina placed a dot of perfume above her upper lip. Inhaling her own jasmine scent heightened her awareness of herself when she stepped into society, a reminder to guard her expression, behavior, and speech.

The kohl lining her eyelids lent her a dramatic aura. Her gaze beckoned but never promised.

A lady should look her best when consorting with a prince. Lord, she felt like a princess in those fairy tales she told her daughter each evening.

Long, white gloves appeared in front of her. Katerina looked from the gloves to Nonna Strega. "No gloves tonight."

The older woman beamed with approval at Katerina. *"Bella, la Contessa."*

"Thank you."

Once the woman had gone, Katerina crossed the chamber to the armoire and opened its doors. She reached for the black, diamond-encrusted reticule. After slipping its gold links handle onto her left arm, Katerina walked down the corridor.

Her pace slowed as she neared her daughter's chamber. Should she enter or not? Seeing her daughter's sweet expression could change her plans for the evening, and she would never forgive herself if she missed this oportunity.

Katerina lifted her head high and rehearsed her grand entrance by floating with poise down the stairs to the foyer. Her brother awaited her there, but her sisters were nowhere in sight.

Her brother shoved his hands in his trouser pockets. "You are going through with this?"

"Hektor, do not attempt to dissuade me."

He shrugged and smiled at her. "Do what you must, sister."

Katerina narrowed her dark, kohl-lined eyes on him. Something was definitely amiss. She had expected an argument but received affable indifference.

The majordomo opened the door. "Enjoy your evening, my lady."

"Thank you, Dudley."

Outside, Katerina paused before climbing into her coach. The sultry July evening reminded her of Naples. Returning to Italy would become impossible after tonight.

Inverary House on Park Lane was a scant few blocks from her home in Trevor Square. Twenty minutes later, Katerina entered the duke's residence and climbed the stairs to the ballroom.

She had arrived purposely late. Her tardiness would whet the prince's desire.

An unexpected wave of uncertainty washed over her. There would be no returning to her old life once she went to the prince.

Katerina had never felt so desperately alone, not even on that long ago night that had brought her to this moment. Her steps slowed. The closer she got to the ballroom, the more her confidence waned.

"Good evening, my lady," the duke's majordomo greeted her.

"Good evening, Tinker."

The man announced her arrival. "The Contessa de Salerno."

Katerina scanned the ballroom before joining the elite throng. She spotted her handsome quarry at the far end of the enormous chamber.

Summoning her courage, Katerina walked into the crush of guests and wended her way slowly around the room. She ignored the greetings from friends and acquaintances, her intense focus fixed on her man. She did, however, spare a nod for her host and hostess like a young queen acknowledging her courtiers.

"Your Highness?"

The prince whirled around, the warmth of his relieved expression tinged with irritation. "Good evening, my lady."

He bowed over her hand. "I despaired of seeing you this evening."

"Tonight is ours." Her voice was a throaty purr. "I have brought you a gift."

He smiled, his irritation forgotten. "One of your priceless gems, my lady?"

Katerina opened her reticule and reached inside. In a flash of movement, she drew a pistol and pointed it at his head.

Several women screamed, drawing the crowd's attention. Guests began backing away out of the line of fire.

"What are you doing?" The prince appeared confused, shocked, and afraid.

"Pulling this trigger will separate your royal head from your royal body," Katerina answered. Her smile was serene, but the hand holding the pistol shook like the palsey.

"You cannot be serious." His complexion had paled to a ghostly white. "What have I ever done—?"

"My name is Katerina *Pavlova* Garibaldi," she interrupted, noting his stunned recognition. "The devil always gets his due, Your Highness, and you will now pay for destroying my family."

"You do not understand," the prince squeaked. "I never—"

"Silence," Katerina snapped. "Die like a man instead of a weasel."

Without warning, a masculine hand materialized from behind her, covering her hand on the pistol, but did not snatch it away. A deep, husky voice spoke, a voice she'd grown to love. "Well-mannered ladies do not point pistols, darling."

Katerina kept her gaze fixed on the prince and her hand on the pistol. "The coward deserves to die for his crimes against my family."

"His Highness *does* deserve punishment," the voice agreed, "but death by pistol is *so* quick."

"Do not deter me." Katerina steeled herself against her lover. "My fingers itch to finish what he started five years ago."

His reply was a husky whisper against her ear. "Do you love me enough to listen before executing His Highness?"

"Speak."

"Do you love me enough to lower the pistol while I speak?"

Katerina tightened her grip on the pistol, her finger on the trigger. *"No . . ."*

Put a Little Romance in Your Life With
Georgina Gentry

Cheyenne Song
0-8217-5844-6 $5.99US/$7.99CAN

Apache Tears
0-8217-6435-7 $5.99US/$7.99CAN

Warrior's Heart
0-8217-7076-4 $5.99US/$7.99CAN

To Tame a Savage
0-8217-7077-2 $5.99US/$7.99CAN

To Tame a Texan
0-8217-7402-6 $5.99US/$7.99CAN

To Tame a Rebel
0-8217-7403-4 $5.99US/$7.99CAN

To Tempt a Texan
0-8217-7705-X $5.99US/$7.99CAN

Available Wherever Books Are Sold!

Visit our website at www.kensingtonbooks.com.

Discover the Romances of

Hannah Howell